Driftwood Chandeliers
A haunting tale of life and death in Bali
All rights reserved
©Mark Eveleigh 2023

Published by Kura Kura Books, 2023
Cover design ©Narina Exelby, 2023

For Narina, who makes life in Bali more magical still.

Foreword

Every six months the lanes and alleyways of Bali are transformed into shimmering tunnels by the great swooping bamboo *penjors* that are set into the ground outside each house.

Penjors are often described as 'Balinese Christmas trees' but they are more beautiful – and infinitely more meaningful – than any mere festive decoration. Each *penjor* is a statement of a family's artistic tastes and a sort of antenna to communicate with the gods. Crucially, if you know how to read it, a *penjor* is also a topographical map of this mystical island.

Each fifteen-metre bamboo pole has been weighted and tied so that its thin tip bows in a graceful arch that represents the cone of sacred Mount Agung – the highest point of the island and the abode of the Hindu gods. The stem of the *penjor*, the river that flows down to the sea, is decorated with leaves that represent the island's varied vegetation.

In the west of Bali, the rain first nourishes the immense tracts of uninhabited jungle that still cover a tenth of the island. This area is known only by a handful of hunters who trap deer and wild pigs or erect great V-shaped nets in the mountain passes to catch giant fruit bats during the season when their meat is sweetened by mangos. From time-to-time rumours of tigers still come out of these forests – flesh-and-blood tigers, not the more common spirit-tigers that can enter a man's body and cause him to run amok in violent and potentially fatal trances.

Although few of the people of West Bali have been to those jungles, they can look at their *penjor* and recognise the spot where the rainwater runs through the highland plantations of coffee, cloves, cinnamon and cacao. Shortly after it irrigates the rubber forests it enters the all-important paddies, governed by the ancient *Subak* organisations that ensure that every farmer gets his share.

At about chest height on the *penjor* there's a platform on which offerings for the gods are placed and below this hangs a coconut. It's fitting that space should be made for a symbol of the trees that still fringe the coast in an area that is yet to be forested with the concrete pillars of resorts and beach clubs. At the foot of the *penjor* there will be a small offering that is splashed with *arak*, brewed from fermented palm sap. This offering at the lower extreme of the *penjor* 'map' is laid down to placate the demons and spirits who inhabit the beaches.

It is on these beaches, and among those demons, that this story is set.

1 – Sacrifices

In later years, when Dewi thought back about that morning, she would blame herself for not recognising the evil omen in the unburnt coconut husk.

Before she led Grandfather out of the house, she'd dutifully wrapped him in a sarong and tied a sash around his waist. She'd held his bony hand as they'd stepped out of their family compound through the redbrick archway, just as the procession appeared at the top of the hill.

Out in the street their neighbour Pande was kick-starting his old Vespa. "Good morning Grandfather. What news?"

The old man bared his toothless gums in the grimace that he imagined still passed as a smile and Pande set off, dragging a blue puff of exhaust smoke along a street that was already smudged with incense. The receding pop-pop-pop throb of the scooter's engine jostled with the clatter of the approaching procession.

Grandfather had long ago reached the age where his name itself had become taboo. "The gods have a list of the old people who are waiting to be called," Dewi's mother had explained when Dewi was still a little girl. "If we speak the name of an old person, the gods might realise they've forgotten to take him."

So, all the elderly people in the village – and across the island of Bali – were known only as Grandfather or Grandmother. Since there were no family names it could sometimes get confusing. If pushed to distinguish, however, they could usually rely on some identifying factor: there was 'Grandfather who worked in the post office'; 'Grandmother who sees the ghosts'; 'Grandfather with the webbed toes'… Dewi's grandfather was known as 'Grandfather the soldier' but never to his face, which was fortunate because that had been a stage of his life – and a part of his destiny – that he preferred not to think about.

Grandfather had mislaid his identification card more than thirty years ago and there'd never been a reason to replace it since he never travelled beyond the village boundaries. For this reason, he'd lost count entirely of how old he was.

Dewi held the half coconut husk before the old man's opaque eyes. "Take this Grandfather."

The old man squatted down. Although he was still flexible, after a lifetime spent doubled over in the paddies, she'd noticed that his arthritis seemed to be getting worse every day. His hands shook as he tried to hold the cigarette-lighter to the husk. The procession was coming closer now and the village musicians were already drowning out the rumble of waves that came from the beach. The heavy gongs clanked like buffalo bells and the *ceng ceng* cymbals joined in with rippling shivers that were crisp as a mountain brook. To the Balinese listeners there was nothing incongruous about the apparently joyful clamour of the funeral.

The early sun sliced between the coconut trees in cardamom-coloured sabres that clashed with the steely-blue smoke rising straight from offerings laid out all along the street. Even now, on the stillest of mornings, it was easy to note the direction of the tradewinds from the way in which they had sculpted the palms.

Dewi imagined that the smoke from Grandfather's offering would act as a sort of veil behind which the old man could hide as the funeral procession passed on its way to the cremation ground beside the Death Temple. It was a barricade that prevented the gods and demons from noticing the old man as they passed with the corpse.

Once the husk was lit and Dewi was sure that the old man remembered how to perform the simple ritual she hurried back into their compound to tend to the rice she'd left boiling.

Grandfather muttered his prayers and gently waved his hand, wafting the essence of the offering on its way.

Only when he'd hauled himself painfully back to his feet did Grandfather turn his moist eyes towards the approaching procession. Of all the people in the village he was one of only a few who recalled the name that had once belonged to the white-shrouded corpse.

"Komang Sari," he whispered under his breath. It had been a long time since those sounds had formed in his mouth but they still had the taste of wild honey. "It feels like several lifetimes since we held hands."

He didn't wait for the procession to pass. He preferred to remember her as she was when they were teenagers – before her family had forced her to marry a man of a higher caste. He turned, heavy with sadness, and hobbled back into the compound.

He'd been back inside less than a minute when the husk stopped smoking.

When Dewi swept the compound out later that morning she noticed that the husk had barely been blackened by the singe of fire. Forever afterwards she was haunted with guilt because she hadn't waited with the old man to make sure the flames took hold.

And who can say for sure that this seemingly unimportant incident didn't trigger the series of bizarre events that began to unfold in the peaceful little village?

><><><><<

From where he sat propped on his boat on the beach Rahim could only just hear the funeral procession. He was blissfully smoking his first cigarette of the day. He'd been intending to give them up because the fishing business was going through bad times and this was one luxury that he could no longer afford. One glance at Rahim's chiselled jaw and sinewy forearms was enough to reveal him as a determined, hard-working man. Strangers always assumed that the barrel-chest, drooping moustache and intense eyes could only belong to a man who had no patience for weakness. But the cigarettes had turned out to be harder to give up than he'd expected.

Life provided enough trials without adding to them needlessly. So, for the time being, he smoked only when his wife Kadek wasn't around.

He'd woken feeling anxious after a restless night filled with dreams that were permeated with the yelping of dogs. If, as the islanders said, dreams were 'the flowers of sleep' then it was cruel that lately so many of Rahim's seemed to have thorns. Unlike some of his Muslim neighbours, Rahim didn't actively dislike dogs. They were just a part of village life, like the pigs that his Hindu neighbours bred for their feasts. He preferred to keep both pigs and dogs at a distance however, and the fact that the latter were now playing an active part in his dreams made him distinctly uneasy.

But now all his worries were being lifted, on a spiralling coil of clove-scented smoke, into the coconut palms over his head. The merest hint of a breeze rustled the spearhead leaves of the bamboo huddled along the bank of the stream. Rahim recalled that some of the old people believed that, if you listened carefully, you could tell

7

the future from the sound of the bamboo. There were times when you would swear that the bamboo was weeping softly. On days when the wind picked up the great green pillars leaned heavily on each other and you could hear them moaning, as they jostled like mournful drunks. On this bright morning it seemed to Rahim that the bamboo stands were singing softly, swaying almost imperceptibly.

It was a good omen, he thought. With luck, by the time he'd finished this cigarette his nephew would have arrived and they could get to work mending that shredded net. He was perched on the diminutive outrigger fishing boat that, in line with an old family tradition, he'd named *Sinar Bulan* – Moon Ray. As he smoked, his free hand roamed over the narrow spine of wood that formed the gunwales. His calloused fingers stroked the cracked blue paint and explored the grooves that had been scoured by countless nets. Fishing was like gambling he thought. And, like gamblers, they worked at night. On particularly favourable nights when boats from every village motored out with spotlights as lures they transformed the normally empty bay into a glittering Las Vegas skyline. Every waterborne gambler doing his best to tempt Lady Luck with the sparkle of diamonds.

The daylight was just for preparation and the never-ending maintenance of boat, engine and nets. As his fingers traced the furrows, he imagined that he could recall every heavy net that he'd pulled in, just as a gambler might remember every winning roll of the dice or a cock-fighting aficionado might remember every victorious rooster. Among all those heavy nets there had been so many others that were disappointingly light. So many years of his life had been spent perched on this boat that his body had adapted to fit the contours of the timber. His spine, cushioned only by a threadbare T-shirt, rested comfortably in the slight curve of the boat's stumpy mast.

When his family had relocated from Java over half a century ago such boats had still been powered by sail. People used to say that these boats 'ate the wind'. Rahim imagined that life had been even harder for his pioneering grandfather, but you had to wonder if some things had advanced for the better; the original *Sinar Bulan* would merely have 'eaten the wind' whereas the voracious Chinese outboard motor of its descendant never ceased to guzzle petrol.

The old ways die hard in these islands and, although within a few years the sails were supplanted by the unreliable little engines, the masts themselves refused to disappear entirely. Instead, like the withered tail of some evolving sea-creature, the masts gradually diminished until they were just hardwood posts rising two metres over the stern. Although this post was still known in Indonesian as 'the hand of the sail' it was now just symbolic and served no purpose beyond a tying point for a tarpaulin shelter on hot days or rainy nights. There was also a sweeping curve of bamboo, brightly painted to symbolise a furled sail, running along the length of the boat at head-height. This fake boom came in handy for drying nets but, other than that, it too was a useless decoration. Mounted on *Sinar Bulan*'s stunted mast was the carved head of a creature with bulbous eyes and a set of vicious fangs that protruded from a snarling dog-like snout. A devilish pair of blood-red horns swooped up from the top of the head.

Few of the foreign surfers who walked past took the time to notice the details of the thirty or so brightly painted boats, let alone the demonic effigies perched on the atrophied masts. Perhaps this was just as well because Rahim, and the other Muslims among his fishermen colleagues, would have been horrified if anyone had ever asked why the boats were mounted with dogs' heads. Despite first appearances, the effigy was not that of a dog but of a semi-mythical deer known as a *menjangan*. The deer were powerful swimmers and it was said that they were sometimes seen far out to sea, migrating between islands. Rahim had heard that these deer still roamed the coastal forests at the far western tip of the island but he'd never seen them for himself. It would be a two-hour journey from the village on his rusting moped and he'd never travelled that far. Nevertheless, there were few fishermen in the village (whether Hindu or Muslim) who would trust a boat that wasn't protected by a carved *menjangan* head.

Rahim's nephew and fishing-partner Yunus had summed it up as they sat out on the tossing waves one night. "All I know is that I have more faith in the power of the *menjangan* to get us home," he said, "than I do in that Chinese motor."

But the fishermen needed to travel fast if they were to compete with the big commercial boats from the fishing port along the coast. Like psychedelic Moorish palaces those big boats seemed

9

to fly across the water in a blaze of dayglo fretwork and flickering lights. The long arms of their ranks of outboard motors leant them the appearance of Viking longboats and, to Rahim and his fisher-folk friends, they were like marauding pirates. If this was indeed a gambling game, thought Rahim as he took a last drag of his cigarette, then those big boats with their crews of twenty or more men were, quite literally, playing with a loaded deck.

He flicked the stump of his cigarette onto the black volcanic sand, wondering irritably why Yunus was late again. As he looked up his eyes caught a flicker far down the beach, a glint of yellow fabric that fluttered as if in a breeze. It was rolling, almost billowing, along the ribbon of driftwood and seaweed that marked the hightide line.

The distant yelling reached Rahim the instant that he realised it was a woman running. The blood started pounding in his ears as he leapt from the boat to run towards her.

>◇◇◇<<

Natalia de Souza had lain awake right through the hours of darkness, listening to the sounds of the Balinese night. She considered herself an experienced traveller and was vaguely ashamed that the series of flights from her home in Brazil had resulted in a bout of jetlag that had stretched on for almost a week. As she recognised each night-call she tried to focus on another more distant one. It was a trick Nat's grandmother had taught her as a little girl when she'd had trouble sleeping and she imagined that it would be as perfectly suited to this West Bali coastline as it was to her family home in the tropical city of Belém.

It had been five years since she'd last visited this island and yet most of the noises were still incredibly familiar. Tokays, those enormous orange-spotted geckos, dominated the night with their bellowing 'Toh-KAAAAY' calls. These giant geckos had become a torment to Nat ever since someone told her that it was good luck to hear a tokay call exactly seven times in succession; now, whenever she heard the first call, she was condemned to stay awake to count them. Sixes and eights were common enough and occasionally they would repeat the call up to an infuriating twelve times. But she'd never heard a tokay make seven calls. Maybe she was just unlucky.

10

In the silence between the tokay calls Nat could hear the croaking of frogs – beckoning the rains – and the ominous hoot of an owl, the Balinese 'ghost bird'. The first hint of dawn seeped into the room and Nat could just discern the paperback copy of *Dona Flor and Her Two Husbands* that lay on the dresser. She was looking forward to delving back into the Brazilian classic by Jorge Amado with the same sensations she might have felt for a long-awaited meeting with an old friend from home. Nat had read it in the original Portuguese version many years before and remembered it as the magical tale of an everyday woman trying to disentangle two sides of her personality. She had the feeling that there might be a benefit in rereading it now.

The distant crow of village roosters and the bickering of the packs of semi-wild beach-dogs almost convinced her that sleep would now be impossible and she'd still been wondering about reaching for the book when, finally, she dozed off.

When she awoke sunlight was flickering through the flimsy curtains. *Matahari*, the sun was called in Indonesian. It meant 'the eye of the day' and she imagined it peering through the woven rattan walls of her room.

Now Nat was aware of the hollow, booming explosions of waves pounding onto the beach. As if in an echo, her heart started hammering in her chest, pumping a rush of adrenalin that jolted her fully awake.

It had been a long time since she'd last surfed and she'd prefer not to face powerful waves before she'd had a chance to ease gently back into the water.

"No worries, no hurries," she reassured herself as she slipped from under the sheet.

There was no obligation to force herself into the surf until she was ready. And besides, the building project here at Bali Moon Eco-resort was progressing slower than expected. She was going to have plenty to keep her busy even before the resort finally opened and she could start on the managerial work she'd been hired to do.

Standing in front of the dresser mirror Nat wrapped a sarong around her back then, holding her unruly strands of thick black hair aside, she tied the ends of the fabric around her neck to create a dress. The yellow print glowed against the toasted caramel of her legs and the shards of early sunlight illuminated green eyes that, according to family legend, had been bequeathed by a Portuguese sugarcane planter. Nat found it intriguing that the Balinese were so often confused at the sight of a *bule* (tourist) with darker skin than their own. While the tourists baked in the sun, aspiring to something close to Nat's natural skin-tone, the islanders spent their hard-earned rupiah on an array of skin-whitening products that promised to bleach them to a deathly paleness.

It was Nat's habit to start the day with a series of sun-salutations but the sleepless night had undermined her motivation for yoga. Surf could wait too. She'd go for a stroll along the beach and simply watch the waves for a while to gauge their power before paddling out into the surf for the first time.

>><><><><<

"The girl was in such a panic that she almost ran right past me," said Rahim. Yunus watched his uncle's hands as he fiddled with the cigarette he'd forgotten to light.

"She'd found the body of a young woman at the end of the beach," the older man continued. "It was half-buried under a log."

"Did anyone recognise her, bro'? Do they know who she is?"

Irritated, Rahim pushed the unlit cigarette back into its pack as he turned away. His nephew was increasingly drawn to the surfer lifestyle. A fondness for Western slang was an annoyance Rahim tolerated. The drinking was more of a problem.

"Maybe the police will be able to find out who she was," he said. "For the moment you and I still have work to do."

They worked in silence but Rahim's mind was as busy as his hands instinctively untangled a net: Who was the young woman? Had she been on the beach the night before? He prided himself on being immune to the superstitions that plagued many of his neighbours, but it still seemed strange that people should want to visit a beach after sunset. When the soaring palms began to throw their shadows along the beach, like slender fingers crawling across the sand, surely anybody ought to realise that it was time to retire to the security of the houses.

Rahim refused to pigeonhole his friends according to religion but, like almost everyone in the village, he classed his acquaintances according to whether they spent their nights working the ocean or their days among the paddies and orchards. The village was almost equally divided into the paddy-people and the fisher-folk. The latter tended to be relatively recent arrivals in the area who had settled on the coastal land that the predominantly Hindu farmers had deliberately left uninhabited because of their traditional fear for the ocean. Many of the fisher-folk hailed from the coast of Muslim Java but, after several generations, they'd long been considered a permanent feature of the community. Rahim considered that, in general, these relative latecomers were less fearfully superstitious; they cherry-picked what was useful from the old traditions but shunned some of the beliefs that made life so complicated for their Hindu neighbours.

As a small boy Rahim learned to use the *tuba* plant to stun the minnows in rockpools so that he could collect them for bait. He learned that the juice from croton leaves would stop bleeding, the *jarak* plant could heal cuts and ulcers and how to treat burns and grazes with the thorny aloe leaves that the villagers called 'crocodile tongue'. Although his family had refused to accept that the moringa trees that once grew in every Balinese compound was a sacred plant that could cure the evil eye, they accepted that it was highly nutritious and wisely incorporated it into feast-day recipes.

In their bravado as youngsters Rahim and his friends would sometimes scandalise the old folks by hanging out on the beach after dark, boasting that they were unafraid of the ghosts and *leyaks* (witches) that so terrified their Hindu classmates. In addition to these, the older villagers especially were intimidated by a whole host of demons: there was a demon who feasted on corpses that were buried on inauspicious days; another who consumed people who walked around after sunset; and still others who ate people who slaughtered four-legged animals, or climbed the coconut trees, on the wrong days. Hindu's among Rahim's fisher-folk friends were even at risk if they wove nets on inauspicious days.

Rahim himself had married a Hindu woman from a farming family. She had adopted his Muslim faith and he was grateful that she had so easily integrated into the fisher-folk community. She'd been born in the village several years after her family arrived as refugees after the great eruption of 1963 when the sacred Mount Agung destroyed their farms, causing a famine across the whole island. Their home city of Karangasem, near the base of the mountain, had been almost destroyed and afterwards its name had been changed to Amlapura in an effort to shake off spectacularly bad karma.

In those days, parcels of land were allocated by the government to any settlers in West Bali who took the trouble to clear the terrain but, even into current times, all land bordering the coast had been left uninhabited.

When you walked up the hill from the beach the house where Rahim and Kadek lived with their two small sons was the first building you came across. Between his simple two-room breezeblock house and the water's edge lay two hundred metres of what might have looked to an uninitiated visitor like untamed jungle. Apart from a section of forest near the village's Death Temple, virtually the entire coast had long ago been conquered. While its ragged-leafed canopy was formed by lofty coconut palms, the shady undergrowth was thick with banana and cacao trees. On a part of the island that had still seen almost no tourism development, these coastal plantations had remained unchanged for a thousand years. Since the first civilisations in these islands coconut palms had provided food, drink, timber, thatch, copra fuel, palm sugar and even alcohol. The families who harvested these crops shared half their yield with the all-powerful landowner Pak Gusti. The banana trees did not even produce fruit and instead the workers scraped together a few rupiah selling squares of banana leaves to be used for disposable packaging. Two families were in the business of brewing illegal arak from coconut sap but these bootleggers operated in remoter areas. Arak brewing was said to be lucrative, but the on-the-spot fines incurred during police raids were so frequent (and perfectly coordinated) that the moonshine families barely scraped together a living in the poorest alleyways of the paddy-people community.

Nobody – even among the most fearless bootleggers or the most progressive fisher-folk – would risk living on the beach itself. The fishermen who worked at night with lamps as their lures would often choose to stay out on a violent sea fighting a storm rather than approach the beach during the hours of darkness.

The only exception was the *warung* eatery, the dining shack at the eastern end of the bay in front of the surf-point, where 'Bu Ana lived. But there were rumours that that strange woman must herself be some sort of *leyak*. After all, the villagers pointed out, only a witch would be brave enough to live there.

Rahim had been a small child when he was first aware of surfers arriving in the village. They rarely stayed more than a couple of days, renting an empty room in a family compound. They were long-haired and semi-naked and people said that they came from some Western tribe called Hippies. Most were merely fleeting novelties but once – an occasion that caused great hilarity among the schoolboys – a group of men and women had been seen *entirely* naked, crouching like cavemen as they gathered shellfish from the rockpools. Now years later, as a middle-aged married man, Rahim still looked upon the *bule* (foreigners) as extra-terrestrials and felt that he was barely any closer to understanding their ways. It was said that there were thousands upon thousands of *bule* in the beach towns in the east of the island. Friends who'd been there had told Rahim that there were more *bule* on the beach at Kuta than there were nuts in Pak Gusti's coconut grove. Rahim had never been to Kuta but he was sure that these accounts must be exaggerations.

He'd been a teenager when the *bules* began to arrive in greater numbers. They complained that the east was too crowded and they wanted space and solitude. They came in search of what they called The Real Bali. At first, they demanded nothing beyond pristine waves and a plate of fish and rice. Although few took time to learn anything of their host's language, most of these travellers acted with respect.

Rahim and Kadek had just married when Pak Gusti decided to build the Bali Bulan Hotel. Although it was grandly designated a hotel, the Bali Bulan was really just a collection of half a dozen bamboo shacks with mattresses, fans and squat toilets.

Despite their different outlooks, the fisher-folk and the paddy-people had shaken their collective heads in disbelief at the suggestion that foreigners would pay for the privilege of sleeping on the beach. It was impossible to imagine that, when sensible people abandoned the shoreline in the evening to make way for the orgies of witches and demons, relatively wealthy tourists would pay good money for an opportunity to sleep there.

Although he could see no future in the scheme, Rahim had been grateful for an opportunity to work as a labourer in the embryonic local tourist industry. He'd made enough wages from that

15

project to build their breezeblock house so that he and his young wife could move out of his father's increasingly overcrowded compound.

Over the course of time it became clear that the *bules* wanted more than just a taste of The Real Bali. Like the god that they'd apparently left back home in their own lands they wanted to create Bali in their own image. They reinvented the island according to their ideals of a beach paradise. Even the witches and demons had to move over to make way for bonfires around which pale-skinned figures cavorted demonically.

It's been said that everyone gets what they wish for if only they can wait for long enough. Pak Gusti certainly got everything he asked for. Two years ago, he'd sold the land on which his hotel stood to an Australian entrepreneur and then he'd moved up to the hills. And that was how Bali Moon Eco-resort was born.

But the old people among both fisher-folk and the paddy-people prophesised that the witches and demons would not stay quiet forever.

>><><><<<

Dewi had been ill at ease ever since she'd noticed Grandfather's unburned coconut husk. When she'd heard at the market about the body that had been found on the beach that morning she couldn't restrain her gasp of surprise. She was haunted by a feeling that she had something to do with the death. When, the woman selling fruit mentioned that the body had been clad only in the bottom half of a green bikini Dewi dashed out of the market gateway, skidding on a floor that was oily with vegetable matter and fish scales.

She'd planned to use the morning preparing offerings. For most Hindu women in the village it was a never-ending task that occupied several hours each day. But it would have to wait because she realised that she needed to discuss this situation urgently with her aunt Ana. Only a presentiment that it would be wise to avoid the beach made her hesitate. To get to 'Bu Ana's dining shack Dewi would have to walk down to the fishing boats and then almost a kilometre eastward along a beach that she would have preferred to avoid. At least for today.

But Dewi considered herself a strong woman who was not easily swayed from her duty. The tricks of an unjust fate – which might have embittered and hardened the character of another person – had, in Dewi's case, instilled a spirit of sweetness and patience. She sometimes wondered if she was paying a penalty for something terrible she'd done in another life but her neighbours agreed that her karmic trials had created a character that was almost saintly. As she walked down the steep hill towards the beach Dewi thought ruefully how they'd change their tune if they ever learned that she was on record with the police in the city as a psychotic knife-wielding mad-woman.

As she walked past the fishing boats Dewi resisted the temptation to look westwards along the beach. She knew that the police would long ago have removed the body – maybe they'd even swept the scene for clues like they did in the movies – but the images in her mind were vivid enough without having to lay eyes on the actual setting just yet.

She tried to think of something else. Since the subject rarely lay submerged in her mind for long it was natural that she thought now about her daughter. Marriage had been a living nightmare but, even two years after it ended, Dewi's separation from six-year-old Ayu was infinitely worse. She'd thought she was in love but in hindsight it had just been a childish infatuation with a man she saw as a romantic rebel. She'd always considered herself homely and there had been something irresistibly flattering in the fact that, after all the women he'd known, it was Dewi who'd tamed this modern-day buccaneer who travelled the islands as a lorry driver. They married within two months of meeting each other and Dewi imagined that the whirlwind love affair was the stuff of soap-opera romances. As a good Balinese wife, she moved into her husband's family compound near the city and, under the watchful eye of his doting mother, she did her best to become a model daughter-in-law.

They'd only been married a month by the time she realised that he wasn't tamed at all. In fact, suddenly back within reach of the attractions of the city, he was wilder than she could have imagined. His driving duties offered the perfect alibis and she never knew if he was at work or simply sleeping elsewhere. The man she'd married was almost a stranger and her new family turned a blind eye to his increasing abusiveness. She hoped things might improve when they found a cheap rented room but he was more dedicated to spending time gambling at the cockfighting pit than either working or being with her. When he won he blew his winnings on whores. When he lost it was even worse and he became abusive and violent. She thought that the maturity of fatherhood would help tame him and, in a remarkably short time, she became pregnant. She had a rough pregnancy and in her darkest days – when she felt least attractive – she even felt that she could understand his straying after other women. When it was all over it seemed that the baby was all she had in the world and for more than three years Dewi rarely strayed from their tiny room.

The last time he hit her she defended herself with a kitchen knife. He spent several days in hospital when the stitches in his arm turned septic and, by the time he returned home, he'd lost his job and they were unable to pay the rent. The police told her that she was lucky not to be in prison and reiterated that, as she was clearly an unfit mother, the baby Ayu would remain in the care of her husband's family. That same terrible week her own mother had died and Dewi returned to her family home to become Grandfather's carer.

It was usual in Balinese society that the children stayed with the family of the father and Dewi personally knew several women who remained married to abusive husbands solely to avoid the certainty of losing their children. She often thought she would prefer the vindictive treatment of her husband – and even the beatings – to the enforced separation from little Ayu. Until she found a waitressing job at the resort, she'd struggled to support herself and Grandfather by making temple offerings, as her mother had done, to be sold at the market. It would still be a long time before the resort opened and the restaurant was just an early attempt by the new owner to at least make some cash while building progressed.

By now Dewi had reached the huge rock shelf that served as the natural breakwater for the section of the beach where the boats sheltered. Her skirt was bunched in a chubby fist and her toes gripped the rubber of her flipflops as she worked her way gingerly over the seaweed-strewn rocks. Powerful waves were crashing against the eastern edge of this raised reef, throwing salty mist into the air. It always surprised her how the sections of beach either side of this headland were so dramatically different. It was often hard to imagine they could be part of the same ocean. Everything in Bali was said to be perpetually swinging in a balance – good and evil, joy and sorrow, peace and violence – and in this spot, more than anywhere else on the coast, the sea itself seemed to be emphasise this philosophy.

Only her aunt would dream of making a home on this wildest section of the beach. Dewi shuddered – no wonder people thought she was a witch.

Farther around the curve of the bay Dewi could make out the *alang alang* thatched roof of the *warung*, standing out among the deep green of the shoreline palms like a terrace of sun-bleached rice plants. A flash of iridescent blue caught her eye as a kingfisher erupted from strangely pink sand that carpeted this part of the beach. The bird's vicious bill, like a dagger dipped in blood, was in startling contrast to its sapphire plumage. Dewi's thick calves ached as she slogged through the soft sand above the hightide line and clambered up the tangle of roots that offered the *warung* scant protection from the waves. She slipped off her flip-flops beside the cracked concrete slab and stepped into the shade of the open shelter with its four rickety tables.

"Good morning Dewi. What news?" came a voice from beyond the ramshackle bamboo bar at the back of the room. "I had a feeling I'd see you today."

Dewi realised that it had been more than a week since she'd visited her aunt. "I've been busy preparing offerings for the funeral and Grandfather needs more and more help," she replied.

'Bu Ana stepped into a triangle of sunlight that sliced through the palms. She had a floral sarong tied over her ample breasts and her long jet-black hair was damp. Another visitor would have assumed that she'd just showered, but Dewi knew that she often went into the sea in the mornings after praying. 'Bu Ana was unusual – perhaps even unique among the paddy-people or the fisher-folk – for the fact that she was in the habit of going into the sea. While she was too fearful of the waves to actually swim, the fishermen would sometimes see her wading waist-deep, wrapped only in a flimsy sarong. Dewi had sometimes heard the gossips at the market tutting with an air of superiority: "it's a shame," they said, "that 'Bu Ana is so careless of her appearance." They pursed their lips at the way she let her heavy hair hang loose and allowed the sun to darken her skin: "like a peasant," they said.

Although their husbands nodded in agreement it was noticeable that they were much more complimentary about 'Bu Ana's appearance among themselves.

Now she signalled Dewi to sit down. The table had obviously been cobbled together from the wood of an old outrigger and Dewi noticed that the edge of the blue timber was curiously runnelled with smooth ridges. "You heard what happened, right?"

It wasn't a question. Dewi was aware that, although 'Bu Ana lived in this isolated location, little happened either on the beach or among the highland homes of the paddy-people that she wasn't aware of.

The older woman nodded. "I was very sorry to hear about the dead girl." She pushed a plate across the table and blocks of sweetened seaweed jelly quivered as if resonating to the husky tone of her voice. Her eyes held Dewi's gaze. "And you've come to see me because she was wearing a green bikini?" she said.

>><><><><<

There was a sense of freedom about this tropical life. It was a feeling that the young woman, barely into her twenties, had never experienced at home in Russia. She relished emerging from her bed and not having to wrap herself in clothing before stepping out into the open air. Just to be able to do this provoked a sensation of liberation in a healthy young body that had yearned for the heat throughout two decades of Siberian childhood. Simply to feel the sun on her body day after day was an almost unimaginable privilege.

Since she'd started learning to surf, three months ago, the doors had been flung open onto a way of life that would have been impossible to imagine for the girl's parents in their bleak landlocked homeland.

Although she'd never have admitted it to anyone, surfing was not all fun, however. There was an edge of stress to the sport that she refused to admit even to herself. If she arrived at the beach to see that the waves were crowded a knot of nervous tension began to grow in her stomach. It sometimes took determination to convince herself that – as a beginner *and* as a female – she had as much right to a place in the lineout as anyone else. A girlfriend had once summed the situation up for her: "When a guy paddles out into the surf he's given the benefit of the doubt until he shows that he *can't* surf. When a girl paddles out everyone assumes she *can't* surf until she proves she can."

Several times she'd been so intimidated that she'd finally paddled away on her own. Then, out of earshot beyond the shoulder of the wave, she gave herself a good talking too, scolding herself quietly in the harsh Slavic tones of her grandmother's voice.

The retro twin-fin surfboard was at least six-inches too short for her but it looked the part. It made it hard to catch waves though and she certainly missed many more than she caught. Twice she'd had unpleasant experiences with surfers in the water. Not with islanders, who were mostly patient and understanding, but with foreigners who were more aggressive in pursuit of their precious holiday wave-quota. She had ended up in tears once after she'd ditched her board to dive under a wave and the board had hit another surfer. He hadn't yelled at her but – what was even worse – he'd given her a look that said more clearly than words that she didn't deserve her place in the lineout. She'd paddled back to the beach with tears in her eyes, convinced that he was right.

But surfing was all about maintaining that positive vibe, chasing the legendary 'stoke' that surfers spoke about as if it were a sort of holy grail of the mind. So, whenever anyone asked how the session had been, she always managed to summon a tone of enthusiasm into her reply. 'Fake it until you make it,' was her philosophy.

She embraced the surf-terminology too and gave it full license to pepper her guttural English. It was all part of the tropical dream she was living. She started her days with 'a dawn raid on the point' and ended with 'a sunset sesh on the beachbreak'.

So, this morning she woke at first light and slipped into her bikini in preparation for another 'dawn patrol'. She wouldn't admit even to herself that the yearned for 'stoke' was probably at its most powerful – much like sex – in the preparation for the surf rather than in the act itself. She went through the ritual of waxing her board, feeling the first rays of the sun kissing her tanned back.

With her sun-bleached hair and bronzed legs, she was an almost unrecognisable avatar of the girl who'd left the frozen north six months ago. She revelled in the freedom to be able to hop onto her scooter. No helmet. No shoes. No worries. Just a healthy young woman in a bikini with her board bungee-ed into the side-rack on the bike. She saw herself as a feminist and, far from mindlessly flaunting her body, she was deliberately affirming her liberation: if anyone, in their misguided narrow-mindedness, thought there was something disrespectful or offensive about her outfit then that was their problem and not hers.

The rented bike was only costing her a couple of dollars a day. It had been giving her some problems lately and this morning it took a few attempts before the engine started.

That delay – only about twenty seconds – made all the difference.

As she eased out onto the main road she heard the roar of several high-powered motorbikes, throttles wound open, as they came over crest of the hill.

She kept cautiously to the gravel at the edge of the road as the first motorbike shot past with a roar. The second bike was so close that a gust of wind blew her blonde hair up in a shimmering banner.

The third rider, following his friends, eased up slightly on the throttle and turned in the saddle to look at the apparition in the green bikini. She shot him a dirty look.

He was still looking directly into her eyes when he hit the oncoming truck.

>◇◇◇◇<

Anyone who saw 'Bu Ana and her niece Dewi sitting across the table from each other in the *warung* might have been struck by how similar they were. They had the same darkly mysterious eyes that contrasted strangely with a mischievous turn of the mouth. But there was something sensual about the older woman's posture that seemed to have skipped Dewi's generation and it was doubtful now that the niece would mature along the same statuesque lines as the aunt.

Despite her love for her aunt, there was something about her that Dewi had always found slightly intimidating. During her painfully insecure teenage years she'd tortured herself by measuring her own development against her aunt's infamous sex appeal. And now, even in the relatively confident maturity of her mid-twenties, she was just accepting the fact that she'd never be blessed with the same carelessly sexy swing of the hip when she walked, or the same hypnotic rise of the breasts when she sighed. Dewi's mother had been a mousey woman, as far removed from her younger sister as a flat-bottomed fishing skiff would be from a full-rigged Sulawesi schooner.

Dewi's father had died shortly after she was born and, realising that it pained her mother to talk about him, she'd soon learned not to mention him at all. Since Grandfather stepped in so effectively as a father-figure, it hardly mattered anyway.

Her mother had looked after Grandfather with such selfless and ceaseless devotion that she rarely even appeared in the street. If pushed into voicing an opinion, people said that she'd been almost a saint but in reality she'd made so little impact on the village that even now, just a few years after her death, it was only Grandfather who seemed to remember her. Dewi's marriage had been coming to a bitter end when a sickness swept through the village, and neighbours told her later that her mother had maintained a sleepless vigil beside the old man's mattress. Word had circulated around the village that the mysterious sickness could be cured with turtle eggs washed down with arak. Every night worried family members scoured the beach with lanterns watching for the bulky forms of turtles emerging from the waves. The creatures would be followed across the sand as they struggled, in single-minded determination, towards the hightide line to deposit their eggs.

So many people were ill with what became known as the Big Sickness that there were never enough eggs to go around. Frustration mounted as the turtles made their painfully slow journeys up the beach. Arguments frequently broke out about who had seen the turtle first and there had sometimes been fistfights on the sand even before she started laying. The great reptiles would industriously dig their nests with kicking rear fins only to be robbed as the eggs emerged from their bodies. The lucky ones would spend another half-hour of panting labour covering the empty nest, before they could shuffle as fast as their stubby flippers would allow them back to the waves. The less fortunate would be killed for their meat although it was not a taste that appealed to many. Some desperate people realised that it was better simply to kill the turtle as soon as it came to the beach, so that they could harvest the eggs straight from the lifeless body.

Dewi's mother spent her savings on turtle-eggs and arak (which tripled in price during the weeks that the Big Sickness lasted). The neighbours said that she'd barely slept the whole time. They heard her through the wall talking to the old man at all hours, reminiscing about crazy things that had happened in the neighbourhood and – when she exhausted those recollections – inventing things that were even more unlikely. She would stop when he fell asleep but the moment he stirred she would continue her discourse as if she'd never paused. Then on the eighth night a powerful fever broke and Grandfather woke the next morning with the bed soaked with sweat. To the surprise of the whole neighbourhood he was entirely cured.

Two days later Dewi's mother contracted the same fever and died.

Despite her mother's disapproval for her rebellious sister, Dewi and her aunt had always been drawn to each other. Even when she was tiny Dewi had her own rebellious streak and she would invent excuses so that she could spend time at Ana's house. If she was sent out on a quick errand she'd make a detour past her aunt's house and stay so long that she sometimes forgot why she'd gone out in the first place. Although Ana's house was one of the humblest in the poor alleyways of the paddy-people community, her hospitality was legendary. No matter what time little Dewi arrived there she'd find Ana's friends sitting on the floor-mats sipping sweet black coffee and munching on snacks. The laughter, chatter and gossip were lively antidotes to the austerity of her own home where her mousy mother and taciturn Grandfather passed their days in monastic silence. Best of all, Ana always had delicious shop-bought snacks in place of the chunks of fermented cassava or steamed rice-cakes that were offered to guests in other homes. These were the days long before Ana owned the *warung* but it had never occurred to Dewi to ask how she could afford such luxuries.

There were some among the neighbourhood gossips who intimated – with raised eyebrows and worldly smirks – that as far as men were concerned Ana's sense of hospitality knew no bounds. Dewi was almost a teenager when such comments started to amount to suspicion in her mind.

"Women are always complaining that men are unreliable," her aunt told her once with a smile. It was the only time Dewi ever heard her mention the subject. "But I've found that once you understand what makes men tick, they're actually the most predictable creatures on earth."

>><><><<

'Bu Ana had never imagined that she'd become a *warung* owner. She'd still lived in the village when Pak Gusti set up the old Bali Bulan Hotel but as the *bule* started arriving in greater numbers she became increasingly nervous. Then she heard that he'd sold the hotel to a foreign developer. She told Dewi that she'd had a dream and woke to the realisation that she must find a way to protect the little temple on the opposite side of the rock shelf from what would one day become a full-blown invasion.

Nobody could deny that 'Bu Ana had more than her share of charm. Even now, edging into her late forties, the feistiness and sexual allure of her earlier years were still obvious enough to provoke men half her age to turn in the street. Nobody knew what hold she had over the – apparently happily married – Pak Gusti but somehow she'd convinced the wealthy landowner to let her build on a small patch of beach-front land that he owned east of the resort.

Everyone agreed that Pak Gusti had struck it lucky when he sold out to the Australian developer and moved his family to his wife's village, as she'd been demanding for years. It seemed too that Ana had caught the local landowner in what must have been a fit of unaccustomed generosity within hours of agreeing the sale. He gave her the piece of beachfront land in the spirit of some vague business partnership and she used the scant savings she'd gathered to build a *warung*.

Suddenly Ana had become a woman of substance. It was agreed without even discussion and by common consent, among paddy-people and fisher-folk alike, that Ana would henceforth be known by the honorary title of Ibu Ana (Mrs Ana).

After a while even the most tenacious gossips lost interest in the intricacies of the business deal. They simply wrote the *warung* off as one of the landowner's less successful entrepreneurial enterprises and – although the landlady, true to form, never got around to hanging a sign, the establishment became known universally as Buana's Warung.

>><><><<

To the few foreigners who visited the *warung* it was unexpected that the open side of the shack faced westwards along the coast rather than taking advantage of the spectacular view straight out towards the pounding waves of the surf-point. To any islander, however, it was logical. Even if you cut a simple path through the forest to the sea you would never cut a straight line along which the wind – and the demons and spirits that are carried on it – could whistle straight inland. It should be obvious to anyone that you must kink the path just slightly so that it sneaks up to the beach at an oblique angle. Everyone knows that evil spirits fly straight, like arrows, and find it hard to negotiate corners.

This aspect of the design was not lost on 'Bu Ana but while the floorplan of the *warung* had been oblique, her intentions had been somewhat more direct: on the day she hammered a series of marker pegs into the sandy soil she pictured the *warung* less as a restauranteur might see it, and more as a general might design a fortress. The view from her seat at the bar offered an unobstructed view along the curve of the beach to Bali Moon Eco-resort. She spent her days like a sentinel, chain-smoking clove-scented cigarettes, and watching over the beach.

"Yes, I remember the girl in the green bikini," she said now. "She came here with two friends last week and she was in tears. It occurred to me then that the green bikini would be the death of her…"

Dewi waited for her aunt to continue but the older woman was momentarily lost in thought, picturing the two *bule* surfers trying ineffectually to reassure the Russian woman that the motorcyclist would survive: "It was so horrible," she'd sobbed. "When they tried to take his helmet off they couldn't. His head was smashed…"

"When I heard what happened with that motorcycle crash I prayed that she'd never fully realise what part she'd played in it." 'Bu Ana spoke so quietly that her niece had to lean close to hear. "The motorcyclist died instantly. There was nothing more that could be done for him but the girl's life had to go on and I hoped that she'd never know how effectively she'd killed him. Then, when I heard that her body had been found this morning it suddenly struck me that it was like a double death."

Dewi shook her head sadly. "Perhaps she never knew…"

"After she came here last week I made offerings at the shrine…" 'Bu Ana interrupted with an expression of such uncharacteristic doubt that the younger woman held her breath. "I prayed that the goddess would never let the girl realise what she'd done."

>><><><><<

The women in the market said that the *warung* was destined for failure. It was the first eatery that had ever been built on the beach. Who would want to eat on the beach? Well, with a few exceptions, it soon became obvious that their husbands did.

'Bu Ana was shrewd enough to keep both her prices and the buttons of her blouse obligingly low. She sailed smoothly between the tables like the figurehead on the front of a galleon distributing miniature pyramids of *nasi jingo* among the castaways at the four tables. Before long it was noticed that some of the fishermen began to take longer to return home once they'd unloaded the day's catch and, after a while, even some of the farmers were making a lengthy detour via the *warung* on their way home from the paddies.

The landlady would allow no indecorous behaviour or rough language to sully her establishment. Occasionally the odd *bule* surfer might stop for a plate of fried noodles but it was doubtful if any ever realised that the water glasses of a few of the men were occasionally topped up instead with illicit arak. Drunkenness and gambling were strictly taboo and the perpetual card games at the *warung* were harmlessly playful affairs. A player was obliged to clip a clothes-peg onto his ear with each losing hand – and, when there was no space on his ears, to then continue around the flesh of his jawline. If, after the game was over, reckonings were tallied up in rupiah according to the numbers of those pegs…well, that was no business of the *warung*'s owner.

It didn't take long for the novelty to wear off, though, and *bule* customers became almost non-existent after the dining room opened at the resort. But in truth 'Bu Ana didn't really mind if the place was deserted most of the time. She was a woman with a divine mission and the *warung* was serving its purpose as a bastion of a unique faith.

High up on the wall hanging over the bar was a small shrine. It was similar to the shrine you'd find in any Hindu house in the village, with sheets of flimsy wood that were tacked together and wrapped in a skirt of shiny fabric. There was one noticeable difference about this shrine however: whereas all the others in the village were coloured yellow the cheap wood frame on this shrine was painted a rich green. As the electric fan above the bar tickled the satin sheen of the skirt it brought to mind water rippling across a shadowy rockpool. Above the shrine hung a printed oil-painting of a beautiful green-eyed woman. Her long black hair and her green robes appeared to billow as she stood, unperturbed and supremely confident, while a huge storm-driven wave reared behind her. There was something in the portrait that was at once reassuringly protective and immensely threatening.

While 'Bu Ana's shrine was unmistakably Hindu in style, the deity it honoured predated the arrival of both Hinduism and Islam because Nyai Roro Kidul was revered by adherents of both religions. She was feared throughout these islands as the Goddess of the South Seas and 'Bu Ana was her disciple.

>><><><><<

Rahim eased the two-wheeled trolley under the boat's bow as his friends balanced the outrigger arms over their shoulders and straightened their buckling legs. *Sinar Bulan* pivoted forward and the trolley took most of the weight. Now they began to haul it over the packed low-tide sand to the sheltered waves in the lee of the great rock shelf. Like a colony of seabirds each outrigger had its allotted resting spot on the beach. When they returned in the morning, after a night spent scouring the waves for fish, each boat returned to its designated spot to roost through the day with its outrigger arms splayed like drying wings. The hierarchy was politely respected in the knowledge that, should an owner one day trespass onto a prohibited nesting site, the entire colony would be thrown into squabbling pandemonium. Rahim was fortunate that he'd inherited

28

his father's position and could launch and land his boat from the sandy section of the beach. New arrivals were allotted outlying spots among the boulders. Life was harder for those fishermen because the trolley could not be used on the rocks and they were forced to struggle into the water with their boats on their shoulders. More importantly, they were also condemned to extra maintenance expenses: launched over sand a boat might, with care, last more than a decade without having her hull re-timbered but regular pounding on the rocks could limit the tortured timber planks only to a five-year lifespan.

'Lifespan' was a term that Rahim would have laughed at. He was not like the superstitious shipwrights from the big fishing port who believed that life would literally be breathed into their big *selerek* boats by boring a 'navel' through the keel prior to launching. Those owners were usually wealthy (despite their expensive ceremonies) and most owned at least two boats. This was because they always fished in pairs and their vessels were considered 'married' until one was destroyed leaving behind a 'widow'.

Rahim and his friends had reached the shallow waters now and the outrigger floated clear of the trolley as a wave lurched under her. Yunus used his surfer's instinct to anticipate the sideways skew as the hull twisted and flipped himself lithely into the boat. "I heard that the *selerek* crews were sent home yesterday because they believe a storm is coming."

Without responding Rahim helped drag the trolley back to the sand then trotted over and swung into the boat himself. Only then did he look up towards the mountains to reassure himself that the peaks were cloaked in the merest wisps of mist. "Let's make the most of it then. Without the *selerek* fleet snapping up the fish we might come home with a real catch."

Let the owners of the big boats listen to the predictions of their priests and fortune-tellers, Rahim thought; a fisherman should feel such things in his blood.

The Chinese motor kicked into life with the third pull of the starter cord. A good omen. Rahim idled the engine as he scanned the waves, watching with practised eyes for a break in the rollers that would allow him to get out to open water. The engine coughed asthmatically as they puttered towards a sunset that entwined itself around the volcanoes of Java like a crimson dragon. On this course they would have met the *selerek* fleet within an hour and, if that were the case, they might expect very little beyond a few spindly fish for their own frying pans. But with the big fleet stuck in the port it could be a promising night.

The lack of competition meant that there was no need for them to expend fuel travelling out too far. They chose their fishing grounds just as the Stingray Star (the Southern Cross) became clearly visible on the horizon.

>◇◇◇◇<<

'Bu Ana was in the temple behind the *warung*, kneeling in front of an altar that had been carved from volcanic rock by some forgotten craftsman long before she was born. She was dressed in a *kebaya* blouse, held with a satiny *selendang* sash around her waist. Her breasts were barely concealed by the loosely crafted lacework of the *kebaya* and her sarong was stamped with the ancient *perang rusak* – the broken knife motif that was traditionally reserved only for the royal family of Yogyakarta.

The object of her devotion was a ceramic figure of a dark-haired woman who, like 'Bu Ana herself, was dressed entirely in green. The figure was about waist-high but 'Bu Ana was careful to stay stooped even as she knelt so that her head never rose higher than the golden tiara on the ceramic head. The goddess's hair was piled high in the Javanese style for Nyai Roro Kidul was still believed by many to be the spirit-world wife of the sultans of both Yogyakarta and Solo.

At the palace in Solo there was a blue tower (penis-shaped, some said) where once a year the sultan – known as 'the Great Mountain' – had a passionate communion with the Goddess of the South Seas. Crowds would gather around the tower throughout the night waiting for the outcome of their tryst. It was only if Nyai Roro Kidul was gratified that equilibrium between the volcanoes and the ocean would continue and peace would reign over Java for the next year.

'Bu Ana's own relationship with the Goddess of the South Seas was more secretive. Now she carefully laid the traditional three-part betel nut offering – red areca nut, green betel leaf and white lime – on the pedestal of the shrine. As always, the demons

30

must be appeased too with offerings of rice wine and palm arak, laid directly on the ground in a small triangular dish made from a folded leaf. She lit an incense stick and as the faint blue coils drifted upwards – carrying her prayers with them – her eyes focussed on the crumbling temple wall. One section of the ancient stonework had partially tumbled, undermined by the relentless landward march of the waves. Through the gap she could see a croton hedge – the spiritual barrier that local people knew simply as 'gold wood' – and beyond the fiery red, orange and yellow leaves she could see the waves pounding.

The crumbling wall was a painful reminder that she was failing in her devotions to the Sea Goddess. The little temple had been here longer than anyone could remember but in recent generations it had deteriorated. It might have been abandoned altogether were it not for 'Bu Ana's care. It was, after all, this shrine that was the sole reason for her determination to build the humble fortress-*warung* that protected it from the influences of the resort. Like most of the Hindus in the community she was weighed down by the never-ending obligations of temple maintenance and her heart sank now at the sight of the disintegrating wall.

She felt the obligation to strengthen that wall far more keenly than any comparatively frivolous ambition to smarten the *warung* or to improve on her own humble living quarters.

>><><><><<

'Bu Ana loosened her sash, unbuttoned her *kebaya* and dropped both onto the sagging mattress in her room. The room was sparsely furnished with just an old rattan chair and a plywood wardrobe against one wall. Four frosted glass bricks, over the bed, allowed some greenish light to filter in from the coconut palms. The other wall had a full-length glass door that opened onto a tiny terrace where a matching rattan chair offered a view over both the surf-point and the precious temple.

By now the ceremonial outfit was lying in a small heap on the bed and 'Bu Ana was tying an older sarong under her arms in preparation for her customary dip in the sea.

Then, just as she pushed the glass door open it was unexpectedly slammed shut by what appeared to be a heavy sack that had been hurled against it from outside.

'Bu Ana reeled back into the room with a gasp and watched in horror through the glass as the slack brown object writhed on the floor of the terrace. Her terror grew as she saw a claw appear from under the folds of leathery fabric. The claw scratched on the floor, as if determined to drag itself closer to the terrified woman on the other side of the glass. Then a dog-like nose emerged from under the leathery sack. As much as she wanted to turn away and run from the room 'Bu Ana was frozen in shock. Her eyes were drawn to the diabolical creature which continued to unfold, revealing a ruff of fox-coloured fur around the nape of its neck. It writhed on the floor for a moment longer and then, with devilish deliberation, began to climb up the back of the wicker chair. 'Bu Ana, backed now against the far wall of her room, watched in fascination as jagged claws, seeking for a hold, crept up the chair and the leathery folds fell loose.

It took a moment more for 'Bu Ana's stunned mind to recognise that the hideous creature was in fact a giant fruit bat. From time-to-time flocks of these 'flying foxes' passed high over the village, on their way from the forests of Java to take advantage of the mango season. She'd never been so close to one, however, and she was shocked by the size of the creature, untangling the last folds of leathery skin that would amount to a wingspan of well over a metre. It hung for a moment from the back of the chair and then, swinging itself free, took off with a powerful flap of its great wings.

The chair fell over with a clatter and 'Bu Ana eased herself down on the bed, her legs shaking. She'd never in her life heard of a flying fox attacking a person and she struggled to make sense of what had happened. Perhaps the giant bat had seen, reflected in the glass, what it thought to be another bat. Or maybe it had seen the reflection of trees and sky in the shimmer of light that glinted across the opening door.

No matter how she tried to reason the situation out, it was such an ominous omen that she decided not to mention it to anyone for fear of the events it might set in motion. Working up her courage, she cautiously opened the door and, alert to any sound or movement in the trees above her, she sidled silently out of the room.

>><><><><<

It had felt like the longest night of Rahim's life. Not even on the awful night when his son had fought his way through the Big Sickness had the hours ticked past so painfully slowly.

Up until just before midnight the fishing had been the best they'd had in weeks and the net kept coming over the side, heavy with fish that flickered like captured lightning in the lamplight. Then Yunus saw something glinting on the black surface of the water and the nightmare began. At first Rahim thought it was the bloated body of a dolphin but as it drifted into their circle of light, he saw that it was draped in a band of cloth. Yunus angled the lamp and its light fell on a human body that floated face-down. Heart pounding, Rahim reached for the paddle and manoeuvred *Sinar Bulan* so that one arching spider-leg of the outrigger passed harmlessly over the floating form. It had seemed vitally important not to inflict some imagined insult by bumping the body.

Yunus reached over the side for a handhold on the body. "Aggghhh!" he gasped, jerking his hand back as if the clammy flesh was hot to the touch.

Rahim heard him mumble a prayer, and this time Yunus steeled his nerve and pulled the corpse towards the side of the boat. It took the strength of both men to haul the body over the side so that it flopped into the belly of the boat. Then the two fishermen eased nervously back to the stern, as if making space for an unexpected guest.

They sat close together, silently watching the figure intently. The face was in deep shadow under the timber gunwales but, as they watched, bubbles of white foam began to blossom from the waterlogged lungs. Then the swaying light shifted eerily, slowly revealing the plump babyish face of a young man with blond hair. He was dressed only in shorts that looked in the darkness to be patterned with army-style camouflage.

"We should take him back straight away," Yunus whispered, as if afraid to wake the visitor.

"We'd have to travel all the way back with him through the darkness," Rahim replied doubtfully, "and then get the boat up the beach on our own."

33

"That's true…and then we'd have to carry him to the village between the two of us. Or we could leave him in the boat and go for help."

"And if the dogs found him first?"

"One of us would have to wait with him while the other went to the village."

Even in the darkness Rahim's glance was all the response that was needed to this. As if unwilling to wake the sleeping form they pulled the net in as silently as possible. The catch, coming from the same patch of ocean as the dead man, made them doubly uneasy and without a word they flicked the fish back over the side.

Yunus leaned over to whisper in his uncle's ear. "Let's move closer to the other boats."

Unwilling to shatter the silence with the raucous cough of the engine, Rahim wordlessly passed the younger man the paddle. The gentle tack-tack of wood on wood was all he heard for the next half hour as they approached the lights of the nearest fishing boat.

"Good evening," Rahim called softly, as if strangely reluctant to disturb their sleeping guest. "We found a body." He could see now that there was one man working alone in the other boat.

"What…?" the voice came back faintly.

"A dead man…"

He didn't know who the other skipper was, but it was a gruff voice that came back in reply: "Stay away! Don't come near my boat!"

Just a moment later they heard the gentle rasp of a net being hauled up the side of the other boat. Then a guttural engine broke the silence as their neighbour puttered away. Although Rahim tried half-heartedly to curse, he realised that in his heart he couldn't summon any rancour for the man's cowardly behaviour. Alone in a boat at night he'd probably have done the same.

So, the two fishermen sat silently as far back as they could in *Sinar Bulan*'s stern and waited. And waited. The hours of the night seemed to drag forever. A storm flickered on the horizon and the air grew thick and heavy as a wet blanket. They sat, unable to doze and unwilling to break the silence. They took solace in the swirl of cigarette smoke that rose like incense. By the time they'd chain-smoked the last of their cigarettes there were still at least three hours left before first light. Rahim yearned for the night to end, wishing with all his heart that this could be just a nightmare and that he would wake, contented and comfortable, in bed next to Kadek's warm body.

Once they saw a fin break the surface and cruise alongside the boat and Rahim heard Yunus's whispered prayer again.

It was the last sound that was heard aboard the *Sinar Bulan* until they saw the first hint of bleaching in the eastern sky. Rahim coaxed the engine to life and an hour later they had already landed their ghoulish cargo at the fishing beach.

2 – Curses

Before Grandfather shuffled onto the street he had to rest for a moment, leaning against the *aling-aling* barrier that partially blocked the compound gateway.

This little wall prevented demons from entering the household, since evil spirits can only move in straight lines and find it difficult to zigzag around such a barrier. Unfortunately for Grandfather, he also much preferred to move in straight lines and the *aling-aling* occasioned an extra series of painful twists for his arthritic knees. The weather, heavy with the threat of a coming storm, had been playing havoc with his joints lately. He'd drunk a glass of extra-spicy *jamu* pick-me-up when he woke but there was nothing that eased the old joints better than the sedative effects of a hot sand-bath.

There was one section of the beach that had particularly spectacular healing qualities but to get to it you had to walk along the sand almost as far as the *warung*. It made for a painful excursion but you only had to look at the height of the palms at that part of the bay – far loftier than elsewhere along the coastline – to see that there was something especially healthy about the place. To many of the old people in the village, that patch of beach had become a sort of informal club, almost a spa where they could relax and feel the life-force slip back into ancient flesh and bone.

With a lamentable lack of respect, some of the youngsters called the spot the 'Hermit Club' because of the way the old people shuffled their rumps in the sand until they half-buried themselves like hermit crabs. Perhaps it also had something to do with the permanent clatter of conversation that carried along the beach like the clink of colliding shells. Sometimes these old day-patients would sit for hours recalling village mysteries and legends that would have passed beyond human memory long ago were it not for the Hermit Club.

When Grandfather, wrapped in a faded sarong and ragged shirt, arrived this morning there was already a group of aged torsos – two men and a woman – propped up in the sand like a row of Russian dolls. He sat down at the end of the row and began to heap the therapeutic sand over his swollen knees. It took just a few minutes for his buried legs to start to throb pleasantly with pulsing blood. Soon the pain in his joints subsided and he entered a state of blissful dreaminess.

He gazed at the darkening sky and tuned lazily into the conversation around him.

"I was still small but I remember everything like it happened yesterday," Grandfather Tabanan was saying. There was a note of characteristic belligerence in his voice. The man he was talking to was a relative youngster whose almost skeletal ribs and bent back reminded Grandfather of a woven bamboo fish-trap.

Grandfather Tabanan was widely said to be the oldest man in the village. He'd been born long before Indonesian was taught in schools and was one of the few people in the entire community who spoke only Balinese. It was a point of honour with him that the relatively juvenile septuagenarians in the Hermit Club often referred to him as 'the old man'. Squatting in the sand, with his angular elbows tucked around his knees and his head pulled between hunched shoulders, he looked like a beady-eyed old heron. A single beaklike tooth jutted from his mouth like a bottle-opener and when he became excited – as he was now – it appeared to be on the verge of rattling loose entirely. Even in normal conversation his voice could be heard halfway along the beach. Grandfather Tabanan had worked most of his life in a small mechanics workshop – yelling over the whine of circular saws and the nerve-bending scream of lathes. Most people assumed that this was the reason for both his lack of patience and his near deafness.

Tabanan was not his real name, of course: he'd given himself the nickname when an ignorant foreigner had once demanded an introduction. Rather than commit virtual suicide by alerting the gods to his presence he'd responded instead by yelling out the name of his hometown: "Tabanan!" he shouted, "I'm Tabanan!" And it stuck.

Sitting next to Grandfather Tabanan was a woman who Grandfather thought of as 'Mang (although he would never have pronounced the name out loud). She was shrunken with age but her clear eyes and defined cheekbones recalled what had once clearly been an arresting beauty. Her hair had remained thick and, when sheened with coconut oil as it was this morning, it gleamed like coiled silver.

'Mang had a dancer's way of fluttering her hand as she nervously patted the sand around her old legs. "They say that it was

37

a moonless night and that the freedom fighters killed the lights on their boat so that the Dutch wouldn't spot them. Perhaps they'd never even intended to land at this village…"

"I remember it clearly," Tabanan interrupted. "We greeted them as heroes. I was just a small child but I remember their leader as if it was just yesterday. He was over seven feet tall and had shoulders as wide as the spread horns of a buffalo. His men handed out red and white armbands with the words *Merdeka atau Mati* – Liberty or Death. It was the first time I saw the Indonesian flag and I remember thinking that it was just like the Dutch flag but without the bottom blue strip."

With its filigree of veins 'Mang's hand floated in the air, fragile as a dried gardenia leaf: "I heard that when they seized an enemy position they would tear the blue strip off with their teeth," she said, "like a cat rips a bird."

Grandfather Tabanan ignored the comment. He straightened his legs and began to heap sand carefully over them, like a man burying treasure. Then his voice blared out with renewed energy. "The freedom fighters stayed in the village to rest until the following night. My father and the other men killed some chickens and a pig, tying its snout first so that it wouldn't make a noise and alert any Dutch informers. They slaughtered some cats too because we'd heard that it was cat meat that gave the freedom fighters their power to see at night. They were here for less than twenty-four hours yet one of the lieutenants fell in love with a village girl and promised he'd return to her after the war."

Grandfather recalled the tales he'd heard of the independence fighters. "My mother told me that, although their arrival was a surprise to the Dutch, those fighters had been expected by us islanders for centuries," he said. "Five hundred years earlier a sage called Joyoboyo had predicted that white-skinned oppressors would be driven out by a race of yellow dwarfs from the north. He said that the rule of those yellow dwarfs – who people said were the Japanese – would last for just one season."

"The people had faith because Joyoboyo's other predictions had already proved accurate," 'Mang pointed out. "Carriages had long ago started to move without horses, wires already stretched around the earth…"

"There was an old woman in the village here at that time who also read the future," Tabanan interrupted her again with his raucous bark. "The old woman looked long and hard into a dish of pig-liver and blood and said that the lieutenant was destined to marry the village girl he'd fallen in love with. He'd return after the war, she said, they would have seven sons and he would die in his sleep at the age of 87.

"Some of the fighters slipped away from the village during the night to hide a stash of arms somewhere in the haunted forest. They were involved in a holy war so they were immune to demons and spirits. They even believed that they were immune to bullets. But destiny played a trick and the future was not as foretold. Maybe because the old woman was unable to imagine the deadliness of a Dutch airstrike. It turned out that none of the freedom fighters were immune to bullets because within a few months all those men were killed in the Battle of Margarana just forty kilometres from here."

The old man's bellowing voice trailed off.

"*Tong kosong nyaring bunyinya*," 'Mang whispered in Grandfather's ear – an empty drum makes the most noise. Her own words were barely audible as she took up the tale: "The lieutenant who was destined to have seven sons in the village left only the first of them here. It soon became clear that the young couple had over-loved each other during his one night in the village. He was dead by the time the baby was born but their son was named after the leader of those freedom fighters. Defying the traditional rules of caste – which was fitting since the father was a rebel fighting for the people – the baby was given the noble name of Ngurah Agung."

Grandfather's eyes were locked on the sand in front of him. It had been many years since he'd heard that name. And he'd have preferred not to hear it now.

>>◇◇◇<<

Nat was walking along the beach shortly after sun-up with the heavy longboard she referred to as 'the log' tucked under her arm.

As she strode along the hightide line she stopped for a moment to inspect a tiny woven dish with offerings of petals and coloured rice. She realised that, even at this early hour, somebody had already been on the beach fulfilling some obscure religious obligation she could never hope to comprehend. You could spend a lifetime on this island and still not understand all the spiritual intricacies. It was enough to confuse most of the islanders themselves: "Who knows why we do these things?" they'd often admit if pressed. "It's just always been that way."

The offerings often included a plastic packet of biscuits, a plastic-wrapped candy or a cigarette and most of this would be pulled apart by the beach dogs within moments of being laid down. Nat often wished, however, that the powerful high priests would issue some sort of edict pointing out that the gods might not appreciate the fact that the countless offerings made in their names were effectively trashing one of the world's most beautiful islands.

How many ceremonies might take place in this one small village each day? Nat didn't know. It was doubtful that anyone could guess but as she walked towards the point, Nat tried to estimate; if each of the family temples had an *odalan* (anniversary) every six months that would probably already amount to about three per week, then there were the bigger ceremonies for the village's three main temples. There were ten days of feasts and blessing through Galungan and Kuningan, also every six months. Then there was the *purnama* (full-moon ceremony) and *tilem* (new moon) each month, and there were weddings, tooth-filings and naming ceremonies. There were ceremonies when a baby was born and then other ceremonies for the child after 12 days, 42 days, 105 days and 210 days. Funerals included separate (normally three-day) ceremonies for preliminary burial followed by another for the cremation itself. Finally, add in days that are specifically propitious for blessing plants, vehicles, animals, boats, tools and weapons, gold jewellery, books (paradoxically a day when it was forbidden to read).

It would be clear that, even in this relatively small village, there was barely a single day when there was nothing happening. But there was one spectacular exception: Nyepi was known as the 'silent day'. For 24 hours the entire island – roads and airport included – closed in a delightful ruse designed to trick the demons into thinking that the island was abandoned by humanity.

Nat walked over the top of the rock shelf just as a squadron of waves rolled towards the end of its thousand-mile journey across the Indian Ocean. She stopped to watch the corduroy lines growing shadowy as they approached. The first wave reared and lacey tongues of spume flickered across its apex as it arced over into a dark barrel that exploded on the reef with the sound of a distant grenade. Nat barely registered that crashing impact because her surfer's eyes were already being lured along the wall of water that hissed along the shoreline like a glinting crystal snake until its venom was finally sapped a hundred metres away at the edge of a deep-water channel. This channel, produced by the run-off after heavy rains, offered an accessible point for surfers to paddle out while avoiding what they called 'the impact zone'. Only the heaviest sets would close out into the channel.

Farther around the bay Nat could see two pink buffalo, peacefully chewing the cud in the shade. She'd heard that somewhere behind that treeline, there was a pristine patch of jungle that was said to be sacred. She hoped to explore it one day.

But for the moment she had other things on her mind. There were five surfers sitting together in the lineout, the noses of their shortboards glinting like shards of ice in the early sun. One turned his board and paddled hard for a wave, then popped effortlessly to his feet as he dropped down the face. He leaned into a carving bottom turn, climbed high and zipped along the face, chasing the curl. His yellow board was a neon flash against the glassy blue of the water. His tanned skin identified him as Balinese and Nat thought she recognised him as one of the fishermen she'd seen near the boats.

There was something akin to a religious ritual in these dawn surf-sessions Nat thought as she placed 'the log' reverently on the sand and knelt to rub fresh wax onto it. The morning breeze gasped out of the forest behind her, hot and wet as the breath of some gargantuan herbivore. It was the tropical breath of the island itself, zesty with the scent of bananas, cloves, cinnamon and vanilla. She limbered up with a quick sun-salutation, loosening muscles that had been far too long out of the water. Then she strapped the leash below her knee and carried her longboard into the small shore-dump breakers that rolled into the channel.

Finding the young woman's body on the beach had set her nerves on edge and Nat had decided that she should get back to the waves before her imagination started to dwell on the various disturbing scenarios. The first wave that washed over her head was like a baptism and, with boosted energy and optimism, Nat began to paddle harder for the take-off spot.

Aware that a longboarder is rarely a welcome sight to a group of shortboarders, Nat smiled and raised her hand in greeting as she neared the other surfers. Through long habit she was already subconsciously reading body language, assessing the hierarchy of the surfers in the water. From the way that two of the *bules* bobbed precariously on excessively short boards she guessed that they were unlikely to successfully negotiate a deep take-off. One of the others turned to paddle for a wave and, although he dug hard and fought to catch it, he was clearly misreading the conditions. The other two held their positions confidently. She'd already seen the Balinese in action and knew that he could surf but the other was pale-skinned – a northern European she guessed, and a new arrival. The jury was out on him for the time being, but he appeared confident and was reading the swell lines patiently, waiting for a realistic opportunity. She was aware that they too would be reading her body-language, trying to estimate her level of confidence. Only paddle for a wave you know you can catch, she told herself…and when you catch it be *sure* to ride it.

Suddenly the other surfers dropped onto their bellies and began to paddle for the horizon. Nat turned to see a thick aquamarine shadow looming as it moved towards her. The others were almost certainly trapped too close to the impact zone to catch this one and, like it or not, they were going to have to take it on the head.

Nat scrabbled hard to intercept the wave farther out on the shoulder where she'd have a chance of catching it without being swiped by its full power. A cumbersome hulk on land, 'the log' surged across the water now like an awakened marine creature. Its added floatation gave it a paddling-speed that was hugely beneficial in this race and its weight produced momentum that would help it drop over the ledge. In surfing – as with most walks of life – advantages usually come with a trade-off; Nat knew that, should this wave break over her, the pounding would be three times as hard with a nine-foot Malibu noserider strapped to her leg.

Above her the lip began to feather, flecked with sulphur-tinged foam like the wings of a cockatoo. She was still too deep for a comfortable take-off so she tried to line her board at an angle across the rearing face. She felt the board's tail rise and the nose started to

42

sideslip towards the beach. The drop, almost vertical, down the face made her reach for the sky, her toes barely maintaining contact with the waxed surface.

Reaching the bottom of the wave she took the shock in her knees and kept her centre of gravity low. The nose of the board was still slipping sideways and, just as she began to think it might slide right out from under her feet, the big nine-inch single-fin bit into the face of the wave to provide traction. She lifted her weight, allowing the board to drive smoothly back up towards the lip. The wall was almost vertical but she fought the urge to drop down to the flatter, slower section at the bottom of the breaker. The only way to maintain speed was to trim high on the steepest section. The board vibrated with the speed and she slapped at the white lip as it snapped, like a slavering dog, beside her thigh.

Nat shot out onto the shoulder, the big board still skating along as she dropped to her belly. She turned to paddle towards the horizon. A dark form broke the surface just a few feet from her and she almost yelped with fright before she saw that it was the head of a large turtle. It would be a female, Nat figured, and might have swum thousands of miles to lay her eggs on the same beach where she'd hatched about twenty-five years ago.

Nat smiled at the thought that she and the turtle were likely to be around the same age. Primal sisters frolicking in the waves.

Then she looked up to see an unavoidable wall of white-water looming upon them. The turtle ducked nonchalantly in the instant before the wave wrenched the board out of Nat's hands.

>>◇◇◇◇<<

Twice a day, old Pak Kolok could be seen driving his little migration along the beach. Even without the swaggering pink buffalo, his perpetually shirtless form would have been instantly recognisable as it shuffled along. Like his outfit – simply a pair of tattered cargo shorts with a big knife hanging from a rope threaded through the belt loops – his job never varied from day to day.

But this morning Pak Kolok had had quite a shock.

He'd been driving his buffalo past Buana's Warung shortly after first light as he always did. 'Bu Ana was doing her best to nurture a shaded plantation of herbs and shrubs under the beachside

43

palms. There was almost nothing you could actually *eat* in that garden but the plants had medicinal and spiritual properties. It was what people referred to as an *apotek hidup* – literally a 'living pharmacy'. Along with infusions for alleviating malaria and dengue it was widely known in the community that 'Bu Ana was the person to see for special potions and poultices of a more intimate nature. She dealt, for example, in the sort of remedies that a man might want to self-administer without the knowledge of his wife. It was rumoured that she dealt in the sort of balms that could protect from the evil eye and from time to time even the most decorous of the women might pay her a quiet visit asking for a small vial of what 'Bu Ana referred to as her 'Devotion Potion'. Just a smear of this magical love-mongering ointment on a man's pillow would lure even the most blatantly philandering husband back to the bosom of his loving wife. There was nobody in the community who had as much intricate knowledge of what was happening in the village's bedrooms as 'Bu Ana. Such cures were not cheap but implicit in the price was the reassurance that the transaction would remain strictly secret.

'Bu Ana had always been famous for her 'living pharmacy', even back to the time when she still had a house surrounded by potted plants in the village. The problem was that, down here on the beach, there were so few nutrients in the sandy soil. So, Pak Kolok and 'Bu Ana had come to an arrangement. Although he was still fine-tuning the process, he was training his four buffalo to drop their dung only when they passed the *warung*.

Pak Kolok had been working with buffalo all his life and knew that they learn quickly if you know how to handle them. The key lay in making sure that the training regimen itself was not complex. In this case, it consisted of a well-aimed kick or a twisted tail for any thoughtless bovine that even momentarily raised its tail in an anarchistic attempt to drop its dung indiscriminately elsewhere on the beach. There were just four animals in Pak Kolok's herd: an old black bull, two fully-grown pink cows and a black calf. The two pink buffalo were sparsely covered with white bristles that offered them scant protection from sunburn, necessitating several hours each day bathing in cool mud. The adult animals could recall a time when indiscriminately dropping their dung absolutely at random had been one of the privileges of buffalo life. During the last few months,

44

however, they'd become dimly aware that it could sometimes be surprisingly painful unless they happened to be in the shady vicinity of the *warung*. The black calf, however, was still too stupid to learn the rules. Or perhaps it was just too nimble on its hooves for Pak Kolok's training methods to be entirely effective.

Nevertheless, the buffalos' twice-daily bombing missions were starting to pay off and 'Bu Ana's 'Devotion Potion' was once again preserving the sanctity of matrimony in the village.

For her part, 'Bu Ana had known Pak Kolok for long enough to know how to train *him*: there was a hefty shot of arak set up on the bar for him anytime that the buffalo completed their steaming deliveries at the medicinal garden.

The most impressive part in the entire negotiation was not the buffalos' accuracy but that 'Bu Ana and Pak Kolok had managed to come to this agreement without speaking even a single word. They'd finalised the entire agreement through a complex dance of acting and sign-language.

Pak Kolok was fluent in only one language, a language that was the primary means of communication of less than fifty other people on the entire planet.

You might assume that it had come as a shock to Pak Kolok's parents when they realised that their second son was unable to hear or speak. As inhabitants of Bengkala village, in Bali's arid northern hinterland, they were more attuned to the possibility than almost anyone in the world might be. Both his parents and his older brother could hear and speak normally but it was soon clear that the new baby had inherited the Bengkala curse.

This 'curse', dating back farther than human memory, dictated that about fifty people in the community at any one time would be entirely deaf and mute. Nobody could say for sure how it came about but there were those in neighbouring villages who shrugged and said that this is the sort of thing that is likely to happen when a woman becomes her own grandmother.

It was almost certainly a fictional invention, but 'the story of the woman who became her own grandmother' made for such lively conversation and speculation that over the generations it had become a sort of word-game in the village. Even into recent times it was played – accompanied by hand-slapping and lewd signals – with hilarity by children in Bengkala's school playground.

It was said that the genealogical anomaly came about like this: a man married a widow who had a daughter; this step-daughter then married the man's father; thus the man was now married to his father's mother-in-law – and therefore was effectively married to his own (step-)grandmother. Things became still more entangled when the man and his 'grandmother' had a daughter. That new-born daughter's mother was now also her own great-grandmother. But, since the daughter of a great-grandmother must be a grandmother... Well, it's clear to see that the new-born daughter was also her own grandmother.

In recent years scientists who took DNA samples had concluded that the Bengkala curse was caused by a recessive gene that most likely derived from a common great-great-great-great-grandmother. The scientists refused to comment on whether the ancestor had in fact been her own step-grandmother but it was immaterial because their version of the story was considered far less interesting. So, the Bengkala legend – and the game it fostered – persisted.

Even up to current times, around fifty Bengkalans were designated with the name Kolok as a precursor to their real name and their only means of communication was the unique sign-language. This language, known as *kata kolok* (literally 'deaf talk'), was unknown beyond the boundaries of the village and only used among the deaf community and their family members and close friends.

Even after years of friendship 'Bu Ana still didn't know her friend's real name. But that was fine with him since abandoning a tainted name was considered as good a way as any to escape an evil karma or a curse. People often found it difficult to reconcile Pak Kolok's wiry, muscular body with a face that was creased like tanned leather, but his athletic frame was perfectly adapted to a language that was founded on movement and agility rather than sound. There was only one place where his muscles had relaxed over the years; the slackening of his right eyelid gave the impression that he was permanently on the verge of a raffish wink. When he was amused by something – which was often – his good eye would sparkle as if he were about to impart the most wonderful joke. The effect was invariably so contagious that the never-to-be-told joke itself was completely redundant and anyone nearby would invariably join him in laughter. He had the sort of barrelling laugh that rolled like a drum from the pit of his stomach. It was a laugh that could only come from a person who is able to give himself to laughter entirely without inhibition. You could always tell when Pak Kolok was present in the marketplace or the cock-fighting pit from the raucous bellow of hilarity that surrounded him like a fanfare. His good nature had made him one of the most popular characters in the village to such an extent that some friends – like 'Bu Ana – even delighted in practising some of the basics of the *kata kolok* sign-language. The people of Bengkala would have been surprised to learn that their unique language was enjoying a minor revival so far away among a handful of Pak Kolok's friends.

If Pak Kolok had a fault it was this: he had the unfortunate habit of a nervous percussionist. He'd tap with sticks or bottles or knives. He'd tap on tables and tins and tree-trunks. On bottles and boxes and boats. And he tapped loudly. Some uncharitable people in the community were convinced that he tapped so loudly that even he – a deaf person – could surely hear it. It was more likely, however, that the mere rhythm, unheard vibrations, passing up through his hand had its own appeal. It would never have occurred to him that hearing people might sometimes wish that they *couldn't* hear something.

This was ironic, however, because there were frequent moments when Pak Kolok ardently wished that he couldn't see things. In the mountain communities around Bengkala people believed that the Koloks had the ability to see ghosts, demons and spirits. In Pak Kolok's case this was entirely true. As such, he was not easily shaken.

And yet he'd witnessed something that morning that had truly jangled his nerves.

Just as his black bull was obediently loosening its bowels, Pak Kolok had noticed 'Bu Ana – in full ceremonial regalia – walk through the *warung* and go into her room. He hadn't given this a thought until he was startled, less than a minute later, by a movement from the back of the building and a giant bat swooped out of the bedroom and flapped past him at such close range that he had to duck behind the flank of the skittering buffalo. He knew that 'Bu Ana worshipped the Sea Goddess but now he was convinced that the rumours must be true. It was well known that a *leyak* (witch) could transform her spirit into almost anything – a creature, a ghostly spirit, or even simply a hovering light – but invariably this only happened at night. It was extremely dangerous for the witch since her human body would be left unprotected at home. Pak Kolok recalled an old man back in his village who had died, supposedly peacefully, at home in his bed. The old man had been suspected of witchcraft and this undramatic death was taken as proof. It was clear that his spirit-form had been destroyed by some more powerful magic, causing the simultaneous demise of his human body back home.

'Bu Ana must be an incredibly powerful *leyak* therefore if she could risk transforming herself into a giant bat during broad daylight.

The thought was so shocking that Pak Kolok kicked his buffalo and hurried away.

When 'Bu Ana finally emerged from her room she was surprised to catch the scent of fresh buffalo dung. Her friend Pak Kolok was nowhere to be seen, however, and – what was truly astounding – his arak had clearly been forgotten.

>◇◇◇<<

'Bu Ana watched from the sand as the young woman threw her board to the side and dived under the breaking wave. The big longboard popped up in the white-water almost immediately, like a marble tombstone in a snowdrift, and a moment later two heads bobbed up alongside it. 'Bu Ana was surprised to realise that one was a turtle and the other a human. The turtle was clearly fulfilling its own karma but, not for the first time, 'Bu Ana wondered why a human would want to flirt with the power of those waves.

She'd just made an offering, petitioning her goddess for luck. Now she hoped instinctively that some of that luck might pass onwards to the dark-skinned woman struggling out there in the breakers. Then 'Bu Ana shrugged her shoulders and walked onwards towards the rock shelf. She was going to need all the luck she could lay her hands on because she was on her way to Bali Moon Eco-resort to speak with the boss.

So many of the *bule* who arrived in the village were solely preoccupied with the waves, she thought. But then, there was no harm in that; perhaps it was the best of them that thought only of waves. In the beginning it appeared that this was all they came for. Then parties began. Fires on the beach. Some tourists arrived with bargirls from the city. The girls were euphemistically referred to by the villagers as *kupu-kupu malam* (night butterflies) but they were treated as hospitably as any other guests in the community. One or two of these butterflies repaid this friendliness, however, by demonstrating in no uncertain terms that they considered themselves a cut above village life. They hankered for cafés and nail-bars and malls where they could go 'eye washing' – to use their trendy island slang for window-shopping. 'Bu Ana remembered one village-born woman in particular who took this haughty city-reared attitude almost to the level of a caricature. She remembered seeing her, high-heels tack-tacking across the pot-holed tarmac of the village street as she squealed in feigned terror, trying to distance herself from a quacking gaggle of four or five ducks. The villagers had watched uncomprehendingly at first until it dawned on them that the image the woman was attempting to portray centred upon the fact that she'd been removed from rural life for so long that she'd forgotten how to deal with ducks.

The girls arguably related better to the chickens however than they did to the men who brought them. But then the men – a couple of decades older than their concubines – had few topics of conversation beyond waves, beer and sex (although that interest was usually already waning by the time they arrived here). They spoke disparagingly of the islanders and, even after decades travelling in the islands, had no Balinese friends beyond the bargirls and the beachboys who helped procure them.

By now 'Bu Ana was climbing the five steps that mounted the scalloped concrete breakwater. Stepping onto a landscape of shallow furrows and tufty grass ridges, she realised that the old gardener who'd planted the lawn must have been working according to the habits of a life spent in the rice paddies. He'd clearly transplanted his agricultural skills directly to the landscaping industry; the bunches of grass had been planted in unswerving lines like rice seedlings and now they were growing in corduroy ridges that gave the appearance of a series of miniature bowling lanes. To 'Bu Ana's left, there was an avocado-shaped pit and a sunken bunker like a machine gun post – destined one day to become a swimming pool and water-level pool-bar. On the other side of these holes and above a steep bank she could see a group of men working on curving breezeblock walls. Bamboo pipes emerged from these garden walls to provide the necessary basics for outdoor bathrooms. 'Bu Ana's own shower behind the *warung* was just a hosepipe slotted through a bamboo stockade but even in the humblest homes in the village it was considered desirable at least to have a roof over the bathroom. She couldn't imagine that foreigners would pay good money to be forced to shower in the rain like the poorest of the poor.

'Bu Ana knew all of the workers and they were all farming people from the highland section of the village. That was to be expected since Pak Gusti had hand-picked the builders for the Australian developer and he'd naturally tried to secure as much work as possible for his relatives and friends. It was also logical, 'Bu Ana mused, that the paddy-people were hired for the construction work since the building began during a period when most of the fields were laying fallow. Life for the paddy-people was a relatively predictable cycle that was dictated by the rains and according to the whims of Dewi Sri, the goddess of rice whose shrines guarded the paddies like miniature watchtowers. For the fisher-folk, however, work was normally only interrupted by storms or the piratical invasions of the big fleet from the port.

'Bu Ana continued towards a swooping thatched roof that reared high, like a whale's tail about to slam down onto the grassy wavelets. The roof was supported on a series of reinforced concrete pillars, rising out of a tiled floor that was the size of a volleyball court. This huge shelter was open on three sides and at the other connected with the kitchen and what would become the reception area and office. Stepping under the shade of this monumental roof she looked up to see two hanging sculptures that drooped from the rafters like the sun-bleached ribcages of young whales. Frameworks of driftwood shards and spikes served as the supports for tangles of gnarled branches that reached down like grasping hands. These two driftwood sculptures were strung with bulbs that gleamed like giant pearls. 'Bu Ana was shocked by the audacity of whoever designed these driftwood chandeliers and the sweeping roof that was far bigger than the tallest of the village's pagodas. Nothing positive could come of such arrogance, she thought.

For the time being there were just four battered tables, huddled together near the back of the room like country bumpkins in a ballroom. There were only two diners at the moment and the tattooed arms resting on the table identified them as surfers.

Dewi emerged from the kitchen bearing a loaded tray. "Here you go, two cheese pancakes with ice-cream." The combination provoked smirks from the surfers. It was often cause of mirth among guests but Dewi could not understand why since it had been part of the staple fare for visitors since the first tourists arrived in the village decades ago. It may have started as a practical joke but by now cheese pancakes with ice cream were here to stay. 'Samidges' had remained too – forever engraved, after the initial misspelling, on the village's gastronomic fixtures.

Dewi was already turning back to the kitchen when she caught sight of her aunt. "Hello! What news?" she asked, noting that the male eyes in the room were already focussed on the voluptuous appeal of the older woman. With a guilty glance over her shoulder towards the kitchen Dewi sat at the table opposite her aunt. "I can't talk for long. There's nothing to do and there are only a couple of guests but the boss always wants us to look busy anyway."

"Is he still worried about how slow the building is going?"

"He keeps saying how it would have been finished long ago if he'd had Australian builders."

"If he'd had Australian builders he'd already be bankrupt."

Dewi giggled into her hand and shot another guilty look towards the kitchen. "He's re-opened Pak Gusti's old bamboo bungalows. They were supposed to be staff quarters or storerooms but now he's trying to rent them on the cheap." She nodded towards the two surfers.

"Drowned *bules* can't be good for business".

"It's all anybody's talking about. They say it's a bad omen."

"Is the boss here now? I have a suggestion that might help him."

"He's back in the city, interviewing again."

"What about the new manageress…? What's she like?"

"Haven't you met her yet?" Dewi asked. "You might have seen her surfing this morning…"

>◇◇◇<<

51

"Today we really need to break our bones," Pande told the building crew, using the slang phrase for hard work. "The boss is still angry that the funeral kept us from working the other day."

Pande had secretly been relieved to hear that the boss had gone back to the city. It bought him some time but he knew that if they'd didn't make headway with the building project there would be trouble when the boss got back. Pande was struggling to deal with the Australian's moodiness. He could be friendly and effusively matey one moment – 'one of da boys' as he often put it – but he had no filter when it came to venting his frustration. Pande had never in his life become so angry that he'd allowed himself to shout. A Balinese would never air his emotions in public to that extent but the boss had no shame and would frequently shout and clutch at the air in what appeared to be a frenzy. Once Pande had even seen him kick a wheelbarrow.

Pande was aware, of course, that *bules* never went through the tooth-filing ceremony, a rite that was designed to remove the bestial impulses. Could this be why so many *bule* were victims to the six enemies of mankind: lust, greed, drunkenness, confusion, jealousy and anger? The body of every living person was said to be inhabited by four creatures – a tiger in the liver, a snake in the kidneys, a black crocodile in the gallbladder and a demon in the heart – and every Balinese looked, with a mixture of fear and disgust, upon a person who was unable to control these animalistic characteristics.

The men on the site also found it hard to know how to respond to the boss's tantrums. Once, during one of the worst outbursts, a teenage labourer had masked his extreme embarrassment behind a sickly smile. Even now, Pande didn't like to recall the effect this had had on the boss. Needless to say, it had been the last time that labourer had appeared on the site.

Pande was determined that his team 'break as many bones' as possible today since there was an *odalan* scheduled at the village's Death Temple tomorrow. The building project was supposed to have taken six months but, at this rate, it was likely to take three times that long. The Australian boss was paying generously and so figured that the added outlay gave him the right to complain when the building crew took days off for ceremonies. The ceremonies involved hard work too and, although it would never have occurred to Pande and his colleagues to resent their religious obligations, there was an obvious financial benefit in working on the site for pay rather than at the temple for free. It was not a choice that Pande or his workmates had ever considered making, however.

Their natural devotion was second only to their fear of being evicted from the *banjar* (their village committee). Every family must send a married male representative to the *banjar* meetings and consistent refusal to fulfil responsibilities would ultimately lead to expulsion. It had happened only once in Pande's lifetime that a man – from a neighbouring village – had been evicted from his *banjar*. With membership of the *banjar* went access to the temple's holy water, without which even the simplest prayer was impossible. The man and his entire family were therefore considered ritually unclean and became pariahs in the community. Pande and his fellow workers would agree that a death sentence was preferable.

Despite the welcome income, many times during the last few months Pande had regretted accepting the job. His family had been poor but life was simpler – and all in all he had been happier – when all he had to do was to worry about whether the rice seedlings would have enough sun or whether the birds would strip the grains before he could harvest them.

As his busy trowel spread cement onto another layer of breezeblocks he thought, for the umpteenth time that morning, how relieved he was that he hadn't had to face the boss to explain that the team would have to take yet another day off tomorrow. The *odalan* ceremony would last for three full days and Pande and his team had had to request special dispensation from the village community so that they only need take one day's leave from work. It was unfortunate that they'd only just returned from an unexpected three-day break to help with the funeral. But funerals and weddings were also obligations that demanded the attendance and support of the entire community. With the exception of the old or infirm it wasn't for them to choose whether to attend or not. Nevertheless, he'd felt uncharacteristically nervous when he told the new manageress and was surprised when she apparently appreciated the situation.

"I know it's a necessary obligation," she'd replied with a level of Indonesian that also surprised him. "It's good though that you'll only be away for one day."

The only worker who would remain on site was the dreadlocked Rasta who went by the name of Bob Bali. He had a famously laidback attitude to life and, although nominally a Muslim, had successfully established a system that ensured that he was under as few obligations as possible. The team would make sure there were ample supplies for Bob Bali to continue working alone for a day while they were gone.

Pande wondered now how he got into the position of being foreman of the work team. He'd never asked to be in charge and initially they had all been paid at the same rate. It was normal that, even working on ceremonial preparations, there would always be someone who was more experienced and whose lead the others would follow. But it was done quietly and politely in the Balinese way and everyone involved in the communal work was considered equal.

In his wild teenage years Pande had gained a reputation as a fearless charioteer in the buffalo-races that took place in the paddy fields on the fringe of the big city. It is doubtful whether any of the other men on the construction team ever wondered why they looked to him for leadership. But, if they were entirely honest, every one of them would have admitted that if he had any doubt he only had to picture his workmate holding the reins and wielding the wooden cosh over the backs of two charging buffalo bulls. Like the mythical hero Prince Arjuna on his fearsome battle-chariot it was certainly a vision that commanded respect.

The boss had no knowledge of any of this, of course. Nor is it likely that he'd have cared had he known. He'd noticed, however, that the rest of the team often turned to Pande for advice and after a few weeks of this he'd taken him aside with a promise to pay him a three dollars per day more than the standard rate. Initially Pande had been delighted; his youngest daughter was starting school soon and there would be books and a uniform to pay for. The trade-off though was that the rest of the team now considered it his responsibility to explain to the boss that they needed another day off.

As his name denoted, Pande's family was descended from the Pande clan, magical swordsmiths who once breathed life into the sacred *kris* daggers that even today remain among the most important spiritual heirlooms of Balinese nobility. But those skills were forgotten long ago. All that Pande had to show for his family's celebrated past was his name and the fact that his family temple was sheathed not in the usual yellow fabrics but in the red of the Pande clan, in tribute to the fire god Brahma. The old skills might be long forgotten but, whether he was laying bricks or planting rice, Pande always tried to remember that he was descended from an ancient line of sorcerer craftsmen.

>◇◇◇◇<<

Some people, Pak Kolok included, thought that there was something uncanny in the way that 'Bu Ana had her finger on the pulse of the beach. It was almost as if she could read the future in the rhythmic rush of the waves. But 'Bu Ana had been profoundly shocked when she'd learned from the fishermen that another body had been brought in that morning on a fishing boat. Her surprise increased when one of them mentioned that the body of the young man had been clad only in green boardshorts.

She'd only been back in the *warung* for a few minutes when Pak Kolok wandered in. There were no buffalo to drop their cargo at this hour but she reached for the arak almost as if by habit at his appearance. The deaf man accepted the glass and stepped to the edge of the concrete floor to tip a few drops on the ground for the demons, as was his habit, before he swilled the rest of the clear fiery liquid down with his usual gusto. 'Bu Ana was grateful for the company and an excuse to take her mind off the mysteries of the bodies. For someone who was unable to talk, Pak Kolok was among the chattiest people she knew and as a natural actress she always found it easy to lose herself in conversation with him.

The *kata kolok* sign-language was so intuitive that she'd quickly progressed far beyond the basic symbolism: a curved moustache on the upper lip signified 'father'; hefted breasts defined 'mother'; a suggestively twitching index finger for 'man'; fingers bent into an oval-shape designated 'woman'. Little was left to the imagination in *kata kolok* and she enjoyed her boisterous conversations with the buffalo herder. This morning, however, he was unusually reserved.

This morning, however, he seemed on edge and stayed only for a few minutes. Then with a motioned 'thank you' – hands swiped together as if wiping a slate clean – he went on his way. 'Bu Ana watched thoughtfully as he walked away along the beach. She wondered what was bothering him and felt more determined than ever to help him if she could.

>><><><<

Since there were no diners at the *warung* 'Bu Ana spent the day re-distributing buffalo dung and tending her medicinal garden. She'd almost finished when she saw the new *bule* resort manageress walking along the beach in her direction. Throughout the morning the waves had been building and now, she noticed, even beyond the sheltered side of the rocks, white horses were gathering. As she watched, a small whirlwind gathered up amongst the boats, raising a skipping mini-cyclone of driftwood and leaves. It danced along the beach, over the hightide line and whipped against the *bule* woman's cinnamon-coloured legs. As the woman skittered coltishly she appeared for a moment to be dancing with the swirling cloud. Then the iron-coloured sand erased her lower half and she appeared to shimmer like a djinn as she pirouetted over the beach.

Nat's head was down, a hand sheltering her eyes from the driving sand. She'd arrived back at the resort after surfing to learn that the *warung* owner had been asking after her. She was intrigued by what she'd heard of the solitary woman who dared to live alone on the beach. Nat prided herself on her gutfeel and, as she walked across the pink section of beach in front of the *warung*, she looked forward to learning more about her. She realised that she was now stepping on a salmon-coloured carpet, draped across the smoky sand. It was as if thousands upon thousands of shells – most long ago crushed – had been drawn to this spot by some sort of vortex. An inveterate beachcomber, Nat squatted down to search among the heap, picking up a handful of sand dollars before she spotted a strange pearly 'penny' that was emblazoned with a curious swirl on one side. There were cowrie shells of all sizes. She'd heard that they were once considered currency in Africa and China, and they were still widely used back home in Brazil in the Candomblé rituals that some people considered voodoo. She picked up several delicate 'money cowries', identifying some by their bulbous mauve-hued backs and others from their curvaceously fluted undersides.

As Nat rose to her feet she saw a Balinese woman watching her from the *warung*. The woman was dressed in work-worn cargo shorts and a tie-dye cotton shirt. Her hands rested on the handle of one of the heavy-duty *cangkul* hoes that the islanders use for any agricultural work, and a cigarette dangled between her fingers.

Many rural Balinese considered that there was something slightly disreputable about a woman smoking. Although not a smoker herself, Nat had been tempted at times to adopt it here in Bali, purely as a mild symbol of feminist rebellion. As Nat came closer, she noticed the few grains of yellow rice pasted to the woman's forehead and in the hollow of her throat, highlighting the healthy golden colour of her skin. From the faint lines around her eyes Nat guessed that she was probably nearing her fourth decade. A few petals in her piled hair, contrasting with its oiled blackness, were poignantly feminine. They contrasted with the slight sheen of sweat that glinted on her forearms and somehow emphasised her air of resilience.

'Bu Ana blew a waft of clove-scented smoke and smiled in greeting. "Did you find anything interesting?"

Nat showed her handful of shells and 'Bu Ana picked out the little 'penny'. "The eye of Shiva," she said. "You should keep this one. Some people say it's protection against the evil eye." She held the eye of Shiva close to her mouth between fingers that were tipped with cracked nail-varnish. The hand that held the cigarette acted as a shield but she appeared to be talking to the shell.

"What are you doing?" Nat asked.

"Some people say that if you whisper to the eye of Shiva you can pass on knowledge to children who are yet to be born."

"What knowledge did you pass on?"

"In this case it's a secret." The Balinese woman smiled as she changed the subject. "I watched you surfing this morning. It was beautiful."

"I'm out of practise and the surf was too heavy for me. I'm glad I had a wave or two before this wind started to blow up though."

'Bu Ana motioned towards a table. "Coffee?"

Nat took in her surroundings as the *warung* owner busied herself behind the bar. The strangely ribbed edge of the table reminded her of the serrated lips of the cowrie shells. Then she noticed the green shrine and the portrait hanging above it. The emerald eyes brought to mind shimmering shards of broken beer bottles.

Nat was still gazing at the mysterious woman in the painting when 'Bu Ana re-emerged carrying two glasses of steaming black coffee. She smiled her thanks. "*Ngopi malu jon*, right?" She spoke Indonesian well but this was one of her few stock phrases in Balinese. It was a line from a popular song and it had resonated with her because of the implication that coffee should be the priority in any meeting. She'd used the line to break the ice more times than she could count. Coming from a *bule*, the phrase was invariably unexpected enough to raise a laugh.

It didn't fail now. The cigarette drooped from 'Bu Ana's mouth and the faint lines around the older woman's smoky eyes crinkled in delight. Only when she had the coffee safely on the table did she flick the cigarette out onto the sand and give herself up to laughter. 'Bu Ana had an infectious way of erupting in a bubbling laugh that swelled in her belly like a hot thermal spring.

"*Adoooh*!" she gasped at last. "Where did you learn that?"

Smiling, Nat blew softly across the top of the glass, sensing even before she sipped it the hot, tarry sweetness that lay under a light dusting of coffee grit. "*Kopi enak*" – delicious coffee. As manageress of the resort, politeness dictated that Nat should communicate in the language of her host country.

"It's only local coffee," 'Bu Ana replied. "The beans were picked in the hills here and roasted in the village. It's not the best but at least it's produced locally."

"Maybe you can put me in contact with the people who roast it, so we can buy it for our guests?" Nat was grateful for an opportunity to reassure the resort's closest neighbour: "We want to support the community as much as possible. I want to buy everything we can from the villagers: rice, vegetables, fruit and fish…and, if possible, this coffee."

As she spoke, she realised that she would not be making such careless promises if the boss had been in attendance at this meeting. She'd convinced him that such sentiments were vital if she were to manage his eco-resort and, although he'd agreed with her terms at the time, she was aware that his outlook was vastly different from hers. "I'm a bottom-line man," he'd quipped once, with only the slightest hint of a leer. For someone who believed in reacting to her gutfeel, she'd overlooked quite a few warning flags since she'd accepted this job. She'd had a bad enough time working at the boss's bar in Australia but, almost half a dozen years after she'd left his employment, the offer to run what he described as an eco-resort for him on Bali's wild western coast had been irresistible. She'd been jobless at the time and nearing the inevitably bitter culmination of a relationship with a man she knew was cheating on her. So, she'd accepted the boss's offer and was on a flight from Rio three days later.

Almost instantly upon arriving at the resort Nat had realised, however, that her view of community involvement was very different from the boss's and that the 'eco' label was nothing but an advertising slogan. Sure, she'd achieved early victories on the environmental front – convincing him to abandon plastic bottles of water in the rooms in favour of filtered water in reusable glass bottles and switching single serving plastic bottles of shower-gel for refillable ceramic containers – but she was under no illusion that these had been cheap victories since the boss had realised that both ideas simultaneously would save him money.

She had done her best to hire local staff but had no idea who the boss was interviewing these days over in the city. She hoped that the *warung* owner would not have reason one day to remind her of her rash promises of community support.

"We're hoping that work on the resort will speed up in the next month so that we'll be finished before the high season." Nat realised that she'd switched back to English.

"Your Indonesian is very good," said 'Bu Ana reassuringly.

"I'm trying to improve…"

"The more I learn about English the more confusing it becomes. How come for example 'quicken' makes something go faster…but 'fasten' stops something from moving altogether?"

The *warung* owner went to the battered fridge in the corner and returned with a small dish of barbecued pork, off-cuts from a *babi-guling* (literally a rotated pig) that had been roasted at a ceremony. She placed it on the table next to her pack of Gudang Garam clove cigarettes.

"You eat pork, right?" she asked.

By way of reply Nat picked up one of the smoke-blackened hunks and popped it into her mouth.

"Pork is one of our specialities back home too," she said when she'd finished chewing. "We have something called *feijoada* that was originally a slave feast and is best described as a pig that has been exploded into a barrel of beans."

They ate in silence for a moment: "I'm sorry that you found the girl. It must have been a terrible shock. Then the fisherman found that second body and people are saying that it's the worst of omens that two *bules* have died even before the resort has properly opened."

"Nobody knows yet how they drowned," Nat pointed out defensively. "Neither of them was staying at the resort, and the police don't even know who the man was."

'Bu Ana came to her point: "Your security guard is a good man. I know him…but, like almost anyone else, he's nervous to patrol the beach at night. I've been trying unsuccessfully to talk to your boss because I think you need an extra security guard – somebody who could be described as a specialist."

As she spoke 'Bu Ana was increasingly aware of a vague feeling of guilt. She'd hit upon this plan with no intention beyond helping her deaf friend, but it suddenly occurred to her now that there might be a benefit in having a 'spy' at the resort who would report to her. Moreover, what better spy than a person who is believed to be incapable of communicating secrets? With Pak Kolok working at the resort she'd have reliable nocturnal eyes as well as Dewi's daytime information to keep her updated.

"I'm not saying you should fire your guard," she reiterated, "but I think you should hire someone to work with him. I can recommend the only person in the entire village who's unafraid to patrol the beach at night."

>◇◇◇<<

The Death Temple's *odalan* (anniversary) ceremony fell on a particularly auspicious day, according to the sacred calendar. For this reason, the temple shared its anniversary with countless others across the island so for several days now thousands of people, all across the island, had been preparing for their big village celebrations.

Men had been busy repairing and cleaning the temples and constructing the temporary bamboo shelters and shrines that would be needed to house the great heaps of offerings. The ceremonies served to reunite the community; the religious obligations that lured workers back from the tourist centres also offered an opportunity for cousins, brothers and old friends to work together towards a common end. During these labours old quarrels were forgotten amid cigarettes and coffees.

Women and girls had been working for almost a week, preparing hand-woven palm-leaf dishes loaded with petals, leaves, coloured rice and the ubiquitous betel nut offerings. The older women were second only to the *pemangku* (priests) in their knowledge of how the rites should be prepared and performed. The younger women and small girls learned from them.

In the midst of all the honours paid to the gods, the demons were not forgotten and the *segehan* low offerings were prepared and drizzled with arak and *brem* (fermented rice wine). The most elaborate offerings were created at the last moment to keep them as fresh as possible. Even relatively impoverished families found funds for imported fruits that had almost doubled in price in the last few days. They had been shipped into the country in individual polystyrene cocoons from as far away as Australia and New Zealand. Oranges (actual *orange* ones, not the usual green of the local variety), red apples and yellow pears of the sort that had never been seen in the local plantations were given pride of place among humble pineapples, dragon-fruit, guavas, mangos and bananas. The whole collection was skewered artistically onto a section of banana trunk and vibrantly coloured rice-flour cakes were pinned above the fruit display. In many cases the offering would be well over a metre tall and an assistant would have to help the bearer stoop through the *kori agung* gateway into the temple's inner sanctum with this tower still balanced on her head. Once the offering had been made and the gods had enjoyed the *sari* (the essence) the towers could be dismantled and eaten by the worshippers.

It was mid-morning and all over the island the women were leaving their compounds with these astounding towers balanced on their heads. The journey was usually a mercifully short one but an experienced Balinese matriarch has no difficulty sitting side-saddle on a moving motorbike with an offering balanced on her head.

Two of Pande's daughters were proudly dressed – like their mother – in the matching yellow *kebayas* and white sash of the female chapter of their local *banjar* council. Each had a hibiscus blossom woven into her hair and, in decorous emulation of their mother, they proudly carried small fruit offering on their heads. Approaching the *banjar* meeting place they saw Dewi and 'Bu Ana, amid a similarly attired swarm of women preparing for the parade through the village to the Death Temple. In the distance the great hollow-log *kulkul* drum boomed out, summoning the devotees.

The elegance and poise of a parade of Balinese women en-route to the temple – even more delicately feminine than usual in matching lace *kebayas* and tight sarongs – is one of the most enchanting sights that the island has to offer.

>><><><<

Pura Dalem, the Death Temple, lay within earshot of the waves farther along the coast to the southeast of the village. It was dedicated to Shiva or, more accurately, to Shiva's wife Parvati who, notoriously unpredictable, could manifest herself in various other guises: sometimes she was Kali (goddess of death) and at other times Durga (goddess of war). Frequently she became Rangda, the demon queen of witches, a terrifying vision with her flashing eyes, black talons, poisonous tongue and pendulous breasts. The Death Temple was a place so inextricably linked to the dark side of magic that it was believed a person could protect himself from a black-magic curse if only he were brave enough to meditate in the complex through the night. Few people had ever been brave enough to attempt such a thing, however, since the *Pura Dalem* was the centre of a *leyak* kingdom.

Even on the sunniest day it was a dank and shadowy place. It was located at the edge of an inlet among the last tracts of what had once been a great mangrove forest that covered most of the coastline. The skeletal trunks and spiked roots of the old trees steamed in a soupy swamp that teamed with life. Low tide revealed colonies of mudskippers – the amphibious fish that resembled the ancestors of the first mammals that crawled from primordial marshes – and entire orchestras of fiddler crabs that shook their oversized scarlet claws at threatening shadows. There were spiders, scorpions, cobras, pythons, and giant monitor lizards that could shred flesh with their shark-like serrated teeth. But these were nothing compared with the fearsome apparitions that were said to exist in the haunted forest that lay beyond the Death Temple.

This forest had remained untouched by humans for so long that nobody could even recall the origins of the tradition that had first dictated its protection. Nobody within living memory had ever attempted to remove so much as a piece of kindling from the haunted forest and few people were even brave enough to set foot there.

It sometimes appeared that the jungle vegetation was doing its best to reclaim still more of its old territory. The walls of the Death Temple were thickly blanketed with moist moss and ferns that sprouted out of the masonry like emerald fountains. Vines scaled the old stonework like a besieging army. As with many of the oldest temples, there was a venerable banyan tree in the centre of the main compound. It was so wide around the trunk that six men could not have hugged it…even if it weren't for the legions of red ants that would have done their utmost to discourage such an inappropriate show of affection. This great tree acted as a Trojan Horse for the patient green forces of the forest that lay in siege beyond the walls. Its upper branches were laden with tonnes of bromeliads and orchids, infiltrated cunningly as seeds by the birds. In the fecund humidity, aerial roots lowered themselves towards the ground at the rate of several inches each week. A single caretaker worked here, swinging his scythe ceaselessly in defence of the ancient stonework, like an aged Crusader standing alone against an infidel horde.

Like every other place of worship, the Death Temple's anniversary was celebrated every 210 days and, despite its spooky atmosphere, the community congregated here as willingly as they did in any other religious complex in the village. Even on the recent occasion of old Komang Sari's funeral, the cremation grounds next to the Death Temple would have appeared to a foreign visitor to be a place of celebration rather than of mourning. Her family had done their utmost to hide their sadness and even the smallest children had been warned that there should be no tears. If the old lady's spirit had sensed that they were unhappy to see her depart for the after-world there was always the danger that it would be reluctant to leave.

Since her family was relatively poor, she'd been buried under the big kapok tree at the cremation grounds until they could raise the money for the expensive cremation ceremony. Before she'd been buried steel had been placed on her teeth for strength, mirrors on her eyes for clarity and a neem leaf on each brow for beauty. Any wounds or scars had been covered with tamarind paste so that they would heal before rebirth. Until such time as her corpse could be exhumed and cremated her spirit would be in a sort of limbo. For most Balinese, this temporary burial was a necessary waystation on the way to the next life. Only members of wealthy families and priests had the luxury of a prompt cremation.

Today was the *odalan* celebration and Pande sat with his friends in the outer courtyard of the Death Temple. The ancient banyan tree loomed darkly against a pewter-coloured sky that was heavy with rain and in front of them reared the *candi bentar* split-gate, with the smooth inward-looking faces that are designed to cleanse the mind of worldly complications. The inner sanctum was protected by another stepped gate known as the *kori agung* and the carving of a grotesquely leering *bhoma* guardian, a spiritual sentry sometimes known as 'Son of the Forest' whose job it was to scare away demons. From within this inner area wafted clouds of incense from sandalwood chips that were smouldering on a coconut brazier. The women of the village had been preparing offerings for several days and it would need sturdier transportation than a mere few incense sticks to carry the essence of all this aloft. But the rites were almost over now and the last tinkle of a brass bell, soft as a handful of coins, drifted from the priest's platform along with the low drone of his Sanskrit chant.

Pande and the other men were sharing packs of cigarettes and joking in restrained undertones that frequently escalated into boisterous banter. The general chatter was no sign of disrespect, merely the natural cheerful sociability of a Balinese Hindu ceremony. They were in the outer courtyard where ritual cockfights are sometimes held during purification ceremonies, the spilled blood providing feasts for the demons that snarl like dogs around the hem of the witch goddess's blood-soaked robes.

The men's ceremonial *udeng* headwear – Pande's, marked with red, denoted his fire-worshipping swordsmith clan – was knotted at the front with two short wings left loose. Some said that it was a depiction of Garuda, the bird-dragon vehicle of the god Shiva, others that it symbolised the *lingga* (penis) and as such denoted

64

Shiva himself. Most of Pande's friends, however, preferred to think that it symbolised a rooster in the final death pounce. At the moment, cockfighting was the only thing that they had on their minds since, once the ceremony was over, they were meeting for one of the season's biggest unofficial tournaments.

Indonesian law stated that cockfighting was illegal but in Bali you're rarely out of earshot of the crowing challenge of a pugilistic rooster. Pande was the proud owner of six good fighting cocks, including the white-feathered, red-eyed Filipino prize-fighter that was expected to become a legendary champion later this afternoon. A row of bell-shaped baskets was on perpetual display at the steep junction outside Pande's house. The birds were left here so that they'd become accustomed to the clamour of the street and the sound of human shouts. Eventually even the frantic din of the cockpit could hold no terror for them. Pande had been happy to notice lately that even the sudden brutal outburst from his old Vespa did nothing to ruffle the prized gladiator's noble white feathers.

Pande had been a regular visitor at the cockpit since he was a teenager. Like most of the regulars, his betting was more often a statement of allegiance than a mathematical wager. In intervillage cockfights he would never risk offence by betting against a local rooster and when the fights were between village birds, he would always back a family member or close friend. Cockfighting was a way to reiterate bonds...just as, occasionally, it was a vehicle for maintaining feuds that might have stretched back generations.

With the acquisition of the Filipino rooster Pande had been promoted in the minds of local aficionados from the ranks of mere enthusiast to the vaunted level of a *juru kurung* (a cage keeper). Such a shift of position was seen as one of honour and – as would appear obvious to any rural Balinese – Pande's owner's honour was now to a large extent inseparable from that of his pugilistic rooster.

The Filipino rooster's fiery eyes shone like red beads. He was clearly ready to fight and Pande was certain he would make a *lot* of money that afternoon.

3 – Promises

The wake of the storm seemed to wash an invasion of surfers into the point, drifting across the rolling waves like pieces of air-sprayed flotsam. The local surfers welcomed these refugees from the more crowded surf-spots of the east, unaware that these were the first trickles of a flood that would one day become as unstoppable as a tidal bore.

Grandfather hobbled across the stream that fanned out over the sand in muddy ripples. He picked his way across the fringe of vegetable trimmings and sundry garbage, the stowaway wreckage of the stream's rush through dozens of private rubbish heaps at the back of the family compounds. Over the last two decades this refuse had increasingly been comprised of plastic. The people continued to claim, as they always had, that if you threw it in the stream it would disappear with the next rains. He passed a swollen pink plastic bag that had burst open like a putrescent corpse, exposing its contents of disposable nappies.

Grandfather could remember when this convenient invention had been introduced to the community through the Chinese general store. The resulting 'epidemic' of nappy-rash was diagnosed by Ibu Putu, the village midwife: "Of course the babies' bottoms are burned," she'd said, "you mustn't burn the nappies after use. It's like burning the babies' bottoms." Ibu Putu's knowledge in such matters was sacrosanct and, from that time onwards, disposable nappies were carefully disposed of in the stream.

As Grandfather struggled over the rock shelf he stopped for a moment to watch the surfers. The act of playing in those rolling breakers just for the thrill of it was ludicrous and, besides, their clumsy acrobatics paled into insignificance beside the dramatic aerial performances of the squadron of frigate birds that wheeled above them.

From behind him in the forest came a riot of birdsong: the piercing whistle of a hunting shrike; the hollow bamboo-knock of woodpeckers; and the cheery cackle of kingfishers. The rain that had kick-started nature into such a frenzy of activity seemed to have temporarily depleted the membership of the Hermit Club. The beach was empty when Grandfather sat down on the humid sand.

As he buried his aching knees, as if hoping to forget them altogether, flocks of swiftlets swooped joyfully over the beach, in pursuit of an airborne buffet of flying ants. Grandfather had heard that in other, wilder islands these birds lived in caves. The Chinese believed that they flew out every evening, sometimes over immense distances, to scoop up seafoam for nesting material. Here, however, the birds were tiny slaves; building their nests in manmade towers so that they could be harvested to increase the wealth of already powerful landowners.

At the soft rustle of a sarong Grandfather turned to see 'Mang approaching.

"Look how the streams are running," she said as she lowered herself onto the sand. "The waterfall must be powerful today."

Grandfather nodded: "Some people say they invented the stories about the ghost waterfall just to prevent children from playing there when the rivers are in flood like this."

"Others say that those stories were started by the arak bootleggers just to keep people away."

"Or maybe the stories are true," said Grandfather thoughtfully, "and only the bootleggers were brave enough to risk living there."

'Mang daintily smoothed the sand ridges in front of her to create two parallel dunes. "People used to talk of a beautiful bootlegger's daughter who once lived near the falls," she said. "Her father kept her confined at their camp and she was allowed to go into the village only when her mother, who suffered from malaria attacks, was unable to go for provisions. During one of these trips the girl fell in love with a boy from the village. His father beat him to make him forget her and the girl's father worked her like a slave, never giving her time to slip away to meet the boy."

"I heard that they invented a secret code," Grandfather recalled. "She would tie knots on a piece of string on the old basket that her mother used to carry the arak to the market. The boy only needed a glimpse of the woman struggling up the hill with the basket on her head to know whether his darling could slip away to meet him. They say that until the day she died the old woman never guessed that she herself was the messenger."

'Mang wiggled her toes, causing cracks to appear in the sand at the end of the twin dunes. "The girl had once seen a dog emerging from behind the waterfall and realised that there must be a cave there. The boy became obsessed with the idea that there might be treasure; if they were rich, he reasoned, nobody would be able to separate them. So, one night they met in the forest and ran away together. The cave held nothing but some rusty old guns that were spilling out of rotten boxes. But the couple stayed there for more than a week, sheltering in the cave, and the girl used her skills to catch fish and frogs and to trap birds."

The old woman fussed at the sand as she talked, her bony fingers as if tracing floral batik designs onto the sandy ridges that covered her legs. "Despite their great differences the two families came together – as if against a common enemy. And that enemy was love. The entire village turned out to look for the missing couple and finally, some men led two policemen to the waterfall. The boy and the girl climbed up the side of the falls and the search-party scrambled up the slippery slope alongside, hauling themselves through the tangled ferns. But when they reached the top they saw that the couple were standing right on the edge.

"'You'll never separate us!' the boy shouted over the roar of the water."

"'Come any closer and we'll fly!' yelled the girl. They said that she was dry-eyed and fearless. 'We'll fly to a better place and you'll never find us.'"

Grandfather shook his head sadly and looked at the old woman beside him. "The police couldn't understand afterwards how it was possible that they never found the body of the boy in that shallow pool," he said.

"But that wasn't the real mystery surely." 'Mang's gaze was piercing. "What could the girl have done to be cursed to remain on earth while her lover flew?"

>><><><<

Pande was trying to light a cigarette but they were sodden with rain. Finally, he threw the whole pack on the ground in disgust. It wasn't the cigarettes he was disgusted with though. It wasn't even the cowardly red-eyed Filipino rooster. Pande was disgusted with his *karma-pala* – literally the fruit of the karma that seemed to be inflicted on him in retribution for something he must have done in a past life.

The fighting cock was a born winner. Pande had known it from the moment he saw it. Although it was still a youngster it had cost him almost a week's wages, but the bird would have been a bargain at double that price. He'd trained it well, teasing its feathers, preening it, mixing its feed with a pugilistic blend of chillies and arak. He fed it maize and jackfruit to thicken the blood and he'd trimmed its comb, wattles and even the tiny earlobes, removing potential beak-holds for an opponent.

The rooster had led a celibate life – never allowing a hen to sap even a fraction of its pent-up aggression. He'd let it spar with the fighting cocks of some of his neighbours, but not too fiercely or too often. Just enough to reassure himself that it was a true warrior and to let it get a taste for battle. Nevertheless, by the time it was in its fighting prime – around three years old – the Filipino's progress had become the subject of choice wherever young men met all along this part of the coast. Pande's heart swelled to see it strut under its fan of snowy plumes, noble and proud as the Aztec warrior he'd once seen in his daughter's schoolbook.

While most of the magical bladesmith arts of his Pande forefathers had been forgotten, Pande still prided himself on an almost alchemistic knowledge of the tempered-steel spurs that were the fighting cock's rapier. His best *taji* were honed from the toughened steel from a truck's suspension leaf-spring. These tiny swords were like deadly darting silver fish when in action. Like any other weapon, tool or mechanical object (including vehicles, televisions and even water meters) they must be blessed with offerings. The *taji* were also guarded from the strength-sapping eyes of women and were handled with extreme care…especially since they must only be sharpened on a moonless night.

The universe had seemed to be aligned with Pande's masterplan: a partial lunar eclipse had coincided with this all-important period of preparation so that he'd been able to remove his finest *taji* from their padded case for specially ritualised sharpening during the most propitious hours possible.

Finally, a man from another village farther along the coast came forward with a suitable opponent to fight this legendary bird. Pande had left nothing to chance. Confident in his success, he'd staked everything he could on the fight. He still couldn't understand what had gone wrong. Standing now in the rain, staring mournfully at the cigarettes that were turning to mush in the puddle at his feet, Pande wondered if there was some way he could have anticipated the disaster. No, he decided; not even the most astute of breeders would ever have been able to foresee such a thing.

Simply to lose the fight would have been bad enough but who could ever have guessed that his great white champion would turn out to be a coward? Pande had been only mildly embarrassed when, after the first initial frenzy of attack, the bird had panicked and ran. The crowd that was hunkered down around the feathered warriors had scattered in a scream of delight, hurling obscenities as they fled, gleefully fearful of the flashing spurs that were nevertheless capable of opening an artery.

At that stage Pande was still smiling too. It had been a moment of unpredictability, that was all. Happened all the time. He and the other owner gathered up their birds and carried them back into the centre of the ring. Holding them almost beak to beak, they ruffled the neck feathers briskly. The white bird's body was almost quivering in Pande's hands, in a veritable frenzy to get at its enemy.

The second time it fled, Pande struggled good-naturedly to join in with the laughter but he knew that his smile was turning rigid and unnatural. The *saja komong* (timekeeper) placed the punctured coconut back in the basin of water. Each round lasted around twenty seconds, or the time it took for the coconut to fill with water and sink. To Pande – watching his cowardly gladiator fleeing its opponent – those seconds dragged forever.

The nausea that rose from his stomach became a knot of bile, choking the back of his throat. But hope was not lost. His bird struck a lucky kick and its enemy – a rusty red creature with the cascading green tail of a wild jungle fowl – was bleeding from its upper thigh.

When the Filipino fled for a third time Pande could not even join in with the laughter. Pande himself was no coward. There was not a single man among the hundred or so in the cockpit who would dare hint at such a thing. But there was no escaping the fact that a man's masculinity was indelibly tied to the performance of his rooster. Especially in the case of a rooster that had become as widely talked about as the Filipino.

70

His friends were joining in the laughter now. Even the ones who had added their wagers as part of the syndicate that backed the Filipino 'champion'. But what else could they do? Bob Bali, he'd noticed, had been betting heavily on each bout and had been winning all afternoon. Loyally, he too had bet on the Filipino…but after a winning streak like that *he* could afford to lose his relatively small wager.

In most of the fights that had taken place that afternoon the *toh ketengah* (the main wager between the two owners) had averaged around two week's wages for a labourer. This fight – the main event – had been deemed so important that almost six weeks wages rode on the Filipino's white-ruffled back. Few people had that sort of money to put upfront so, as usual, the wager was made by a coalition of Pande's friends and neighbours.

The drama was still playing out when the storm that had been threatening all afternoon finally broke with a crash of thunder. The rain began to pound on the corrugated iron roof of the barn that served as the village coliseum. Pande was grateful that the clatter drowned out the laughter and the sound of his own blood, throbbing in his temple.

The humiliation reached almost unbearable proportions when the referee finally announced that if the Filipino refused to stand and fight there could only be one solution. In a situation where such a 'stalemate' occurred both birds would be put together under an oversized basket. There, like two prize-fighters in a cage, there could be no alternative to fighting to the death. As it turned out, there *was* an alternative: the white 'champion', Pande recalled bitterly, had behaved with legendary cowardice. It had been something closer to cold-blooded murder than a fairly matched fight.

It was only afterwards that Pande wondered if his mistake had been in opposing a bird that was marked with the fiery colours of his own swordsmith clan.

By now, the winning owner would be back in his village celebrating and the referee would be enjoying his reward in the form of a leg from the losing bird for his pot. The meat of a fighting cock that died in a ring was the most delicious, marinated as it was in its own adrenalin.

Pande was no coward. He'd stood in the rain for a long time but sooner or later he would have to go home to tell his wife and daughters what had become of his great white hope.

>◇◇◇◇<<

Things had not gone well for Rahim since he and Yunus brought the young man's body back to the village. It was shortly after dawn when they'd reached the beach but, even at that early hour, a crowd of helpers – along with some ghoulish spectators – gathered to carry the corpse up to the village. It was mid-morning by the time statements had been taken and the two fishermen were free to return to the boat to collect their catch.

By now the beach dogs had already pulled the fish out of the belly of the boat. Rahim felt some initial rancour towards the other fishermen who could have saved the catch for them, until he realised that he too would have preferred to distance himself from a boat that had made such an ill-starred catch. Between the dead man and the dogs, Rahim and Yunus had no appetite for what was left of the catch. They simply hauled it to one side and left the heap of dead fish in the shade for any scavengers – whether human or beast – with a stronger stomach.

Despite their sleepless night it seemed vital to both men that they stay awake now to attend the midday prayer-call. When Rahim finally arrived home, he was so exhausted that he'd gone to sleep without even eating. He woke around sunset and Kadek – clearly reassured to see how famished he was – sat with him while he ate two plates of rice and fried fish. He was soothed and reassured by the caring eyes that still had the same effect upon his body as they had when he'd first gazed into them. He caught her hand and, ignoring her laughing excuses, kicked the door closed and pulled her down onto their mattress. Wrapped in Kadek's smooth limbs he was able to pretend for a while that the terrible night had been nothing but an unsettling dream.

Figuring that both he and Yunus would benefit from a night away from the *Sinar Bulan*, it wasn't until after breakfast the next morning that he went back to check on the boat. Slow parade of fishing boats was still coming back in and at the far end of the beach he could see the bulky forms of a small herd of buffalo. The wind whipped around their legs so that they hovered above the sand like pink zeppelins. Trailing behind them, as if tethering them to the ground, was the unmistakable stick-figure of old Pak Kolok.

As Rahim crossed the ankle-deep stream he was aware of a strangely sweet scent hanging in the air. It was not unusual for a dead animal – the carcass of a dog or even a bag of drowned kittens – to wash up along the banks.

He was puzzled to realise that the smell became more powerful as he approached *Sinar Bulan*. Wrinkling his face, he examined the boat. Maybe an animal had crawled in to die. He raised the flimsy slatted bamboo deck but there was nothing inside. Somebody – presumably Yunus – had been back to clean the boat yet it was as if the timbers themselves were saturated with a smell of rotting meat. Reluctantly he forced himself to recall the morning that he and Yunus had returned with the body. There had not been even a hint of odour while they were on the boat. But perhaps that could be explained by the fresh sea air. Neither had he noticed anything during the awful half hour it had taken to carry the corpse up to the village. Now, however, the boat was steeped in the scent of death.

These thoughts turned over in his mind as he re-crossed the stream heading homeward again. As he stepped onto the narrow strip of tarmac that ran up to the village he happened to glance through the tangle of fishing boats beyond the trees. Someone was sitting on a log staring out to sea. The lone figure shifted slightly and he saw it was Yunus. They hadn't spoken since that awful night together. As he made his way between the boats he saw his nephew slump forward, his face in his hands.

Rahim stopped in surprise. He had the uncomfortable sensation that he was intruding. Spying even. His instinct was to back away – but the young man turned and saw him.

Yunus rose to his feet slowly, a look of horror on his face. "Oh my god! You know, don't you?" The words tumbled out like fish cascading from a net. "You've discovered what happened…and that it's all my fault. The smell of death on the boat. It's a curse. It's as if I killed him."

"What are you talking about?" Rahim's mind whirled in confusion. "Did you know him? Who was he?"

"No, no. I have no idea who he was. But it's part of my punishment that we had to find him. And the boat. Your boat. The

Sinar Bulan is cursed. I've tried incense, disinfectant...everything. The smell of death won't disappear."

>><><><<

Nat had slept badly and even a dawn surf session had not eased her mind. The waves were only knee-high and, reflected in the early golden light, they had the colour and mellowness of warm honey. It was only as she was wading thigh-deep that she realised that the murky water was treacherous with floating driftwood that had been carried down by the heavy rains.

She was the first in the water and was grateful for the rash-vest in the chilled morning air. She'd only caught one wave, however, when an older Frenchman paddled out on a longboard. Jean-Pierre and his wife Marielle had checked into one of the bamboo bungalows a few days before. He paddled to where she floated on her board and they chattered aimlessly about the conditions as they watched the horizon. They took turns catching waves but, to Nat's increasing irritation, she began to notice that whenever dark lines started to form, indicating that a set of waves was moving towards them, Jean-Pierre would tunelessly whistle a few notes. He did it so consistently that she started to expect it the moment she discerned the approach of swell-lines.

Among sailors the world over it was once believed that there were people who could whistle up a storm. Nat had read that men had been thrown overboard by crewmates who believed the Jonah was deliberately courting disaster by whistling on deck. She wondered now if they sometimes did it out of pure exasperation. In more recent times surfers had turned the same superstition on its head with the belief that it was possible to whistle up waves. Nevertheless, in the near silence of the Balinese dawn, it was a habit that she found irritating. Even more so because he insisted on whistling the same four chords over and over. It was only the fourth or fifth time that she recognised the monotonous notes as the introduction to the traditional French tune *Frère Jacques*.

The heavy rains had brought floating bamboo poles and branches that sliced the wave-faces as ominously as fins. Eventually the whistling, along with the unpleasant prospect of getting her leash tangled around a floating branch or being impaled on a bamboo punji trap, began to play on Nat's nerves. She decided that her time could be better spent with a short social visit to Buana's Warung.

She'd found her thoughts returning frequently to the intriguing Balinese woman. It wasn't surprising, she told herself. Despite the company of the resort staff, her life was increasingly one of solitude. There was more to it than that though. There was something about the healthy splendour of the woman's laughter, a sense of freedom that Nat wanted to become more familiar with. As she started up the shallow slope of pink sand with her board under her arm, she was still telling herself that this visit was just a whim. By the time she'd laid her board against the natural ramp that separated the *warung* from the beach, however, she was close to admitting to herself that her short surf-session had just been a ruse to bring her to this end of the bay. Perhaps she hadn't even really intended to surf and, in her heart, she should have been grateful to Jean-Pierre for the maddening whistling that had provided the perfect excuse to abandon her self-deception.

When she stepped into the *warung* 'Bu Ana offered a change of clothes along with the ubiquitous glass of coffee. "Would you like to borrow a sarong?" she asked, glancing at the wet rash-vest.

"No, it's fine, thanks. I was barely in the water long enough to get wet," Nat replied. "There were too many logs and trunks. It makes it a little risky." She nodded towards the waves. "And that man out there keeps whistling the same tune over and over and over…"

"There are some who would say that makes it even riskier."

"What do you mean?"

"Haven't you ever heard that whistling on a beach summons ghosts?"

Nat shook her head. "I never knew that."

"Was he whistling anything in particular?"

Her lips were already pursed when Nat hesitated, laughing: "How can I tell you?"

'Bu Ana smiled too: "There would be no risk if you hummed it in my ear."

Nat stood up and leaned close. A wisp of jet-black hair tickled her lips and she was struck by the warm scent of coconut oil and cinnamon. In that instant she realised that her heart was beating so violently that the other woman must surely hear it.

Nevertheless, she began to hum the repetitive series of chords quietly. She'd only just started when 'Bu Ana turned her face in surprise and she found herself staring into her almond-shaped eyes.

"I've watched you surf," 'Bu Ana said, as the Brazilian woman sat back down, trying unsuccessfully to hide her confusion. "You don't strike me as a woman who's afraid to take risks."

>\<>\<>\<>\<<

A moonlit night. The waves hammer the sand with hollow booms, sounds that echo with the promise of a strong swell for the next morning. The tops of the palms, lost now in the darkness, rustle in a brisk offshore breeze.

The young Russian woman parks her scooter behind the shack that the coconut pickers use for midday shade. After the brightness of the headlamp her eyes take a few moments to adjust to the darkness. But since the moon is climbing she decides to wander down onto the dark sand. The waves could be big tomorrow and she wants a closer view of the glint of white-water as it rolls towards the shoreline from the breakers out on the reef.

The tide is still going out so she wanders slowly down to the hightide line feeling the wind-blown silica prickling her calves. There she stops, breathing deeply. It's as if she's inhaling the essence of this paradise – trying to trap it in her lungs so that she might be able to live off it, atom by atom, eking it out through a later life in what might be less benevolent latitudes. It's the sort of perfect tropical night she knows she'll remember forever. She imagines describing it in years to come to her friends. Maybe even her grandchildren.

If only that nightmarish motorbike accident hadn't happened. She tries, once again, to drive it from her mind. For several nights after the accident the villagers had guarded the patch of tarmac where the motorcyclist's blood had been spilled. They erected a *magagabag* – a small bamboo frame covered with a net over it. She tried not to look at the spot, but when she rode home one evening she'd noticed that it was even illuminated at night with a kerosene lantern. The little tent was a traffic hazard in itself but the Javanese police officers would not risk ordering it to be removed before three days were up: the Balinese believed that great danger could arise should witches be lured by the blood. This *magagabag* would confuse them since they would be unable to find which of the many holes in the net was the one through which the victim had passed.

She drives the memory from her mind, rejecting visions of witches or even – although this is more difficult – of the ghost she'll always refuse to acknowledge. Perhaps she can rinse the memories clean with seawater. Her own nocturnal purification ceremony.

She glances around cautiously, then in one impetuous movement pulls her T-shirt up over her head. She unties the string at the front of her boardshorts and lets them fall onto the sand. Then her green bikini top, like a wisp of seaweed, drops onto the top of the pile. As she hooks her fingers into the waistband of her bikini bottoms, she looks around again. More cautiously this time. She decides to keep the bikini bottoms on and smiles to herself; it wouldn't detract from the story as far as the grandchildren are concerned. As she walks down the hard sand tiny shards of graphite flicker in the moonlight. The warm water rushes around her ankles and she kicks happily, sending up faint sea-lightning sparks of phosphorescence. She walks farther in until the waves are breaking around her waist.

Suddenly she hears laughter from the blackness of the beach. Some men are walking down the sand. They are on a tangent that will surely lead them directly past her discarded clothes. She ducks down in the water. The black liquid slips like a veil over her breasts and laps around her shoulders. The men have reached her clothes and the sound of laughter reaches her in a series of harsh guffaws. In its raucous tones she can sense drunkenness. And the threat of sexual aggression. Her senses are taut like the nerves of a hunted animal. She prays that the waves will hide her.

She can see four men now. Coming closer, towards the waters-edge. Something glints as it's passed from hand to hand. A bottle. Or a knife. A low call reaches her over the water. It sounds guttural and menacing. Although she understands nothing, she realises that the call is intended to lure her out of the water. She panics and starts to back away. She is safe while she stays in the water. So, she eases out farther and although her feet are still on the sand she can now see bigger waves sucking up in rearing barrels behind her. One of the men shouts again and this time the sound is distinctly commanding. Three of the men sit on the sand, patiently waiting. They know that she will have to come out sooner or later. She strains her eyes and realises that the fourth man is removing his shirt, preparing to follow her. He's calling to her now as he wades in. It's a low crooning that, somehow, sounds doubling menacing to her ears — a masculine siren-call designed to lure this half-naked mermaid back to the sand.

She swims just a little farther. She realises that she can no longer touch the sand and hovers there, treading water in the cocoon of darkness that she imagines will protect her.

The pull of the current on her body — the last sensation she ever feels — is like the gentle caress of an insistent lover.

>◇◇◇◇<<

Pak Kolok continued to accept the proffered arak at the *warung*. He reasoned that it might be unwise to risk offence by refusing, but he took care to spill an extra-large share for the demons and he'd taken to carrying sliced onion in his pocket. It was a known deterrent to witches.

'Bu Ana was sorry to see that her old friend had drifted away from her and she'd wracked her brains to recall some offence she might have caused. The *warung* was quieter than ever these days, but around mid-morning the French surfer and his wife had stopped by and ordered drinking coconuts. 'Bu Ana was aware that flourishing businesses do not bloom out of balance-sheets showing only complimentary arak and young coconuts. Not here at least. Over in the tourist areas a coconut could be sold for ten times the local price — more still if it was adorned with a cherry and had a paper parasol. But over there, palms only grew in hotel gardens and were, in any case, consistently kept free of the heavy fruit that endangered sunbathing guests.

The Balinese had always believed that the domain of the gods began at the tops of the tallest palms. For this reason, no building should ever exceed that height. The island's tourism developers had firmly entrenched beliefs of their own, however. They believed that even the gods could be bribed and in some parts of the island four- and five-storey hotels loomed high above the treetops.

Nevertheless, Bali had so far remained mercifully unmarred by the skyscraper hotels of neighbouring islands. In 1966 President Sukarno (like 'Bu Ana, a devotee of the goddess) built a hotel that was nine-storeys tall. He lost his power, however, before he had a chance to fulfil his promise to dedicate a room to Nyai Roro Kidul. When a huge fire swept through the hotel the Balinese claimed that it was divine wrath provoked by the sacrilege of such an audacious attempt to 'reach for the skies.' Others claimed that it was caused by the goddess. The proof, they said, lay in the fact that only one room survived the conflagration. While even the metal railings in the hallways melted in the intense heat, everything in room 327 (including even the fabrics and plastic telephone) remained miraculously untouched. Even to this day room 327 at Grand Inna Bali Beach was decorated in green and remained a shrine to Nyai Roro Kidul.

Out here in the western hinterlands the skyline was still shaggy with the tops of tousled palms. Even the looming apex of Bali Moon's audacious restaurant-lobby barely reached the canopy of palms. The tallest buildings in the entire village were a pair of two-storey 'towers'. They were inhabited not by people but by tiny swiftlets and were built by Pak Gusti so that his men could harvest the valuable crop of miniscule nests, smaller than a new-born baby's ear and yet each one worth several days' wages.

Pak Gusti's family had been the richest in the village for as long as anyone could remember. Then he'd married a woman from an even wealthier highland family – owners of vast rubber, chocolate and coffee plantations – and these days his business empire encompassed almost everything that the community produced. He accepted tythes of half the profits from the farmers who worked his rice paddies and orchards and he even got a cut from people who harvested the wild honey and who produced palm sugar. It was whispered too that he was not above financing the arak distillers – a reasonable supposition because Pak Gusti also potentially had the power to deflect, or at least delay, police raids. As the local entrepreneur he'd even set up a small *bengkel*, a mechanic's workshop, where the battered minibuses that carried schoolkids were fixed. Some of the villagers joked that, just as the swiftlets were on his payroll, perhaps he was even bankrolling the kids to inflict maximum damage on the school buses.

Only a few of the paddy-people owned the land they worked. Most were tenants, working along lines that would have been familiar to mediaeval European peasants of the feudal era, and sharing half their harvest with landowners like Pak Gusti.

Still, Pak Gusti was generous enough in his way. 'Bu Ana was grateful for the land she'd built the *warung* upon and for the fact that he did not add to her pressure when business was slow. She was aware, too, that the village mogul was probably only maintaining his shrinking buffalo herd as a source of employment for Pak Kolok.

>>◇◇◇<<

Just as Rahim began to think that the smell of death on his boat had disappeared for good it would return, more overwhelming than ever. It was almost as if it had an energy of its own, surging and swelling as inexorably as the tides.

After three days Rahim and Yunus made the decision to put to sea anyway, but the stench increased even as they hauled *Sinar Bulan* down to the waterline. It became so unbearable that they had to drag the boat back up the beach and neither man had even suggested that they try again until something could be done.

Rahim noticed that the other fishermen now kept their distance. It was as if both the boat and the crew were cursed and, worse still, that the curse might be contagious. Rahim noticed that the boats that rested near *Sinar Bulan* had larger, more expensive, blessings than usual.

"There might be a *balian* who can help," one of these Hindu fishermen suggested, using the local word for a shaman. The fisherman had clearly been working his nerve up to make this suggestion. "There's a powerful *balian* who specialises in demon chasing. Maybe he can scare away the demons that have taken over your boat…"

Like so many Hindu ceremonies Rahim knew that it would be complex and costly. Even for a relatively simple household ceremony it would often take well over a week for a woman to prepare everything that was needed. Although his wife Kadek had been raised a Hindu and would be familiar with the skills needed to make many of the offerings, she was now a Muslim and all the preparation would therefore need to be outsourced. There was a

80

more important consideration; Rahim was also worried that, as a Muslim, taking part in a Hindu ceremony would put him in an uncomfortable position with the elders at his mosque.

There were so many complicated implications that the decision kept him awake all night. Somehow it symbolised a fork in the road of his spiritual life and he wondered how, even if he could afford the ceremony, he could emerge from this situation without causing offense. Yet he had to try something or resign himself to the fact that he would have to abandon his boat.

The next morning before first light, while she cooked the last of their fish for breakfast, Kadek too was lost in thought. "This is a problem involving the spirits of the sea," she pointed out hesitantly.

"And so…?" he replied, distractedly.

"Perhaps it's a problem that's older even than the Hindu and Muslim religions."

"And if it is…?"

"What we need is somebody who can perform a cleansing ceremony that's related specifically to the sea…"

The suggestion was unexpected. Yet, it was so entirely logical that Rahim could hardly believe he'd overlooked it. The Goddess of the Sea was a deity who transcended religions. Although such idolism was forbidden by the Koran she was worshipped with utmost devotion by Muslims right along the southern coast of Java.

As the early morning prayer call began to wail out Rahim wrapped his green-chequered sarong around his hips and, carrying his *songkok* prayer-hat, hurried up the hill to the small mosque. He greeted his friends in Arabic as they made their ritual cleansing at the fountain beside the domed building.

"*Salam alaikum*" – peace be upon you – he said.

"*Wa-alaikum salam*," they replied – and unto you be peace.

A few of the men were Muslim paddy workers and farmers but the majority were fishermen. They were his own kind, he thought, and yet the fishermen in the group were colder towards him, turning their backs just an instant too quickly and clearing just a little more space than necessary around him at the fountain.

As he prayed he wondered if a purification ceremony would be considered an act of disloyalty. The inside of the mosque was totally bare. Unlike the gaudy imagery of the temples there was a total lack of decoration apart from the prayer mats they laid out on the cool tiled floor. The walls and pillars were painted pale green, the colour of Islam. The Koran condemned idolatry yet, for generations, Muslim fishermen along this coast had been making offerings to the Sea Goddess. Surely even the staunchest elder in the mosque would not consider it more disrespectful than the 'graven image' of the *menjangan* head that adorned almost every mast in the fishing fleet.

By the time he'd finished praying Rahim was not only convinced of the wonderful practicality of the solution, but he'd also entirely forgotten that it was Kadek who had suggested it.

>><><><<

'Bu Ana was more doubtful when Rahim asked for her help later that morning. "I'm not a priestess or a *balian*," she said. "I just make the simple offerings for the Sea Goddess and tend to her temple."

"I've thought about this and even prayed for a solution," the fisherman replied. "Perhaps it's only the Sea Goddess who can cleanse my boat of the smell of death. If you can help me I'll make a donation with my first good catch and you can use the money for your temple."

A vision of the crumbling temple wall loomed in 'Bu Ana's mind like a broken vow. She was convinced that as a would-be priestess she had none of the spiritual skills that Rahim was hoping for. On the other hand, since the money was for her own temple, maybe the Sea Goddess *would* intervene in the case. It seemed sacrilegious to refuse.

"You have to understand that I can't promise anything..." she said hesitantly. "I'll try to help. You pay for the offerings and if the smell of death doesn't disappear then you don't have to pay with the catch."

It was a better deal than Rahim could have hoped for. Besides, if the Sea Goddess were not able to help then it seemed almost certain that he'd never see another net hauled into *Sinar Bulan*.

>><><><<

It was the hardest thing Nat had ever been forced to do. Yet she could see no way around it. She had to fire Pande and his entire team.

The boss had phoned her from the city and, in his fit of temper, had yelled that even Dewi the waitress would have to go.

"But why her?" she'd asked in exasperation.

"Because she's a fucking paddy-person," he'd yelled. "She'll also drop work the moment there's a ceremony. I can't run a business like that!"

Only Bob Bali could stay on. She liked the easy-going Rasta, with his no-worries swagger, and she realised that there must be many who secretly envied a stance which appeared to be perfectly designed to sidestep religious complications in general. "If Bob says don't worry, I ain't gonna worry," was Bob Bali's grinning response to pretty much everything.

In fact, the discussion with Pande had gone even worse than Nat had feared. She'd have preferred it if Pande and the others had shouted at her as she deserved. But they responded with inscrutable politeness and calm.

"You *bules* come to our island because we have a rich culture," Pande pointed out sadly as a parting comment. "Then you fire us because we insist on respecting that culture."

She explained that the boss had left her with no choice but she was still apologising uselessly when Pande and his team picked up their tools and silently walked out without a backward glance.

She despised herself even more for the tears she'd shed in her room afterwards. She had no alternative now but to follow the boss's orders and try to drum up a new work-crew from among the fisher-folk.

>>◇◇◇<<

'Bu Ana recalled a recent event at the famous Tanah Lot Temple when exactly 1,800 young women – identically dressed in the green sarongs and gilt headdresses of the Sea Goddess – performed a ceremonial dance. Nyai Roro Kidul had clearly been angered by what was primarily a record-breaking attempt and a publicity stunt; television footage showed dozens of young dancers being carried out of the temple when they were overcome by trances. Fortunately for the victims, seawater is said to be a preferred cure for trances and – with the waves around Tanah Lot crashing ever more violently as the performance progressed – there'd been an unlimited supply.

The power of the gods was not a thing to toy with and 'Bu Ana had prayed hard for inspiration before she decided to try to harness the goddess's energy in this purification ceremony. She had performed occasional blessings and boat-naming ceremonies for the fishermen but she'd never tackled something as formidable as a curse. Curses rarely appear by pure chance; there is almost always someone – or *something* – that instigates them. In attempting to remove this one there was a very real danger that 'Bu Ana might be going into spiritual battle against a potentially powerful foe and she hoped that her goddess would protect her.

It was just after sunrise when 'Bu Ana, wearing her green *kebaya* and sarong, arrived at *Sinar Bulan*. Through the lacework of the blouse a black vest shimmered with the satiny sheen of shadows in a moonlit rockpool.

Dewi, now jobless, accompanied her as an assistant and Pak Kolok acted as bearer for the three heavy baskets of offerings. Rahim and Yunus arrived moments later and the boat's owner promptly passed around a pack of clove cigarettes that only partially disguised the pungent smell of rotting meat. Pak Kolok grunted as he accepted a cigarette. His right eye – glinting mischievously from under its sleepy hood as if he were about to share the most hilarious joke – was more effective than any words could have been in reassuring the boat's owner that all would be well.

Of the five people who had gathered for the ceremony only Dewi refused the cigarettes. Trying not to wrinkle her nose at the stench that surrounded the boat, she busied herself with lighting a fistful of incense sticks and propping them up in the seams in the boat's timbers.

Then she helped Pak Kolok unpack the baskets. There was a young chicken that had been sacrificed, flattened out and fastened onto a woven palm-leaf dish. To the uninitiated this *banten caru* looked like a roadkill stapled to a dartboard. 'Bu Ana had spent a lot of time creating a figure – like a stylised two-dimensional doll – from the bleached inner leaves of palm fronds. This doll had an oversized dish-shaped head and dangling pendant earrings made from fragrant jasmine blossoms. Any Balinese Hindu would have recognised it as a version of a *cili*, the sort of fertility symbol that usually represented Dewi Sri, the goddess of rice. 'Bu Ana had never witnessed – or even heard of – a purification ceremony of this sort but she hoped that, if the request came from the heart and in a good cause, there could be no harm in improvisation. She'd reasoned that Nyai Roro Kidul (the Goddess of the Sea) and Dewi Sri (the Goddess of the Land) might be sisters of a sort. Dewi Sri was the deity who protected farmers just as Nyai Roro Kidul was the benefactress of fishermen. Looked at in this light, it stood to reason that their preferred offerings would be similar.

It was vital to get it right, though. as in every other part of Balinese spirituality, these two usually kindly deities could – if angered – also bring pestilence and suffering. Just as evil demons could occasionally do works of charity, so the gods could be ruthlessly malicious.

The universe was all part of some spiritual tug-of-war between the forces of good and evil. The early Balinese believed that their island was balanced on the back of a giant turtle, restrained by two dragon-snakes. When these dragon-snakes dozed off, or simply failed to concentrate, the turtle moved and the result was perceived as an earthquake. The *Mahabharata* holy book told how the gods' enlisted the help of the turtle and the dragon-snakes to create the Sea of Milk by stirring elements of the earth (along with living beasts including elephants and rhinoceros) into the sea. The elixir they created granted immortality to the gods. Some say that the story related to a legend of a giant tsunami at the dawn of humanity.

'Bu Ana's beloved goddess was, in fact, more often feared for her wild and vindictive nature than loved for her benevolence. Countless people, living along the brutal southern coast of these islands, feared her for the human sacrifices she took every year. Throughout these islands few would tempt fate by wearing green clothing near the sea. It was said that the Goddess of the South Seas would take people who wore her favourite colour; the women served her as slaves and young men would often be carried into her world as lovers.

'Bu Ana's shrine – in full sight of the sea – was itself green and she habitually wore the colour as an act of faith. It was this, more than anything else in her controversial nature, that caused the villagers to treat her with respect and fear. As Rahim had begun to realise in the last few days, a haunting sort of solitude was reserved for people who appeared to have invited a curse upon themselves.

Dewi spread two green sarongs on the shady sand beside the boat and the two fishermen sat cross-legged. The bitter-sweet scent of death hung in the air more insistently than ever as Yunus looked up to see the soaring *menjangan* head snarling from the *Sinar Bulan*'s mast. He'd never noticed how malevolently the eyes stared and he looked away quickly.

Yunus tried to concentrate on the ceremony but the sacred chants – including the few phrases of Sanskrit that the Sea Goddess's disciple knew – were unintelligible. 'Bu Ana tied the woven *cili* figure to the top of the mast, placed other offerings in the boat and sprinkled blessed seawater over everything. It was a common misinterpretation that the sea was unclean but 'Bu Ana knew that its purification potential was great, especially in ceremonies relating to fishermen.

Next, she took two small oblong dishes, that had been made from folded banana leaves, and poured liquid into them. There was coffee to keep the guardian spirits awake and arak to keep the revelling demons happy. She asked Rahim for his cigarettes and, after lighting two propped them against the banana leaf dishes.

Now Dewi reached into the biggest basket, straining to lift out something heavy. It was wrapped in a wet cloth but, as the woman laid it down on the ground, a fold of the fabric fell away and Rahim saw a scaly flipper. 'Bu Ana peeled back the covering to reveal a sea turtle with a shell that was about fifty centimetres long. Its watery, tear-filled eyes appeared almost resigned and it moved its fins mechanically, ineffectually shuffling the leaf litter and driftwood backwards as it etched smooth arcs in the sand.

Rahim had seen enough turtles to estimate that this was a relative youngster, falling far short of the allotted eighty-year lifespan she might have reached under more fortunate circumstances. As a Muslim Rahim would never eat a reptile, but he considered it a fortunate day when one became entangled in the nets. If you were lucky, they could fetch a good price. Despite the fact that trade in turtle meat was illegal they were still sought after by some Hindus to make traditional *lawar* (spicy chopped meat and blood) during Galungan festivals. At other times Ah Beng, the owner of the Chinese general store, could sometimes be helpful in finding a buyer. Rahim had heard that the Chinese believed that turtle meat promoted long life.

The reason for this belief was about to become clear. At a signal from the Sea Goddess's disciple, Pak Kolok unsheathed the knife from his rope belt and stepped forward. With one well-aimed hack he beheaded the turtle. Blood gushed onto the sand as the reptile's muscles thrashed. It was as if, somewhere far off in the spirit world, she was suddenly swimming free. Pak Kolok glanced towards the 'priestess'. Her eyes were moist and she raised her right hand in a symbolic miming gesture, as if she was holding a powerfully throbbing object. Careful not to allow any part of the offering to be polluted by contact with his feet, the deaf man flipped the turtle onto its carapace and carefully sliced around the edge. In less than a minute 'Bu Ana had reverently laid the pulsing heart of the turtle in a palm-frond dish at the foot of *Sinar Bulan*'s mast.

The Sea Goddess's disciple raised her joined palms over her head and, watching her intently, the others copied the pose.

"*Om santi santi santi,*" she intoned. And the ceremony was over.

Rahim and Yunus moved silently back to the other end of the boat and lit fresh cigarettes. While the two women gathered the baskets and remnants of offerings, Pak Kolok cut away the turtle's flippers and innards, leaving the meat in the intact carapace.

"May I have a cigarette?" the priestess asked when her belongings were back in the baskets and Pak Kolok had rinsed his knife. These were the first words she'd addressed to Rahim since the ceremony had begun. He gave her a cigarette and offered the pack to her deaf assistant. As they added their clove-scented smoke to the incense that swirled around the boat, Dewi took out her phone and snapped a few photos.

"There are just two things you have to remember," 'Bu Ana told the boatman. "The woven figure of Nyai Roro Kidul must be left on the mast until it falls off. Secondly, the turtle has now become a sort of totem animal. It is a spirit protector for your boat. Neither you nor your family must ever, from this day forward, harm a turtle."

'Bu Ana realised that there was no need to urge secrecy about the ceremony; as practising Muslims, the two men would be unlikely to gossip about the part they'd played in such animistic practises. As she reassured herself about this 'Bu Ana glanced along the boat and her gaze fell on the *menjangan* head. "One final thing," she paused. "Please give me another cigarette."

When the group turned away from the boat a cigarette was smouldering between the pearly white fangs of the sacred deer, and the heap of turtle innards – as if tenaciously clinging to life – was still writhing diabolically on the black sand.

>><><><<

"I thought maybe you were avoiding me," 'Bu Ana smiled as Nat climbed up the root-strewn bank in front of the *warung* just as the afternoon breeze was beginning to ruffle the tops of the palms.

"Of course not," the Brazilian woman replied. "I've just been very busy with work." It was an understatement. Since she'd been forced to fire Dewi, Nat had been covering as a waitress and even lending a hand as a chambermaid.

"I haven't been able to replace the building team since the boss made me fire Pande and his crew so there's been no advance on the work."

"People always need work here," 'Bu Ana told her gently, "but the fisher-folk know that they'll be unpopular with their paddy-people neighbours if they take the jobs."

Nat's frustration was evident in the way she stabbed her bamboo straw through the drum-like membrane in a young coconut. "We're trying to bring money into the village." She wondered uncomfortably if her voice was rising to a whine. "If we don't make progress on the building work soon there'll be no jobs for *anybody*. Probably not even for me."

"Is there anything I could do to help?"

"People listen to you. I've noticed that the men here respect you no matter what walk of life they come from."

The upwelling of bubbling laughter this provoked in the older woman was so tumultuous that she had to put down her glass of water. "I think you might be over-estimating my credentials in this neighbourhood," she gasped finally. "The women claim that I'm a bad example of the fairer sex…and the fact that so many of their men seem to think the opposite," – here she glanced down at her ample cleavage – "doesn't improve matters."

Nat's eyes were drawn over the Balinese woman's shoulder to the painting of the emerald-eyed beauty that hung behind the bar. "I heard that you tried to help the fishermen who found that man..." she said, slowly.

"But I don't see what I can do to help you. Nobody will work for the resort just because I suggest it. And to be honest – although I would gladly help you personally any way I can – I'm not even sure if I want to help establish the resort. It's no secret that the boss and I aren't exactly kindred spirits."

"I want this resort to be a success for the community. Not for him. If you can think of a way to help I'd be very grateful."

'Bu Ana considered the situation: The demise of the Bali Moon Eco-resort was not a prospect that would fill her with regret but she felt sorry for this young woman who was now caught between the villagers and an unfairly demanding boss. It was true that many local families might benefit from extra income. While she had no urge to actively support the resort there might be a way she could help. And, if so then did she really have any right to sabotage their opportunity to improve their standard of living?

"I'm not sure there's anything I could do," she said hesitantly, "but if I could convince a team of builders to get back to work there are two things I'd ask in return."

"Anything!" The manageress smiled without reservation.

"You must hire Dewi again and you must give my deaf friend a job as night watchman. He's the only person with the balls to guard the beach at night in any case."

"...apart from you," the Brazilian woman added.

>><><><><<

Rahim was dressed and sitting on the bench in front of his ramshackle bamboo kitchen long before sunrise. When the first prayer call of the day started with a shriek of feedback from the speaker at the neighbourhood mosque it was exactly five o'clock and he was already down to the muddy dregs at the bottom of his coffee glass. If he left instantly there'd be time for that first long-awaited cigarette during a leisurely stroll through the darkness up to the *masjid*.

He knew that it was childish to be so excited, but as soon as the prayers were over he hurried down to check on the *Sinar Bulan*. Even before he was halfway across the shallow stream, the weight began to life from his shoulders and by the time he'd arrived at the boat he could tell that the smell of death had completely disappeared. Moreover, it was replaced by the heady scent of jasmine blossoms.

"Getting 'Bu Ana to do that ceremony was the best idea I've ever had," he laughed delightedly, when he told Kadek later.

He felt sure that they'd turned the pages onto what was sure to be a new and more promising chapter in their lives. So, it was fitting now that Kadek should come up with an idea.

"Why don't you rename *Sinar Bulan*?" she suggested tentatively. "You know how after the eruption they renamed Karangasem city…? In the time since then – when it's been known as Amlapura – there hasn't been another big earthquake."

Once again, the idea was suddenly so sensible that Rahim couldn't believe he hadn't thought of it himself. "A change of name would secure a fresh start for the boat. A new beginning."

The new name, when they finally chose it, was so well-suited to the boat that Rahim could never remember afterwards which of them suggested it. It was almost as if the name itself had condensed out of the cloud of jasmine that hovered around the outrigger.

He painted the name on the boat's hull in a vivid red that matched the colour of the *menjangan*'s horns and it was '*Putri Laut*' – Maiden of the Sea – that put out to sea that evening with Rahim at the helm and Yunus upfront nursing the nets.

>>◇◇◇<<

"I brought you some fish," said Rahim as he stepped into the shade of Buana's Warung the next morning. He placed a wicker basket on the table.

'Bu Ana had just finished her prayers and Rahim struggled to keep his eyes from straying to the golden globes of breasts that were barely concealed by the lace of the *kebaya*. "I haven't forgotten that I promised you the first big catch. This is all we caught last night. I'm ashamed that it isn't much and I'll bring you more as soon as I can."

'Bu Ana nodded her thanks and took the small bunch of fish back behind the bar. "I heard you renamed the boat," she said. "I think the goddess should appreciate the new name. Please sit down. I'll be there in a moment."

In a few moments she returned – already changed into shorts and T-shirt – and carrying a package wrapped in banana leaves. "Half the fish for you and half for me," she said. "Feed your family first and you can repay me later."

It had been a miracle when the smell around the boat had disappeared and 'Bu Ana had been sure that Rahim's luck would change. It was still too early to know whether she'd simply cured the symptom without affecting the disease. There was something about the fisherman's honesty and determination that she liked. She would have been happy to release him from the debt but it was not hers to wipe out. He'd undertaken a solemn oath to Nyai Roro Kidul.

No, she decided not to relinquish the debt too promptly. 'Bu Ana for her part intended to sell the fish to cover some of the costs of the collapsing wall but, now she thought of it, there might be an unexpected benefit in Rahim remaining in her debt for a while longer.

"Fishing has been getting harder and harder for a long time now, my friend," she said. "It's not easy to feed a family from the sea with the competition from the big *selerek* fleet. Maybe it's time to think of something else you can do…?"

>◇◇◇<<

For three more nights the crew of the *Putri Laut* had scant luck.

Yunus was now pulling another net over the boat's side. Rahim couldn't see much in the shadowy lamplight, but he didn't have to ask; from long practise he could tell instinctively that the net was, once again, disappointingly light.

If fishing was a gambling game, then Rahim was beginning to think that the cards were always stacked against him, no matter how he cut the deck. This was the worst losing streak of his life and he was struggling to find reasons for his bad fortune: after all, the big fleet had not sailed into these waters for over a week and he knew that the other boats in the village were making reasonable catches. Even in the brisk offshore breeze he caught the scent of jasmine that

91

had continued to hover around *Putri Laut* long after the woven *cili* doll had blown off. He'd imagined that the perfume was a blessing that would bring him better luck but now it was just an added mockery.

Even on the worst nights the fishermen could hope to bring home at least enough to feed their families. The fishing community had its own informal welfare system, perfectly designed to avoid any of the stigma of charity. Anyone who was in need could simply appear – as if wandering casually on the beach – when the boats arrived. In return for their help in hauling the vessels back up the beach they could expect an *oleh-oleh* (a 'souvenir') of a couple of fish. For those who were even more needy and were unable to lift – widows, the elderly, or the infirm – each crew would leave a few 'forgotten fish' on the decks. Thus, the poorest of the poor – whether fisher-folk or paddy-people – could help themselves from these abandoned fish without appearing to accept charity.

For the last couple of days *Putri Laut*'s hauls had been so paltry that they could barely leave a handful of sad fish in the boat for the needy. Yesterday, Rahim had been shocked to realise that the few 'forgotten fish' appeared to have been overlooked by even the most desperate of the people who came to look for free food. It was irrefutable proof that *Putri Laut* still carried the curse. Word had gone around and the curse of the drowned man now hung so heavily over Rahim's boat that it even infected the 'forgotten fish' they left as charity.

Conversation in the village still revolved around the police investigation into possible connections between the body of the woman that the Brazilian manageress had found on the beach and the young man the fishermen had pulled out of the sea. Rahim barely regretted having been on the scene of that first discovery but he'd have given anything to turn the clock back and to let the drowned man drift harmlessly past their hull. Some people pointed out that it was a strange coincidence that the same fisherman had been involved in both discoveries. "And bad news often comes in threes," they said. It would be foolhardy to associate too closely with Rahim until they knew what would happen next.

As a waterman it seemed unlikely to Rahim that the bodies of two people who died at the same place and time could have drifted so far apart. Given the same state of the tide it was very doubtful that one could have been washed onto the shore while the other drifted so far out to sea. But the police had assumed that there was a connection and their investigation had been centred on trying to track down the man's accommodation among the few homestays and guesthouses along this part of the coastline. The fact that both corpses were wearing green had inspired hushed talk among the villagers but it barely reached the ears of the Javanese police officers. There were whispered suggestions that the Goddess of the Sea might be embarking on one of her legendary slave-driving binges. It was the sort of talk that was usually only heard when larger maritime tragedies took place – the capsizing of an inter-island ferry or at least the sinking of a *selerek*. So far it had only been two *bules*, but there was a mood of impending doom in the air and people began to warn their children to stay away from the beach.

Then word filtered out from the police station that an Australian surfer had gone missing from a beach far away in the east. Apparently, he'd been warned not to challenge the powerful swell but had recklessly paddled out alone in a state of arak-fuelled bravado. It was believed that, once he found himself trapped in the rip current that was carrying him out to sea, he'd broken one of the golden rules of surfing: figuring that the board was hindering him, he unstrapped his leash to try to swim back to the beach against the current. It was astounding that his corpse had been carried so far, especially since his board had washed up just a few kilometres along the coast from where he went missing.

The reason for the death of the girl was still unknown. Until, that is, Yunus broke down in tears on his uncle's boat and revealed the tragic story.

>><><><><<

Yunus's hands were mechanically untangling the few spindly fish that flapped in the net. As the lamplight shifted with the gentle roll of the boat, Rahim could see that the young man's shoulders were shaking. Rahim had no idea exactly what a nervous breakdown was but it occurred to him that this might well be what one looked like. Despite his better instincts, he was intensely irritated. After all, it was he Rahim who was in trouble with the boat; Yunus could probably find work elsewhere and, free from the responsibility of a

93

wife and children, the young man could afford to move on without looking back.

"What's the matter with you?" Rahim snapped. He'd been working up his nerve for the last hour and had finally suggested to Yunus that perhaps the young man might want to leave and look for work on another boat. "We both know that there's a curse on *Putri Laut*," he'd said. "It's my boat and my responsibility. There's no reason why you should be tainted with it too."

The outburst this suggestion provoked had shocked him.

"It's not you. It's me who…" The unexpected response was choked off by a sob. "Oh! Allah forgive me!"

The young man held his head in his hands. "This is all a curse because I was there the night the girl died." His words came out so unexpectedly and with such force that he might have vomited them up. And, as if in reaction, his uncle rocked away as if to distance himself from the statement.

"What? You were there?"

"We were just walking on the beach when we came across her clothes. She was in the sea. We weren't going to hurt her but she was nervous and thought we were waiting for her." He broke down again, his shoulders shaking in the darkness.

"When was this?"

"The night before her body was found." It was as if the truth had been restrained too long. It was bubbling out now and, despite himself, Yunus was almost relieved. He kept his back towards his uncle as the words began to tumble out. "We'd been drinking. She heard us and swam into the waves. We tried to make her come out because it was dangerous. But she got scared. After a while we went away. We couldn't see her, but we left so that she'd feel safe to come out. We tried to convince ourselves that she'd swam back in farther up the beach…"

"Didn't you try to save her?" Rahim barked. He scrambled forward and wrenched his nephew around by the shoulders. He only barely resisted the urge to slap at the triangle of light that illuminated the tear-streaked face.

"I tried to swim to her to convince her to come back. She was afraid of me and swam farther out. I even called in English but maybe the waves drowned my voice. Or maybe she was just too scared. I realised she thought I was chasing her so I came back to the beach. We tried to save her...", he crumpled onto the net, sobbing uncontrollably, "but in the end we killed her."

His words were like an echo from the sea. "We killed her. Allah forgive me, we killed her..."

4 – Turning the Tide

Grandfather was so engrossed in the effects of the hot sand – an electric current buzzing mildly through his legs – that he hadn't noticed the buffalo herder walking along the beach towards him until he was a few metres away. They nodded at each other, and it was only when the deaf man nodded a second greeting that Grandfather realised that 'Mang was sitting behind him. The beach had been deserted when he arrived and Grandfather had wondered if the same villagers who were warning their children away from the beach had started to give the same instructions to their old folks.

'Mang had a habit of appearing soundlessly next to him. It crossed his mind that she'd never lost the floating step of a dancer. She carried her fragile frame so weightlessly that he was unable to discern even the shallowest impression of her footprint in the black sand around them.

"Life must be strange for that man," she said as they watched the buffalo herder's wiry figure crossing the rock slab. "Not only to be deaf but also to be so far from anyone he calls family…"

"For a people who consider family ties so important, we certainly have a knack for separating ourselves," Grandfather replied thoughtfully. "They say my father died before I was born. Maybe Dewi's daughter has also been told that her mother is dead. Will little Ayu ever get to know her, I wonder."

They sat for a while as the sand worked its magic. Then Grandfather spoke again.

"I remember a man who was born on Sulawesi but raised on Bali by the people he thought of as his mother and father. His biological parents had emigrated to Sulawesi for work but they decided in advance that any children they had must be raised on Bali. So, when he was still tiny the baby's uncle travelled to Sulawesi to collect him and raised him as his own here. He never met his biological parents."

This time it was 'Mang who broke the silence in a voice that was so soothing it was almost a caress. "I think often about one of my best friends when I was small. Three generations of her family lived together and yet they were not related in the way people would assume."

"How could the three generations all be unrelated?"

96

"My friend explained it to me once. The grandmother was not even from their family but she had no sons. She'd have been left alone in her old age so when the little girl's father was born his real parents gave him to the grandmother to raise as her own."

"So, she was his milk-mother then?" Grandfather clarified.

"Exactly. It was a normal case of what we call milk-fostering. She loved him like her own son and raised him so she'd have someone to look after her."

"That's not so unusual," Grandfather nodded. "But the little girl…?"

"The man she considered to be her father (the adopted 'milk-son') was really her uncle. Her biological father was his brother. When she was still a baby she was moved into his house because his grown children had left home and he could better afford to raise her. The little girl still frequently visited her biological parents and she was great friends with her older sisters, who all lived in the same street. That family was one of the closest I ever met yet the little girl's father was really her uncle, her brothers were really her cousins and their grandmother wasn't actually related to *any* of them."

>><><><<

As he reached the beach Rahim did his best not to glance towards the shadowy palms. He still felt guilty about his decision to work on the resort's building crew and imagined *Putri Laut* watching him accusingly from her place of abandonment under the palms.

After painful soul-searching he'd decided that it was best if nobody learned of the part that Yunus and his friends had played in the death of the young woman. Luckily for them, the tide and breeze had obliterated all footprints by morning. It had simply been a horrifying misunderstanding, and there was nothing to gain by condemning them to prison for manslaughter. Rahim knew nothing about the law but it seemed highly likely that if the case went to court Yunus would, in all probability, be seen as the most culpable. It would be unlikely that a judge would take the viewpoint that he'd acted bravely by risking his own life to try to convince the girl to come out of the sea.

By now it was generally accepted that the girl had died simply of drowning and the police had closed the case. Nobody could imagine why a *bule* would want to swim alone at night in any case. Among those who knew about the accidental death of the motorcyclist there were those who suggested that the girl's drowning might have been a case of suicide.

As it stood, the young men were condemned to carry the secret (and perhaps the curse) to their graves. What was worse, Yunus had now implicated Rahim in a secret that would haunt him too until the day he died. He was sure now that the young woman's death was the reason his boat his boat had been cursed. He didn't want to know who else had been present that night but he had a good idea. When he found himself avoiding not only the boys themselves but also their families he found another reason to resent Yunus. He would never be able to look at those people without being reminded of the awful secret he was party to.

During restless nights, the entire scenario played and replayed itself like a looped movie in Rahim's head. Although he could imagine that the boys could be crude when they were drunk, he knew without a shadow of a doubt that they could never be rapists or murderers. The girl had clearly misread the situation and had taken Yunus's approach as a threat. Nevertheless, she'd died. And to Rahim their drunkenness was a major factor in the tragedy. He'd pointed this out in no uncertain terms to Yunus that night on the boat: "She would still be alive," he'd yelled in an explosion of rage that flecked the young man's face with spittle, "if it had been me or others among the village men who came across her that night."

"I know. I know," the young man had cringed, not even deigning to wipe the droplets of saliva. "I promise I'll never drink again as long as I live."

"I don't care," Rahim replied, as if the last of his energy was draining out of him. "I don't care what you do for the rest of your life. I never want to lay eyes on you again."

He'd fished alone for three more nights but his heart was no longer in the business. Nor were the fish in the net. The boat was already tainted in the eyes of the other fishermen and, even if he could have found a new assistant, there could be no question of potentially infecting someone else with the dark karma so contagious that it had been transferred from *Sinar Bulan* to *Putri Laut*. After decades working at night on the sea, Rahim now had to steel his nerves to take to the dark waters alone. Maybe this was what life had in store for him from now on. Maybe, he wondered, as he worked through those dark lonely hours, it was part of his own *kismet*, his own destiny, that he must pay for the sins of his nephew with a lifetime of solitary confinement on the dark waves.

When the big *selereks* invaded the fishing grounds again it was a fatal blow to the last of Rahim's optimism. Now, even the luckiest fisherman among them was barely making ends meet.

The building project had been completely stalled since Pande's team had been fired, and when 'Bu Ana had first suggested that he and Yunus should agree to work on the site he was reluctant. He couldn't understand how it would benefit the *warung* owner but a promise was a promise and – although the curse had stuck – she'd succeeded in erasing the smell of death from his boat. She agreed to erase his debt if he helped to get a work-crew together among the fisher-folk.

He'd talked the decision over with Kadek. He hadn't mentioned the dead girl, of course, but he hoped that by voicing his concerns he could assuage the contempt he felt for himself at the idea of working at the resort. Kadek had agreed with his reluctance to refuse 'Bu Ana. He'd made a promise to her after all. He was still in her debt and if she asked for his help he couldn't refuse now, could he?

So, at 'Bu Ana's suggestion Rahim visited the homes of some of the other fishermen. He went only to those he knew were struggling to haul in a catch that was sufficient even to pay for petrol and feed their families. Although they were reluctant, few of them could refuse an income that would at least tide them over until the fishing improved.

Word of his mission soon spread and it became clear that some among the paddy-people looked upon him as a traitor. Nobody had accused Rahim out loud and in the beginning he wondered if he was imagining it. Then, in the market one morning he'd turned to see three farmers who were obviously talking about him. They didn't even bother to look away or to hide their disdain when he smiled at them. They just remained still, coldly staring at him. He'd had to force himself to make his last purchases rather than simply fleeing.

But he'd left as quickly as possible and he hadn't returned to the market since.

The paddy people acted as if he was a 'strike-breaker'. They clearly felt that it had been he who'd turned the tide. And it was true that, only after he'd agreed, had others – equally desperate for work – followed his lead. Once he started asking around it became obvious that many of the fishermen had been waiting for someone to lead the way and now there were nine fishermen working on the site.

The indomitable Bob Bali, due to his relatively long service, had become foreman. Even though they were now working together on the building site, Rahim couldn't look at Yunus without thinking about the poor girl. He went out of his way to avoid the young man and had noticed that Yunus himself was becoming more withdrawn and solitary, rarely speaking even to others in the small team. It was said that Yunus had given up drinking and had even sold the old yellow single-fin surfboard he'd been riding for more than a decade. Since he'd stopped working on the boat Yunus had begun to look pale and haggard. Older than his years.

Thinking back about the whole affair afterwards, it seemed to Rahim that the entire situation, leading to his employment at the resort, had built up momentum as inevitably as a boulder bouncing down a gully. It was as if the big fishing fleet from the port and Bali Moon Eco-resort were in collusion; the over-fished waters had been a deciding factor in forcing the fisher-folk onto the resort's payroll. Perhaps this too had always been part of his *kismet*.

>><><><<

As he walked past the great bamboo restaurant, with its roof sweeping upwards like a whale's tale, Rahim waved at Dewi. She was taking orders from two tattooed and bearded hipster surfers; an older couple sat nearby, and all were dwarfed by the gigantic driftwood sculptures that hung from the ceiling like timber stalactites. Rahim had never stopped to wonder if whales would have testicles, but perhaps that was what these sculptures were meant to represent. Maybe sperm whales.

It was fortunate that when Pak Gusti first established his humble Bali Bulan Hotel on this spot he had – with an islander's traditional respect for the beach – located his six woven-bamboo huts as far back as possible. They didn't interfere with the boss's layout plans for Bali Moon Eco-resort so there had been no reason to remove them. When the new guest suites were finished the huts would all be used as storage rooms and for basic staff accommodation. For the moment, however, the boss had decided to rent them out at a discount backpacker rate. It was a desperate attempt to recuperate at least some of the money he was haemorrhaging while building continued.

Nat – who slept in the most westerly of the huts – was proud of the fact that she'd fought for relatively generous payrates for the replacement builders. Work had progressed well in the three weeks since the fisher-folk team started so the boss should have no reason for complaint: "You're learning how this works already Nat," he'd said. "Once the villagers have had a taste for working wages they're unlikely to turn them down. You just have to give a little tug on the chains from time to time."

Rahim had been doubtful about working at the resort but he'd been reassured that, through three weeks of earning a real wage, living conditions had markedly improved for his wife and two small sons. It was the only period of reliable income that his family had enjoyed since he'd worked as a labourer erecting those old bamboo huts for the original hotel and Pak Gusti protective breakwater wall.

Although he still stayed away from the marketplace, Rahim was coming to terms with his decision which was justified more readily with each weekly payday. His priority must always be towards his family. If there was anybody among the paddy-people who didn't accept that, then he'd be happy to explain to them.

Some of Rahim's building colleagues had started spending lavishly. It hadn't been overlooked up in the village that a new television had been purchased by one fishing household. A week later a satellite dish was installed at another. Almost drunk on his unaccustomed wealth, one of the fishermen had sold his boat and bought a scooter. There was likely to be no turning back for him from that decision. The multi-coloured planks from that boat would be hacked into tables for the resort's swimming-pool bar and the faithful *menjangan* head had already been hung on the restaurant wall, dwarfed by the oversized whale testicles.

Like water seeping through fissures in the bedrock of the island, the 'fair wages' that Nat had fought for had widened the gulf that was dividing the community.

Some of the paddy-people became openly antagonistic and, in a fit of pique, a few of the farmers' wives refused to buy fish from their fisher-folk neighbours. To Rahim it was the height of hypocrisy that the people who had branded him a traitor were now openly buying their fish from pickup trucks belonging to the fishing port. Kadek was naturally among the group of fisher-folk women who retaliated by boycotting the rice and vegetables of the paddy-people.

Ah Beng the Chinese owner of the general store rubbed his hands. His produce was less fresh and more expensive and yet he was now doing a thriving business with both sections of the community.

>><><><<

Pak Kolok had never been happier.

He was now supplementing his buffalo-herding income with wages from nights spent as a watchman at the resort. It was the best job he'd ever had: the paramilitary uniform and army surplus jungle boots came, apparently, with a license to make money in his sleep.

The other night watchman was a nervous fellow who counted himself lucky since the night his fearless deaf reinforcement turned up for duty. He'd spent his nights shuddering at the sound of the wind blowing through the trees or the haunting call of the 'ghost bird'.

Pak Kolok was, of course, immune to these things. He was only expected to stay awake until the last *bule* had disappeared from the beachfront and then to take a quick look around a couple of times during the night. He was a fitful sleeper anyway and would wake instantly to the mere vibration of a footfall that might have been indetectable to a hearing person. He took his duties seriously and when such a sensation – real or imagined – woke him he would get up from his sleeping mat in the storeroom and wander out to check that all was well.

Pak Kolok could end his night shift with the habitual delivery to Buana's Warung and enjoy a pre-breakfast arak shot before he went back to his shack up in the village. As a livestock worker who worked primarily on the beach Pak Kolok successfully transcended the boundaries between the fisher-folk and the paddy-people. Some in the community assumed his deafness left him ignorant to problems that arose occasionally in the village and Pak Kolok did nothing to dissuade them of this belief. The 'curse of Bengkala' had deprived the *kolok* people of hearing but it had also ensured them immunity to most of the petty squabbles that other people suffered from.

Nobody begrudged Pak Kolok taking the security job. In fact, nobody in the village had ever felt any envy for Pak Kolok whatsoever…and he was shrewd enough to realise that this could sometimes be a rare blessing.

Back home in the north of the island the *koloks* of Bengkala were famous for two things: they were talented martial-arts experts and they were said to be immune to black magic. In the highland villages around Pak Kolok's hometown, people respected the *koloks* for their fearlessness, both in the face of human enemies and even when confronted with witches and demons. For this reason, they were often hired as security guards and gravediggers. Pak Kolok had arrived on the south coast many years ago when he'd been working his way around the island with a group of fellow-*koloks*, doing martial arts exhibitions and acrobatic displays in marketplaces. They had a small run of success performing in the forecourts of petrol stations during a fuel shortage that had people queueing for hours at a time. Most of the time their nomadic life had been spartan, however, and they barely scraped together enough for a plate of rice. Often they had to sleep rough among the rats that over-ran the market stalls at night with the sickly-sweet stench of fermenting fruit in their noses. Finally, during an all-time low-point, hungry and homeless, he and his friends had drifted into the village that would become his home. When his friends moved onwards Pak Kolok had stayed behind, grateful for a chance of a small steady income as Pak Gusti's buffalo-herder.

That was about fifteen years ago when the buffalo herd had numbered more than a dozen. Even by that time though, there were very few buffalo left working the fields. While Pak Gusti occasionally rented his beasts out for ploughing, the minimal profit he made from the buffalo trade came from sales to Sumba and

Sulawesi where the animals were in huge demand for funeral sacrifices.

In Bengkala there were those who claimed that the *kolok* were doubly cursed: the loss of one sense had apparently been balanced by the boosting of another – a sixth sense – that gave them the ability to see spirits, ghosts and demons. Some people joked that this was because the *koloks* were themselves part demon; their almost unquenchable thirst for arak proved it.

By the time his first week of work was over, Pak Kolok realised that he was to be part of a bigger team than he'd imagined. The building was slowly nearing completion and an entire convoy of trucks had come down the private dirt-track from the village road, delivering air-conditioner units, mini-bars, fans, kitchen appliances, ovens, flat-screen TVs and light-fittings. There was also a whole pile of expensive 'antique' wood that was destined to clad the concrete pillars and beams that supported the restaurant roof.

To the builders it was just scruffy old wood – not even fit to patch up the oldest fishing boats – but the boss was adamant that this 'antique' timber would bring a note of timeless venerability to what would finally become the resort's lobby. With so many valuable accessories and materials piling up on the site, the boss decided that it would be wise to put a security wall around the side of the resort that faced the village. Apart from the razor-wire compound around Pak Gusti's precious bird-nest towers, this was the first time that such security measures had ever been seen in the village. The wall with its sprinkling of broken bottles, like green ice, had just been completed when the boss arrived back from the city.

He considered himself a man of the world and prided himself on his shrewdness. "Most robberies are inside jobs," he explained to Nat. "I want you to hire a team of paddy-people as guards so that they can protect the property from inside *and* out."

Showing, for once, a rare understanding of village psychology, he figured that the ex-fishermen who worked as builders would by now have few friends among the paddy-people. Nat had pointed out to him that, since they'd fired the paddy-people builders, it might be hard to find others who would agree to work at the resort. But the boss was a better judge of human character than she'd imagined and Nat was surprised at how easy it had been to hire security guards among the paddy-people. The original catalyst for

104

the whole situation – the firing of Pande and his team – had apparently been forgotten among more recent grudges. The fisher-folk no longer bought paddy-people produce since the farmers had boycotted local fish. The result was that life had become so expensive that few people were now able to turn down an offer of work.

When Bob Bali passed the word in the paddy-people section of the village there was no shortage of applicants for the security jobs.

Just before he jumped into his double-cab 4x4 pickup to drive back to the city the boss summoned this new security force for what he jokingly called a 'council of war'. Using Nat's talents for translation he clued them in on the specifics of their duties.

Pak Kolok, of course, understood little of what was going on but the new security guards were thrilled by the turn of events and hurried back to report to the village: "We've been hired as guards to watch over potential thieves among the resort's fisher-folk workforce," they said.

>><><><><<

The Southern Cross – known locally as Bintang Pari for its resemblance to a stingray – hovered in a diamond-studded sky that was mirrored by hundreds of powerful lights that glittered from the selerek fishing-fleet. Occasionally this view tricked bule into thinking they had seen a ghost city; at night they were certain that they had gazed at a Javanese cityscape that sprawled across much of the horizon, and yet sunrise the next morning would reveal a stark and empty seascape.

Pak Kolok sat on a driftwood log with the reassuring weight of a heavy torch resting across his knee. Like the uniform and army surplus jungle-boots, the torch was a badge of his profession. It was also a potentially useful tool in the unlikely instance that he might need to frighten somebody away from the beach. He preferred not to use it; such a powerful appliance must obviously be very heavy on power and he wasn't sure yet whether the cost of batteries would be deducted from his wages. More importantly its harsh white blaze disrupted his night-vision.

To Pak Kolok's eyes the beach was far from deserted after dark. Most people can only see the obvious things that the daytime brings but Pak Kolok was one of those who could also see at night. The night held no fear for Pak Kolok because he had the sort of vision that brought the night into focus with vivid clarity. He'd become so used to it – after a lifetime spent on the hinterland of the spirit-world – that he sometimes found it hard to understand that other people *couldn't* see such things. It was like imagining that there were people who could have stared at this beach, on this particular moonless night, and *not* seen the icy phosphorescent shimmer of the sea lightning that flashed along the lip of every wave.

Perhaps there was a certain justice in the fact that a man with only one good eye (and no ears to speak of) should be granted a form of vision that few people are even aware exists. Even Pak Kolok could not have said categorically whether this was a blessing or an added cross for his old shoulders. There were many times when he wished that he didn't see things so clearly. He would have given anything, for example, to be able to walk past a site where ancient executions had taken place and not to see them re-enacted in his mind's eye as if he'd witnessed them personally only yesterday. At this moment, he particularly wished that he could *unsee* the diabolical vision of 'Bu Ana transformed into a giant bat. He'd counted her as perhaps his closest friend in the village but witnessing the awesome power of her dark magic had driven a wedge between them.

'Bu Ana too had noticed the change. There had been times before when she'd realised that there was something unusual about her deaf friend. Once as they sat together at the *warung* shortly after sunset she'd noticed him suddenly look up in surprise at the patch of beach right in front of them. Although there was nothing she could see, his eyes had moved from left to right across their field of vision – not once but twice. The gooseflesh had sprung up on her arms with the realisation that he'd watched two forms – entirely unseen to her – drifting past them.

Pak Kolok sat now with the torch over his knees and watched as the moon rose over the horizon. As far as he could see in watery blue light, the beach was deserted. On certain nights under similar conditions he'd sometimes seen this beach almost thronging with crowds of spirits and ghosts.

Pak Kolok assumed that the majority of these might be the spirits of people whose family had failed to hide their sadness during the cremations. He could communicate with these denizens of the night even less effectively than he could with his average island compatriot but, growing up among the gravedigger community in Bengkala, he'd witnessed such tragedies in person and he'd recognised the wandering wraiths who were subsequently torn between two worlds.

This beach was the haunting grounds too of small, dark-skinned spirits known as *wong samar*, the warriors of an ancient Javanese king who were trapped on the wrong side of the spirit-frontier after a battle. There were the white-shrouded Muslim *pocong*, the ghosts of corpses that had refused to leave the realm of the living and there were dangerously vindictive Hindu *banas* with human bodies and fireballs for heads. Many Balinese believed that merely seeing spirits of this sort could cause a particularly intense sort of post-traumatic stress disorder that they knew as *ngeb* and which was manifested most clearly in a state of muteness.

There was one apparition in particular who was such a regular visitor that on nights when there was just the right sort of opaque light Pak Kolok would almost *expect* to see her. If she was absent on such a night he would search worryingly for her – trying to spot her, almost like an old friend, among the floating wraiths and mournful waifs. To others among the villagers who saw her she was memorable primarily because she was a *bule* woman draped in the sort of long dress that might have been worn more than a hundred years ago. She was instantly recognisable too because of the ash-coloured hair that hung almost to her feet. To Pak Kolok she was irresistibly and spectacularly unique as the only creature that he had ever heard *sing*.

He didn't recognise it as 'singing' of course. Since he had no concept of 'sound', the sensation came to him as a sort of vibration. Nevertheless, her voice was the only thing that had ever triggered the receivers that were buried in the silent catacombs of Pak Kolok's brain. The sensations it provoked were so intense that he'd sometimes gone to the beach on those strange opaque nights specifically in the hope of hearing her sing.

The first time he'd heard her song, he'd thought he'd imagined it. The second time he wondered if it was a recurring dream. Sometimes on peaceful evenings he would sense the vibrations of that song but he would be unable to spot her. Then he'd be tortured by the uncertainty that he might not really be hearing it. Perhaps it was just the wishful side of his memory. Maybe she'd departed already. He dreaded the day that she might disappear from his life forever...although the possibility had crossed his mind that it might be he himself who was the spiritual anchor that tethered her wraith's form to the living world.

She was a common sight among other villagers who were attuned to such sightings and they all admitted that the beautiful singing was mysteriously foreign. The old people said that it wasn't Dutch but that perhaps she'd been a traveller on one of the Portuguese ships that sailed through these islands. Others said she might be singing in Latin. Children often have the clearest eyes for such sightings and once a little *bule* girl had reported that the ash-haired woman had followed her into the village, singing sadly all the way. The little girl was similarly unable to recognise the language until, several years later and back on the other side of the world, she'd heard the French song *Frère Jacques* and had recognised it immediately.

How this French ghost had been condemned to spend eternity on a remote West Bali beach nobody could guess. It was noticed that when she appeared another figure would often be close by. She was a silent, thin woman who wore Balinese ceremonial clothes and who hovered over the ground, as if the lower part of her legs had simply disappeared. Some claimed that she might be the female spirit who was known to reside among wild banana trees and was believed to be as old as the island itself.

Some of these *hantu* (ghosts) appeared, by their clothing, to be more recent departures from the world of the living. There was a man in Western-style trousers and shirt but since he was headless nobody could say for sure if he was local or *bule*. There was a weeping wraith who old-timers identified as a teenage labourer who'd been crushed by a bulldozer when the big bridge was under construction on the highway. There was a beautiful girl who was said to have been an arak brewer's daughter. Parents told their children that she had gone crazy with remorse for disobeying her mother and father. Pak Kolok had seen her sometimes, running wildly along the beach flapping her arms, as if trying to fly. There was also a handsome young man in a military uniform who had been recognised as a freedom fighter who passed through the village on a reconnaissance many years before. Some said he'd fallen in love with a local beauty and had been condemned to remain on this beach until his 87th year on earth. There was a legend that his ghost could lead you to hidden treasure. Pak Kolok saw the freedom fighter almost on a regular basis, so it was perhaps unfortunate that nobody had been able to tell him of this legend.

None of these apparitions held any fear for Pak Kolok. If you are a good, respectful and honourable person there was no reason to be intimidated. Just as he was able to see through the spirits, he believed that they too could look into a human form as if it were transparent. Should they instinctively divine evil hidden in a person's soul he had no doubt that, in that case, they could be very dangerous indeed. Pak Kolok was not ostentatiously religious or morbidly superstitious. He'd made mistakes in his long and stumbling trek along the path of life. He was essentially a good man, however, and believed that he had nothing to hide from the all-seeing spirits of the night.

Only Ibu Putu, the old *balian manak* (traditional midwife), had an inkling of just how common the phenomenon of paranormal vision was in the village. She always took careful note of which babies were born with their eyes open, believing that these – babies that had cried while in their mothers' wombs – were cursed with the vision. In recent years, however, women tended to give birth in the maternity ward of the city hospital. And the training of the doctors there naturally fell short in many of the traditional intricacies of midwifery.

An almost total lack of formal education had left Pak Kolok with only a bare understanding of the history of his island. He knew that during World War II many of his countrymen had been sent to force-labour camps and the country's propaganda machine made certain too that schoolchildren learned of atrocities that took place under the Dutch. The *puputan* – the mass ritual suicides of entire Balinese royal families and their followers – had passed into island lore.

Pak Kolok was still a small child when his country went through the horrific communist purge of the mid-sixties. It was never taught in schools and the historical context of the genocide was lost on Pak Kolok along, perhaps mercifully, with the fact that America had abetted what the CIA described (in a top-secret 1968 report) as 'one of the worst mass murders of the 20th century' by supplying names to the death squads. He knew nothing of the statistics yet during his nomadic years his gift for paranormal vision meant that he effectively became a living eyewitness to many of the shameful atrocities of an era when as many as one in twenty of his island's population were murdered. The effect of witnessing so many firing squads, massacres, mob-beatings, castrations and rapes would almost certainly have been enough to provoke *ngeb* muteness, if Pak Kolok had not been mute already.

In all the areas he had visited – and during his young martial arts days Pak Kolok had travelled through most of the island – he'd never come across a place that was so densely populated with spirit-life as the beach near the village he'd chosen as home. On particularly powerful nights when that opaque glow made the beach appear to shimmer and the phosphorescence lit the waves like gas flames, his vision would reveal an entire ghost palace out on the rock shelf near Buana's Warung. Pak Kolok didn't question whether the palace was real or an illusion. To him, the fact that it became visible only occasionally made it no less tangible.

Some said that it was the palace of Nyai Roro Kidul and they were more terrified of that phantom castle than they were of all the ghosts that walked on the beach. It was said that the beauty of that enchanted building – like the irresistible Queen of the South Seas herself – had the power to lure people into the waves.

This evening was unusually quiet, however, and Pak Kolok was surprised that, despite the glowing light, there was nothing to be seen along the beach. A black shape caught his eye, luring his vision far out among the waves. From the way the object bobbed he recognised it as the head of a large turtle. His eye continued to follow its course along the beach and suddenly he caught a hint of movement. His vision backtracked, like a sniffer dog retracing its steps, until it locked onto the form of a distant figure. It was walking towards him and, from the way it kept deviously to the edge of the treeline as if trying to hide, he was sure that it was human and not a member of the spirit world. It came closer and, as it ducked under the fringe of pandan leaves, he rose cautiously to his feet and stepped back into the deep shadows.

Pak Kolok circled back behind the boats. If he had a disadvantage in his work as a night watchman it was in his stealth. He had only instinct to tell him which things were silent when trodden on and which were noisy, and the heavy jungle boots had effectively dulled that intuition entirely.

Even through the boots, however, he could sense that the pile of cut palm-leaves he stepped on as he crept behind the bungalows must have sent out a vibration that could be heard right through the resort. The skulking figure had clearly heard him and was able to duck through the darkened restaurant to dash out of sight.

In the moment before the figure disappeared, however, Pak Kolok caught a fleeting glimpse. He was almost certain that it was the *bule* manageress Nat.

>><><><><<

Rahim and Kadek lay sweating on their thin mattress. The window was closed to keep mosquitoes at bay and the air was as dense as the thick black honey they harvest in precious spoonfuls from the tiny stingless bees. It was long before dawn and Rahim had woken with the impression that somebody had spoken to him.

The memory of a dream returned, like a swimmer labouring towards the surface of a black pool. First he remembered the dogs. A pack of them had chased him down onto the beach. Although they weren't exactly vicious, they were strangely insistent. It was almost as if they were herding him, deliberately turning him back onto the beach when he tried to veer off towards the road. The dogs had pursued him relentlessly until they'd backed him down to the water's edge. He'd walked in up to his knees, trying to distance himself while keeping his eyes locked on theirs. Suddenly – as if at some unknown signal – they backed off and trotted away. One of the dogs looked back over its shoulder, gleaming eyes fixed on something in the sea behind him. When Rahim turned the water behind him was smooth and dark like the water at the bottom of a well. With the total absence even of a ripple, the warm water wrapped comfortingly around his legs like a warm pelt. Then he was aware of a movement.

It was as if a solitary drop of rain had landed on the surface, causing a circle that spread and grew until a series of ripples was expanding across the surface towards him. He imagined that they could spread without diminishing until they circled the world if he had not been standing in their way. He felt a growing apprehension as the wavelets reached out inevitably towards him, but when he tried to move he was unable to react. It was as if his legs were bound by the water. He could only wait in spellbound horror as the circle spread towards his knees. The first ripple swirled around his legs, seeming to gather strength as it touched his skin. It tugged gently yet deliberately. It was more coaxing than forceful and he tensed his legs, easily resisting the pull. It was far from overwhelming – merely like the swirling current he'd felt a thousand times when he and Yunus had launched their boat out into the waves. Even so, he had the feeling that its pull would ultimately prove irresistible and that it would finally succeed in luring him deeper. He looked down at the surface, half expecting to see hands gripping his legs but there was just his own reflection. The face that looked back at him became distorted by the colliding circles and was tinged by the greenish sheen of the seawater. Then he realised that the face was not his own but that of the girl whose body had been found on the beach. Her long blonde hair swirled over her creamy breasts like seaweed in a sunlit rockpool. Her blue Slavic eyes were also tinted by the green gauze of the water and had the piercing gaze of a cat. His heart started pounding. He was staring into the cut-glass eyes of the goddess he'd seen in the portrait in the *warung*.

"Come back to the sea," the voice demanded.

Rahim woke with a start, the thrum of adrenalin pumping through his veins. The voice was so real – so loud, and so filled with a note of inexorable command – that he was surprised to realise that Kadek was still snoring softly beside him. The house was silently smothered under the heat and stillness of the night.

>><><><<

A glass of arak waited on the table but Pak Kolok, uncharacteristically, appeared not to have noticed it. There could be no clearer signal that something was on his mind but 'Bu Ana preferred to let him get to it in his own time. Besides there was not much she could do to force conversation from a man with no words. So, she sat opposite him, running her fingers over the rough-hewn table, and waited patiently.

Finally, he picked up the glass. As was his custom he carefully poured a few drops onto the ground before, less cautiously, tipping the remaining contents into his mouth. He gulped, grimaced and wiped his lips with the back of his hand. Then he leaned his elbows on the table and tapped the glass thoughtfully on the wooden surface. Just as 'Bu Ana thought that he was finally about to come to the point, he apparently began to sense an appealing rhythm in the tap-tap-tap vibrations. In his nervousness he started tapping more forcefully, unaware of the noise he was now making. 'Bu Ana winced and restrained herself from reaching over to still his hand. Her friend was building up his nerve so she continued to wait, hoping that her own nerves would withstand the increasingly brutal pounding of glass on timber.

Finally, he set the glass on the table, took a deep breath and looked up. 'Bu Ana watched as he cupped his hands to his chest in the unmistakable shape of breasts, his eyes inadvertently moving simultaneously to 'Bu Ana's ample cleavage. She took a deep breath which apparently did nothing to divert his gaze. Then he pointed towards the resort and made a waving motion with his hand. She realised that this was his way of symbolising the surfing manageress of Bali Moon Eco-resort.

Over the course of her friendship with Pak Kolok she'd become adept at understanding his signs. She followed his movements now as one hand pointed towards the beach and the other symbolised the rising moon. She pictured him watching the beach, his searching eyes suddenly focussing on a mysterious movement. She imagined a skulking figure creeping through the trees. A nocturnal prowler scuttling guiltily into cover before the deaf night-watchman could intercept. Then once again he re-enacted the breast-resort-surfing sign. She had to double-check to be sure that he really thought the figure he'd seen skulking through the darkness was Nat.

'Bu Ana shook her head dubiously. Pak Kolok nodded confidently and renewed his rhythmic tapping on the table.

>><><><<

The boss would be back in a couple of days and Nat was anxious about how he'd take this latest disaster.

Bob Bali had finally finished preparing the antique wood cladding for the concrete pillars in the restaurant. The boss had recounted with enthusiasm the story of the precious lumber that had been dismantled from a traditional house in Central Sumatra. The considerable expense and the cost of transport was worth it, he said, since it would provide a splash of colour and sense of timelessness the restaurant – soon to double as the resort's lobby – so desperately needed. The wood was reamed and creviced with more than a century of household blunders and where the blotched paintwork was scratched and peeling the slapdash brushwork of generations of house-owners showed through. The boss had even pointed out the marks of old graffiti in Javanese and in Dutch. They were unintelligible but Nat imagined that they were the hand-scratched devotions of lovers who had disappeared from earth long ago.

"With all the money that the boss is spending on this place, why doesn't he buy good, new wood?" Rahim had asked Nat when the men were offloading the timber from the truck that had carried it across half of Sumatra and the entire length of Java to arrive here at the resort.

As the only construction worker who had been with the project right from the outset, Bob Bali had been given the important job of cutting the beautiful old timber to size. He'd spent two days measuring the concrete pillars and had then disappeared around the back of the cement suites that still looked unappealingly like prison cells.

An entire week passed before he reported to Nat that the wood cladding was ready. As they walked behind the concrete walls Nat was surprised to find herself shuffling through snowdrifts of sawdust and curlicues of pastel-coloured shavings.

The easy-going Rasta stopped proudly, hands on hips, surveying a pile of what appeared to be half-inch shutter board: "The boss is gonna be so happy," he grinned. "I finally finished sand-papering all that scruffy old wood down. Now it's as good as new."

>◇◇◇<<

Grandfather had been wandering dejectedly around the compound since he woke. "Have you seen Semut?" he asked Dewi – have you seen the ant?

His granddaughter squatted in front of the steaming rice-pot in the bamboo kitchen and, just for a moment, she thought his mind was wandering too. Then the penny dropped. When the puppy had been given to them by one of Grandfather's old friends, it had been a busily bumbling ball of black fluff. Pande's oldest daughter – the one with the problems – had laughed delightedly when she saw it and had quipped that it was as small as an ant. The girl rarely spoke and the reaction was so uncharacteristic that the name stuck. By now the dog had grown substantially and Semut seemed, more than ever, the most unlikely name for a dog.

"That dog's always off doing his own thing," Dewi replied distractedly. "Don't worry."

"I didn't see him all day yesterday…" the old man mumbled as he went out. A few minutes later she heard him calling in the street.

The dog was a fine specimen of the Kintamani breed. He looked like a miniature husky with his cheerful tail curling to the right (a lucky sign in a dog) and a dense mane that had served him well in fights. The thick jet-black fur that was perfectly adapted for life in Bali's mountainous Kintamani region was a torment here in the lowland heat. Because the dog never stopped panting, a visitor's first impression of Semut was invariably of his startling blue tongue. There were those who claimed that the blackberry stains on the Kintamanis' tongues proved their descent from blue-tongued Chow Chows that were imported centuries ago by Chinese traders as gifts for the island's kings and princes. Grandfather had always shared the common belief that the blue tongue had magical properties. Dewi remembered her mother's anger when, after Grandfather had sliced his foot on a bamboo spike, she caught the old man removing his bandages so that the dog could lick the wound. After that he'd always made sure that his daughter was out of the house before allowing the dog to administer its magical treatment. It hadn't surprised him that the wound had healed within a very short time…despite his daughter's professed astonishment that he never caught an infection that would have cost him his leg.

Some said that a Kintamani dog was a sort of canine nobility, of a higher caste than other dogs. They claimed that it would never breed with a common street dog. In any case, aficionados pointed out, pure Kintamani bitches were so secretive that they only whelped in secluded mountain caves. In the Kintamani highlands the myth persists even today that you never found a new-born Kintamani pup until its mother had decided to return from the hidden caves.

Dewi was increasingly doubtful about many of the myths surrounding these dogs, however. Since Semut had reached maturity she'd seen him mating with several of the scraggy piebald bitches in the street and she was pretty sure that before long there would be a fair population of half-breed Kintamanis in the village...and it was extremely unlikely that *any* of them would be born in caves.

Grandfather was back in the kitchen now. "I didn't see Semut all day yesterday," he said again, more loudly this time.

"Oh, he'll be back soon." She thought how uncharacteristic it was that the old man had become so attached to an animal. Raised from tough rural stock, Grandfather knew that wanton cruelty to animals was a waste. Actual fondness, however, was a ridiculous affectation reserved for Westerners, perverts and people with a vitamin deficiency. He had no time for the sort of pampered women who had nothing to do but sit all day, watching endless streams of Bollywood soap operas, with fluffy dogs on their laps. Dewi could no longer recall who had given Grandfather the dog. Lately, she'd noticed that he'd become increasingly obsessive about the animal – as if Semut somehow represented a last strand in the mooring rope that tethered him to some powerful part of his personal history.

The dog was still missing when Dewi returned from her shift at the resort later that day. Grandfather was intensely worried and, although she felt he was over-reacting, she finally agreed to report this at the police station. As she walked there Dewi became increasingly puzzled to learn from neighbours that at least three other dogs had also disappeared from homes along the road.

The policeman at the desk was from Java and, as a Muslim, had zero inclination to follow up on a case for a missing dog: "Just go home *ibu*. Dogs know how to look after themselves. He'll be there when you get back."

Word in the village was that more and more dogs were disappearing and the paddy-people began to speculate. An influx of migrants from other islands – specifically Northern Sulawesi and the Maluku Islands – had imported their own gastronomic traditions. There were scores of restaurants in the capital that openly served curried dogmeat, the spiciness helping to disguise the gaminess of carnivore flesh.

The restaurants made no secret of their culinary speciality, although casual by-passers might not decode the cryptic signs that showed only the letters 'RW'. *Rintek wuuk* (literally 'fine hair') was slang for dog in a Sulawesi dialect.

Then rumours about the missing dogs took another direction after someone remembered hearing about an amusement park in the east of the island that had been struggling until the entrepreneur had come up with the idea of opening a crocodile exhibit. Half a dozen monstrously obese crocs had been imported from Indonesian Borneo. They munched chickens like children eat jellybeans and in desperation their owner came up with a clever plan: why not harvest the packs of abandoned beach dogs that were becoming a nuisance anyway?

He offered half a day's wages for each dog carcass that was delivered to him. Guns were both illegal and expensive, and poisoning was forbidden lest it sicken the precious crocs. It soon became apparent that it was impossible to get close enough to the timid beach curs to club them. Tame village dogs, on the other hand, were much easier to approach. Word circulated around the village that a team of dog-hunters collecting for the amusement park might have been operating in the area, but nobody could add anything that amounted to more than a vague suspicion.

Others among the paddy-people kept their theories to themselves. Mostly. They hinted that they were party to proof that supported an entirely different theory. If pushed, they merely pointed out that there were those among the fisher-folk who'd always hated dogs…

Whatever the explanation, neither hide nor hair was ever seen of Semut again.

>>◇◇◇<<

Grandfather hadn't left the compound for a few days – just in case Semut wandered back. Dewi, meanwhile, was busy at the resort. For these reasons, neither of them heard when a violent sickness first infected the fisher-folks' cats. In fact, communication had broken down to such an extent between the two sides of the community that few among the paddy-people were aware that cats were suddenly dying by the score down in the fishing village.

Up until now, those cats had lived a charmed life. They grew fat and lazy on fish innards and their coats were sleek and shiny from a diet rich in fish oil. In comparison with the scabby beach dogs that bickered over scraps and yelped at flying pebbles, an unhealthy cat was a rare sight. They bred so successfully that there would surely have been a population explosion were it not for the fact that female kittens were frequently tied in sacks and drowned. It was an unpleasant task, but sterilising the animals was prohibitively expensive and the alternative was to be over-run by cats within the course of a few years. There were only a couple of old folks who were trusted with the drownings and most among the fisher-folk preferred to turn a blind eye to the institutionalised slaughter.

But now something akin to a plague was sweeping through the cat population. Such a thing was not unheard of and some of the old folks said they could recall a time when every feline in the entire village had been wiped out. It was said that after that plague the current population stemmed from Siamese kittens that had been procured from a neighbouring village, which lay at the other side of a river that had presumably served as a barrier to the virus.

This case appeared to be different, however; people started noticing that the virus only attacked cats in the fishing community. The relatively small population of pet cats that managed to hold their own among the dogs in the paddy-people community were apparently in fine fettle.

One morning Rahim returned from the mosque to find Kadek fussing over her beloved pearly grey Siamese. The pretty cat was staggering as if drunk, rolling blue eyes that had become strangely opaque liked cracked ice. The cat reeled from side to side, turning a confounded gaze back at its hind quarters as if trying to work out why its legs failed to obey it. Kadek tried to get it to drink water and forced charcoal into its mouth to try to soak up any toxins. It was all hopeless. The poor animal's belly swelled and it died in pain within two hours.

"You think it's just a sickness?" Kadek asked him through her tears. "You know how the dogs died up in the village? I think the paddy-people poisoned our cat."

Although Rahim couldn't quite put a finger on it he realised there was something poignantly worrying in the fact that it was Kadek – herself born into the paddy-people community – who first voiced what would become a growing belief that the cat-killing had been deliberate.

>><><><<

The building work at Bali Moon Eco-resort was almost finished by now. The builders had been scrupulously honest about the resort's equipment and materials. Not so much as an empty paint tin had been removed to serve as a plant pot nor even a shred of packing crate for firewood. It was as if the fisher-folk construction team was doing its best to make the paddy-people security staff appear ineffective.

These days Dewi was busy from breakfast until well after sunset since five of the bamboo huts were now full of guests. Among them were two couples, from Australia and France. The two men and one of the wives surfed when the tide was high but the French woman, Marielle, spent most of her time on a sunbed, massaging oil into a tan that already reminded Dewi of goat leather.

Marielle had discovered that Dewi had a basic talent for massages and these hour-long sessions became a highlight of the French woman's holiday. As a small girl Dewi had picked up the natural Balinese skill of *pijat* (therapeutic massages). She'd learned at an early age how to mix coconut oil and champak blooms and to give a simple yet thorough rubdown that had soothed Grandfather's aching back after he returned from a day bent-double in the paddies. Nat had checked with the boss over the phone and he'd jumped at the idea that the resort could offer massages to the guests; Dewi would get a cut of the fee and the resort would pocket the rest.

>><><><<

'Bu Ana was happy that both Pak Kolok and Dewi were benefitting from the jobs she'd managed to secure for them. She'd gone twice to visit Dewi at work to be told that her niece was massaging a guest in one of the huts. So, this time she decided to wait around until Dewi finished her hour-long therapy.

'Bu Ana estimated that (even after the resort's 'commission') Dewi could double her daily wage at the resort with the three hours of massages.

Nat agreed to cover for Dewi's waitressing duties but this afternoon the place was deserted. 'Bu Ana could see that the roofs of the suites were now being tiled and the window-frames fitted. It was during the hot sultry mid-afternoon hours and she was just thinking about abandoning her vigil and going back to the *warung* when the Brazilian woman trotted up the steps from the beach with her board under her arm. She lowered her board carefully onto the grass and sat down next to 'Bu Ana on the restaurant's concrete steps.

"I don't know how you're brave enough to tackle those waves," 'Bu Ana commented.

"I love it," the Brazilian woman replied. "I feel privileged when I get a chance to spend time out there. It doesn't happen as often as I'd like." She motioned with a light-hearted grimace towards the dull thud of hammering that had just started up again, as if on cue, from behind one of the suites.

"Thank you again for helping Dewi and for giving my friend the job on your security team," said 'Bu Ana. "He's a good, kind man and he deserves more support."

"It's fine. Between you and me, I think he might be the only guard who's even awake during the night."

'Bu Ana paused thoughtfully: "It's funny you should say that. A while back he told me that he saw somebody on the beach around midnight. She was acting very suspiciously but she got away before he got a good look."

"She…?"

"What?"

"You said 'she'. Did he say it was a woman?"

"Oh, yes. He was pretty sure it was a woman creeping back from somewhere over there," 'Bu Ana motioned westwards along the beach.

"Did he report it to anyone?"

"It's not so easy for him to make a report," the older woman smiled. "He asked me to tell you but I kept missing you."

'Bu Ana watched the manageress's eyes carefully. "Do *you* have any idea who it might have been?" she asked.

Nat shrugged. "…I'll ask around," she said finally.

><><><><<

"I'm thinking of changing my trade," Bob Bali joked one day as the construction crew chatted through a coffee break.

"What work are you thinking of taking up?" Rahim asked, as he kicked a few pieces of chopped kindling under the battered pan that served as a kettle. "Think you might start being a builder…?"

The others laughed.

"I'm going to take up massaging and waiting on tables. You realise that it's possible to be paid for both simultaneously…?" Bob Bali jabbed a calloused thumb over his shoulder in the direction of the huts.

"It's true," Yunus nodded. "She's paid more for three hours of massages than we get for half a day's hard labour."

"What do you know about hard labour Yunus?" one of the men chortled.

"It's worse than you think though," Bob Bali steered the conversation back on track. "On top of the waitressing and massaging she's also making money selling *jamu*."

Although the men were unaware of it, the unwitting entrepreneur in the burgeoning business of homemade *jamu* production was actually 'Grandfather the soldier'. The traditional herbal super-remedy made from turmeric, ginger, cinnamon, nutmeg, mace, cardamom, honey and a secret mix of mysterious roots and leaves was produced according to an old recipe that had been passed down through three or four generations. Some advised mixing the raw yolk of a duck egg into the concoction and others said that a turtle-egg worked wonders for the libido. Dewi rightly assumed that the *bules'* adventurous spirits might not stretch to raw egg and, from the experience of her hour-long massage sessions, she figured that it might be unwise to do anything that would offer a further boost to their libidos.

On the first day that Grandfather brewed up the magical concoction Dewi offered free samples to the guests, resulting in orders for two large bottles. Two days later Grandfather made more money selling *jamu* than Dewi was earned from waitressing. But by now in any case she'd began to think of waitressing as something to do when she wasn't making money from massages.

She'd gone to the market before work that morning to buy ingredients so that Grandfather could mix a fresh batch of *jamu*. As much as she liked the guests at the resort, she had to agree when one of the stallholders at the market quipped that the *bules* had too much money and not enough clothes.

$$>>\diamond\diamond><<$$

After the fiasco with his Filipino rooster, Pande had rarely been seen around the village. He left early each morning to work the two small beach-side paddy terraces that he now farmed for Pak Gusti. He'd built a stilted bamboo shelter on the dyke between the terraces and took some cold rice and vegetables wrapped in a banana leaf so that he could stay there throughout the midday heat without coming home.

It was the height of the *mepuah* season when the voracious birds swooped like locusts to plunder the crops. Pande had spent the last week rigging the terraces with ingenious webs of string that he could activate simply by pulling a bamboo lever tied to the corner of the shelter. From this position he could flutter shreds of flapping plastic bags and rattle noisy tin cans that were loaded with stones. He'd also mounted a scarecrow (decked in an old conical hat) and a cunning mechanical windmill that rattled a bamboo stick against a paint-can and swivelled in the breeze. As he was building that contraption it struck him that the old paint-can had turned out to be the only lasting benefit from the months he'd spent leading the construction team at Bali Moon Eco-resort.

Pande was aware that this land (about equal to half a soccer pitch) had been shamefully neglected during the time he was at the resort. This despite the fact that, like all the other farmers, he'd continued to make the required offerings at the shrine to Dewi Sri and on auspicious days at the irrigation ditches and dams. To overlook such obligations would be tantamount to a sin. He was proud now that the dykes and sluice gates that interlinked his paddies with the neighbouring ones were once again perfectly maintained.

'The land does not belong to us,' went an old refrain that had always been one of the central tenets of island life, 'it's only loaned to us by our children.'

It was a code of practise that had been handed down from his forefathers and was as firmly rooted as the Subak organisations that defined exactly when the precious water supplies must be shared. The system was flawlessly orchestrated throughout the island over a thousand years of experience. It ensured that the water that flowed out of Pande's terrace onto the burning black sand of the beach had already been used to the absolute maximum of its life-giving potential during its journey down from the flanks of the volcanoes.

Tradition, religion and sheer magic flowed through the entire ecosystem like the tendrils of some ancient vine until the great steps of the terraces were inextricably interlinked all the way down to the black sand beaches. In the old days, the islanders would harvest their own rice but now poorer Javanese migrant teams roamed the country doing the hot, hard work that few Balinese wanted to do these days. Once these teams had packed up their plastic-covered squatter camps and moved on, the *pengangon bebek* (duck-herder) would march through the paddies – like a Balinese Pied Piper – leading his flightless migration of quacking ducks to gather the precious dropped grains. At the same time, these flocks would pluck out pests and aerate the earth with their splashing bills. The ducks marched as if hypnotised behind the herder's magical *penyisih* staff. People said that an evil person could ruin the entire flock – so that they would never lay again – merely by shaking that feather-tipped bamboo with its cloth flag.

Some things had remained the same and in the old days, as now, most farmers still gave half their harvest to the landowners. Much had changed however in Pande's lifetime: the arrival of pesticides and toxic fertilisers had wiped out the natural ecology of these wetland environments. As a child Pande could remember his father working the paddies, simultaneously plucking water-plants for vegetables and even catching edible eels between his toes. He could recall 'fishing' for edible dragonflies with a stick tipped with sticky jackfruit gum and catching snails, frogs and monitor lizards in the paddies to supplement their meals. That way of life belonged to another age. These days you still grew your own rice...but everything else had to be bought.

Pande had, in his own small way, become one of the community leaders among the paddy-people, counted upon as one of the most valued workers when it came to temple preparations. Before he'd began working on the resort's construction crew, he had also been a popular visitor among the fishermen who were used to seeing him in the hot afternoons leading his two small daughters down to the waters-edge to splash and play. The little girls had almost forgotten those afternoons; once he started at the resort, he'd had neither the time nor the energy. Now, having lost his savings at the cockpit he owed it to his family to ensure that the next rice harvest would be the most lucrative possible. Inexplicably, a gulf had opened between him and the fishermen he'd once considered friends so that he no longer felt welcome at the beach. So, he spent every daylight hour at the paddies.

Pande wondered again if all that had happened was just the latest manifestation of his bad karma, perhaps for something he or his wife had done in another life. The fact that they'd had three daughters in a row without yet having a son was in itself proof of a curse. One day two of those daughters would marry and leave home and there would be no son to look after Pande and his wife in their old age. Wayan, the oldest of his daughters would remain with them...in fact she would doubtless be a demand upon them until the end of their days.

When talking about Wayan, people habitually drew a line with their finger across the middle of the forehead: as if indicating that the blood had only filled her body up to that level, without reaching her brain. Pande had learned, however, that medical science defined her condition as *sindrom Down*.

There were two teenage boys in their street who also had Down syndrome. One was quiet and shy and he got a thrill out of life by just waving silently at passing vehicles. He was well known and most people played along with this and waved back. The other boy was often seen swaggering up the street with his phone playing pop music at maximum volume. Usually he had a jaunty cigarette in the corner of his mouth and would only take it out from time to time to wail tunelessly along with the chorus.

As a female, however, Pande's daughter was carefully protected and remained almost a prisoner in the home compound. She was delighted by animals. Orphaned puppies and pregnant cats were irresistibly drawn to her and she was often to be seen with a kitten or even a hen dozing contentedly in her lap. Wayan's closest friends were the birds that inhabited the overgrown riverbank at the back of the house. The strutting waterhens – known as *kerquack* for the noise they made – would come to take rice from the palm of her hands. She loved how they would grab miniscule pecks for themselves and then grab a bigger beak-full and dash, tripping over toes that were almost as long as their bodies, to drop the rice in front of the tumbling black fluff-balls that were their babies. Wayan had learned to mimic birdsong perfectly, luring entire squadrons of bulbuls that serenaded her from the branches and performed aerial acrobatics for her by catching morsels in mid-air. At dinner when she thought her parents weren't watching, she would slip a handful of stodgy rice into her pocket for her feathered friends. Her parents turned a blind eye, understanding that the harmless crime of the smuggling itself gave her an added pleasure.

Pande barely saw his wife and three daughters now and he'd lost touch with his friends. His youngest daughter – five-year-old Nyoman – was about to start school. She was mortified at the potential embarrassment of being the only child without a uniform on the first day. Even if everything went like clockwork there would be a considerable delay before the rice could be harvested and the deal struck with the buyer. Pande sat, cross-legged in his stilted hut, like a meditating hermit. Half of his mind was alert for the thieving flocks of birds. The other half was searching for a way to raise the money that would pay for Nyoman's uniform.

The shameful disaster with the Filipino rooster had been a public display in cowardice and Pande was determined to be an honourable example to his family from now on. It was he who'd led them into this situation and he could see no alternative now but to swallow his pride. He would have to ask the boss for a job at the resort. Another *odalan* ceremony was approaching but Pande would offer to work straight through the ceremony to show his willingness to get the building finished. His presence would be expected for the temple preparations and to turn his back on those obligations would put him in an uncomfortable position with the *banjar*…but perhaps he could ask forgiveness and maybe they would understand. He'd do his best to make it up in the future, once he was back on an even keel.

Perhaps if the boss saw that he was prepared to make such a sacrifice, he'd be sure to allow Pande to come back to work.

The islanders had a saying: the heavier the load on the rice plant, the lower it will be forced to bow.

>><><><<

Pak Kolok was doing his best to avoid the Brazilian manageress. There was no doubt in his mind that it was her skulking figure he'd seen that night on the beach. Yet 'Bu Ana had assured him that it wasn't Nat.

The deaf man pondered this as he watched his buffalo wallowing like pink whales in the muddied waters of the inlet. The way he saw it there were only two possibilities: either Nat was lying, or 'Bu Ana was. He didn't know the manageress well but, try as he might, he couldn't imagine what secret she could possibly have that would take her along the deserted beach in the middle of the night. Was it possible then that 'Bu Ana was protecting Nat because the manageress was also somehow involved with the Sea Goddess? It stood to reason that a woman who had the power to turn herself into a giant bat at will, could wield a power that would easily subjugate a naïve *bule*.

Nyai Roro Kidul had claimed two victims recently. With her inexplicable nocturnal skirmishes on the beach and her audacity in the waves maybe the Brazilian surfer-girl was also a disciple of the Sea Goddess. Or was she destined to become the next victim?

As the only effective set of night-eyes on the beach, he'd have to be more alert than ever.

>><><><<

Pande waited over an hour while the boss finished a leisurely lunch with the regency police chief.

The resort's ex-foreman restrained his impatience and nerves behind a gently wafting curtain of cigarette smoke. The buttons on the policeman's uniform shirt strained against the bulk of his belly when he laughed. The policeman had transferred here from Java several years before and he was about as well respected as any other in his profession. A free lunch at the resort was the least he had a right to expect (and probably there was substantially *more* due to him than that). And why not? Pande had no misconceptions on that front. The man had almost certainly paid good money to buy his way into that rank and he had every right now to start to recuperate some of that loss. That was not what people called *korupsi*. It was merely the way the system had always been.

Out of the corner of his eye Pande noticed that the police chief's uniform was strained almost as tight as the miniskirt of the Balinese girl who strutted over while the two men were saying their goodbyes.

"So, you want to come back to work?" the Australian asked without preamble when he finally deigned to see Pande. He led the would-be construction worker on a short tour across the front of the site. "As you can see, it's come a long way. There's really not much left to do…"

"More than half of the building was done with me as foreman. I have a lot of experience and know the project better than most," Pande was aware that his desperation was probably too obvious. "I'm not asking to come back as a foreman – I'll be happy to work again as a simple labourer."

"What about this new ceremony that's coming up soon? Full moon isn't it? What then? I guess you'll expect time off as soon as you've started work."

"No. I'll work straight through from tomorrow – today if you want – until the project's finished. I need the work and will work every day." If Pande had to beg he was prepared to do so. He owed that much to his family. Sometimes it seemed to him that they were, all of them, cursed.

Fortunately, the boss saved him from the necessity of begging. "Ok. Let me think about it. I'll let you know."

The boss kept him waiting for three days, then sent word that he had all the workers he needed.

It seemed to Pande that sometimes life was like throwing salt into the sea. No matter how hard he tried he could never make a difference.

><><><<

Putri Laut still lay abandoned under the trees. It had been so long since her decks had been rinsed by the waves that dead leaves filled her to the scuppers in rust-coloured heaps and fallen coconut fronds draped like frayed bunting over her fake boom. Her desiccated timbers – used to daily basting in the foamy breakers – dropped flakes of blue paint like cracked ice onto the black sand.

Since he started at the resort Rahim had had little time to think of the never-ending maintenance work that is a fact of life for a timber boat in a tropical climate.

Now he'd been offered an unexpected opportunity to return to the ocean. It was difficult to imagine, however, that this was what the Sea Goddess had meant when she commanded him to return to the sea in his dream.

Nat had waited until he came down from the roofing work for a coffee-break before she wandered over to talk to him.

"So, the boss is trying to start some activities that the guests can do," she said as Yunus handed them each a steaming glass of tarry black coffee.

"He wants to find reasons for them to stay longer."

"You mean like the massages?" Rahim nodded towards the restaurant where Dewi was now mopping tables in preparation for lunch.

"Sort of. There need to be things that guests can do even when there's no surf. We had the idea that fishing trips could be perfect for times when there's small swell."

Rahim nodded: "Less likelihood for them to get seasick."

"I wondered if you could find a couple of fishermen who would agree to take *bules* in their boats for short fishing trips. Just for two or three hours." Nat suggested a payrate and Rahim quickly figured that – even after the resort's commission and fuel costs were deducted – the income for a fisherman would be about equal to what the builders made in a day's work.

"Perhaps I could do it myself when the building is finished," he suggested. It had been worrying him lately that work at the resort would be coming to an end soon and yet he couldn't know for sure until he went to sea whether the curse still lay upon *Putri Laut*.

He yearned for the relatively carefree days when his only obligation – fraught as it often was – was to maintain his boat and to catch enough fish to feed his family. But that was back in the old

128

days, before the curse. As much as he missed the sea, he wasn't convinced that he really wanted to return as a hired guide.

Watching Yunus passing the coffee glasses to the rest of the workforce, he wondered momentarily if he should suggest that Yunus take guests out in *Putri Laut*. It might do the young man good to get back onto the ocean before the fear of that watery element – and the memory of their horrifying night together – had time to gnaw more deeply at him. He still intensely resented the position the young man had put him but perhaps it was true that everyone deserved a second chance.

The *bule* manageress was also watching Yunus and, as if aware exactly where Rahim's thoughts were taking him. She spoke cautiously. "I think the fisherman should ideally be somebody older…" She obviously felt that she ought to qualify the statement. "We have a responsibility for the safety of the guests so it would have to be a boatman with a lot of experience."

Rahim nodded. So, the *bule* woman had an inkling then that Yunus might not be entirely reliable. He was momentarily overcome by an almost tearful sadness for his nephew, before he forced himself to recall that the young man had brought this situation upon himself. Did Yunus also suffer from dreams of the sea?

"I'll do my best to find someone," he told the manageress. "I'll ask around and let you know."

Even after the Brazilian woman returned to the restaurant Rahim continued to sit apart from the others, and his thoughts stayed on Yunus. Maybe the offer of the building job had been another part of the young man's curse. Maybe he'd have been better had he been forced to continue fishing. Endless nights out on the boat would have provided less temptation. The young man used to be light-hearted and jovial but his increasingly melancholic personality had coincided with this period of unhabitual wealth. Rahim knew that, despite his promised abstinence, his nephew was drinking heavily again. He was paid more for labouring than he'd ever earned before and a small bottle of bootlegged arak – enough to lead to unconsciousness – only cost a couple of hour's pay. Rahim hadn't seen Yunus at the mosque in over a week. He'd begun to think that Yunus was already beyond help.

5 – Bali Moon Shine

"This is just the latest kind of sickness," Grandfather Tabanan bellowed.

Even though only he and Grandfather were in attendance at the Hermit Club, the old man's voice had risen to a decibel level that would have been sufficient to address a political meeting. They were watching three *bule* surfers – hefty, well-fed, sunburned boys – strapping themselves to their surfboards with plastic leg-ropes. They reminded Grandfather of Pak Kolok's tethered pink buffalo.

"It's like a virus that's sickened the whole village," Grandfather Tabanan roared. The surfers glanced back in surprise. "In the past we suffered from malaria and dengue but at least we all suffered together. Now we suffer from tourists and it's driven a wedge into our community like never before. We fight like cats and dogs…in fact, we even fight *over* our cats and dogs."

Seeing the way that the conversation was going, Grandfather was relieved that 'Mang hadn't turned up this afternoon. It had been she who'd given the dog to him although he could never quite figure out her motivation in doing so. Had she meant it as a tender display of affection? A subtle way of reminding him of her, perhaps? Maybe she just needed to get rid of more damned puppies and knew he was too kind-hearted to refuse. He was never really sure but, in any case, he was dreading telling her of Semut's disappearance.

"Don't worry," Grandfather adopted the soothing tone he reserved for his friend's particularly cantankerous moods. "Like any other virus it'll die out in the end and the village will still be here. Next year or the year after they'll leave and things will return to normal."

Grandfather realised that he missed 'Mang's soothing personality and gentle distractions, the perfect balance to Tabanan's raucous complaints. He could never tell, however, whether his two friends got along with each other. 'Mang appeared to let the old man's bitterness wash over her and, for his part, Tabanan simply bulldozed through any comments that the woman made.

Grandfather Tabanan was believed to be the oldest person in the village ever since Grandmother Moyang had died. She'd been so old that her nickname meant literally 'Grandmother ancestor'. "But she was barely 90 years old," Tabanan had yelled at the time. "Nothing at all wrong with her and she dropped dead. Just like that."

According to government records Tabanan had never married. Among the villagers, however, he was accorded immense respect because he was said to be married to a woman of unique and fearful power. Although he'd only talked about it on one or two occasions, every nugget of detail had been greedily picked up and then generously shared until, finally, their love-story had been incorporated into the communal treasure-chest of the village's most prized legends. It was said that he met his wife while he was fishing for freshwater shrimps near the spot where the river flowed into the sacred forest. Grandfather wondered why he would have been so reckless as to fish that close to the Death Temple and almost within earshot of the ghost waterfall. Nevertheless, according to the legend, he'd caught something infinitely more valuable than shrimps that afternoon.

It was said that Grandfather Tabanan was married to a *wong samar* ghost, but Grandfather had never personally seen evidence of the existence of this spiritual spouse. Several times during their many years of friendship he'd seen Tabanan with various unknown females. He'd always looked closely, but there was never anything unusual about their upper lips. The two little ridges under a human nose – Cupid's bow to the Ancient Greeks – are known to medical science as the philtrum. Textbooks described the philtrum as 'a vestigial medial depression with no known function'. To the Balinese, however, these tiny ridges serve an immensely useful purpose; they were the only fool proof way to be certain that a person is a human. Everybody knew that ghosts invariably had a flat upper lip that was devoid of the philtrum ridges.

For this reason, Grandfather was sure that he'd never seen Tabanan's otherworldly wife. He accepted this spirit world union as fact, however, since there was nothing particularly unusual about a person being married to a spirit. There were some villages where marriages of this sort were relatively common; if it was an accepted fact that the sultan of Yogyakarta was married to the sea goddess Nyai Roro Kidul, then why should it be considered strange that a normal person might marry a more humble ghost? In his memoirs Sultan Hamengkubuwono IX had described the vaguely schizophrenic character of his Sea Goddess wife, who would

131

sometimes appear – especially during a full moon – as a beautiful and obliging young woman and, at other times, as an old crone. When the sultan died in 1988 palace servants reported apparitions of the goddess, apparently in mourning.

The *wong samar* too were said to be devoted wives but, perhaps predictably, they could be dangerously vindictive if betrayed. Grandfather assumed that his friend's ghostly wife must be a woman of super-human patience to put up with her husband's angry rants. People sometimes said that the old man must have done something really saintly in a past life to have lived to such a ripe old age. After all, they quipped: 'There wasn't too much that was saintly about him in this one.'

The few who were more charitable – and who knew the old man's story – said that he had a lot to be angry about. At the age of eleven he'd been a clever student and on the verge of a scholarship. Then, in an ill-fated writing contest, he won a place on a school trip to Java. As it turned out, he barely set foot on the neighbouring island. The boat capsized at midnight, just as it was nearing the Javanese port of Banyuwangi. More than fifty people drowned that night, among them some of Grandfather Tabanan's schoolfriends. He'd forced himself to jump from the vessel's listing hull into what appeared to be a bottomless pit of inky blackness and had plummeted so deeply into the water that both his eardrums had been burst by the pressure. The dirty water had caused infections and his hearing had never recovered. With it went his chances of an education. After his return, people shunned him fearfully as one who had been to the realms of the dead and returned. They noticed that he even spoke with a different voice, shouting his words as if trying to send a message from beyond the grave.

Grandfather Tabanan never ventured onto the sea again and seventy years later, he still woke in a panicked sweat from nightmares in which he was swimming endlessly, struggling to the surface through a cold, oily syrup.

"Those *bules*!" he roared now, almost spitting in his rage. "I saw them riding through the village on their hired scooters. Too fast. No awareness for children or animals. Worse still, none of them wearing shirts. You'd think that the whole village already belonged to them!"

>><><><><<

The paperback copy of *Dona Flor and Her Two Husbands* still lay, unread, where it had been placed on Nat's dresser. During the first weeks the hot sea-breeze had sometimes blown in through the open window so that the pages fluttered like a trapped bird. More recently it had fattened as if in reaction to a lazy island lifestyle and lack of exercise – swelling in the tropical humidity it had developed a curvature of the spine, as if struggling to sustain the weight of its inflating belly.

Fortunately island life had the opposite effect on the book's owner. Nat had been so busy that there was little time left to read but surfing, yoga and hard work had honed her muscles and heightened the sun-blessed tone of her skin.

The boss had been over in the capital 'interviewing' for the last two weeks. He hadn't deemed it necessary to offer any details, but Nat needed only to take a glance at her new 'deputy' Suzie to have an idea of what form that 'interviewing' had probably taken.

Back home in the Amazonian port of Belém there were people who claimed that they could see the coloured auras around a person. Nat had never really believed such a thing but she was quite sure that if Suzie had an aura it would be the peachy-pink shade of *nusa indah* blooms. Translated into English the name meant 'beautiful island' but – having ordered a veritable forest of seedling trees to adorn the steep rock-gardens in front of the suites – Nat knew too that their Latin name was *Mussaenda pubescens* in reference to their soft, downy leaves.

Nat guessed that Suzie was about twenty years old and, despite her manicured pink talons, the dangling earrings and her flickering false eyelashes, there was something distinctly pubescent about her. In spite of the artificial accoutrements there was something about her that paradoxically embodied simple girlish femininity. Her green contact lenses gave the impression that you were staring into a mossy well, and Nat could imagine the appeal that this young creature had held for her boss.

Suzie also had a surprising amount of brash confidence to go with a professional name that she'd almost certainly not been christened with. She was from the highlands of Sumatra where, if the legends were true, her people had once dined on Christian missionaries. Those days had long disappeared but it struck Nat that there was something of the man-eater in the cat-eyed young beauty.

Suzie simply arrived one morning bearing a scrawled message for Nat from the boss. It had done nothing to clarify exactly why she'd been given the position of deputy manager: 'I've explained Suzie's duties carefully,' it read. 'She can handle it. She will take some of the guest relations load off you.'

There was something familiar about Suzie and it was only later that afternoon that Nat recalled what it was. A woman called Marjorie with whom she'd shared a room in Australia seemed to have the same vividly peachy-pink aura. Marj had been such a perfect name for her old colleague that when she got to know her better she had to assume it was a working name. After all, when Nat applied for that job she'd also been informed that the more exotic Natalia would be more appreciated in her new line of work.

Nat had been backpacking around Australia for two months at the time and was almost entirely out of money; it was either a case of finding a job within a week or giving up and heading home to Brazil. She'd bought a cut-price rail-ticket, gambling her last dollars on the vague offer of a job as a receptionist in a Sydney hostel. Around two o'clock in the morning the train had stopped in the Western Australian town of Kalgoorlie-Boulder. It was an unlikely time to go for a wander but the guard had told her that the train would not leave for two hours so, unable to sleep in her cramped seat and intrigued primarily by the air of adventure in the town's name, she'd made the typically reckless decision to explore. She was amazed to find that the bars in the high street were still boisterously busy.

There had been something irresistible in the Dodge City atmosphere. But, as the only woman on the street, it was also intimidating. As she turned a corner, she almost walked into a punch-up in a side alley, where a group of men were watching two others slugging at each other with a lack of coordination that was so perfectly choreographed as to leave the two almost entirely unscathed. As she hurried past one of the spectators noticed her, instantly losing interest in the fight. He shouted something that was, mercifully perhaps, unintelligible and stumbled after her.

It was the drunk's pursuing footsteps that made her turn into the first open doorway she passed. It would be an exaggeration to say that her arrival occasioned a stunned silence but there was a noticeable lull in the ear-splitting din and a momentary cessation of the crunch of broken glass underfoot – and that was the closest that The Railhead would ever get to silence during opening hours. Given the attention that was suddenly focussed on her, it was not a moment for gazing around. Instead Nat kept her face forward, took a deep breath and marched purposefully for the bar like a floundering swimmer heading for the edge of a pool. Although Nat didn't realise it at that point, she would have ample time to contemplate the beer-soaked atmosphere of the Railhead with its cracked plaster, cobbled-together furniture and creaking spit-and-sawdust floorboards.

The boss had spotted her instantly, which wasn't surprising since she was hardly inconspicuous as the only female customer on the public side of the bar. By the time the train had moved on, she'd accepted his job offer, collected her backpack and moved into the twin room on the second floor that she'd share with Marj for the next three months.

"Tonight, Natalia, the drinks are on the house," the boss had said grandly. "You can try your uniform on in the morning and start pulling schooners when we open tomorrow afternoon."

Schooners, ponies, middies, shetlands, butchers, pots and pints were all part of the bartender slang of the Outback bars. There were other terms that would become familiar as well. Most of them she preferred to forget. It had been years since anyone had called her Natalia and, since she associated it mostly with her grandmother, it made her uncomfortable to have it used in her new workplace. She made no real effort to use it in introductions and it made no difference anyway because within a week or so The Railhead's new barmaid was universally known as Nat and was already a favourite among the regulars. It wasn't like the punters were there for conversation anyway. Kalgoorlie was a gold mining town and The Railhead was what was known in Outback slang as 'a skimpy bar.' It attracted large crowds of drinkers who were willing to pay slightly inflated prices for the simple reason that the barmaids all wore 'skimpy' French-style lace lingerie.

The tequila girl had just resigned so Nat's job was to walk around the bar in basque and panties, with a leather bandolier of shot-glasses strapped across her chest and two bottles of tequila slotted into holsters that swung from her sashaying hips.

Even from her first evening shift her exotically dark skin, surfer's physique and startling blue eyes were enough to entice generous tips even from the most single-minded drunks. She shuddered with embarrassment for the first two evenings but she'd never made so much money and within a week she'd learned that just a hint of flirting had an exponential effect on the tips. If she could upgrade a punter to one of the more expensive tipples there was extra commission to be made. One evening – towards the end of a shift that had involved several invited shots of Herradura Reposado (The Railhead's vintage tequila) – she climbed onto the bar, to great applause, and gave an exhibition of the Samba that was said to have evolved from a slave dance born in her city. Like so much else, the dance was believed to have come to her country via African slaves and – while her skills might not have won a glance at the Rio Sambadrome – it was quite clear from the fistful of banknotes she climbed down with that it was appreciated. After that it became a part of her repertoire. She wondered sometimes how her strong, independent grandmother might have felt if she could see her at work. There were days when she felt guilty at profiting from a sexuality that had been exploited by men since her ancestors arrived in the 'New World' generations ago. There was even an enduring legend in her own family of a maternal ancestor – a beautiful negress concubine who had, in line with many local legends, 'enslaved' a wealthy landowner. It was said that Nat's family descended from that union. According to the legend the slave-girl enhanced her natural allure with Candomblé spells, from which no mere white man could ever have escaped. Although the landowner could never acknowledge her – or the several children he had with her – the family legend claimed that she was the only woman he ever genuinely loved. That slave-girl was just one speck of dust in the fifteen million-strong horde of 'black gold' that was transported out of the hellish gates of Elmina fortress, in what later became Ghana. She brought with her the religion of West African tribe-lands and the family still claimed that she was the first in a long line of *mães de santos* (mothers of saints) who oversaw the initiation of new disciples to the ancient religion in the New World. Nat's own grandmother was the last in that celebrated line of priestesses.

An estimated four million slaves had been transported to Brazil by the time that African Holocaust officially ended, in 1888.

Through the course of more than ten generations of suppression and persecution her grandmother's religion had been driven almost underground. Their martyrs clashed dramatically with the saints of the ruling landowners. The *escrava-de-ganho* (profit slave) Rosa Maria Egipcíaca da Vera Cruz, who was a sex slave for 25 years, became an established saint in the Candomblé religion along with Escrava Anastácia (Slave Anastácia), who was always depicted with an iron collar around her neck and a cruel, muzzle strapped across her mouth. To this day, any worshipper who wanted to petition the blessings of 'the girl in the iron mask' was expected to do so through three days of strict silence, mimicking the torture of the saint. It was a powerful image of the most heart-rending of silent protests yet it was said that Anastácia's piercing blue eyes could speak volumes.

Nat had accepted the job at The Railhead by free choice, so she too stayed silent and tried to keep the contempt for the miners from showing in her own blue eyes. The miners were lonely, bored and ridiculously overpaid. And they were Nat's first experience of just how easily pleased men could be. Before long, her shifts at The Railhead started to feel almost like any other job. The early evening was a breeze. The worst part of the shift was when the miners started to get drunk and she had to move fast to keep away from clawing hands. Then again towards the end of the evening things improved slightly because their coordination and reflexes made them easier to avoid.

Fights broke out every night and, during her first month, they seemed so often to be fighting over her that Nat thought it was her fault. Someone would try to grab her and another drunk would, in a fit of gallantry, hit the offender. The Railhead had a solid staff of bouncers who – being, for the most part, relatively sober – usually managed to swing their own fists with enough accuracy to ensure that it was rarely necessary to evict a customer. It was actually very difficult to get thrown out of The Railhead since it was the boss's considered opinion that the bouncers had failed in their job if a paying punter needed to be thrown out before he'd had a chance to empty his wallet.

Nat had left Kalgoorlie three months later with enough money to travel onwards for the next year. She was aware that she could have made considerably more. Nat knew that her roommate Marj had capitalised on the situation far more effectively. She knew this because of the many evenings she'd had to doze across the benches in the bar while her roommate made effective use of their pokey bedroom. Nat had no regrets of missed opportunities on that score. There had been offers of course but that was a line she refused to cross.

Although she considered deliberately burning bridges so that she'd never be tempted to return, there was something in her cautious nature that had convinced Nat to keep lines of communication open in case she ever needed The Railhead as a financial fall-back in the future. Even so she'd been astounded when, five years later, the boss had called her to say that he'd sold The Railroad: 'I remember you telling me once how much you loved Bali – and that you speak bahasa. I need a team-player who I can be sure is speaking the same language.'

She recalled – along with his befuddling habit of confusing metaphors – that she'd once mentioned to him that she'd spent six months in Bali, studying yoga and the Indonesian language. She was surprised, however, to realise that he recalled any conversations from those drunken Railhead evenings. She'd been more surprised still to learn that he wanted to hire her as manageress for what he'd described as an eco-resort that he was building on a remote West Balinese beach.

>< <> <> <> ><

A dancer shimmied across the lawn, fans fluttering in imitation of a hummingbird. The gold thread in her traditional dancer's costume glinted in the spotlights that had been mounted in the palms next to the resort's new lobby. Waitresses clad in ceremonial sarongs and *kebaya* blouses appeared to be involved in dances of their own as they flitted from table to table with bottles that dipped beaklike into tulip-shaped glasses. The tables were arranged like a laagered wagon-train and somewhere out beyond the circle of gilded light the village snoozed. The steady rumble of the waves was drowned by the reverberating sound of a dozen bamboo xylophones and the throb of double-ended drums and cymbals in the hands of the village orchestra. The throbbing clatter of the gamelan produced a beat that travelled up the table legs like the insistent pulse of a distant earthquake.

The dancer wafted across manicured grass that was finally more like a billiard table than a rice paddy. The rough timber of the tables – the venerable planks from five decommissioned outriggers – were covered with Indian sarongs printed with multicoloured Mandalas. The dance had no religious importance and its significance was purely in flirtatious entertainment.

The woman held out the ends of the flowing sash around her waist and strutted – one slightly plump thigh pushing through the slit in the front of her sarong – past the first two tables. Nat's stiffened, avoiding eye-contact with the dancer. 'Please don't make me dance,' she muttered under her breath – although not so loud that the boss, sitting by her side, could have heard.

But she needn't have worried. The woman passed onwards beyond their table…and then abruptly turned, as if in afterthought, and tapped the boss on the shoulder with her fan. She'd been well cued and had known all the time exactly where she was heading. The crowd laughed, a few people clapped and the boss feigned surprise as he got to his feet.

The woman, a veteran dancer, was performing the *joged bungbung*. Despite her years of experience, she was a less adept dancer than the teenage performers who'd been dancing on the grass for the last hour. While easy to appreciate because of the dramatic movements and gorgeous costumes that represented butterflies, princesses and goddesses, their complex choreography told tales that were way beyond the understanding of most of the audience at the inaugural evening of the Bali Moon Eco-resort. By comparison, the *joged bungbung* was simply a slapstick parody of flirtation; the aging dancer would entice one man after another to dance with her…and the more awkward her victim, the more the crowd enjoyed the performance. In the old days, these veteran dancers – nearing the end of their careers – sometimes had a reputation as women of easy virtue. The suggestive dance – at times developing into something unmistakably sexual – was said often to be just a preliminary to arrangements of a far more intimate sort.

The boss was familiar enough with the concept to make a play-act of attempting to pinch and grab at the dancer. She parried his advances and fended him off with playful slaps of her fans, causing even more hilarity among the spectators. It was a sort of ritualised flirtation that transported Nat's mind uncomfortably back to bar-top Samba exhibitions at The Railhead.

Across from Nat the village headman applauded delightedly – his oversized signet ring flickering under the lights. The local police chief sat next to him. Although he smiled politely at the dancers the policeman was obviously more engrossed in something that Suzie was whispering in his ear.

The official launch of Bali Moon Eco-resort had gone well. The religious ceremony had taken place that afternoon under the auspicious patronage of a powerful *pedanda* (Brahman high priest) who ensured that the *melaspas* rites would 'breathe life into the property'. Despite his reticence to run to a bill of several thousand dollars for a half-day ceremony, the boss was attuned enough to the island philosophy to realise it would effectively be a curse on the resort to overlook the ritual. He knew that should anything go wrong – however minor – in the day-to-day maintenance of the property it would inevitably and forever after be explained by the omission of these crucial rites.

There had even been a suggestion that he commission a *balian terang* to guarantee that the weather would remain clear for the afternoon of the ceremony. It had turned out to be expensive however since this shaman-for-hire must be prepared to enter into dangerous spiritual battle with any other *balian* (hired perhaps by wealthy plantation owners) who were using their magic to bring rain. For huge temple ceremonies it was even possible to skip the middlemen and go straight to Ida Ratu Sila Majemuh, the god of weather. But that was more expensive still. Nevertheless, the Balinese weather worked a spell of its own and, after an early-morning drizzle, the sun had beamed benevolently down through the afternoon.

The *pedanda* had returned to the capital before dinner and the fifty or so diners, seated around the tables on the lawn now were a mix of *bule* guests, friends of the boss and local bigwigs. The boss was shrewd enough to keep the local politicians, the village headman and – especially – the district police chief happy. It was clearly not coincidental that the delectable Suzie was seated next to the local law-enforcement crusader since this evening she was sporting long dangling earrings in the shape of handcuffs. Her eyelashes fluttered faster than the dancer's fans. Subtlety was not her strongpoint, Nat thought again.

Pak Gusti, the original landowner and the community's petty nobility, was sitting at another table – his belt already loosened after the feast. He was talking to a representative from the tourism office and the regional newspaper editor. A photographer had been circulating and everyone hoped that their photos would appear in the next issue of the weekly advertiser. Tomorrow morning there would also be a brainstorming session to try to ensure that everyone was onboard for the 'mutually beneficial' future of the resort and most of the same dignitaries were invited. With only a couple of exceptions they'd already claimed prior engagements, however: since the meeting was mid-morning it was assumed that neither breakfast nor lunch would be served. More important still, the newspaperman and photographer would not be present so nobody would have the thrill of seeing themselves in print.

Throughout the meal the boss had been expounding on fresh ideas for activities: "Wives and girlfriends can do yoga, for example, while the men are surfing," he said.

"That could work," Nat agreed, "but maybe wives and girlfriends will want to surf too...then they can all do yoga together."

"Even better! It's lucky that both you and Suzie are qualified yoga teachers. You're likely to be busy with managerial work but I'm sure she can make time for both." He leaned closer to Nat with a lewd smile. "Suzie's *extremely* flexible."

The diners had finished heaping their plates from the buffet of local specialities that was lined up under the two great driftwood chandeliers. The great aluminium trays of fried rice, fried noodles, vegetable *cap cay*, peanut sauce *gado-gado*, beef rendang and fried chicken had been refilled several times. There were *satays* made of chicken and goat (but no pork, in deference to the Muslim guests). Even the most intrepid diners among the *bules* were challenged by specialities like bee larvae *lawar* salad and plates of baked sago grubs, which looked like severed thumbs.

By now everyone had moved on to after-dinner cocktails. The suites were fully occupied for the first time, although most of the guests had been invited by the boss. His welcoming speech had rung all the notes of bravado and boasting that Nat had expected but she'd been surprised when towards the end he had thrown in a mention of thanks for her – his 'gorgeous manageress' – and the staff 'who had worked so hard to get the place up and running.' He paused for the round of applause before adding, '...just four months over schedule.'

His final mention had been for the resort's 'signature cocktail'; the 'Bali Moon Shine', which he hoped everyone would be keen to order after dinner. Nat was aware that it had been concocted as a particularly high-profit beverage. If enough was consumed it would make inroads towards offsetting the hospitality bill for the evening. The boss ordered a jug of Bali Moon Shine for their table and poured them each a glass of the kaleidoscopic mix of mango juice, grenadine, arak and a cheap domestic version of blue curaçao.

The drink's potency was camouflaged by the sensory overload of these colours and cloying flavours but underneath it all the distinctive medicinal flavour of locally distilled palm arak was discernible. Technically the sale of this local arak was illegal but from the way the police chief leaned towards Suzie it wasn't statements he was planning on taking down this evening.

>◇◇◇◇<

"The *bules* will pay twenty-five dollars for a boat for three hours fishing," Nat had explained to Rahim. "The boss's offer is that the fisherman gets ten and the resort gets fifteen."

"I can ask around and see what they say..." the fisherman replied, with a nod.

"But...wait a moment," Nat interrupted with a sigh. "This is strictly a secret between you and me okay." She'd hoped that Rahim would haggle over the price. Now his Balinese politeness put her on the spot so she felt she had to continue: "Between you and me, I think the payment is unfair. Let's pretend that the fishermen refuse and that we had to offer them fifteen. The resort will still get ten and if the *bules* catch something they can pay extra to the resort to get it cooked."

Rahim nodded. "That seems fairer."

"But if the boss ever hears that it was my suggestion and did not really come from the fishermen I'm in big trouble. Understand?"

There were several old fishermen – past what would have been considered retirement age in another place – who still spent long arthritic nights at the work of hauling nets into their increasingly decrepit boats. Rahim figured that these ought to be the first candidates for what should prove to be a far easier living. When he passed them sitting together, smoking by one of the boats that afternoon, he stopped to explain the boss's deal. As he talked he became aware of a growing sense of embarrassment among the old-timers. As their reluctance became clearer it dawned on him that they sensed something disreputable in the suggestion. Finally, they thanked him for the offer and sent him on his way with a polite refusal.

Could it be that the old men thought they would somehow be prostituting themselves by turning their boats – a means of livelihood that went back to their great-grandfathers – into one more plaything for the *bules*? The more Rahim thought it through the more he began to suspect that, in some way he couldn't define, there *was* something dishonourable in it.

>><><><<

As a younger man Pande had been a local legend at the buffalo chariot races in the paddies south of the city. He'd been smaller then – almost fifteen kilos lighter. His frame had bulked out in the last decade but hard work had maintained the tone of his muscle. From time to time he still rode over on his old Vespa to watch the Sunday morning races. Officially, betting was illegal on such occasions but there was always a quiet wager that Pande found irresistible. He had an eye for the form of the buffalo – refusing to be swayed by the gaudy harnesses, cloth-sheathed horns and ornate chariots of the richest owners. He could usually pick a pair that were perfectly matched and which he was sure would run well together.

The racing buffalo were a breed apart. A different species from the bulky specimens that trudged along the beach in front of Pak Kolok. They'd been carefully bred and nurtured almost like racehorses for the West Balinese sport of *mekepung*, a form of racing that existed nowhere else in the world. The lightweight wooden racing chariots of modern times were simply trimmed-down versions of the carts that the first pioneering rice-farmers used to transport their crops.

There was a rare skill involved in racing these chariots along the rutted paddyfield dirt-tracks. Pande knew better than most, however, that all the skill in the world amounted to nothing without the sheer wrought-iron nerve that allowed a charioteer to stand tall while his wooden platform – the size of a large coffee table – veered wildly around bends at speeds of up to 60 kilometres per hour. The charioteer who knew the animals well and consistently refused to give in to the almost irresistible temptation to slow the buffalo by hauling on the reins was the winner.

Pande was a popular face at the racetrack and there were two or three owners who from time to time had tried light-heartedly to tempt him back onto a chariot. In recent years, as he'd felt his age kicking in, he noticed that the offers were increasingly made in jocular tones, but it was still pleasant to know that his racing past was not entirely forgotten.

It was only two weeks before the big Jembrana Cup meeting, one of the biggest fixtures in the *mekepung* calendar. The fact that Pande was still respected at the course after all these years was a balm to his injured soul and he wondered if it was his battered pride that had provoked him to come back here this morning. His daughters deserved the excitement of a rare trip out of the village, he told himself. Little Nyoman was standing on the footplate of the Vespa between his knees with her hands gripping the centre of the handlebars while her bigger sister sat behind with her arms around Pande's chest. His oldest daughter Wayan was home, of course, protected as always within the family compound. In any case, with her love of animals she'd have surely been traumatised by the brutality of the races.

Even before Pande propped the Vespa up onto its centre-stand two old friends had come over to chat and offer cigarettes. The two girls ran off to explore the paddock-side marketplace where snake-oil medicine vendors hawked potions that were displayed across rattan mats and snack stands had ingeniously been folded out from the panniers of scooters. There was even small tin carousel – driven by a moped motor which supplied barely enough power to turn the six multi-coloured seats – and another motorbike mounted with a rack displaying row upon row of waterfilled plastic bags.

Each of these swinging bubbles held a goldfish, presumably calmed now by amnesia after what must have been a truly horrifying ride down the highway from the city.

The two men who'd obeyed the pop-pop-pop summons of Pande's Vespa were clearly hoping to benefit from his judgement. Although Pande had no money for wagers this morning his practised eye was already analysing the pairs of buffalo that were being harnessed together around the edge of the grassy meadow. Even in gambling – as in every other walk of life – there was a sort of karmic justice; if either of the men backed a winning team on Pande's recommendation it was a dead cert that he would remember the man who had given him the tip afterwards. There were several teams that looked to be well-matched but, in many cases, there was an imbalance somewhere: one bull significantly stronger, another too old for its partner, one too wild, another too unpredictably nervous. One team was already harnessed up near the starting line. They were keen and the bulls looked strong but the tough hides on their hindquarters already showed the scars of the brutal nail-studded cosh that served as a *mekepung* jockey's whip. The scars were a sure sign of a losing team: almost certainly inflicted by a frustrated rider. A winning team would not require such heavy-handed use of the cosh.

Pande and his friends had to raise their voices over the thundering of hooves on timber boards as a pair of feisty pink buffalo were unloaded from a battered truck. The race-teams were assembling the decorated carts, the wealthiest of them mounting the carvings of snarling dragons and tying on the vertical posts from which team pennants would fly like battle standards as the chariots charged. There was one particularly ornate cart, with golden trimmings that gleamed in the early sun. It belonged to an ex-army colonel who Pande knew well. The two pink bulls had striped red-and-white fabric – unmistakably emphasising the colonel's patriotic zeal – covering their horns. They were pampered creatures and it was certain that the colonel's family would have been awake since well before dawn making offerings that would bring luck in the race. The buffalo were well matched but they were still young and inexperienced. They were more than likely purchased as a pair and Pande guessed that he might have paid as much as US$6000. What could he, Pande, do with that sort of money? But to the colonel this was merely a hobby – or, at most, an investment that might turn a profit in two or three years when the bulls reached their racing prime. While they were still so young, and relatively weak, it would be difficult even for the best charioteer to make much of them.

There was another team of sturdy black bulls that Pande spotted as probable winners even at first glance. Of course, a weak or nervous rider would destroy their chances but in the right hands they would be certain winners. In fact, they were so superior that it would be difficult to find someone to bet a substantial amount against them. He pointed them out to his friends but they too could see that there would be little money to be made from them unless sufficiently strong competition arrived later in the morning.

"Pande. Good to see you here." He felt a hand on his shoulder and turned to look into the beaming face of the colonel. "We've all been wondering where you'd got to. I guess you've been busy lately?"

Pande smiled back and shook hands with a man whose closely cropped hair would have identified him as a soldier even if his khaki shirt hadn't. A response to the question had clearly not been expected because the colonel was already talking again: "What do you think of my beasts? They're good but they're still young."

"I think you might have champions on your hands within the next three years," Pande said diplomatically as his friends drifted away.

The buffalo soldier held open a pack of imported Marlboros. "I hope you're right. My oldest son is riding for me these days. He's only sixteen and – like the bulls – is also still young and inexperienced. I think he'll mature too and I'll have a winning team in a couple of years. The boy's ambitious but he's too heavy with the whip."

"When the bulls are faster there'll be less need for the cosh."

"Right. *Lebih cepat, kurang darah*." More fast, less blood. It sounded like an equation the colonel may have picked up from some boot-camp training session.

They wandered together for a few minutes through the preparing teams until Pande's daughters ran up. He was grateful that the colonel saved him embarrassment by instantly inviting the girls to *es cincau* from a vendor with polystyrene iceboxes strapped to the panniers of his motorbike. The plastic cups of iced drinks with sweetened jelly made from crushed leaves were splashed with luminous syrup in a variety of different colours. Aware that all the syrups tasted the same, the men shared smiles of amusement when both girls chose pink.

"One of these days I'll convince you to come back and relive the glory of your youth," the colonel smiled. "Do you realise, girls, that your father was one of the greatest riders who ever raced here? You should be very proud." Then, leaning towards Pande he whispered, "let me know if you ever want to make a comeback. I'd be proud to have you on my team."

>><><><><<

Pande and the girls wandered towards the finish line. The U-shaped course stretched for almost three kilometres through the paddies, ending about two hundred meters down the road from the starting point.

The chariots thundered past – racing in groups of twos and threes – with a deafening clatter of bouncing cartwheels and the bellowing battle-cries of frenzied riders. Pennants billowed over the jostling horns of the buffalo and the nail-studded cosh thudded onto backs that were already spattered with glistening blood. The fearsome vehicles looked more like some sort of hellish battle chariot than the descendants of humble farm carts. It was not unusual for charioteers to lose control and Pande warned the girls to stay back when he saw them playing too close to the course. Occasionally riders had been killed in crashes and spectators had been badly hurt when chariot, rider and animals flipped into the paddies.

The colonel's team was one of the last to race. Pande was sitting on the grass bank next to the edge of the heavily rutted mud track and the girls were playing on the grass farther on, near the finishing line. The team with the sturdy black bulls was leading the charge but the gilded paintwork of the second chariot that came around the corner was instantly recognisable. The sixteen-year-old charioteer was fearless. He was heavy-handed with the cosh, however, and the pink buffalo's rumps were streaked with fresh blood from incessant blows that would have crushed a man's skull.

As the colonel's team galloped up to the finishing line his son hauled back hard on the reins with a blood-curdling cry that was a mixture of frustration and fury. The animals almost skidded to a halt and by the time Pande rose to his feet he could see that waiting team assistants were already leading the panting buffalo to the side of the track. When Pande walked into the paddock the young rider, still on the chariot, was cursing bitterly and the colonel's handlers were trying to calm the snorting bulls. Suddenly and without any warning the young charioteer began flailing again, flapping the reins wildly. The nail-spiked cosh hovered threateningly above the crowd for a second and then slammed down on a blood-spattered rump. The buffaloes surged forward, and only the straining power of the group of men who grabbed hold of the harness prevented them from charging into the crowd. Bystanders rushed forward to help restrain the bulls and Pande vaulted onto the chariot. He grabbed the charioteer's raised arm before it could descend onto the buffalo a second time and grappled him around the neck. The youngster was small but the demon that had entered his body charged him with astounding strength. He almost broke free in the instant before Pande realised gratefully that other men were now beside him on the chariot. It took the combined weight of three strong men to haul the young charioteer to the ground. Still Pande struggled to pry the club from his clenched fist. In the moment before the charioteer passed out entirely Pande looked into the young man's glazed eyes. In them he saw something that sent a shiver of fear through him.

Realising now that the colonel was kneeling beside them, Pande forced the vision from his mind.

"He'll be fine in a few minutes," the old buffalo soldier shrugged. "It's just the speed craze."

In the world of *mekepung* violent frenzies of this sort were relatively common; as likely to be caused by the tense prelude to the race, with its magical talismans and religious blessings, as by the adrenalin-overdose of the event itself. Pande had seen many young men fall into *mekepung* 'speed crazes' of this sort. Such trances were a common occurrence wherever emotions ran so high that a person's soul was left momentarily unguarded so that his body could be temporarily occupied by a tiger-spirit. Usually such trances were not dangerous and holy water was enough to return the victim to the world of the living. In this case – armed with a cosh and a battle chariot – there had certainly been considerable risk. The boy had quite literally run *amok*, to use the common Malay word.

"I hope his mother doesn't hear of this," the colonel muttered as the boy's eyes began to clear. The young face was pallid, the chin flecked with saliva but he was unharmed. "The boy lives to race but this has happened five times now and his mother has already warned that if it happened once more it would be the end of his *mekepung* days."

They sat on the grass beside the recovering boy. The colonel lit a cigarette and handed Pande his pack of Marlboros. "The Jembrana Cup is in two weeks and I'm going to need an experienced rider." Furrows creased his forehead.

"There are lots of young riders who would give their right arms to ride for you," Pande reassured him.

"With these young bulls I'm going to need someone with experience. I'll say this once. If you'll agree to race for me you can name your price. I'll pay half in advance and half after..."

"I'm already too old," said Pande slowly as he lit a cigarette.

But there was something in his voice that eased the colonel's brow. "Keep the pack," he said.

>>◇◇◇<<

Little Nyoman had been so proud to go to school in the brand-new uniform, paid for with the colonel's advance. Although anxious, Pande was excited about the race. He'd had several early-morning practise runs getting to know the buffalo and getting used to the way the chariot handled. A good racer could ride any sort of chariot but each had slightly different characteristics.

Pande's wife was worried and spent hours preparing special offerings for their family shrine. Offerings that would bring him luck and keep him safe. He could tell that hidden behind her fear there was a sense of pride. Few of the village women would ever waste their time going to watch buffalo-racing but their husbands were enthusiastic about seeing the village hero make his comeback, so the Jembrana Cup was the talk of the moment all through the market. Pande was becoming a celebrity yet he continued to maintain a low-profile in the week before the race. He'd never have admitted – even to himself – that the prospect of the race went a long way towards balancing the shame of the cockpit. And even in a small way towards the painful memory of the day he'd been reduced to begging for a job from the boss.

On the day of the race Pande prayed and said the quickest of goodbyes to his wife before he left home. The girls begged to go with him, but he didn't want any distractions. It was still dark when he started the Vespa and puttered up to the main road. It hadn't rained recently and the track would be in perfect condition. He rode to the colonel's house on the outskirts of the city and in the spacious compound he had a second blessing, performed by the *pedanda* (high priest) the colonel had hired. The sixteen-year-old son, subdued and sulky, refused to even watch the race.

When, later that morning, the boy heard how the cart had flipped at full speed over the steep bank he collapsed instantly into a sort of comatose trance that only ended three hours later when the *pedanda* completed the exorcism. His mother often told friends who asked after him that he'd never been quite the same after he learned that the powerful farmer who'd taken his place had been crushed to death beneath a writhing buffalo.

Little Nyoman never realised her new school uniform had cost her father his life.

6 – **Full Moon**

The Hermit Club was unusually crowded when Grandfather arrived there on the day of Pande's funeral. There were seven or eight old people shuffling their bottoms in the black sand, burying legs like driftwood sticks under carefully tended embankments.

They'd taken the opportunity for an outing after they emerged from their respective family compounds to prepare their smoking coconut-husk barricades.

"Sometimes the tricks that life deals us can be so sad," said 'Mang. Although she was sitting close, her voice was so soft that Grandfather could barely hear her.

"We exist only to serve out our *samsara* – our cycle of reincarnation," Grandfather replied pensively. "Many of us might have chosen another path…other people to share our lives with. But such choices were not always open to us."

"Our destinies are all written in advance," the old woman replied, "but our lives are often interlinked in the most unexpected ways."

"Sometimes you have to wonder if it's fair for destiny to play such merciless tricks," Grandfather twisted his stiff old torso so that he could look directly into 'Mang's eyes. She dropped her gaze quickly and her nervous leaf-like hands fluttered across the two small dunes she'd built in front of her. He'd never seen her looking so fragile. It was almost as if she was fading before his eyes.

"I remember Pande when he was a small boy," she said, steering the conversation back to the events of the day, rather than dwell on older – and even more troubling – times. "Even when he was small he was strong and fearless. He just never had much luck. I suppose it was part of his *samsara* that he accepted with good faith what life dealt him."

"He reminded me of a Sumatran soldier I served with in the army," Grandfather said looking back at the waves. "He was as tough as they come but life always did its best to trip him up. He'd gotten into trouble back in his village for distributing pamphlets. That was during the Communist uprising and, as you'll remember, there was more than enough trouble to share right throughout our 17,000 islands. He claimed though that he was innocent and it was probably true since he couldn't even read. It might have been this alone that saved him from execution. Instead, the judge gave him the choice of signing up for nine years in the army or going to prison. There was a girl the soldier was in love with back in his village and he believed that another man denounced him to the government in a fit of jealousy."

'Mang sighed. "The terrible things people do for love…"

"But love endures, doesn't it?" Grandfather gazed out to sea, speaking so quietly that it was almost as if he was conversing only with himself. "That's what he believed, anyway. When we were in the army together he never doubted for a moment that the girl was waiting for him. One day he received a letter from a friend telling him she'd married someone else. We were all amazed that he took it in his stride: 'It didn't matter,' he said, 'nine years was a long time for her to be alone.' Nevertheless, it meant nothing, and she'd still be waiting for him when he got out. They did their best to train us to hate and they forced us to stand-by on guard-duty while the anti-communist militias did their slaughtering right in front of us. Through the middle of all that it often struck me as strange that so many of us were in the army because of love…"

"*Lain lading, lain belalang*," said Mang thoughtfully – different meadows have different grasshoppers. "People only have so many solutions to their problems."

Grandfather looked at the old woman, but her own gaze was now fixed on the horizon, preventing him from reading anything in her eyes. He remembered how he too would avert his stare for years after the so-called 'communist emergency' of 1966-66, troubled by the thought that other people could see the slaughter, suffering and the ghosts of mutilated corpses reflected in his own pupils. Some said that within the course of a few months of mindless violence as many as 80,000 Balinese – one in twenty islanders at that time – were slaughtered. Such strange things happened in those days, he thought. He recalled hearing of a priest, supposedly a communist sympathiser, whose magic was so powerful that his would-be executioners were physically unable to behead him…until, that is, they were able to summon another priest who sprinkled holy water that 'diluted the magic'.

These weren't the sort of stories he could tell an old woman. Or anyone else for that matter. So he blocked the images from his mind as he had so many times in the past: "Anyway, a couple of years passed and he heard that the girl now had a baby. Unbelievably, he *still* said that when his time was up she would be certain to run away with him. This no-good grunt private with no money and no future… Of course, he was kidding himself, right?"

"Of course. He must have been but how did he find out?"

"Well, I bumped into him again many years later, long after we'd left the army. He was a truckdriver and I wasn't surprised to hear that he never got together with the girl he loved. But it hadn't happened how I'd expected it. He told me the story of what had happened when he finally served out his nine years. 'I had almost no money by the time I'd hitchhiked back home to Sumatra,' he told me. 'Even when I saw their modern two-storey house and the shiny car I was still confident. I waited on the corner until I saw her husband leave. Imagine how I felt when I recognised the man who'd denounced me. I thought about killing him. By then I'd seen so much killing that it would have been easy. But then I decided that I was about to have my revenge in an even better way."

Grandfather paused as he scooped handfuls of hot sand towards his scrawny buttocks. "*Of course*, I'd have bet anything that she was about to turn him down. I'd been expecting that outcome ever since I first heard him talk about her. Well, I was wrong. She leapt into his arms. Said that she'd been waiting with a packed bag under the bed for months. She would walk out with him right that instant and didn't care in the least about his poverty.

"They were still madly kissing in the doorway when a little boy came down the stairs. My friend told me, with tears in his eyes, that that he couldn't do it and as he stepped away from her she saw it in his eyes. She was wailing, begging him to take her with him because she'd waited nine years to abandon her life and family for him. My friend just ran down the street and never looked back."

>><><><><<

It had been two weeks since the resort opened in earnest. At first Rahim had decided that tour-guiding was not for him and he'd gone back to fishing alone. After the first few nights he began to think that his nerves were returning to normal. The catches had improved but lack of demand for local fish meant that most fishermen were barely

153

showing a profit and, even with a reasonable catch, it was not easy to make ends meet.

It was increasingly common these days for fishermen to work alone at night. The most superstitious of the older fishermen would never work alone but for many it was the only way to ensure a profit. Many of the young fishermen were now out of work and those with connections had found jobs in the resort as cleaners, bartenders and pool-boys.

Surely it could only be a matter of time before the paddy-people got tired of paying transportation costs for fish from the big port rather than buying directly from their village beach. Then the fisher-folk too would happily stop buying fruit, vegetables and rice from the Chinese store. Rahim imagined that the village was like an outrigger that had been broadsided by a wave. It had been through countless storms before; the buffeting might last for a while but surely it would get back on an even keel sooner or later.

It had been his wife Kadek's suggestion that Yunus deserved another opportunity. But then she didn't know about the part that his nephew had played in the curse: "Don't think I'm not aware that you made some mistakes of your own before we got married," she'd teased. He wondered uneasily what she might be alluding to. "Yunus is too young to be written off as a bad character forever," she continued. "Everyone deserves at least one extra chance. You would make a good team and what could be so wrong with making a little money by taking tourists fishing until the situation improves?"

He thought it over as he left the mosque after the mid-afternoon prayer-call. By the time he was halfway back down the strip of hot tarmac he'd decided that the only logical solution for *Putri Laut* was to ride out this storm with a few *bules* for ballast. After all, his responsibility would merely be to run tours; if the fish continued to steer clear of the boat it would simply be blamed on the *bules* fishing skills. Kadek's suggestion to take Yunus back would also make undeniable sense. While Rahim could understand only the gist of English conversation, Yunus's command of the *bule* tongue would prove extremely useful if *Putri Laut* was indeed destined to put to sea as a tour boat.

There was one problem, however. As soon as Yunus had collected his bonus for the end of the building job he'd disappeared to the city to visit friends; Rahim left three messages without getting a response from his nephew. During one fitful sleep he dreamed that he was alone on the boat at night when another body drifted past. When he reached out to grab it the body twisted in the dark water and he saw that it was Yunus. His grip slackened in his surprise and the body drifted out of sight into the blackness behind the boat. Rahim woke from the dream with the feeling that the young man had almost slipped out of reach. He enlisted Kadek's help to continue calling until Yunus answered.

Rahim had already caulked the boat's hull and given her a smartening lick of paint by the time Yunus arrived back in the village, just in time to help with *Putri Laut*'s first tour.

The resort would be supplying packed breakfasts – along with the bundle of cheap plastic fishing rods and tackle. Kadek had insisted that, since the *bule* were guests on Rahim's boat, it was only right that he should show his hospitality, so she'd spent the previous evening steaming *jajan bantal*. The pillow-shaped coconut-leaf packages, stuffed with stodgy rice, palm sugar, grated coconut and peanuts were coloured bright green with *pandan* leaves. She'd even spent money on a new thermos so that they could offer strong coffee and had ordered a bunch of fresh young drinking coconuts.

Rahim had pounded the root of *tuba* shrubs to stun minnows in pools on the great rock slab so that there was no shortage of bait. It was not fatally toxic and would wear off after a while so that any fish he overlooked would eventually wake unharmed. He was confident that – with Kadek's help – he'd thought of everything.

Now he settled himself into his habitual position against the stunted mast. It was like old times. Even the fact that Yunus was late made the situation reassuringly familiar. He ran his hands over the timbers he knew so well and puffed contentedly at the first cigarette of the day. Farther along the beach he could see a group of people in Hindu ceremonial clothes, squatting around an oversized cockfighting basket.

"Good morning bro. What news?"

Rahim was so pleased to get back to what felt like old times that even the young man's surf-slang was not enough to jangle his nerves.

"How many are coming fishing with us?" Yunus asked.

"There's a husband and wife – *orang perancis*," Rahim replied – French people. "And one other man too."

155

"How long will we be out for?" Yunus was wearing a white T-shirt that he must have bought in the city. 'Don't bro me, if ya don't know me' – the words, stencilled across his chest, meant nothing to the older man. Rahim shrugged and silently offered his cigarette pack.

As his nephew plucked at a filter tip Rahim noticed that he'd started growing his thumbnail, so that it already stuck out like a stubby talon. While this affectation was often seen in the city, the extended thumbnail was rare in the village. Traditionally it had been a status symbol of the upper-classes – effectively advertising the owner's disdain for manual labour. The inference was that it was impossible to work with nails like that but among the paddy-people and the fisher-folk there were few who were in a position to make a show of rejecting manual labour.

They smoked in a strained silence until Yunus answered his own question. "I guess we should be back by lunchtime," he muttered.

The grimacing *menjangan* head hovered over them like a grinning dog.

>◇◇◇◇<<

In the three months since he was born the baby had never seen so many people gathered in one place. It was true, however, that he had never been left entirely alone. Not for a single instant. His immature spirit was not developed enough to withstand the powers of the earth, so he'd spent his first 105 days in the arms of adults or his older sisters.

Today the extended family had come to witness his *Telubulan* ceremony and the moment when he would first touch the ground. He'd been taken from his home in the city and was back in the village of his grandparents, where his placenta (the most important of his spiritual siblings) had been buried the day he was born. When the baby was 12 days old, and still nameless, a *balian* had been hired to enter the spirit world in a trance. The old woman's eyes had rolled back in her head and – in the strange whining voice that seems to be almost the lingua franca of the spirit-world – she reported that the baby was a reincarnation of his great-uncle. That ancestor was still remembered by some as a famously talented flute-

156

player, and the baby's parents were happy to know that their son had inherited such musical skills. Had the choice been a less favourable one, however, all would not have been lost since his parents could simply have hired a different *balian* for a second opinion. They could try as many times as they liked without risking any offence to a whole series of powerful – and potentially dangerous – *balians*: everyone knew that even the most reliable *balian* might accidentally contact the wrong ancestor. After all, even with modern telephones it was possible to get crossed lines.

Today would be one of the most important days of the baby's life. Not only would he touch the ground for the first time, but this was also the day upon which the gods would decide his name. His parents would find it written on a piece of *lontar* palm tucked between the offerings. The entire congregation would dutifully gasp in wonder at this miracle (despite being fully aware that his father had hidden it there in advance).

A tiny wooden doll had been carved in the baby's likeness and, from the way the baby was wailing, he undoubtedly wished the humiliation he was undergoing today might have been inflicted instead on the lifeless figure. The baby was not enjoying the attention. First an egg had been rolled over his squirming body to give him strength and virility. Judging from the way he kicked and yelled it worked like a charm and he'd had to be restrained while lengths of white cotton were laid over his head and tied around his wrists to promote long-life. He'd wriggled and screamed even more while bunches of hair were cut from his head – to be thrown later into the sea – and onion juice was rubbed over the crown of his skull to deter witches from entering through the soft fontanel. He'd been further protected with three talismans: an old Balinese coin; a copper amulet containing a piece of his dried umbilical cord; and a sliver of what was said to be a tiger's tooth.

During the first part of his life he'd symbolically been an angel but today he would be ritually 'planted' on Earth. It was a risky period because for some time his soul would be lighter than a feather – liable to drift away or to float back up to the heavens. For this reason his chubby arms and sausage-like legs were weighted with heavy bracelets and anklets. They would effectively shackle him to the planet until his soul had developed enough human weightiness to withstand the magnetism of the heavens.

His uncle launched the wooden doll into the waves in a miniature outrigger while, amid great laughter, his father dashed after trying to catch it in a net without getting his sarong wet. Up until this moment, they believed, that the baby's soul had been drifting loose in the ocean but now they had captured it and he was finally 'returned to the earth'.

Now they laid him down on the beach and lowered a domelike basket – something like a cockfighting basket but this time symbolising the amniotic sac out of which he was born – over his head. It was the first time in the latest of his chain of incarnations that the baby had touched the ground. As he felt the damp, gritty sand under his hands the baby let out a mournful wail: "Oh no," he seemed to be saying. "Not again!"

>><><><<

Nat had planned to start her day off with some yoga but – rather than join Suzie's repetitive class – she decided to do a series of sun salutations on the western end of the beach, far from the resort and fishing boats. As she walked down onto the crisp sand, waves of tiny baby crabs scuttle in front of her like froth-bubbles. Life on the island revolved around an endless cycle of burgeoning life that bordered almost on plague proportions. After the recent rain great masses of swarming flying ants had appeared, shedding their wings under the driftwood chandeliers and making dinner inedible. Croaking frogs devoured the night's silence and the air above the beach was thick with darting dragonflies and swooping swiftlets. Now billions of these tiny crabs – each smaller than a fingernail – emerged, swarming on the banks of the streams; Nat could pick them up in writhing handfuls that spilled over like living sand. What was it that fed on these crabs, so tiny that a human might crunch scores in a single mouthful? Nat had no idea.

There was something about this abundance of life that recalled her home beach in Belém, darkened not with lava but by the tannin-rich run-off of the great Amazon Basin. Perhaps it was a momentary sense of homesickness that convinced Nat to abandon her yoga plan and to practise some of the *capoeira* moves she'd learned as a teenager. Nat pulled her hair into a ponytail and began to move as she hummed the African rhythm under her breath. The

Brazilian martial art had been cunningly disguised as ritual dance to mislead slave-owners. She focussed her mind to conjure up the echoing twang of the *berimbau* gourd instruments and the *atabaque* calfskin drums. The word *capoeira* was said to have been borrowed from an Amazonian indigenous name for the small birds that engaged in fierce ritual fights during courtship. As Nat crouched low, swayed rhythmically and swivelled in slow-motion kicks her strong body took on a bird-like elegance. She was rusty from lack of practise; the *corta capim* (grass cutter sweep) came back to her effortlessly enough but the *meia-lua de frente* (halfmoon kick) felt very clumsy. She attempted a *vôo-do-morcego* ('flight of the bat' drop-kick) but realised that it was too ambitious so she practised a sequence of *chapa baixa* (low kicks), a technique that incorporated the celebrated *malacia* (cunning) of a capoeirista streetfighter by appearing to start as a high kick that finally made contact at the opponent's knee.

By the time she stopped to return to the resort for breakfast she was breathing hard and her skin shimmered like oiled teak.

Nat knew that if she remained at the resort all day, she'd surely be called to deal with some minor disaster so she'd jumped at 'Bu Ana's invitation the day before to explore the forests beyond the *warung*. A chance to visit what the Balinese woman described as 'a ghost waterfall in a haunted forest' was irresistible to her adventurous spirit. Nat justified it as 'research' since it might ultimately turn out to be an excursion she could arrange for resort guests.

She'd been busy for the last few days arranging a menu of excursions and activities. It had been surprisingly hard to find a boatman who was willing to run fishing trips and Nat had begun to realise that in some obscure way the fisher-folk saw the suggestion as an insult to their professional pride. She'd been relieved when Rahim had agreed to take the first group himself. The buffalo-chariot racing, initially appealing, had been reluctantly removed from the list when she learned of the sport's brutality and gore. More shocking still, local gossip – the coconut wireless – had it that a charioteer had been killed in a recent race. Like the cock-fighting that took place most Saturdays, it wasn't the sort of holiday experience the guests would appreciate.

As she made her way towards the *warung* after breakfast Nat waved at the two fishermen who were smoking beside a brightly painted blue boat. Rahim signalled a thumbs-up, confirming that all was ready for the guests' fishing outing. That was a relief. This was the first free day she'd had since the resort officially opened. The boss was back in the city and, for at least one day, surely she could trust Suzie to handle things alone.

Farther along the beach just beyond the last fishing boats Nat could see a group of people in ceremonial clothing gathered around a cockfighting basket. It must certainly be a particularly huge rooster because the basket was much larger than the usual woven cockfighting domes. As she approached she focused on what appeared to be unusually brightly coloured plumage inside the basket. Then, with a shock, she realised that it was a child in ceremonial clothes. Judging from the wailing emanating from the basket, it didn't appreciate the experience.

A man walked away from the gathering, carrying a chicken and a young duck towards the waves. They squawked and clucked in terror as he swung them by the legs, tossing them high so that they splashed down, a sacrifice to the ocean.

A moment later the duck was contentedly dipping its head, ruffling its wings and twitching its tail, as if it had been through the entire performance many times before. Water off a duck's back, Nat thought. The hen was less fortunate; freedom in her case meant instant waterlogging and almost certain drowning. Nat wished she could help but this appeared to be one of those cultural situations when she must resist the urge to get involved.

Suddenly she heard 'Bu Ana's voice calling cheerfully in Balinese to the man who had made the offering. He replied with a smile and the *warung* owner continued, walking straight into the sea, until the shore-break waves were already wetting the hem of her bush-shorts. She wore a tie-dye T-shirt and had to shrug her arms into the straps of a green knapsack before she delved into the water to hook the floundering chicken out. She emerged from the water swinging the dripping hen by its legs in front of her.

The duck was already waddling farther along the beach and the baby was now being released from his wicker cage. The ceremony was over.

"Once the offering's been made it's immaterial what happens to the hen," the Balinese woman explained as the two women made a detour past the *warung*, to deposit the hen at her new home. "Just as it makes no difference if dogs eat the offered rice the moment it's laid on the ground for the demons."

The chicken and duck would be taboo to the family that made the initial offering, but any passer-by could freely wade in with an ambition to save (or to eat) the sacrificial creatures.

"I hope this trek is not too rough for flipflops...?" the Brazilian asked once the traumatised chicken was secured under a dome of its own behind the *warung*.

"No, flipflops are best because we have to cross streams and it's easiest to walk barefoot in those sections." 'Bu Ana held up a machete in its battered wooden scabbard. "I don't want to actually cut a path but I can use this to clear the worst if necessary."

It was not often that 'Bu Ana took a day away from the *warung* and she too had woken to an unusual sense of freedom. When Pak Kolok had stopped by with his buffalo she'd considered asking him to come along on the excursion as a guide. But she was surprised at an instinct that told her that it would be more enjoyable to have the undiluted company of her new Brazilian friend. Although it had been a year or two since she'd entered the sacred forest, she didn't doubt that she could find the way without a guide. It would simply be a matter of following the stream through the haunted forest.

>><><><><<

Suzie couldn't understand why Dewi had been hired as a waitress in the first place. She was so slow and frumpy. She didn't add anything to the image of glamour that Suzie wanted to instil at Bali Moon Eco-resort. It was convenient that Nat had disappeared for the day so that Suzie could finally get the lazy staff in line.

The interns – little more than schoolgirls – who'd been brought in from tourism school in the city were keen enough. The boss had said that the maintenance team and cleaners should be hired from among the fisher-folk since they'd be liable to less time off for ceremonies. Suzie wished that the boss would replace Dewi too.

"Dewi! Can't you see that there's a table waiting to be emptied?" she hissed as the waitress emerged from the kitchen with a loaded breakfast tray.

"Right away." Dewi took a deep breath. "As soon as I've delivered this breakfast."

Nat would have lent a hand herself if she saw that the restaurant was busy. Perhaps Suzie was scared of cracking a nail. Dewi delivered mixed juice, a pancake, coffee and a toasted banana sandwich to the table that had become the habitual breakfast-time territory of an English couple. They were tranquil, easy-going people but almost rigidly fixed in their habits: after an early-morning stroll along the beach they spent every day snoozing and reading by the pool. No activities or exploring for them, although the Englishwoman had become a regular for massages in the few days since they'd arrived. With the massages as a lucrative side-line, Dewi could afford to put up with some bullying from Suzie.

"Thank you Dewi," the Englishwoman said when the breakfast tray was offloaded. "We had a lovely walk on the beach this morning."

Dewi sensed that some small talk was expected. "The volcanoes on Java were unusually clear this morning," she nodded.

"It was the nicest morning since we arrived. The only thing that's upsetting is to see so many stray dogs on the beach."

Dewi realised that Suzie was hovering by her shoulder. Some brief response was expected before she moved away: "Lately there have been more of them than ever. Some of the other guests were complaining about their barking. Have they bothered you?"

"No but we feel so sorry for the puppies especially."

"People often abandon the females you see, because they can't pay for operations and can't risk having even more puppies in the village."

The pressure from Suzie was mounting and Dewi was already moving away as she spoke. As she piled dirty crockery onto the tray her thoughts turned to other things. If the rumours were true, then Suzie had established an even more lucrative after-hours massaging service of her own. Talk around the village was that she'd frequently been seen in the police chief's double-cab pick-up. The gossips said that it might not be a coincidence that the chief's wife and kids had been sent for a holiday to her family's home in Java.

162

Pretty young Suzie didn't restrict her law enforcement networking to after-office hours – and the boss apparently didn't have a problem with her being collected by a police car in the middle of the afternoon.

"Dewi! Stop daydreaming and bring a bill for those people." Suzie tutted quietly to herself. "These village girls…"

>><><><><<

'Bu Ana hoped that her Brazilian friend wasn't wishing that she hadn't come on their little jungle trek. The vegetation was unexpectedly dense after the rain and in the humidity it was easy to imagine that they could *hear* the trees growing. Although 'Bu Ana didn't want to use the machete more than necessary, it had come in useful almost immediately when they turned off the beach. They'd walked through the first row of *pandan* trees, dripping with bulbous prehistoric-looking fruits, to be confronted by a riotous tangle of brush. It had obviously been a long time since anyone had passed this way.

Nat had watched quietly while 'Bu Ana opened the knapsack and took out a small plastic bag full of religious paraphernalia. She arranged the first offering in a square dish made from leaves that had been carefully folded and pinned: this *canang sari* contained a slice of banana, a 500-rupiah coin, the three ingredients of the betel nut offering (signifying the red, white and green of the gods) and petals in the same colours (the green represented by sliced *pandan* leaf). Then with an elegant flick of a few ylang ylang petals, she sprinkled holy water and finally she wafted a swirl of incense that raised her prayer towards the spirits of the forest, asking permission for their visit. 'Bu Ana beckoned with her finger and Nat stepped forward so that her friend could tuck a miniature bouquet of petals into her hair and dab a few grains of rice onto her forehead and the base of her throat.

Before long, the rice had been loosened by the sweat that ran into the women's eyes and dripped in rivulets between their breasts. Their plastic flipflops had instantly become unbearably slippery on the dank undergrowth that invaded the track, and both women were now barefoot.

163

The myriad winged creatures were poignantly familiar to the Brazilian woman. There were irritating biting flies like Amazonian *pium* flies, winged bloodsuckers that would have been called *borrachudos* back home and *pólvora* sand-flies small as powder-grains. When she wiped her forehead she smeared pinhead-sized stingless bees into a gritty paste.

"In Brazil we call them eye-lickers."

"They are wonderful honeybees," 'Bu Ana replied, "a whole nest produces just a couple of tablespoons of tarry black honey that tastes like the nectar of the gods."

The first stream they'd crossed had been delightfully cool and they stopped to splash the water up their arms. The rocks midstream were treacherous and they had to hold onto each other, shrieking like drunken comrades.

"There are places in my country where the butterflies drink turtle tears," said Nat as they moved onwards. "I think they do it to get salt…The turtles don't seem to mind sharing."

"Nature can be beautiful."

"Sometimes more so than it might first appear. A researcher who'd worked in the Amazon once told me that it was only the males who harvest the salt like that. They collect it as a gift for the females who need it to produce their eggs."

Twice they'd had to backtrack when they veered away from the low ridge that marked their route, and it was already late morning when 'Bu Ana gratefully caught the distant sound of rushing water coming from upriver. But the hike to the 'ghost waterfall' was not over yet. The cascade had been given this name not only because it was haunted, but because it had the habit of disappearing entirely. People said that wanderers had sometimes circled, befuddled, for hours around the sound of the falls without ever finding them. The village children were terrified by tales of the ghosts, spirits and demons that haunted the falls and there was a threatening air of mystery about this part of the forest that kept people away.

It was easy to imagine how people were misled because the falls had a strangely shifting will-o'-the-wisp nature. The sound grew fainter. Then, when they next heard it clearly the thundering water sounded like it was downstream from their position. Nat wondered if they'd accidentally passed it, shielded from view perhaps by the stands of towering bamboo that grew, impenetrable as a stockade, along the banks of the river. It seemed, however, that these two wayfarers were not about to be duped by the disappearing cascade because just then the sound of crashing water filtered louder than ever through a relatively open part of the riverbank. Nat realised that they had indeed passed the falls because they were now approaching from the upriver side. As she stepped into the stream once more the chilled water tugged at her knees, as if hurrying along the last part of its journey from the mountain peaks to the rim that was still hidden behind the bamboo. On the opposite bank the ground was swampier, slippery with mud that squelched between their toes. They had to grab branches of ferns to slow their descent as they eased down the bank on their bottoms – "on all-sixes," as 'Bu Ana said.

Finally, the Balinese woman stopped to point. Beyond the last curtain of bamboo Nat could see a wall of cascading white water on the far side of what appeared to be a deep pool. "Wow! I hadn't expected it to be so dramatic!"

"It was worth the walk, right?" Their voices echoed through the glade and 'Bu Ana pointed at something that was moving on the far bank. Where the fringe of plummeting white-water cast a veil across the black rock a pure white dog was slinking away, its tail curled high like a flag of surrender. "There's a rock ledge there that is a path into the cave behind the falls." 'Bu Ana leaned close to make her voice heard, "I wonder if that dog was inside the cave."

The bars of light that cut through the bamboo were reflected on the dog's snowy back and it looked nervously back, frightened by the unaccustomed presence of humans. Behind it, Nat could just make out one, two, three fat piebald puppies. By the time the two women had slithered down to the water's edge the dogs had disappeared.

'Bu Ana slipped the knapsack off and lowered it onto the thick bed of spear-shaped bamboo leaves. Laying the machete beside it, she knelt to prepare a fresh *canang sari* for the high spirits and gods.

"There are many stories about this place being haunted," she said as she lit a second incense stick for the resident demons. "Many of them are probably true but it's fair to say that, over the years, there have been many people who found it convenient to keep

165

strangers away from this place. There's a cave that goes back into the rock under the falls and, during the independence war, freedom fighters hid guns and ammunition there. Later it was used as a hideout by illegal arak distillers."

"Aren't you nervous to come here?" Nat asked.

"Very few people come here but if you are respectful there's no danger."

"Thank you for bringing me here. If you prefer, I promise not to tell anyone about it."

'Bu Ana now reached into the knapsack and took out a little bottle of rice wine mixed with arak and a small ladle-shaped dish made from a folded banana leaf. She added slices of red onion and ginger to the offering; the 'cold' onion and the 'hot' ginger would remind the demons of the balance that must be preserved for the universe to function smoothly. 'Bu Ana held the dish aloft in her left hand, wafting the alcoholic essence with the prescribed *ngayab* hand-gesture to notify the spirits of the presence of the offering. She recited three magic Sanskrit syllables under her breath "*rang, ring, tah*" – born, living, dead. Then she transferred the dish to her right hand (the 'sweet hand' people called it) and, grasping her elbow with her left hand, reverently poured the liquid onto the ground. Unseen by the two women, the demons would already be snarling and fighting over the offering.

'Bu Ana's silence continued for so long that Nat wondered if she'd forgotten her question. Most likely her friend was simply giving herself wholeheartedly to the offerings, almost drifting – body and soul – into another realm, as only a Balinese could do at such moments. But now 'Bu Ana returned to the present. "Yes. I think it's better if you don't tell anyone about this place. Maybe we can come here together from time to time…"

Nat nodded. "Is it okay to swim? I'm so sweaty and also I'd like to explore the cave." She was glad she'd worn lightweight boardshorts. They'd be able to dry during the walk back.

'Bu Ana rose to her feet. "Of course. Let's go," she hesitated, "– these bush-shorts are too heavy to swim in though…"

Nat found herself looking into the older woman's dark almond eyes. She shrugged: "Take them off then." She turned away quickly, vaguely surprised at her juvenile embarrassment. "There's nobody here but us."

'Bu Ana's eyes swept the water's edge, scouting for signs of monitor lizards or snakes. "It's going to be lovely to cool off," she said as she grabbed the bottom edge of her T-shirt and swiftly raised it over her head. She dropped it on the ground and, almost in the same movement, reached behind to unclasp her bra. The touch of the forest breeze was pleasant on her sweat-dampened skin. The Brazilian woman sidled around a clump of young bamboo to undress. 'Bu Ana unbuttoned her shorts and – without a glance at her friend – let them drop on the ground, taking her underwear with them. Naked now, she took a few cautious steps across the sharp stones at the edge of the pool. Only when she was in up to her knees did she turn around to look at her friend. "It's deliciously cool," she said.

Nat was still holding her shirt when she looked up to see the older woman standing in the water. The sunlit pool formed a curving green backdrop and Nat had a fleeting impression that she'd seen this vision somewhere before. She recalled the portrait that hung in the *warung*, but then her eyes took in details of the reality, the copper urns of the Balinese woman's heavy breasts and the matronly spread of her hips. Nat's instinct was to look away but her eyes were lured to the triangle of jet-black fur, tangled below the curve of the older woman's belly. She hoped 'Bu Ana hadn't heard her involuntary intake of breath; caused, not by the sight of the first naked woman she'd ever been alone with, but by the intricate tattoo that almost entirely covered the woman's right thigh and hip.

Realising that she was still standing with her shirt scrunched protectively in front of her chest, Nat lowered her hands with exaggerated carelessness, revealing small breasts as smooth as varnished teak. She'd intended to swim in her boardshorts but suddenly it occurred to her that this would now appear prudish.

>><><><<

Putri Laut rocked like a cradle on the gentle swell that curled around the distant Javanese headland. Rahim had draped a roof tarp across the bamboo boom and lashed it to the fake mast, just below the snarling *menjangan* head. It was hot and they'd already eaten their snacks and this gentle swell was making Rahim sleepy. Yunus sat in the bow baiting hooks for the two *bule* men. They'd caught a surprising number of fish – including two that were almost the length of Rahim's forearm. More often the bait was simply snatched and Rahim was doubtful there'd be enough to last much longer. The Frenchman had been turning pale over the last hour, however, and it seemed likely that the sickly rocking coupled with the faint smell of leaking petrol would drive them towards shore before long.

The midday breeze was just picking up but the sea was reassuringly smooth and there was no sign of the storm that was supposedly approaching. The previous day he'd been shocked to hear one of the younger fishermen questioning a *bule* surfer on the beach about the rumour of a coming storm. He was not sure where they found such accurate information but it was said that the surfers knew the details of weather conditions even beyond the coming week. They certainly had a mysterious way of coinciding their arrival with the coming of bigger waves. Somehow, there was something shameful in a Balinese fisherman asking a foreign tourist for advice on sea conditions around the island.

The Frenchwoman was content simply to sit with her brown legs draped over the side into the water while her husband fished alongside their Australian friend. The sea rippled around chubby ankles that were polka-dotted with mosquito-bites and her blonde hair was frizzy with the humidity. Loudly confident and with a hissing hint of French accent it had been she, Marielle, who'd made the introductions when they first arrived at the boat: "This is my 'usband Jean-Pierre and this is our Aussie friend Eric. He's searched fish all over the world."

Eric was a man of few words, but he was certainly a dedicated angler. The fact that he'd been catching the bulk of the fish all morning hadn't helped to curb the Frenchman's growing moodiness.

Rahim understood little English and had no knowledge of French at all. There was no need for language skills, however, to be aware that some very weighty emotional ballast had been brought aboard *Putri Laut* this morning. The tension was becoming as taught as Eric's fishing line.

"Don't you want to grab a rod Marielle?" Eric broke a long heavy silence. "The fish are biting beautifully."

"They seem to be biting on your side of the boat for sure," she replied. "What about you Jean-Pierre? *Ça marche*? You don't seem to be having so much luck."

"It's not *only* about finding the fish," Jean-Pierre's grin was sickly. "But then it's not about sitting around all day displaying your legs either."

"I don't think these men are offended by a view of my legs," she stroked her knee and, whinnying with forced mirth, turned towards Rahim. "You don't mind if I bask my legs, right Rahim?"

Rahim grimaced in mortification and in his confusion glanced down at the woman's brown knees. When he looked up, she was looking at him, one eyebrow raised coquettishly. He felt his face grow hot and he looked along the boat to see Yunus watching him. The woman was a deliberate troublemaker. Infuriated, he resolved to have as little as possible to do with her until the trip was over. Luckily, he'd established an onboard protocol as soon as they started out; it was he who dealt with the boat and Yunus who was responsible for keeping the guests happy.

Half an hour of strained silence followed the incident of Marielle's legs, then Jean-Pierre suggested – to Eric's obvious disappointment – that they head back to the resort. It was with relief that Rahim felt the surge of the swell as they neared the beach and shore-bound rollers passed under them. *Putri Laut*'s stern raised, her bow dipped and she started to surf towards the sand. Marielle shrieked and the two *bule* men whooped with laughter. To the fishermen who came to help haul the boat up to the beach the trip must have looked like a great success.

As he reluctantly accepted a tip Rahim did his best to laugh off a feeling of sickness mingled with embarrassment.

>>◇◇◇<<

The pool under the falls was shallower than Nat had expected at first glance. She'd been able to wade most of the way across, swimming only for the last section as she followed 'Bu Ana towards the curtain of falling water. It pounded powerfully on her head and Nat had to work up the courage to follow her friend blindly through. Only when 'Bu Ana reached out with a guiding hand had she steeled her nerve and ducked through.

When Nat's eyes adjusted to the flickering darkness behind the cascade she saw that there was a rock ledge. The two women struggled to find a spot to clamber up the slippery rocks then, straightening cautiously, Nat realised that the cave was tall enough to stand upright and that it stretched about four metres back. It was surprisingly dry underfoot, carpeted with a thin layer of bamboo leaves that must have washed in during flood periods. This cave must have served as a perfect den for the puppies and Nat could see that, except in the heaviest rainfall, it would make an ideal hideout. The only danger might be the snakes that would likewise consider it a wonderful lair, but hopefully the recently departed dog had ensured that it was vacant at least for the time being.

They stood for a while, shoulder to shoulder, in the shimmering light that filtered through the cascade. Then, without a word, Nat eased down to the edge of the rock ledge and slid back into the water. The falls hammered on her shoulders and, accustomed now to its pressure, she paused to enjoy the pummelling massage as she ducked back out into the glaring daylight. She struck out across the water, feeling the sun on her back. Reaching out with her hands to touch the gravel, she gave one last kick to propel herself to the edge of the pool. Her left foot jarred painfully against a piece of submerged wood and she yelped in pain. Limping out of the water she edged over to a huge stone slab and sat down to inspect the damage. Blood was running freely from a cut on the end of her big toe.

She looked up to see 'Bu Ana rising out of the pool, her wet skin tiger-striped under the slatted light of the bamboo canopy: "Did you hurt yourself?"

"Nothing serious, just kicked a stump or something."

"Let me see." Suddenly the older woman was kneeling on the edge of the slab with Nat's foot in her hand. Nat propped herself up on her elbows, looking down the length of her shimmering legs to where the woman knelt, as if in prayer, concentrating on the injury.

"It doesn't look too deep…but we should probably find some antiseptic. Protect it from the mud on the walk back." She glanced around the edge of the pool until she saw what she was looking for.

Nat watched as the Balinese woman swam across the pool to a stand of plants that was leaning over the water. She carefully picked a handful of young leaves and put them into her mouth. She was still methodically chewing as she walked out of the pool and, within a moment, was kneeling on the slab with Nat's foot in her hand once again. She took the mulched-up lump of green paste from her mouth and eased the injured foot into her lap. The change of position made Nat's thighs splay slightly wider. She glanced inadvertently down to where water droplets from the pool glinted like diamonds on her sable curls and when she looked back up she was staring straight into 'Bu Ana's eyes. Her heart began to pound with the realisation that she'd never felt so naked in her life.

The Balinese woman took a wad of green mulch out of her mouth before she spoke: "You don't mind do you?"

Nat shook her head, wondering whether the pounding of her heart was audible. The Balinese woman daubed the paste carefully onto the cut. Nat was grateful for the stinging sensation that distracted her mind from the burgeoning feeling of warmth between her legs.

"Now we should relax and stay here for a while until the leaf paste has dried."

"Don't worry," Nat smiled, "I'm sure it won't be too long before my toe is back on its feet."

The arched pillars above them reminded Nat of the vaulted ceiling of Belém's Lady of Grace Cathedral with shards of light that filtered through emerald windows. She had no idea how long they lay still for, but she sensed the sun's passage into the western sky. She arched her back on the heated boulder. She'd rarely felt so utterly, blissfully relaxed.

"This is better than a spa," She said finally as she rolled onto her side.

"Who needs hot-stone massages?" 'Bu Ana replied without opening her eyes.

Nat was grateful that the fleeting eroticism had passed. Just the foolishness of a moment, she told herself. A juvenile fantasy that was best forgotten. She propped herself up on an elbow and allowed her eyes to travel down the length of her friend's flank.

'Bu Ana breathed steadily, almost dozing, and Nat could examine the details of the unexpected tattoo, depicting a beautiful woman in a green sarong with a billowing mane of dark hair that swirled up towards 'Bu Ana's right hip. Nat wondered if the woman was a mermaid since, as with the portrait in the *warung*, the lower half of her legs were covered by a breaking wave.

Nat hesitated: "Can I ask you something?"

"Of course."

"It's just…I was surprised to see your tattoo."

"There are people in the village who love to gossip. *Omong kosong*, we call it – empty talk." 'Bu Ana's voice was drowsy. "They believe that only bad girls have tattoos."

"Tattoos are so common where I come from that few people would think that."

"*Lain lubuk lain ikannya*," 'Bu Ana replied quietly – different pools have different fish. "Anyway, in my case the gossips might be right. I don't mind admitting that I haven't always been the respectable spinster you see before you." She rolled over, propping herself on an elbow so that the two women lay face to face. "I've noticed that you don't have any tattoos. I presume that means you're a good girl…?"

"I think it's safe to say that being unmarked by ink is not a sure sign of what you'd call a good girl," Nat smiled. "I've had a less respectable past than you'd probably imagine." Without thinking she reached out to flick a mosquito away from the sun-warmed skin of her friend's shoulder. "Perhaps I'll tell you one day."

"There are many things that I regret from my life," the Balinese woman spoke thoughtfully. "But this tattoo isn't one of them. She's the Queen of the Southern Sea."

"She looks familiar. My grandmother was a priestess who worshipped Yemanjá, the Brazilian goddess of the sea. She'd light incense, then lay candles out in a star-shape and place food, drink and flowers inside for her goddess."

"It sounds very familiar too," 'Bu Ana said. "Who knows, maybe Yemanjá and Nyai Roro Kidul could be sisters…despite the fact that they're separated by half a world."

Soothed by the warmth of the rock and the gentle glow of sunlight that flickered through the bamboo they lay side by side. Two statues washed up by the floodwaters: an Amazonian athlete sculpted from polished teak and a Balinese goddess with curves of burnished copper.

>◇<◇<◇<<

Nat was back at work in the restaurant the next morning because Dewi was busy with massages. It was useful extra revenue for the resort but Nat was irritated that her managerial position was slowly being eroded into that of a stand-in waitress.

The Australian couple had checked out and the Frenchman Jean-Pierre had decided to go with them – ostensibly to catch some waves in the east. His wife Marielle had been noticeably relieved to see him go and had stayed on alone at the resort. Even though she'd retained their double room, she'd driven a hard bargain in getting the price down for single occupancy. Nat had been nervously waiting for the boss to blow his top when he realised the rate had been reduced. But now she had something more important to deal with: one of the cleaners had come to her, visibly embarrassed, to report that she thought the Frenchwoman was sharing her bed with someone. After mulling it over she considered that it would be best if – for the moment at least – they turned a blind eye. There was nothing Nat could do about that. She was running a resort, not a convent.

On top of this there were the inexplicable absences of her deputy Suzie. It turned out that yesterday afternoon she'd disappeared again, leaving the resort without a manager. Nat was grateful Dewi had enough experience to handle things by now.

Nat had reprimanded Suzie about her absence and the girl had calmly suggested that she call the boss. The boss's response had been unexpected: "Suzie has duties of her own, apart from resort administration," he'd growled. "You don't need to worry about that. Just let her arrange her own time-table."

Nat ended the phone-call feeling that it was her and not Suzie who'd been told off. There was more going on than she knew about, that was for sure. She was also reminded that it was the boss's lamentable people skills that had goaded her into swearing never to work for him again after she hung up her 'skimpies'.

But now, in the quiet period of the late afternoon, she sat on the restaurant steps with Dewi and watched the sun sink over the five Javanese volcanoes on the other side of the straits. As she poured the frosted bottle of Bintang into their glasses, she realised there was nowhere in the world she'd rather be at this moment. "This is what Balinese call the Southern Sea, right Dewi?"

"It's really the Indian Ocean though," the waitress frowned. "Isn't that right?"

"I was reading something recently…" Nat began in Indonesian. She paused and her aversion to an outright lie forced her to correct herself. "Actually, it was a picture I saw of a goddess they call the Queen of the Southern Sea. Have you heard about her?"

Dewi turned to look at the manageress but the blue eyes reflected only the ochre of the setting sun. "Many people say that it's unlucky to talk about gods or ghosts in case they overhear you." Dewi paused for a moment, then lowered her voice. "I think it's probably okay though if we continue to speak quietly in English, since she wouldn't understand…"

Nat nodded: "Okay, in English then,"

"Few tourists would ever hear of the Queen of the Southern Sea but she's well known to us. Especially over there on Java and along the southern coast here. There was a luxury resort on the north coast where, a couple of years ago, many of the staff suddenly started suffering from trances. A priest said they must put up a shrine to the sea goddess and after that there were no more trances. Sometimes she takes human sacrifices. Few people here will wear green on the beach because they say that it's like an invitation to the Goddess of the South Seas."

"Like a red rag to a bull…Do the fishermen here on Bali worship the Goddess of the Sea too?"

"Some of them. The old ones do, but they won't let on about it in public. Most of the fishermen are Muslim you see."

"Oh! I didn't realise that she's worshipped by both Muslims *and* Hindus?"

"Sure! Well, you know about my aunt Ana, right?"

"Of course." In fact, Nat had forgotten momentarily that Dewi and 'Bu Ana were related but then she was only slowly unravelling the entwined kinships among the resort's relatively small staff. In his efforts to limit absenteeism because of ceremonies the boss had instigated a rule – common among employers all over the island – forbidding employees from marrying each other. Nevertheless, whenever there was a family-level ceremony (a tooth-filing, a child's naming ceremony or a marriage) Nat was often astounded how many people turned out to be related.

"Well, my aunt Ana prays to the sea goddess. When you went to the *warung* did you notice the shrine behind the bar? The one that's wrapped in green cloth?"

"Is that a shrine to the Queen of the Southern Sea?"

"Yes, and that's not all," Dewi was warming to her subject now, encouraged by the unaccustomed sensation of cosiness that came from the paradoxically icy beer. "Most people don't know this, but my aunt also has special powers, given to her by the Goddess of the Sea."

>◇◇◇◇<<

By the time Dewi was halfway up the hill on her way back home she was thoroughly confused. She'd been enjoying her conversation with Nat...although it would take a while to acquire a taste for the bitterness of beer.

An easy-going friendship had been growing between herself and the Brazilian woman. When all was said and done, however, *bule* were often hard to figure out. There was so little common ground between their lives of leisure and the working lives of the islanders. It stood to reason that not all *bule* could be wealthy but how many islanders could choose to fly to the other side of the world merely to have fun, without the slightest intention of doing any work? Aside from that, the majority of *bule* didn't seem to have any religious impulses at all. A couple of them had admitted to Dewi that they had 'no religion'. She'd thought about that comment many times since and it still made no sense; to say you have no religion would be like claiming you had no soul...or that you were somehow living and breathing without a heart and lungs. How could such people ever honestly relate to people whose days were governed by the never-ending task of balancing the forces of good and evil that kept their island in equilibrium?

Somehow Nat was different, however. Most importantly, she was working and not on holiday, she spoke the national language (if not that of the island) and she had at least a vague understanding of the local culture. Moreover, with her cinnamon skin she bore more resemblance to the islanders than to the white-skinned Westerners.

Dewi was mortified now to think that, in some way she could not figure out, she must have caused offence. She analysed every part of the conversation yet she couldn't imagine what could have provoked Nat's sudden and inexplicable iciness. Dewi had been enjoying their talk and was happy to enhance Nat's knowledge of local culture. It wasn't often that a *bule* showed more than a fleeting interest.

Everything had been so pleasant. Nat was so obviously enthralled that Dewi had pulled out her telephone to show the photos of the purification of Rahim's boat. It was only then, too late, that the thought crossed Dew's mind that she shouldn't be showing the photos: "Please don't tell anyone about this," she asked. "It might embarrass the boat's Muslim owner."

Still flicking through the shots Nat agreed. "Of course. No problem..." She zoomed in with her fingers on one of the photos.

Dewi was nearly home now but she was still unable to understand the look of shock – almost abhorrence – on Nat's face. Turtles were protected, of course, and it was illegal to kill them. She couldn't recall a single instance though when the police had made a fuss about a turtle. Nat didn't strike her as such a stickler for the law.

7 – Moonstruck

"The *Buana Alit* – the world of living people – is only a part in the immensity of the universe." Grandfather Tabanan's voice carried halfway along the beach as he expounded on one of his favourite theories. "Few people are aware of the ways in which our own experiences interact with the forces of the spirit world within the *Buana Agung* – the universe as a whole."

"Our paths were laid out long before we were even born." 'Mang was speaking directly into Grandfather's left ear in a voice that only he could hear. "We never had an opportunity – you and I – to choose our destiny."

Meanwhile Tabanan's volcanic rumbling continued on Grandfather's right side: "The realm of the occult is constantly exerting its force on the world of the living but it takes a special vision to see into the spirit world."

It was an old refrain that Grandfather had heard many times.

The voices of his friends, buffeting him from either side, mingled clumsily in his befuddled brain, as if reaching him through the thick fog of a malarial hallucination. He wished he could lie down and pull the hot sand over his head like a heavy blanket. Dewi, worried about his health, had forbidden him from going to the beach on such a hot and sultry afternoon. Maybe, after all, she was right but he'd obeyed the rules all his life and now, at this age, he had a right finally to choose his own path. If he was destined to die on this beach, then so be it. Let this charcoal-coloured sand be his burial shroud.

"Old people like us," Tabanan intoned, "we who can smell the grave, are already on the doorstep of the spirit world…"

"Only in old age do we finally get a chance to choose our path," the old woman cooed.

The voices buzzed in his head as the effects of the sand pulsed through his legs. Grandfather Tabanan was still discoursing on the spirit world. And it was a world that the old man knew well; after all, he claimed to be married to a citizen of that shadowy realm.

'Mang was talking softly in words that tinkled like the *kantil* xylophones that played in delicate undertones in gamelan orchestras. She was saying…? What was she saying? Grandfather listened carefully – tuning out the *kendang* drum-roll of Tabanan's soliloquy.

"Life moves on from one generation to the next," 'Mang was saying. "And the best that we can hope for is that we all do what is right…"

"You and me," Grandfather said quietly. "We did what was right…"

"What's that you're saying?" Tabanan barked.

"*We* did what was right!" Grandfather repeated more forcefully.

"What's that got to do with anything?" the old man whined. "I don't think you're listening to a word I'm saying."

"Sorry, I thought you were talking to Grandmother," Grandfather said, consciously avoiding 'Mang's name.

Tabanan sighed deeply, uncoiling his long limbs like a man laboriously erecting a tripod, and pulled himself to his feet. He was still brushing the sand off as he stomped away. He was famous for his lack of patience. "There's nobody else here," he shouted over his shoulder. "You just sit around here all the time mumbling to yourself. You're *pusing kepala!*"

Grandfather shrugged, watching him leave. The old man might be right – he was indeed getting dizzy in the head.

'Mang too watched the old man walking away. "*Lidah dia tidak bertulang,*" she said – his tongue has no bones. Grandfather smiled ruefully. He liked Tabanan but it was true that the old man often let his tongue run away with him.

Now, alone on the beach just the two of them, the haze began to lift from Grandfather's mind. It was like the dawn mist rising up the flank of the volcanoes, bringing the cloud-forests into focus and finally revealing the treeline, above which everything was unobscured.

Grandfather's mind trawled through every afternoon he'd spent with his two friends since the day of the old woman's funeral. Not once had Tabanan ever greeted 'Mang or responded to a comment from her. Grandfather had put it down to Tabanan's grumpy disposition but suddenly he realised that 'Mang had been entirely invisible to the old man. Grandfather Tabanan, the man who claimed so readily to see spirits and to be married to a *wong samar* had never even seen the old woman who'd spent these afternoons with them.

Grandfather turned towards the old woman who sat next to him. He'd never stopped loving her for a moment. From the time he first set eyes on the girl he knew then as Komang Sari, he'd loved her. He thought he would never survive after her father forced her to marry a man of a higher caste and she left for the city. He came close to drowning in a depression that suffocated him and by the time he struggled to the surface he'd joined the army. The atrocities he'd been forced to witness had the unexpected effect of tempering him against pain, as the Pande swordsmiths hardened white-hot Damascus steel in their forges. Finally, he'd left the army and, through sheer dogged determination, had carved a life for himself. A marriage of his own. A family.

Although he tried, he never forgot 'Mang Sari. A part of him never let her go and he continued to love her through to the day, several months back, when he could not summon the last ounce of courage necessary to hide his grief as her funeral procession approached. As she passed down the street in her burial shroud she'd seen his tears through the spiritual barricade of the burning coconut husk. He'd been unable to trust himself to attend her burial – and he hoped to have departed himself before the final cremation. But she'd sensed his heartbreak just the same and her corpse had reacted to the yearning that formed a knot in the pit of his belly and caught like a fishbone at the back of his throat. He'd re-entered the compound before she passed, but it was too late. Her spirit had already refused to abandon him.

Grandfather took her hand, delicate as a dried leaf, and studied her face. The teenage girl he'd fallen in love with had the same bright eyes and the same quizzical dimples when she smiled. Now, however, her hair was silver and the story of her life was written in lines that were as clearly decipherable as if they'd been etched into the old *lontar* palm scriptures.

Only two lines were missing that had been there before: her upper lip was flat, unmarked by the two ridges of the philtrum.

>◇◇◇◇<<

When Pak Kolok arrived at the *warung* to make his morning dung-delivery 'Bu Ana guessed instantly that there was something on his mind.

'Bu Ana was still far from fluent in *kata kolok* but the finger-probing sign for 'jiggy-jig' would have been unmistakable even to an utter novice. As the resort's only effective night guard, he was worried about a situation that he was both reluctant and unable to disclose to anyone else.

It took less than a few minutes for 'Bu Ana to understand that a *bule* woman at the resort was taking a local man into her room at night. Without any experience of 'resort etiquette' poor Pak Kolok wasn't sure if it was the sort of thing he was supposed to overlook or whether it was his duty to report it. Added to this was his natural reluctance to initiate the Brazilian manageress into the fine-points of his language through the particularly vivid symbolism of 'jiggy-jig'.

So, he'd come to talk to 'Bu Ana, who he figured would know exactly what to do. She was unable to establish who the local man was but she was not sure if this was because her deaf friend preferred not to reveal his identity or whether he genuinely didn't know.

'Bu Ana was disappointed when the morning passed without a visit from the Brazilian woman. At the same time, she was relieved because she was absolved from the guilt of sharing the secret and had little wish to carry it to the resort herself.

Then, just after lunch while 'Bu Ana was still clearing the table from her only guest of the day, Dewi arrived.

"I don't want to *omong kosong* – to tell tales – but I can't keep things to myself anymore," said her niece. "Suzie, the deputy manageress, has been disappearing most afternoons and apparently she's having an affair with the police chief."

"I think that's common knowledge," 'Bu Ana pointed out. "She's hardly subtle."

"But that's not what's worrying me. I was doing a massage yesterday, for an older Australian man, and when he went to get his wallet from the dressing table he knocked something onto the floor. I picked it up for him and realised it was one of Suzie's earrings."

"You're certain it was hers?"

"I recognised it because it was shaped like handcuffs."

"Like I said, 'hardly subtle'…Does she have any reason to go into the rooms?"

"There's no reason why she should go into his room…and I can only think of one reason why she might take her earrings off."

>><><><<

These days Nat avoided the busy hightide surf sessions, preferring to catch her waves when the jagged rocks made conditions less appealing to the inexperienced masses. As the tide pushed more and more water onto the rocks it would invariably start to get busier, not only with resort guests but also with the surf guides who were driving over from the east with increasing numbers of travelling surfers. The fame of the once virtually unknown surf-spot had increased since the boss had started his marketing drive to coincide with the opening of the resort. Now, minivans arrived most days, their roof-racks stacked with foam boards. The local surfers had retained their naturally hospitable attitudes; there were none of the ignorant manifestations of localism that had spread like a rash across so much of the surfing atlas.

There was one aspect of these amphibious invasions that was sure to lead to trouble sooner or later, however. The tour groups populated the break with learners – who knew nothing of the norms of surf protocol or the rules of etiquette – and then they would leave immediately for the long drive back to the east. It was rare that anyone stopped even for a coconut or a fruit juice at Buana's Warung, so most of their excursions were completed without spending a single rupiah in the local community. The foreigners were still being greeted with traditional politeness; the locals viewed them with indulgence – impolite children who could not be expected to know better. The guides from the east, however, were increasingly gaining a reputation as parasites.

The tension was summed up by one of the local surfers as he watched yet another minivan pulling into the beach road one morning: "Wherever there's sugar, there'll be cockroaches," he muttered bitterly.

Local surfers had only appeared with the latest generation. The paddy people had traditionally been fearful of the sea, few among the fisher-folk had energy to squander on leisure and, in any case, surfboards were both rare and expensive. Even a block of surf-wax cost almost half a day's pay for a labourer. Nevertheless, a few boards had been left in the village – donated by travelling surfers who recognised the injustice of a situation where local kids were

181

deprived of the wherewithal to ride their own waves. The handful of local surfers – riding these battered hand-me-down boards – had always been a splintered group. Now, in the face of this invasion, they decided that a united front was necessary.

Yunus had somehow acquired the money to replace his old yellow single-fin with a newer model and, through friends among the *bule*, he'd been instrumental in collecting donations to establish a surf club. Soon the local surfers were walking around with T-shirts stating that they were the 'Ombak Merah Gang' (Red Wave Gang). It was a reference to the colour of the wave when the heavy rains flooded out of the mountains; the inference was that tourists shunned the wave when it began to turn from its customary blue, to café-au-lait and then to a rusty red. There was an added deterrent in the fact that the floodwaters, laden as they were with offal and detritus, lured bull-sharks. These powerful predators – notoriously indiscriminate in their attacks – were doubly unpredictable because they were rendered almost blind by the murky waters. There was a positive side to the red wave though and those who regularly surfed the point under such conditions agreed that an almost alchemic transformation in the consistency of the water meant that the wave was often at its most powerfully barrelling best under such conditions.

The Ombak Merah Gang put up hand-painted signs: 'If you not from here, don't surf here'; 'OMG! Lokals Ownly'. Another sign farther along the beach paradoxically pointed an arrow at another – hitherto almost unknown – right-hand break; 'OMG! Private Rightender' it read. Guests in the area were still welcome to surf anywhere but the surf club set up roadblocks and instigated a fee to be collected from every tour group that visited the local breaks. The fee was minimal but, nevertheless, the tours tapered off temporarily. In part this was due to the rains that were provoking heavy red barrels at the point. The revenue raised by the collections was so little that by the time the rain ended and the tours started again the roadblocks had already been abandoned.

Around this time three surfers rode in from the east on retro-style motorcycles with blaring four-stroke engines that announced their impending arrival long before they turned into the resort's private lane. Any villagers who were alert to evil omens might have listened with terror to the sound of those booming engines which heralded the start of one of the most shocking incidents in the village's history.

They would be remembered as The Playboys but initially the three young men passed almost unnoticed among the guests at the resort. They spoke only a smattering of English and even less Indonesian and communicated among themselves in their own language. Some said it might be Russian, others that it could be Yiddish.

They surfed fearlessly but with limited skill. They had an attitude of brashness in the surf that was out-of-proportion with their talents, but the boys of the Ombak Merah Gang perceived something appealing about their reluctance to do anything by halves. When they weren't surfing they drank beer with equal dedication. The afternoon they spent drinking at Buana's Warung was the biggest boost to business that 'Bu Ana had in weeks. They didn't even notice when they exhausted the chilled bottles in the fridge and had to move on to warm beer. One of them – 'Bu Ana thought she heard the others call him something like Lexi – plucked occasionally at the strings of a blue ukulele. When Pak Kolok paraded past with his dung-dumping pink buffalo The Playboys walked outside to watch. Their laughter subsided eventually and 'Bu Ana thought they'd left. But she found them later, still sitting on the root-strewn ledge near the *warung*. The Playboy with the ukulele was singing softly but 'Bu Ana's bare feet carried her silently forwards until she could make out the words.

"Ain't no such things as the Bali blues..." He slurred slightly. "Life's just better when you're not in shoes."

The voice was surprisingly angelic and the English, which grated so harshly when he spoke, was almost flawless.

"But it's a rocky road to tread,
With the voices in your head,
Whispering your fears,
Will it all fall to pieces? ...Like driftwood chandeliers."

As 'Bu Ana retreated silently back into the *warung* she had no idea that the wheels of destiny were already accelerating along a collision course that would ultimately claim the lives of three people.

>><><><><<

Nat imagined that she was alone within the island's immense tropical backdrop. The dragon's back of Java's volcanic peaks lay on the western horizon and, in the other direction, the forest-fringed bay arced eastwards until it finally faded entirely in the sea mist.

As 'the log' slipped down the wave Nat leaned, feeling the big Malibu longboard turn smoothly out back up the face. It was one of those unblemished morning-of-the-earth dawns when she imagined that it was almost a crime to allow her nine-inch fin to slice the mirrorlike surface of the water.

As the board climbed Nat stepped forward towards the nose. Resisting the temptation to shuffle in an ungainly crablike motion, she cross-stepped instead. One foot over the other as elegantly as possible. When, in moments of thoughtless panic, she found herself shuffling hurriedly back towards the tail she cursed herself in the harsh Portuguese street-slang of her childhood. Reaching the lip Nat cross-stepped backwards now, smoothly back-peddling. Practised casualness could turn the manoeuvre almost into a strut. With her weight back over the fin again, the nose rose out of the water, unleashing the heavy board's manoeuvrability for a cutback.

It was only when Nat kicked out at the end of a wave that she realised how focussed her mind had been while she was riding, her brain concentrated entirely on execution of the nose-riding dance that defined longboard surfing. It sometimes seemed as if even her breathing was on hold – her entire being lured into a sort of animated hibernation that allowed for nothing but the existence of the wave itself. The slightest clues in the ripples of a wave's surface allowed her to anticipate how it would break. She sometimes thought that it was like reading the future.

This feeling of heightened perception lasted until the moment she kicked out over the back of the wave.

The other part of the experience was no less intense in its own way. She sat on the board, her hips gyrating gently to the swaying samba rhythm of the waves. Her eyes were fixed on the horizon, analysing the deepening shadow lines that betrayed the early promise of a burgeoning peak. Like the ride itself it was an effective form of meditation and, only after the surf session was over, would she realise how much closer she'd unconsciously come to resolving the minor niggles – or outright problems – of her other life on the land.

In the words of the yogis she'd spent time with in shalas of the east 'there were things she wanted to internalise' and this was her chosen 'mind-space' for doing so. The pristine perfection of the Balinese morning was finally vanquishing the feeling of uneasiness she'd felt ever since she'd first paddled out.

As Nat had lowered her board onto the sand and prepared to stretch her sleepy limbs she'd glanced casually eastward along the bay. She'd been surprised to see somebody standing waist-deep in the water. The swimmer turned at the same moment and, even at that distance, Nat could discern – or maybe she imagined – 'Bu Ana's warm smile.

The time would come when the two women could become cheerful acquaintances again, perhaps. But a rekindling of actual friendship was impossible since Nat had learned of the Balinese woman's turtle sacrifices.

She chided herself for being melodramatic. Unlike most *bule* on the island Nat was far from a stranger to the act of sacrifice. The backstreets of Belém city were no place to be freaked out by such things. From an early age she remembered Candomblé festivals where her own grandmother made sacrifices to Oxolufan (the creator), Xangô (the thunder god) and Yansan (the goddess of the wind). Nevertheless, there was something about the turtle sacrifice that had hit Nat like an act of betrayal. She could not decide, however, whether it was the act itself that she so intensely resented or the effect that it had had on her growing affection for the bewildering Balinese woman.

Nat waved vaguely before pushing her board out into the waves. When she'd paddled out to the take-off spot that she turned and looked towards the *warung*. 'Bu Ana had already crossed the pink-sheened section of shell-strewn beach. There was something unsettling about the scene – something unexpectedly ominous – that Nat could not quite place. Then 'Bu Ana had walked through the sheltering wall of palms and the slanting rays of the early sun made her wet sarong flash like green neon.

>><><><>><<

'Bu Ana smiled at Suzie. She didn't feel like smiling. She smiled because there was an empty well where the pit of her stomach should have been. She smiled because, for the moment at least, she could think of nothing else she could do.

"Does Nat know you've come?" 'Bu Ana asked, straining to keep the bitterness from showing in her eyes as she poured coffee for her unwanted guest.

"No, Nat's still surfing."

"So, she doesn't know about your 'business offer'?" 'Bu Ana didn't try to disguise the hint of sarcasm that was injected into the term.

"No. Perhaps the boss doesn't think that it's anything to do with her."

'Bu Ana's smile was wearing thin now, turning to a strained grimace. "And why does the boss imagine that I need a partner in the *warung*?"

Now it was the city girl's turn to smile. She looked around in silence and her gaze took in the deserted dining area with its rickety chairs and its scarred tables. As her eyes swept the *warung* it was as if her curled eyelashes were sweeping the cobwebs from the corners of the room. "Would you say business is booming?"

"That's my business and as far as I'm concerned it's doing okay..." 'Bu Ana raised her coffee glass. I'd like to clink this glass against those pearly white teeth she thought.

"That's where you're wrong."

"What?"

"You say 'it's your business,'" the girl's smile was slipping now too as if a mask was slowly being removed – revealing the true face of the unwelcome visitor. "As we both know, it's also Pak Gusti's business and he's accepted the boss's offer to buy out 51% of the *warung*."

"Why would Pak Gusti do that?"

"Because he's a businessman and you can't run a business the way you've been doing it. Don't look so horrified though. It's good news for everyone. The boss is not interested in just taking a share of your profits."

"So, what *is* he interested in?"

"You think he's interested in making a few measly rupiah on every coconut you sell? He's going to put far more *into* this place than he'll take out...at least in the short term. He'll modernise the whole place: beanbags on a bamboo platform outside to watch the

186

surf. A music system and maybe even a big screen to show surf movies. We'll turn this rundown *warung* into a cocktail bar with a license to stay open all night."

"What do you mean, 'we'?"

"What?"

"You said 'we'll turn it…'"

"It will be my job to run the cocktail bar. With your help of course. You and I will be partners and Nat will continue to run the resort."

"You think you can get an alcohol license and permission…Oh, wait. You have law enforcement connections, am I right?" 'Bu Ana immediately regretted her tone. Not only had she shown a card she might better have kept hidden until later, but she realised that this was a time for stalling, not for accelerating the antagonism. As it was, the situation was already gathering momentum at a pace that made her head reel.

"There's no need to be like that." The smile had disappeared and the green contact lenses were piercing under their fake canopy. "But yes. We *do* have connections."

"So, you've come to tell me that you've spoken to Pak Gusti already. And he's agreed. Now tell me what happens if I simply disagree to the offer."

"Maybe I shouldn't say this, but I like you and – believe it or not – I respect you. The thing is that this is less an offer than an announcement. A warning. Or even a demand if you want me to put it more clearly. If you don't accept then the boss will make an irresistible offer and Pak Gusti would certainly sell this land. Then the boss would just knock the *warung* down – and perhaps the temple too – to make way for a bar here without your help."

'Bu Ana looked away, hoping that Suzie wouldn't sense the knot of fear that was tying her throat closed so that she couldn't trust herself to speak. She felt the tears welling and was unable to raise her eyes even when she heard the girl's chair slide back from the table.

"I'd suggest you think it over for a couple of days. I'd hate you to make a hasty decision."

>◇◇◇<<

187

Anyone who saw the beach in first light the next morning might have assumed that there'd been an invasion during the night. Perhaps the spirits of the freedom fighters had returned, disembarking this time from some ghostly amphibious landing-craft and reclaiming the beachhead in armoured vehicles.

The sand was etched with the heavy tread of tracks, each almost a metre wide. It only took a second glance to notice, however, that the tracks did not run in parallel lines but swayed drunkenly up the beach in erratic curves. There were ten of these lines running from the edge of the water, across packed black sand that was otherwise as featureless as an empty parking lot. They passed onwards over the driftwood rubble of the hightide line and finally disappeared under the spiky *pandan* trees.

An onlooker at this early hour would have been astounded to see Nat darting across the sand, erasing the tracks – like a frontline spy, removing evidence of the nocturnal invasion. But at this hour of the morning only Pak Kolok could have been watching the beach. Nat knew that he'd finished his nightshift half an hour ago and was already heading for the eastern end of the bay, to the spot where his buffalo were tethered during the night. She had the beach to herself and was determined to obliterate the evidence before the first fishermen appeared.

Nat didn't need to waste time analysing but her practised eyes told her instantly that these tracks were made by five mature turtles – possibly around forty years old. She could see where they'd come doggedly up the beach, exactly where they nested, and where they descended back to the waves. She'd worked for a summer as a volunteer with a conservation project on Brazil's Ilha Grande (Big Island) and as she scuttled around – disguising the tracks by sweeping with a branch of brushwood – she tried to remember what the researchers had told her. At the start of the laying season it was often the young, immature females who arrived first. Their eggs might very often be unfertilised and would be sacrificed to the hungry predators: dogs, snakes and monitor lizards. At the tail-end of the laying season would come the oldest and slowest females, some arriving in what might be the last migration of their eighty-year lifespan. Their eggs – often also substandard – would also be sacrificed to any predators that were still hungry after the rush of the mass landings. The healthy young females in the prime of their life

188

would therefore tend to arrive in the middle of the laying period when the predators were so stuffed that they were unable to eat.

There was only one predator that had learned to conserve nature's bounties and to save them for another day. Modern man was that predator but in his greed he entirely overlooked the logical essence of conservation – considered mere common sense by even the most voracious of stone-age hunter-gatherers. Nat knew that if certain members of the community knew about this landfall they would raid every nest without leaving a single egg. There would be well over five hundred eggs from these five females alone, maybe closer to a thousand. In the village market they would sell for about 1,500 rupiah each for some vaguely conceived medicine or to enhance the sorry sexual performance of some insecure male.

It was only on a whim that Nat had even decided to head westward along the beach this morning to practise some *capoeira* moves on the sand.

By the time she finished the previously unmarked virgin sand below the tideline was graffitied with the marks of dancing feet. The beach was still empty so she slipped off her clothes and trotted into the waves, revelling in the cool water that rinsed the sand and sweat from her naked body.

>><><><<

'Bu Ana made her offerings at the shrine on the wall behind the bar at sunrise, as she did each morning.

She wafted her hand, gently pushing the incense, and the prayer it carried, towards her goddess. Then she looked westwards along the beach in time to watch the row of suites at the resort burst spontaneously into flames, as their windows simultaneously reflected the fiery glare of the rising sun.

Although merely an illusion, it seemed to 'Bu Ana each morning that it was a reiteration of a blessing from the goddess to her disciple.

She'd prayed particularly fervently this morning, asking for the guidance that she hoped might be delivered through her dreams. She could see no alternative to accepting the boss's 'offer'. She couldn't kid herself though: she would not be able to remain for long with Suzie as a manageress. She was aware that there would be no room for 'Bu Ana in the cocktail bar that they had in mind. It was like the cockfights when a worn-out old cockerel was shoved into a domed basket with a powerful young adversary. In such a scenario it was rare to find a backer who would put his money on the veteran.

'Bu Ana was disappointed in herself for being pushed into a position where things had to be weighed up in terms of profits. But these days that seemed to have become the dominant attitude throughout the entire community. The fishermen were barely making any profit because the paddy-people refused their catches. So, they were forced to sell at reduced prices to middle-men who haggled them down to the last possible rupiah and then made their profit in the city. The little profit the fisher-folk made from this they then bought expensive produce from other middle-men rather than from their paddy-people neighbours. The paddy-people had the same problem. With half the community boycotting the local produce there was no market for the rice or the harvests of dragon fruit, watermelon, mangos, papaya, durians and bananas. Only Ah Beng, the Chinese trader who worshipped profit like a god, was doing well.

The contagion – another Big Sickness – had become so widespread that now even 'Bu Ana was wondering how to boost her profits.

The sun was already high and the inferno in the resort windows long ago extinguished when 'Bu Ana saw two people walking along the beach towards the *warung*. The figure on the right, a *bule*, was the stockier of the two and she recognised the other as the young fisherman from the cursed boat. As they came closer, 'Bu Ana recognised the Frenchwoman who'd come to the *warung* with her husband. She recalled that they'd been out fishing that morning in *Putri Laut* and remembered that they had been arguing in undertones. The bitterness had intensified until they'd left eventually without talking to each other. This, 'Bu Ana suddenly realised, must be the woman that Pak Kolok had described.

Although the work-habits of 'Bu Ana's younger years had scarred her with what might be described as a professional cynicism, she had an unusual respect for the sanctity of marriage. While it was true that she still maintained a side-line in providing clandestine cures and bewitching balms, she never did so without weighing up the benefits that it would bring to family life. If a man had some affliction he wanted to hide from his wife, why would she not help?

190

If a wife wanted to lure her man back to the marital mattress, who was she to refuse?

In her experience the game of love was almost always played out between predator and prey. The seducer and the seduced. But in this case, who was who? Had the frumpy Frenchwoman lured this young man, or was he living out some juvenile macho fantasy? Either way, no good could come of this situation and it doubtless was the woman's husband who was the injured party. Maybe they thought they were safeguarding their secret by coming to the *warung* rather than being seen together at the resort. If this was the case they were deliberately embroiling her in their lies. Perhaps the young man, knowing something of 'Bu Ana's past reputation, assumed that she was in no position to judge. Maybe he was right and she was being a hypocrite.

Their assumption that she was no better than them seemed to echo the boss's attitude that he could force her into becoming an accessory in their cocktail bar. That too would implicate her just as surely as if she were involved in some sordid orgy with the boss, Suzie, the police chief and god-knows-who else. She was in one of the bottle-shaped fish-traps that the fishermen wove from bamboo slivers. There was no alternative but to continue swimming steadily deeper into the trap as the wicker walls closed in around her.

As the Frenchwoman and her Balinese lover stepped up the bank towards the *warung* 'Bu Ana's heart hardened towards them. Yet her animosity was outweighed by the islander's natural sense of hospitality towards foreign visitors.

"Good morning," the Frenchwoman called. Her forehead was sheened with sweat and as she wiped a slick of wiry blonde hair away from her eyes, 'Bu Ana noticed the tan-line on her finger where a wedding ring had been.

She wondered if she should explain that the *warung* was closed for the day. Since, typically, it was deserted at the moment the lie would be a believable one. But that too would be a form of dishonesty.

"Good morning," she replied. "What news?"

"The usual news," the young man said, cheerily confident, as they kicked off their flipflops by the steps.

They were only halfway towards the closest table when a note of sternness in 'Bu Ana's voice stopped them. "What do you want?"

"Two fresh coconuts and can we see the menu?" the woman asked. "Please and thank you." 'Bu Ana remembered now that the French couple had ordered coconuts the last time they were in the *warung*.

"I have one fresh coconut only," she said stiffly.

"It's ok, you have the coconut," the young man said to his companion with exaggerated gallantry. "I'll have a beer. The breakfast of champions."

"I don't think you understand," 'Bu Ana interrupted. "I have a coconut for the lady. That's no problem. But I have nothing for you."

"No, I don't understand." Yunus's smile was turning to a sickly mask.

"The lady was also welcome last week when she came here with her husband." 'Bu Ana spoke slowly and clearly in English so both would understand. "As a guest in our country – and a person with foreign values that are different from our own – she's still welcome now. If she returns with her husband he will be welcome too. But you...," she looked steadily at the young man. "You are *not* welcome."

"From what I hear of your younger days, I'm surprised you're in a position to judge..."

"Nevertheless, it's my right to refuse to serve you since this is my place – for the time being at least. Later it might not be mine anymore and I doubt that the new owners will be so fussy. I assume though that you'd prefer to leave now, since it could be a very long wait."

As she watched the couple walking stiffly back down the beach 'Bu Ana realised ruefully that she'd just successfully frightened away what would probably be her only customers of the day.

>><><><><<

A huge mango-coloured moon rose above the islands of the Far East. It loomed out of the wild valleys of West Papua, drawing a scarlet

192

blanket across one of the world's last tropical glaciers before passing high over the church spires of Ambon. Among the stilted villages of the Alor Islands, the great glowing disk provoked tales of the days when the skulls of enemies still hung from the rafters. In the whaling communities of Lamalera, elders among the men who still hunt sperm whales with hand-held harpoons said that this blood-red moon could only be an evil omen.

The apocalyptic light crept along the 666 demonic kilometres of the dragon-shaped sprawl of Flores and across the tangled isles of Komodo – where the villages are still besieged by dragons of their own. The moon reflected the bubbling lava in the craters of Sumbawa and threw purple shadows across the flanks of Lombok's Rinjani volcano.

At last its rays illuminated the volcanic plume above Bali's mighty Mount Agung before they delved into the lakeside community of Trunyan where, even today, 'Hindus of the Wind' lay their dead out on the shore of the crater lake. In the highland villages people recounted the story of how, every night, a vengeful demon called Kala Rauh chases the moon across the sky. The demon had stolen some of the elixir of immortality and the *tirtha kamandalu* ambrosia was just entering his throat when Vishnu – reacting almost instantly to a tip-off from the moon and the sun – beheaded the thief. Kala Rauh's head remained immortal while his body died and he occasionally revenges himself (as can be seen during an eclipse) by swallowing one of his informers.

On this particular night, however, Kala Rauh was not fast enough and the moonlight continued unimpeded, as it swept along the coral sand of Central Bali and within moments was reflected in the shimmers of volcanic glass on the black sand beaches of the west. The moonlight picked out shimmering sparks of sea-lightning – blue phosphorescence that glittered in the shallows like tiny gas flames.

Throughout that entire chain of islands, vast numbers of turtles were counting on this mango moon to guide them. They had been making these migrations thousands of miles across the oceans since long before humans made what was believed to be their first sea-voyage (on a bamboo raft between Bali and Lombok) a mere 850,000 years ago.

The moonlight created a faint parody of a sundial – a 'moondial' – as it threw the shadow of a short stick across the sand. Rather than being used to tell the time, however, this marker was one of several that indicated the position of turtles' nests to a lone figure who crept across the remote West Bali beach. Although it was just past midnight, Nat had already dug up three nests and had removed more than 350 eggs, taking great care not to disorientate the embryonic reptiles by rotating them as she placed them carefully in a bucket. The chances of a hatchling surviving to adulthood, she knew, was said to be around a thousand to one so statistically there was virtually no hope that any of the unborn refugees she was spiriting away would return to these beaches as a laying adult. Nevertheless, she'd already smuggled one bucket into her room and brought another one for the last two nests. The biggest risk was in slipping past the deaf night-watchman who, she now realised, might be particularly keen to know about the existence of the nests. But she knew now where he made himself comfortable among the shadows of the boats and it was usually easy to spot him from the glow of his cigarette. Tomorrow, before first light, she'd transport the eggs to a rarely visited section of the beach where she would carefully bury them again.

She muttered one of her grandmother's favourite sayings as she carefully removed the last batch of eggs: *Os deuses ajudam quem cedo madruga* – the gods help those who wake early.

Nat was anxious to get this covert mission completed as soon as possible. When she'd first walked down the beach – guided by the light of that spectacular moon and marvelling at the blue fringe of phosphorescence around her footsteps – she'd been surprised to hear voices coming from the coconut grove above the beach. Now all was quiet again but she worked with her headlamp shielded in her hand all the same, so that her work in the nest was illuminated only by the subtlest glow. If these nocturnal activities were noticed it would make her appear extremely suspicious. There'd been one night when she thought that the deaf nightguard nearly spotted her and she'd almost confided in 'Bu Ana. After seeing the photos of the turtle sacrifice, however, she could only shudder at her naivete. In hindsight she was grateful that Dewi had inadvertently given her an insight into the truth before that silly infatuation took a firmer grip on her.

Her turtle-smuggling skirmish was almost over now and she could get some sleep. The voices among the trees had been getting louder. From the slurred shouts she guessed that they had been drinking. Perhaps they were Javanese men who'd come across on the ferry from the neighbouring island and were sleeping rough among the trees next to their motorbikes. She'd never travelled in a country where she felt as safe as she did here; even in the poor areas of Indonesian cities she'd always appreciated a sense of welcome that was a far cry from the tension of Brazil's *favela* slums.

There were times, wandering the backstreets of cities like Jakarta and Makassar, when people back home would certainly have considered her foolishly naïve. So, even now – alone in the moonlight on a deserted beach in remote West Bali – she felt no trepidation.

Then six dark figures emerged from the trees and turned in her direction. They were still far away, but Nat saw that even if she started for home now their paths would intersect long before she reached the lights of the resort. As her thoughts turned to the half-naked body of the girl she'd discovered on this same beach the first tingle of fear dripped like melting ice down her spine, Suddenly her complacent feeling of confidence was shattered – like a brick going through a shop-window – by an awareness of danger.

Nat rose to her feet and, with exaggerated casualness, began to stride towards the resort. She was suddenly aware of the bucket swinging absurdly in her hand and racked her mind for a plausible reason for being out alone at this time of the night. There was no way to explain the bucket but she certainly didn't want to clue these men into the presence of turtles on the beach.

A dog! She would pretend she'd been walking a dog and had lost it. Ideally a *big* dog. She put two sandy fingers into her mouth and tried to whistle. Her mouth was dry, and now gritty, but at the second attempt a piercing whistle cut through the silence of the night. The men stopped. Noticing her for the first time. They adjusted their route to intercept her. It struck her that the whistles might alert someone at the resort and she tried another blast – even louder this time. After a moment's rueful thought, she cursed her luck. The only security guard who was likely to be awake was deaf.

By now she was now less than a hundred metres from the approaching men. Their faces were hidden in the moon-shadow but their drunken stumbling was unmistakable. Their chatter had stopped and there was something ominous about the way that they whispered among themselves.

>><><><><<

The light of that gleaming red moon made it easier tonight to slip between the tangle of boats that interlinked their outrigger arms like old friends. Yunus was doing his best to avoid the owl-like eyes of the deaf security guard. He figured that he'd only narrowly avoided being seen when he sneaked into the resort the previous night.

Now, as he ducked cautiously between the boats, he caught sight of the guard who appeared to be dozing against a driftwood log. Yunus grinned. Once beyond the boats, he need only duck past the restaurant – which would be long abandoned at this hour – then he'd have a clear run to Marielle's suite. Just a few more minutes and he'd once again be engulfed in the warmth of her ample thighs.

He was aware that this was not a relationship that was going to last much longer. In fact, it wasn't a relationship at all. Just some fleeting fun and Yunus still couldn't understand why that damn hypocrite at the *warung* had insisted on making such a big thing about it. The fling had almost run its course in any case. Perhaps Marielle would end it herself before her husband returned to the resort. But if Jean-Pierre wasn't coming back then Yunus would be forced to put an end to it himself before much longer. For the time being the meals, drinks and spending money she lavished on him was enough to support a lifestyle that was far more pleasant than fishing had ever been. She was past her prime, that was plain to see, but she had an ardent enthusiasm for resurrecting a sexual appetite that had apparently lain dormant for too long. In short, she was infinitely superior as a nocturnal companion to Putri Laut.

Yunus had passed the last of the boats and had almost reached the restaurant when the sound of a whistle reached him from far along the beach. Cringing down into the shadows, he turned back to see if the security guard had noticed. Then he shook his head and grinned to himself. Of course, he hadn't. And it was certain that the other guards would be sound asleep by this time.

As he rose and started to move forward the whistle came again. He was tempted to ignore it but, driven by nothing more than vague curiosity, he detoured from his usual skulking route through the shadows and trotted to the edge of the resort's lawn. From this slightly elevated vantagepoint over the sand he could see a group of people far along the beach in the moonlight.

One figure was slightly separated from the others and appeared to be deliberately trying to maintain a distance from the dark crowd that was formed by five or maybe six others. Although they were too far away to be sure, instinct told him that the lone figure was a woman.

The whistle came once more. There was something desperate about the shrill note this time and without another thought Yunus jumped down the five steps to the beach and started off at a run across the sand.

He was only halfway along the beach when most of the men started walking away in the opposite direction from the resort. Perhaps they had seen him. He couldn't be sure. As the woman came closer he recognised Nat the resort manageress. Only one of the men was still following her closely.

Even before Yunus reached them he could hear the man's voice. He registered the coaxing tone but the words were unintelligible. The woman was moving now on an angle to the beach – in a strange crab-like shuffle that was taking her closer to the water with every step. With a sickening feeling Yunus realised that she was trying to maintain a distance not only from the man but also from this unrecognised stranger who was running across the beach as if to intercept her. Clearly she figured that she was trapped between the two of them and was edging towards the water as if for safety.

"Good evening Ibu," he called in his most reassuring voice. "What news?"

"The usual news," she said – deliberately non-committal – as she continued to hurry past, nerves tensed but apparently doing her best to ignore him too.

"You don't remember me, do you Ibu?" he asked in a soothing undertone. He'd reached them now and, although he spoke to her, he kept his eyes fixed on the stranger. "I worked with Pak Rahim on the building."

The man was about Yunus's own age, but tall. Almost a head taller. He was watching this new arrival carefully and, even in the moon-shadows, Yunus could sense undisguised aggression in his eyes and in his posture. Without taking his eyes off the young man Yunus noticed from the corner of his vision that the others in the group were now perhaps fifty metres farther away up the beach.

"Oh! Yes!" Nat said finally. There was undisguised relief in her voice now. "I *do* remember you."

"And you?" Yunus stepped in front of the man, allowing a touch of belligerence into his voice. "Who are you?"

The man began to reply in Javanese and his speech was slurred. Yunus couldn't understand what he said, and it was immaterial in any case since he didn't allow the man to finish his explanation. "You should leave now," he said, pointing along the beach to the spot where the rest of the gang were still walking. "Just go!"

The man continued walking forwards as if he intended to walk right through the meddling stranger who was interrupting his fun.

"Carry on walking Ibu," Yunus muttered over his shoulder before turning quickly back. "You, my friend, need to leave. Right now."

The man advanced another step and pushed him roughly in the chest. Yunus allowed himself to step backwards and tried to inject a soothing note into his Indonesian words. "You don't want to have any trouble here...better you go with your friends."

The man looked like a fighter and, if he refused to go peacefully, Yunus knew that his only chance was to lure him farther from his friends. The distance between the three of them and the dark group farther up the beach was increasing with every second. But now the gang had stopped to watch and Yunus knew that it would take moments for them to come racing back. The last thing he wanted was to be entangled with this man, wrestling on the sand when ten more feet arrived to start kicking.

It was beginning to look like a fight was inevitable but the farther he could draw the man away from the gang before any trouble started the safer their position would be. So, the next time the man blundered forward to push him in the chest he allowed himself to take three or four steps backwards, ignoring a wavelet that washed around his ankles. The man followed, as by now Yunus knew he would. The manageress was still walking steadily. "Let's just go," she called to Yunus.

"He won't back off," Yunus replied in English, without looking at her. "You just keep moving and I'll keep him away."

"Don't make me do this," he suggested half-heartedly to the man. But the man was coming forward again and Yunus realised without a doubt that there was going to be no alternative. The next shove gained them a precious metre or two extra distance from the gang. Yunus took one last glance up the beach, estimating the time they might have before the others sprinted back.

"I warned you," he shrugged. He half turned his back as if he was simply going to walk away. Then, almost in the same movement, he swivelled his upper body and slammed his right fist as hard as he could against the man's cheekbone. A boxing match was out of the question because he would almost immediately be outnumbered. The only hope lay in that first punch and the instant Yunus's knuckles collided with the man's face he knew it was the best he could have hoped for. Yunus caught a glimpse of the whites of his eyes glowing in the moonlight – indistinguishable from the eyes of people he'd seen in ritual trances – as the man crumpled onto the sand. Pole axed. A sheen of phosphorescence momentarily outlined his inert body before the water revived him and he rolled groggily over.

"Don't run," Yunus told the woman, trying to maintain a steady, calm tone. "Just keep walking but walk fast!"

The man staggered, dizzy as he got back to his feet. Yunus was already backing away, a rear-guard for the retreating Brazilian. It was unlikely that he'd been knocked out, after all, but he was dazed. He was moving after them now but with noticeably less enthusiasm than he'd shown before. Unfortunately, the other five men had already started running towards them. Yunus guessed that he and Nat would make it to the resort steps before the gang got there…but it was unlikely that their momentum was going to be checked merely because they arrived on resort property.

Nat and Yunus marched briskly towards the resort lights, their legs straining to break into a run. Even when he thought back afterwards, Yunus was unable to define why running had instinctively felt like a bad idea. There was something about the obvious pack mentality of their pursuers that made it potentially fatal.

The two of them reached the five steps up to the lawn just a minute before the gang arrived, but now Yunus realised that he'd merely succeeded in delaying the inevitable. The guest accommodation was back beyond the pool and the staff quarters, where the security guards would be dozing, was farther still. It was doubtful that anyone would hear their shouts and very little chance that reinforcements could possibly arrive before it was too late. He'd prefer to take the beating on the open lawn rather than back among the buildings. As Yunus turned to face his attackers at the top of the steps he saw the deaf security guard trotting towards them from the darkness of the restaurant with a puzzled expression on his face. There was just a fleeting moment of reassurance before he the thought struck him that the odds were barely diminished; three against six – when the three included a *bule* woman and an old man – was still likely to add up to a pounding for him.

"Go Ibu," he said quietly. "Take the old man and get out through the back of the restaurant."

By now the six men had slowed to a walk as they reached the bottom of the steps. One of them was rubbing a shining sheen of blood across his left cheek with the back of his hand but the rest all looked equally determined to exact vengeance. Fists and feet were likely to be the least he could hope for – a gang like this could very likely be packing knives too. The only advantage he had was the strategic benefit represented in five shallow steps. If it had to come to a battle at least let him fight from an uphill position where he could try to prevent them from surrounding him.

"No!" The woman's decisive voice came from his right side. "We stay together."

One of the gang made the first move to mount the lower step. If they reached the top there would be no going back. Yunus stepped forward as if to meet him. On the ledge beside the top step there was a large Bintang bottle and he grabbed it around the neck and raised it like a club.

"Act crazy!" he rasped at the manageress. "Just back me up."

He stepped forward with the bottle raised over his head. "C'mon! You want this?" he roared. "Come on up then! Who's first?"

Two of the men mounted the bottom step and Yunus lunged at them with the bottle swinging. His aggression was sufficient to drive them back to the sand from surprise alone. Another tried to circle the edge of the steps to the left. Yunus sensed the old security guard step forward beside him. He heard a strange grunt and was astounded to see the old man's jungle boot swing high towards their attacker's head in a very respectable karate kick. It missed but the unexpected determination was enough to drive the attacker back down to the sand. The young gang member smirked as he retreated but the security guard advanced down three more steps and his smile disappeared as he rapidly backed off farther. Yunus jumped down in line with the old man threatening again with the bottle. The gang was hesitant now but it was crucial to keep the pressure on. A hint of weakness in the eyes of the defenders on the steps would be enough to reignite their belligerence.

Then, from Yunus's right side a hand grabbed at the bottle and the man almost wrenched it away. Yunus couldn't risk relinquishing his only weapon but while he wrestled three other men were closing in on him. He swung his fist at the man holding the bottle but missed. The others lunged at him from the left and he threw a punch so wild that it almost threw him off balance. Just as he thought they were about to close in on him the man who'd grabbed at the bottle howled in pain and crumpled to one side. Nat had descended the steps to protect their flank on that side and had swung a low sweeping kick – a perfectly executed *chapa baixa* that jarred the attacker's knee sideways. His weapon released, Yunus swung desperately in a wide sweep that would have smashed the face of anyone who had not jumped out of the way.

It was enough to take the fight out of the men. They slowly backed away from the bottom of the steps. One of them was still holding the back of his hand to a split cheekbone and another clutched his knee, in considerable pain. Their hearts were no longer in the fight and – with an angry threat or two in Yunus's direction – they turned to walk away westwards along the beach.

That great red moon had continued its journey westwards too – with lofty unconcern for the petty dramas that were taking place on the planet below. Its light had already swept onwards, over the Javanese coast, past the smouldering cones of Merapi and Bromo and the mystical temple of Borobudur. It illuminated the volcanic cloud above notorious Krakatao and threw its shadows into the jungles of Sumatra. Finally, it left the Indonesian archipelago to transform the great expanse of the Indian Ocean into a sheet of burning copper.

>><><><><<

When Yunus thought about the incident later he tried to muster a feeling of guilt about the violence but the feeling faded almost instantly, like phosphorescence dissolving on a moonlit beach. He knew he'd been left with no alternative.

Moreover, it was as if all the stress of the previous weeks – every bad thing in his body – had concentrated in the shoulder and forearm that had been honed to steel by years hauling heavy nets. He had the impression that all the pent-up poison had passed through his fist directly into the young man's jaw.

In that fleeting moment of impact his curse had been transferred to the body that lolled helpless in the foamy water.

>><><><><<

The case of Alexi Romanov – also known as The Playboy – was destined to be recorded among the village's most disturbing legends.

The details leaked from the sound-proofed interrogation room at the back of the police station as surely as if the building had been constructed of mosquito-netting. Almost before the beatings were over it was common knowledge that the night-duty police had failed to establish the source of the drugs. Under normal circumstances, the villagers might have viewed the police brutality as unforgivably barbaric. In this case, most felt it was justified and there were some who would have appreciated an invitation to assist with the enquiries.

The few details that were established during that questioning became public knowledge the next morning via the police chief, who had a habit of chirping like a blue-rumped parakeet during his courtship dance with Suzie. Then a pair of officers stopped by Buana's Warung and shared their inside knowledge in return for a complimentary shot of arak.

It was said that Alexi Romanov had been tripping on magic mushrooms when the tragedy took place. Romanov and his two playboy friends were staying at the resort and had requested some spoons and a big thermos of hot water from Dewi because, they said, they wanted to make coffee before an early-morning surf the next day. But they used the water instead to make ticket-to-the-moon tea. Around sunset they started drinking and ended up eating the cloggy 'shroom mulch at the bottom of their glasses with the spoons.

For more than an hour there had been no effect at all and, just as they began to complain that they'd been duped, the hallucinogenics kicked in. All around them oily psilocybin rainbows swirled as if slicked across the face of a shimmering wave. The psychedelic lightshow was apparently so real that at one point Alexi Romanov tried to photograph it. Time was also fluctuating fluidly and between the decision to take the photo and the actual move to find a phone, there had been an estimated delay of a further forty-minutes or more. The phone was confiscated so that the shot could be used in evidence, although even the police couldn't explain what the photo proved.

Nevertheless, snapping the photo was possibly the last relatively lucid decision in Alexi Romanov's life.

One of the playboys conceived the idea that the sun was going to rise again at any moment from the same spot where it was already bleeding crimson across the sky. They waited in vain for something to happen as time played its psychedelic tricks.

"Think we're going to see a sunrise or not?" Alexi asked, exasperated after what seemed like an hour.

"Got to," someone said. "The fuckin' thing can't just stay down there all night."

As his friends staggered down the beach, beseeching the sun to rise again, Alexi sat still, trying to calm a wayward hammering heart.

It was the first time that twenty-three-year-old Alexi had taken psychedelic drugs of any sort, and he was already beginning to regret it. About the time he took the photo he began to suffer from increasingly intense paranoiac hallucinations. Alexi had tried to tell his friends that the 'shrooms were poisoning him but their giggling response jangled his nerves still more. While his friends shouted on the beach, trying to bully the sun into rising, Alexi spent the next hour pushing his fingers down his throat in the bathroom in an unsuccessful attempt to vomit. Next he tried doing callisthenics in a desperate effort to distribute the toxin through his system and so clear his mind.

Nothing worked, however, and finally Alexi decided that a quick spin on the motorbike would be just what was needed to clear his head. Riding along the sandy beach-side dirt-track that connected the resort to the village was a struggle but once his tyres accelerated onto the tarmac Alexi began to feel better. Had he been able to continue onward for another kilometre or two he probably would have cured himself not only of the effects of the evening, but also of the urge for any further psychedelic experiences.

But his journey was an unexpectedly short one. Less than a kilometre from the hotel there was a tight righthand bend that coincided with a steep drop. With the wind in his eyes and the shimmering 'shroom kaleidoscope projected onto the tarmac, he overshot the corner at speed. He dropped the bike in a slide, leaving much of the flesh from his right leg on the tarmac, and sending the bike careening over the ledge and into the sidewall of a house. People from neighbouring houses – woken by the scream of grating iron and crashing masonry – arrived within seconds. Dewi, who lived just across the road, was one of the first on the scene and said afterwards that apart from the leg – which, because of the adrenalin and the drugs, he barely appeared to notice – Alexi was unhurt.

The heavy bike brought down the wall of the house and part of the roof. Normally there were three children sleeping in that room but the oldest of the three – people often described her by drawing an imaginary line across the middle of their forehead – had snuck out of bed and was curled up on the terrace with two orphaned kittens (victims, perhaps, of the fisher-folk plague). The weight of the motorbike and the roof was enough to kill Pande's second daughter and to gravely injure her little sister Nyoman.

>◇◇◇◇<<

The reunion between the Balinese *warung* owner and the Brazilian resort manageress, when it finally happened, was one of mutual distrust. It might never have happened at all if not for the fact that Nat had finally convinced herself that it was not professional to allow an unbridgeable chasm to develop between her and the woman who was, after all, the resort's nearest neighbour. They could never now be friends, she told herself, but since the woman operated the only other property on the beach it was ridiculous to try to avoid her entirely.

Nat's attitude, when she finally deigned to call in at the *warung* during an afternoon walk, was merely one of professional politeness for a woman she considered a heartless turtle killer. Nevertheless, she was taken aback by a corresponding iciness in the Balinese woman's attitude and the two women circled each other warily – like two jet-maned roosters sizing each other up as enemies.

"I'm sure you know that Suzie came here to threaten me," said 'Bu Ana, after the cold formalities had reluctantly been exchanged, like congealed soup.

"Threaten you? With what?"

"I'm sure the boss has told you his plans already."

"He doesn't tell me much."

"He's going to steal my *warung* and give it to Suzie for a cocktail bar."

"That's ridiculous. He can't just take your *warung*."

"Of course, that's not how it will appear. Are you really saying you didn't know?"

"Certainly not!" Nat's curiosity began to get the better of her icy resolve. "Please explain from the beginning."

"I'm going to be allowed to run the *warung* as a cocktail bar jointly with Suzie, but they're sure to make the situation so impossible for me that I'll have to leave. They won't have to actually *steal* it…but the result will be the same."

"But what about the landowner? I thought he was a friend of yours."

"I thought so too, but he's a businessman. If I don't accept the offer to share the *warung* then Suzie says your boss will simply make an irresistible offer and buy it. Then I'll have nothing."

"So, what will you do?"

"I'll probably have no alternative but to accept. At least that way perhaps I can protect the temple for a little longer."

They were sitting at the same table where they'd talked when they first met and now, as then, 'Bu Ana's pack of Gudang Garam clove cigarettes lay between them. The older woman picked up the pack and Nat watched her fingernails, with their cracked red varnish, shaking slightly as she plucked one out.

"Can I have one…?" Nat asked.

It was a symbolic statement of peace, perhaps as old as the first cultivated tobacco patch of the ancient Mayans.

"I'm truly sorry to hear about this," the Brazilian woman said as wisps of blue smoke danced between them like spirits. "I promise I had no idea about any of this. The boss seems to have more secrets with Suzie than I'd guessed."

"I was angry and hurt when Suzie first told me but, to be honest, the more I thought it over the more certain I was that you couldn't have known. I'm sorry for doubting you."

The moment of honesty was like a door opening to a familiar and comforting room. It was only with a determined effort that Nat summoned the will to slam it closed before she could be tempted to walk through. "Well. Like I said, I'm sorry this is happening. I hope the landowner will protect you. But I guess there's nothing that I can do and I should get going now."

As Nat pushed her chair back from the table the older woman reached across to grasp her hand. "What's the matter? I thought we were friends…What's happened?"

"I thought we were friends too. But don't worry. I think it was my misunderstanding. I just got carried away…" Nat gently but resolutely freed her hand.

"What happened?" 'Bu Ana persisted. "You're like the *bunga malu* – the 'shy flower' that shrivels its leaves and shrinks away almost before you've even started to reach out to it. At least you owe me an explanation…"

"I don't think I *owe you* anything at all," Nat exploded, with an angry curl of her upper lip. She stubbed the remaining half of her cigarette out in the shell that served as an ashtray, extinguishing their short-lived peace. "I heard about the sacrifice you made at the boat. I heard about the turtle you killed."

"Aaah. That…"

"Yes *that*. There are great differences between you and I and, although you might think it is a small thing, it made me realise that I could never understand you. And perhaps never forgive you."

"Could you forgive me if you knew how many turtles I've saved?"

"*Saved?* I'd never have taken you for a hypocrite…"

"At least you can listen while I explain. Ok? Take one more cigarette and if you haven't understood by the time it's finished then you never will, and I'll agree that you should leave."

>><><><<

Some of the villagers were sorry for the harsh karmic justice that was inflicted upon Alexi Romanov. Most thought, however, that he got what he deserved.

Romanov's befuddled playboy friends slept off their stupor far along the beach and it was only in the morning that they began to piece together the events of the night before.

When they finally tracked their friend down at the police station he was almost unrecognisable. According to the police report, Alexi's collision with the wall had resulted in two black eyes, a fractured cheekbone and enough broken teeth to make speech unintelligible.

The Playboys spoke no Indonesian so it was only after an hour that somebody was found who could inform them of the death of the little girl. Learning that Alexi would be transferred to the city jail that afternoon and would eventually stand trial for manslaughter, the two remaining playboys left immediately to alert their embassy.

Late that afternoon, while the police van was still on the way to the city, a call came through on the police channel that five-year-old Nyoman had died in hospital from a punctured lung.

Alexi Romanov himself died of internal haemorrhaging in the van before he arrived in the city. According to the post-mortem report, it was a delayed after-effect of his crash.

>><><><<

Despite her family tradition as practitioners of dark Brazilian rituals and her increasing familiarity with island superstitions involving spirits and demons, Nat considered herself a sceptic. Until, that is, the afternoon that she found herself on a collision-course – in the most literal sense – with a living demon.

It was late afternoon when she set off in the boss's double-cab pickup to run the last errand of the day, collecting some ingredients from the night-market in the village. Although the air-con was blasting at full power, Nat always found it pleasant to drive with the window down, arm resting on the door frame, the breeze running fingers through her hair.

She drove out of the resort gates and along the dirt-track that ran parallel to the beach, then turned up the steep hill. She passed Rahim's house at the southern edge of the village and then swung right past the crumpled wall where Pande's widow lived. The road dipped steeply to cross a narrow humpback bridge in the bottom of a shadowy gorge that was arched with bamboo. As she dropped to second gear and accelerated up the hill Nat was dimly aware of a single strand of palm leaf that fluttered down from above, as if carried on the breeze. It touched her arm so lightly and fleetingly that she only barely registered it. She glanced in the rear-view mirror expecting to see the strand lying in the road but there was nothing there.

Unbidden, her mind replayed the moment when the strand brushed her arm. Only now did she realise that there was something unusual about the dappled surface of what she'd taken to be a dried leaf. There was something improbably weighty too in the way the paper-thin strip of vegetation had brushed her arm. In the instant when her mind formed the word 'snake' she also realised that from the way it had landed on the edge of the open window the object could just as easily have fallen *into* the car instead of falling out. After all, if it had fallen out surely she would have seen something in the mirror, even if only the flick of a tail disappearing into the thick vegetation that flanked both sides of the road.

At the top of the slope ahead a small barbecue stand was smoking dimly and a group of young men sat in the gathering twilight watching satays sizzle. Nat's reluctance to look foolish in front of the local hoods was more powerful than her fear of a snake so she waited until she had passed the group before easing slowly to a halt.

Trying to convince herself that there could not possibly be a snake in the car she pulled the handbrake up gingerly with just the tips of her fingers. She opened the door and slid smoothly out until her bare toes gratefully touched the tarmac. Now she leaned down cautiously to try to see into the darkness under the seat. She switched on the torch on her phone and trained the light under the seat.

208

Nothing. Feeling gingerly for the edge of the rubber mat on the driver's side she pulled it out and flapped it onto the road. She spent a few minutes searching cautiously but by the time she'd opened all the doors and shone the light around the seats and under the dashboard she was convinced that she must have imagined the entire incident. With all four doors opened like spread wings surely any wild creature would make a bolt for freedom, she thought.

The equatorial evening was fast descending by the time she was ready to drive onwards to the market. As she looked back across the valley in the direction from which she came she saw an electric cable silhouetted high above the road at about the spot where she estimated that the thing, whatever it was, had landed on her.

"Maybe…" she mumbled to herself. It seemed highly unlikely – almost impossible – that a snake had fallen off that wire in the exact moment she passed underneath and passed through the open window. "I'll never know for sure." She shrugged again and – determined to put it from her mind – hurried on towards the night-market.

>◇◇◇<<

"I know you've been friends with Ana for a long time," Dewi was saying nervously. Pak Gusti had sat on the top step at the resort so she'd positioned herself a step lower. It was an instinctive sign of deference to the landowner's Satria caste.

"I don't have to tell you that she's a proud and independent woman," she continued hesitantly. "Life has treated her harshly – as you know – but she's rarely ever asked for help."

"That's true…" the celebrated businessman replied guardedly. Despite his little empire, he was a rare visitor in the community. His business strategy was built on delegation and he had minions (most of whom preferred to think of themselves as 'business partners') all over the village. Aside from these chosen few it was rare that anyone – either paddy-people or fisher-folk – had reason to speak to Pak Gusti personally.

To Dewi he was an intimidating character. He'd been a friend of her family – inasmuch as he was a friend to *anyone* – as far back as she could remember and he'd visited her family compound several times when she was small. As a little girl he'd sometimes brought her gifts but his gruff manner and serious demeanour meant that she shared the shyness that the other village children felt in his presence.

Today, however, for the first time she'd worked up the nerve to speak with him face-to-face. The phrase she'd just uttered was the longest she'd spoken to him in her 26 years but *something* had to be done to save her aunt's *warung*. Dewi understood that, in her aunt's eyes, the *warung*'s importance was primarily strategic. It was the fortress that defended the temple of the Sea Goddess. She also knew that – even for the most important thing in her world – her aunt's pride would not allow her to beg. So, Dewi had chosen to sacrifice herself. She would beg for her aunt.

Pak Gusti had come to the resort for a lunch meeting with the boss and Suzie and both had been visibly put out when the waitress approached the local mogul to request a few minutes of his time after lunch. Dewi had been prepared for a rebuttal and was surprised when he accepted with what she took to be an expression of uncharacteristic nervousness. After lunch, as he smoked his imported cigarettes with the boss and flirted mildly with Suzie, she was surprised to notice him watching her from time to time. But it was already late afternoon when he signalled to her to join him on the step.

"I know you were very generous to help her set up the *warung*," she continued. "It's all she has and to lose it would be incredibly painful for her."

"Nobody is trying to take the *warung* away from her," Pak Gusti interrupted brusquely. "As it is the place barely pays for itself and under the resort management it will be a flourishing business. She's not going to be kicked out. She'll work with Suzie."

"That's very convenient, if you don't mind me saying so." Dewi's nerves abated, making way for an anger that she fought to control. "It's convenient for you and it's convenient for the boss. You both know that 'Bu Ana could not work as a partner with Suzie even for a week. Then you'll both be able to assuage your guilt by claiming that she left of her own accord."

The businessman was silent while he dug into his packet of Marlboros. "What do you suggest?" he asked, as he searched his pocket for his gold-plated Zippo.

"I'm not saying you owe her anything, but I know that piece of land is not important to you. I'm suggesting you should think carefully before you make a decision. That small patch of land is very, very important to her, to my aunt…"

The suggestion, innocent though it was, hung in the air and suddenly it seemed to Dewi that it was pregnant with an ominous tone that she'd never intended. There was no possible threat she could imagine that would weigh on Pak Gusti, yet she was taken aback now by the effect her words had on the landowner. Gone was the brashly confident Satria businessman, and in his place sat a chubby old man. An old man whose face was suddenly etched with worry.

To Pak Gusti the words were heavy with foreboding. It was as if a court sentence, which had been pending for almost three decades, had been pronounced. The words the waitress had spoken hung in the air like a swinging noose.

"She told you, didn't she?" he stammered. His cigarette remained unlit, ignored between his long fingernails. "I couldn't understand how nobody ever guessed. I watched you growing up and it was always so obvious that you were so incredibly like Ana. So, she finally told you that I'm your father."

><><><><<

Nat had almost forgotten all about the snake by the time she left the market. It was almost totally dark when she set out to retrace her drive back to the resort and once again she was feeling carefree as she drove, arm out of the window past the now-deserted barbecue stand and down the dip to the wooded gorge.

Then her headlights what she first took to be a coil of rope in the middle of the road. As she approached the rope moved. She braked hard, coming to a halt so that she was almost blocking the entire road. She could see now that the uncoiling rope had transformed into a large cobra. As it moved up the hill towards her, hood fanned out and head raised off the ground, she jabbed at the window switch, praying for the protective glass to slide up before the snake reached her.

The mystery would have been solved had she been able to convince herself that this was the creature she'd collided with. It would have been convenient – and intensely reassuring – to consider that the snake had been stunned and was only now recovering, dazed in the middle of the road. But Nat guessed that this snake was almost two metres long and about the same thickness as her wrist. It was unfeasible to imagine that this hefty and imposing creature could have been the leaf-like creature that so lightly and fleetingly brushed her arm.

She'd seen several snakes during the months when the construction of the resort had disrupted the shoreline habitat, while at the same time creating idyllic open areas for opportunistic sunbathing. But this was the first time that she'd seen a king cobra – known simply as *ular raja* (king of snakes) to the Balinese.

Two unconnected cobra sightings in the same evening seemed very unlikely. Yet this was unquestionably not the same creature she saw – or might have seen – brush against her arm.

The cobra stared malevolently at her through the glass, hood flared wide as a man's hand. Her hypnotised gaze was distracted by glimmer of light among the trees on the opposite side of the gorge as a motorbike appeared at the top of the slope. Frantically Nat flashed her own headlights, trying to alert the driver to the slithering obstacle that now blocked most of the road. The heedless rider came barrelling down the hill. He pipped his hooter twice as he crossed the bridge, perhaps in irritation at the driver who was blinding him, Nat imagined.

The motorcyclist saw the snake at the last minute and swerved violently as the cobra struck at the spot-lit shape that zapped past. Nat couldn't tell if the snake had struck at the man or the machine but the rider continued accelerating out of the sight. Clearly he had no intention of stopping.

She expected the snake, surely intimidated by its brush with danger, to move into the safety of the thick vegetation that lay just a metre away. Astoundingly, the creature continued to display almost unnatural aggression, apparently determined to hold its ground in the centre of the road.

It seemed to be watching her as Nat, separated by a few millimetres of glass, puzzled over what seemed to be a show of almost supernatural belligerence. Dimly she became aware of a vague recollection tugging at her brain. She recalled reading, many years before, something about cobras mating for life and about how

212

they were said to be among nature's most devoted partners and parents. Dimly she remembered an Indian folk tale – perhaps a story from Rudyard Kipling, although she couldn't be sure – about how a cobra will sometimes seek vengeance upon any person who had harmed its loved ones.

It was an unlikely scenario, she realised, but this incredibly aggressive and determined behaviour was in itself almost inconceivable. Nat's mind baulked at the sudden thought that she'd inadvertently kidnapped the cobra's mate. That it was, even now, a prisoner in the vehicle, perhaps curled behind a door panel or twisted tightly into a gap at the back of the seats.

She tried to put such thoughts out of her mind. Besides she was now running very late and the kitchen staff were waiting for her at the resort. She eased the car back into the road, passing gingerly within a metre of the waving head. Even as Nat drove cautiously across the bridge she could still see the cobra in the rear-view mirror. The hair on the back of her neck tingled as she watched its flared hood staring after her taillights.

She tried to put the incident out of her mind but after that evening she tried to avoid driving the pickup – almost as if there was a curse on the car. She considered warning the boss, imagining how terrible she would feel if somebody reached for the gearstick or jabbed the brake to feel the sharp stab of a venomous bite on hand or ankle. But she couldn't face the boss's ridicule so the only person she mentioned the incident to was Dewi.

"Do you beep your horn when you go across that bridge?" her Balinese friend asked when Nat shakily recounted her experience later that evening.

"No. Why would I?"

"Didn't you notice that people always *pip-pip* their horn as they cross that gorge? They say that there's a demon that lives there and you must salute it so that you can pass safely."

Nat continued to consider herself a sceptic but it always gave her a subtly feeling of hypocrisy afterwards whenever she crossed that bridge, politely tapping a double-hoot to placate the cobra as she went on her way.

It's not exactly that I believe it, she told herself, but it can't do any harm to be respectful.

8 – Waning Moon

The night was as hot and damp as the sheet that shrouded Grandfather's sweat-slicked chest. Dewi mopped his fevered brow and opened the door to entice a breeze into the room. She paused to take in an unusually powerful scent of jasmine that she'd never noticed before in the compound.

She'd left work the previous afternoon immediately after Pande's widow had dashed down to the resort to tell her that Grandfather was ill. Her mind was still spinning after the conversation with Pak Gusti but she'd not yet had an opportunity to speak to Ana. She tried to reconcile the thought that the woman she'd thought of all her life as her aunt was actually her mother. Dewi wished she could talk the situation over with somebody – but by the time she returned home Grandfather was already burning with fever.

"You spent too long buried in the sand, you silly old man," she had scolded tenderly. "You'd think you were some sort of hermit crab. You shouldn't stay there for so long."

Dewi wondered if it was just heatstroke. When she forced him to drink rice-water mixed with life-giving *daun kelor* (moringa) he vomited it up almost immediately. She recalled the story of how her mother – aunt, she reminded herself, aunt – had nursed Grandfather through the Big Sickness. When Grandfather finally slept she decided that now she too would talk to him, regardless of whether he was in any condition to make sense of her words.

So, despite the fact that he made no sign of hearing her, she recounted her conversation with Pak Gusti. She told the old man of her confusion over the revelations that threw into question everything she'd considered true about herself. Once she even dared to voice her optimism that Pak Gusti would live up to his promise to return her daughter to her. If there was anyone in the village powerful enough to bring the little girl home to her mother would be Pak Gusti.

"My father might be able to fix it," she dared to say aloud. It was the only time in her life that she would ever refer to him in that way. "He alone could return little Ayu to me."

Dewi's voice penetrated Grandfather's fever only for brief moments so that, when he woke in the morning, he believed that he'd dreamed that she'd learned the truth about her parents. Grandfather's hallucinations had continued through the night and at one point his visions were remarkably similar to those experienced by Alexi Romanov at the last moment of his fateful motorcycle ride.

It was possibly a sign of how close he was to what his prophetic friend Tabanan called 'the smell of the grave' that he dreamed also of 'Mang Sari. She'd returned from the dead and transported him back to the time when they were young lovers. They were walking on the beach hand-in-hand: "No matter what happens in our lives," she said, "I will always be yours."

It was only when he turned to look at her that he realised her dress was the shade of vibrant green you only see in the luminescence of a field of young rice shoots. Or the chartreuse glow you see through the breaking lip of a backlit wave.

>><><><<

Pak Gusti had departed for the city but he'd promised to return in three days. There were still things to talk over and Dewi would have to be patient until he set the wheels in motion for her reunion with little Ayu.

As he'd recounted the tale of Dewi's birth, the façade of his confidence had slipped like crumbling stucco on a damp wall. She'd almost felt sorry for him, until she imagined his privileged life as a wealthy young high-caste man. No doubt when Ana had told him of the pregnancy he must have thought that the voyage of his life – a voyage that had been carefully mapped out since before his birth – had been thrown into turmoil. On the day he learned that he was the father of Ana's child he must have imagined that the noble vessel he was privileged to sail in was being swept irretrievably towards a jagged reef.

As they sat together on the steps at the resort, he'd told Dewi the whole story. It had spilled out as if her words had shattered the clay urn that had contained it for almost three decades. He admitted that, for the five years their affair had lasted, he'd been jealously in love with Ana. He was entranced not only by her beauty and her air of sexuality, but by a strength and confidence that he'd never come across in another woman. He didn't mention that when he met her she'd made a living from offering herself to men and that he'd paid

215

what was needed so that she could retire from this profession. Ana had asked nothing of him, but even after he married a Satria woman (as was expected and planned) he continued to cover expenses that allowed to her keep a small house, almost as his secret second wife. The shock of the pregnancy had rocked his world.

"I was sure my wife would learn of it." His eyes pleaded with Dewi for understanding. "Her family was powerful and would ensure that she kept custody of our children. On top of this they would have been furious enough – and influential enough – to bankrupt me, and that would have cost the livelihood too of all the people who worked for me."

There were some things he didn't tell her though. He didn't mention that he'd once suggested to Ana that she terminate the pregnancy but her fury had been so frightening that he'd never mentioned it again. He didn't tell Dewi either that he had spies in the village whose duty it had been to reassure him that Ana never slipped back to her easy-going ways and resumed her previous professional activities while he still supported her. He didn't admit that he'd considered accusing her of disloyalty and claiming that the father was someone else. The existence of his own web of spies had backfired on him. In hindsight they'd been his biggest mistake. After all, if they were convinced that his 'courtesan' had had no other lover then others in the village would be sure to know the same thing. There were few secrets.

He explained how Ana had come up with the solution herself. The fact that Ana's sister had recently married was the ideal cover. The young couple had been trying for a baby with no success and they circulated the rumour that they had a job to go to in the city. As if in a typically spontaneous last-minute decision, Ana decided to go with them. Pak Gusti had paid all the bills and it was accepted as the normal way of things when the young couple returned less than a year later with a new baby and the doting 'aunt' in tow to assist with the necessary ceremonies.

The custom of milk-fostering was so deeply threaded through the fabric of the community that, even to the family themselves, it had been easy to accustom themselves to the lie.

Milk-fostering was, however, typically an agreement that was equally known to all parties and so such news as this – 27 years after the fact – was hard for Dewi to digest. Her close bond with Ana

216

was now explained, but she felt betrayed by the memory of her now deceased surrogate-mother who'd had a habit of blaming Dewi's occasional attacks of rebelliousness as 'the bad influence of your aunt'.

"I'm almost relieved that the secret is out," Pak Gusti had concluded. "Whatever happens next is up to you."

Dewi realised that it would be an additional torment to admit now that she'd had no inkling of this situation and that it was Pak Gusti himself who had revealed the secret. Perhaps unconsciously he'd been waiting for even the vaguest invitation to smash that urn.

Despite herself, she was sorry for him. "I didn't come to blackmail you," she said. "I came to see if you could find a way to let Ana keep the *warung*."

"I can try but I think it's already out of my power." He gesticulated towards the resort that now spread across the expanse of what had once been his family's coconut groves. "Even if I try to delay the inevitable, I think they would win in the end. There might be something else I can do for you, though."

Dewi hardly dared to breathe, as he outlined a plan to bring little Ayu back to the village. "After all, she's also my grand-daughter," he added. "Since your marriage broke up I've been trying to figure out how I could get involved without anyone suspecting my connection. Your ex-husband is not a suitable father and I think I can put pressure on him through my connections. You help me keep our secret and I'll do everything I can to get little Ayu back to her mother."

Before she could even think what she was doing Dewi had thrown her arms around the old man's neck. It was only later that night, as she sat talking to Grandfather, she realised guiltily that she'd forgotten all about her attempt to save the *warung*.

>><><><><<

Nat never quite understood how she ended up reconciling herself to 'Bu Ana's explanation about her turtle-conservation successes. Even after she'd accepted the facts, there remained something unforgivable about the turtle sacrifice.

"Firstly, let me admit that it's not the first time I've sacrificed a turtle in a ceremony concerning fishermen." It had only been the

Balinese woman's strong hand on her own that had prevented Nat from leaving before 'Bu Ana could continue. "In the process I have certainly saved hundreds of turtles. Potentially thousands."

"Please explain." Nat's voice was bitter with sarcasm.

"An important ceremony must always include a sacrifice, as you know. Sometimes a chicken, a pig, a goat. Occasionally they will fatten a puppy to make satays for a feast. You have no problem with that…?"

"I was raised in a community where animal sacrifices were common. So, no, I don't have a problem with that."

"Before we sacrifice an animal we must pray, uttering special mantras, asking the animal's permission with the promise of reincarnation to a higher lifeform. But none of the normal sacrifices ever involve an aspect of conservation…"

"And this one did…?" The sarcasm had not diminished.

"An average fisherman like Rahim might sell 12 to 15 turtles a year, even if he only catches turtles in his nets accidentally. Those turtles will most likely be mature females on their way to the coast to nest. As you'll probably know, the males are usually much farther out to sea with no responsibilities beyond feeding and mating – much like the males of many species." 'Bu Ana's smile died on her face under the Brazilian woman's stare.

"I'm still not sure where you're heading with all this." Doubt and curiosity were now struggling to oust the sarcasm, but the green eyes still blazed like the flickering flame from ignited copper.

"In the old days tens of thousands of turtles were killed for traditional feasts during the Galungan festivals. Even today the trade in turtle meat continues. By convincing Rahim that turtles are a sacred totem animal that should be protected at every opportunity then we could directly save, let's say ten adults a year. Those ten turtles might lay as many as 200 eggs each season and would be mature for at least 30 years. And it doesn't end there. I don't think Rahim was an active egg-collector, but perhaps he and his family used eggs, like many in the village, for their supposed medicinal properties."

"Ok. I can see the benefit in convincing him to protect them. What happened to the turtle you killed?"

"Pak Kolok helps as an assistant during my ceremonies and, in return, he gets the turtle meat, which is considered a great delicacy where he comes from. He's sworn that it is only on these occasions that he will ever eat it. He helps me test the efficiency of my system by quietly inviting the fishermen to share the feast. They always refuse."

The Balinese woman's hand slowly relinquished its grip. But now, however, Nat – brow creased in thought – ignored the opportunity to withdraw her own.

"You consider yourself a conservationist with your dangerously solitary nocturnal expeditions…" 'Bu Ana enjoyed the surprise in the Brazilian's blue eyes, "but I think my own statistics speak for themselves."

"How did you know about that?" Nat's voice was almost a whisper.

"I have ears everywhere. And when I don't have ears, I have eyes. Pak Kolok realised what you were up to on the night of the fight. It was a relief to him, actually, because until that point he'd assumed you were a witch."

"My grandmother would be so proud!" Nat laughed. "She was a *mãe-de-santo* priestess practising what some people consider to be Brazilian voodoo. There is no concept of good or bad in the Candomblé religion – merely an obligation to fulfil your own destiny to the utmost regardless of what's required of you."

"You're not saying your grandmother really was a witch?"

"She always worked good magic – sacrificing painted guinea hens and black roosters and cutting the hearts out of turtle doves. Things like that…"

"My god. What did she want turtle dove hearts for?"

"People say that they're the only way to tame a she-devil. You have to put it into her anus while she's sleeping."

"I imagine that would be easier said than done," 'Bu Ana smiled.

>><><><<

Yunus had been caulking split seams in *Putri Laut*'s hull with resin made from tree sap when he saw Pak Kolok walking along the hightide line on his morning buffalo migration. As the young fisherman had a few hours before he and Rahim had to take four tourists out fishing, he decided on a whim to walk down the beach to meet the buffalo herder.

They greeted each other with just a smile and a nod and walked in companionable silence as far as Buana's Warung. Yunus watched in amusement as the buffalo dropped their steaming cargo. The *warung* owner stepped out from the shade of the thatched roof and beckoned. Yunus approached nervously, recalling his recent eviction from this establishment.

"I'm glad to see you here. I heard what happened the other night," 'Bu Ana said. "Pak Kolok told me everything. He's a real chatterbox when he has a dramatic story to tell."

Seeing them smile, Pak Kolok sauntered over to enjoy the joke.

"You acted well and bravely," she continued. "I heard that you single-handedly saved the *bule* manageress and I wanted to apologise for misjudging you."

'Bu Ana reached behind the bar for the plastic bottle of arak and poured three shallow glasses. Yunus took the proffered glass. "It's ok. You were right. It's all over with the French woman and she's gone back to her husband. It was me who was in the wrong. I have to say though that what happened the other night was not single-handed. For much of the time I think the deaf man and the *bule* woman were protecting me. Without that unlikely pair of street-fighters I would have taken a beating for sure."

"Never underestimate Pak Kolok. He's a martial arts expert from way back. And I think there's more to the Brazilian girl than meets the eye too."

"She's an Amazonian warrior!" Yunus laughed. "I'm ashamed that she would need to defend herself in our country though. Lately everything seems to have been turned upside down."

"I've been noticing bad omens too. Drunks on the beach and angry people in the village might be the least of our problems. When I looked into the well this morning the water looked like it was boiling. At first, I thought maybe a monitor lizard was trying to climb out but there was nothing in there. Yet the water appeared to be boiling all morning."

'Bu Ana reached over to pour more arak but Yunus put his hand over the top of his glass. "Thank you, but I've decided to slow down with this stuff."

Pak Kolok didn't refuse. Before he sipped it, however, he made sure to spill an extra-large splash onto the sandy soil for the demons.

>><><><<

The next day was brutally hot. The afternoon sunlight filtered through 'Bu Ana's bedroom window and crept up the tangled sheets that lay across the foot of the bed. When 'Bu Ana felt the sun's heat touch her leg she stretched luxuriously. Nat was curled next to her, like a sleek, dark cat.

When the Brazilian woman had arrived at the *warung*, after a low-tide surf session that morning, she'd been animated and talkative. It was as if she was intent on making up for their lost conversations. The resort was almost empty since most of the guests had checked out to make way for a big group that was due to arrive the next day, so the manageress was free to enjoy a day of relative laziness.

'Bu Ana had been uneasy since noticing the omens. Something threatening was hanging in the air but she couldn't define it, so she was grateful occupy her mind instead with Nat's questions about the Goddess of the Sea. Only Dewi had ever assisted with 'Bu Ana's offerings to Nyai Roro Kidul but, persuaded by Nat's obvious curiosity about the goddess, 'Bu Ana had decided to invite her Brazilian friend into the humble temple.

Even the simplest offering would be unthinkable in surf shorts and rash-vest, however, so she loaned Nat her spare sarong and *kebaya* blouse. The two women went into the bedroom to change. Afterwards Nat couldn't even recall what had happened. Like waves borne across the ocean from opposite sides of the world, their collision had been inevitable from the outset. The intimate tenderness of that long, hot afternoon would linger with Nat for the rest of her life.

Now as the sun creeped into the west Nat rolled over and looked up with sleepy eyes to see the Balinese woman gazing at her.

"Your eyes are the colour of the special stone we call *sukabumi*," Ana whispered. "I guess you could translate it as earth-lover stone."

221

"That's nice. People used to say that I got them from my grandmother, but hers were much more startling."

"You miss your grandmother, don't you?"

"She was a legend in our city. She had dark skin and there were people who said she was a black witch, although she never did any harm in her life. With two exceptions. She had the most alluring walk of any woman I ever knew. It tortured men and the way she danced Samba made them want to die."

"It must have taken a strong and independent woman to live her life in those days."

"Probably a similar type of strength and independence that I see in you…"

"My life-story has been quite predictable by comparison. You know Pak Gusti?"

"The landowner?"

"Yes. Well, his father was the first man I slept with. I was just fifteen and I guess you could say that I was his concubine. For him it was more than just a fling, and I was young enough and naïve enough to be satisfied because he bought me dresses and gave me some cash. Two years later I told my father that I'd been offered a job at a shop in the city but in reality Pak Gusti's father set me up with a small apartment where he could come to visit me…"

"You don't have to tell me anything you don't want to."

"It's not a period of my life that I'm proud of but I want you to know. Realising that I could make money without getting out of bed was a revelation to me at that young age, but when my sugar-daddy found out he kicked me out of the apartment. Then I really had to get to work and spent most of the next few years working out of bars near the beach. I never had a relationship worthy of the name with any man until years later, when I finally moved back to the village. Pak Gusti was probably more astounded than anybody to realise that he'd fallen in love with his father's ex-concubine. I can't say that I was in love with him but he treated me with respect and, for the first time, I began to wonder if maybe I was something more than just a whore."

"Did you marry him?"

"No! He was already married then. It could only be a fling to me, although in the end we had a child together. I want you to know

222

everything…but there are some subjects we could save for another day."

>><><><><<

Things were going to plan at the resort but, even so, the boss was in a pensive frame of mind this afternoon. The meeting with Pak Gusti had gone well but there'd been something strange about his attitude that the boss couldn't quite put his finger on. The landowner had been unusually quiet – far from showing his usual enthusiasm – and the boss hoped he wasn't having second thoughts about the *warung* deal. Could whatever was bothering Pak Gusti have something to do with that waitress? The boss couldn't guess. And, for the life of him, he couldn't imagine what they might have in common. The boss prided himself on being a shrewd psychologist, but there were always so many complex details going on behind the scenes with the Balinese.

And now Nat and that bimbo Suzie had disappeared at the same time. You could hire a staff of hundreds and still never be able to find a single employee when you needed one. They were a few people around here who were walking on thin ice. They'd very soon find themselves in hot water.

It seemed that, around here, if you wanted something done it was best to do it yourself. The boss had decided to meet personally with that crazy woman who ran the *warung*. He'd entrusted Suzie with dealing with her, but she'd reported that the Balinese woman was going to put up a fight. It was important now to keep the pressure on.

It was his bad timing that he'd decided to walk to the *warung* at hightide and the slog through the soft sand was straining his legs as well as his patience. At least the walk gave him a chance to think things over. All in all, plans were coming together well. It had been a quiet week for the resort but the first big group – eighteen people – would be checking in tomorrow for a week of yoga and surfing. Apart from the classes, accommodation and meals he'd also charge a supplement on tours and fishing outings. Then there were minor money-spinners like massages and cocktails. The trick was to make sure that the guests didn't stray too far under their own steam so that, one way or another, the majority of their holiday budget circulated back into the resort. The fact that those two bodies had been found near the property had not been great publicity. It didn't gel well with his marketing drive for a hidden island paradise, that was for sure.

Then there was the situation with The Playboys. That had been more dangerous for business still and it was only through Suzie's charms that he'd managed to distance the resort from the police investigation.

Still, every cloud had a silver lining. These incidents seemed to be an effective deterrent to guests who might otherwise be tempted to wander out after dark to spend their food and booze budgets in local eateries rather than adding to the resort cashbox.

By now, the boss was crossing the big rock slab, stepping carefully to keep his white tennis shoes – already heavy and uncomfortable with sand – out of the salty rockpools. Unusually, the beach was almost deserted. There were no surfers in the water and up ahead just a solitary old man was sitting on the beach, appearing to be merely a torso propped up on the sand. As the boss came nearer he saw that the old man was so deeply immersed in animated conversation with himself that he didn't even look up. He was entirely alone yet he spoke so emphatically that it was hard to believe there was nobody sitting next to him.

Despite the stifling heat an icy shiver prickled down the length of the boss's spine as he hurried past.

Apparently this beach was over-run with lunatics but once he'd set up the cocktail bar they would get the resort security guards – or even off-duty police – patrolling this part of the beach. He'd make it a no-go area for villagers and crazy old men like that one would have to find another place to sit and talk to themselves.

This happy thought turned his mind to the problem at hand. Pak Gusti must have a real soft spot for that crazy woman to allow her to run the *warung* into the ground like this. Nevertheless, once she started working under Suzie it would only be a matter of time. Suzie would know how to rattle her cage and it wouldn't be long before she flew the coop. Even if Pak Gusti changed his mind the time would inevitably come when he needed to sell in any case. Every Balinese Hindu – and especially those with a big family – would always have an expensive ceremony looming somewhere on the horizon. That was usually the moment to strike and get the best deal. Then, once the crazy woman had been ousted, the place could *really* be turned around.

The boss's tennis shoes were now crunching over the pink-sheened sand but he ignored its scattering of shells. He slogged onward and within a few minutes was clambering up the short, steep bank beside the *warung*. "Hello!" he barked "Anyone here?"

He was short of breath from the walk through the soft sand and he was short-tempered by nature. After a moment, he shouted once more. Still nobody appeared. The place looked abandoned. He shook his head in irritation and decided to sit down on the edge of the root-strewn bank, to gather energy for the walk back. 'Bu Ana's medicinal garden lay nearby, and its spattering of fresh dung made his nostrils flare. 'Keep 'em in the dark and feed 'em bullshit,' he thought to himself.

That was when he noticed the mushrooms.

It took just a few seconds for the roots of a plan to spread through his mind: these tiny beige-coloured buttons reaching for the sky on their flimsy stalks, might provide all the leverage he needed. He slipped his telephone out of his pocket and snapped a shot, making sure that the location was obvious. Surely, this would provide the necessary momentum to push the deal through. After all, it didn't do to let the grass grow under a rolling stone.

"Good afternoon. What news?" The voice, calling from the darkness of the *warung*, startled him.

He got up and walked into the shade beneath the thatched roof. With his eyes still adjusting to the shadows, it took him a moment to make out the *warung* owner, standing next to the green shrine.

"News is good," he said. "I hope it's equally good for you…?"

'Bu Ana waved her hand around the empty room. "Sit down anywhere. Don't be shy."

The boss settled himself at the nearest table while 'Bu Ana walked to the fridge. The silence was broken only by the soft pop of three bottles being opened and the gentle tinkle of the caps dropping onto the concrete floor. 'Bu Ana handed him a Bintang and put another on the table. Ignoring his questioning glance, she took a sip from the neck of her own bottle and sat down.

There was a movement back in the shadows and Nat walked out of the backroom in surf shorts and rash-vest.

"Going surfing?" the boss asked, with arched eyebrow.

"I surfed at low tide." Nat picked up the third bottle and held it above the table so that they could clunk the green glass together. She pulled a chair out from the table –unconsciously distancing herself from the conversation – and sat down with her legs crossed.

To the Australian, who liked his beer as icy as possible, the atmosphere in the room was substantially colder than the beverage. But he hadn't got to his position by shying away from conflict: "I've had another meeting with Pak Gusti…" he began.

"Yes, Suzie came the other day and explained your plan," 'Bu Ana was equally direct. "I haven't made a decision yet…"

"The way I see it, there's nothing to decide. You work with us and we'll make a success of this place. All you have to do is to come along for the ride and not drop the ball…"

"But I'm not sure I want to ride with you and Suzie."

"Nat also works for me." He let a deliberately sleazy eye slip towards the Brazilian's crossed legs. "Maybe you can ride with her…?"

Nat struggled to keep the anger out of her voice. "You hired me to run the resort and I think Ana would prefer to run the *warung* her way."

Mimicking 'Bu Ana's earlier gesture, he waved his hand around the empty room. His finger picked distastefully at the runnelled edge of the table. "I don't think this is any way to run a business."

"It might not be a great business in your eyes but it's *my* business," 'Bu Ana's expression was fixed now in what Nat recognised as the defiant smile of a Balinese person who is on the verge of fighting back. "The villagers here might not have much in the way of Western luxuries, but life has been peaceful and decent here for as long as anyone can remember. There were rarely any arguments – and there were no outcasts – in this village until you started your business here…"

The woman's inscrutable smile did more than her words to strain the boss's notorious temper: "Bali Moon has brought a *lot* of money into the community! I don't hear anyone complaining about that!"

"Bali Moon money is cursed…" 'Bu Ana paused to let the boss's inevitable guffaw of laughter subside. Then she continued without letting her patient smile slip for a moment. Nat had the unmistakable impression that she was explaining to a child. "The community has been divided ever since you sacked your builders for respecting the very culture that brings tourists to this island. Then you instilled further distrust by hiring paddy-people security to watch over imaginary thieves among your fisher-folk staff. A few people made money but ultimately the only ones who benefited are you and the Chinese trader, because the farmers now refuse to buy from the fisherman and the fisherman refuse to buy from the farmers. The young men with money are turning to drunks and your guests do drugs and…"

"You can't make a mushroom omelette without breaking a few eggs…"

"What?"

It was the boss's turn to grin now, and he did so with an effect that the two women found chilling. "Are you aware that Alexi Romanov made a statement before he died?"

"I heard that there was no statement."

"As a personal favour I asked the police to keep silent about it because I want to help you."

"So, what did this statement say?"

"According to the police report the mushrooms came from this property and the deaf man delivered them to the guest's room…"

"That's a lie!" 'Bu Ana was aghast.

"The police believe it," the boss shrugged. "Either way if you open that particular can of worms you might be surprised by what it contains. If you want a word of friendly advice you should probably destroy any evidence…and there's a whole plantation growing right beside your front step." The boss was a shrewd poker player and, although he was enjoying toying with her, his face now wore an expression of kindly concern. It would be interesting to find out if, after he'd gone, she incriminated herself still more deeply by removing the mushrooms that she'd possibly not even realised existed until now.

But it didn't really make a difference now because he still had an ace to play: "It might be too late for that though. I was told that they already sent somebody here to investigate. You might have been busy at the time, though." He glanced lasciviously at Nat's legs again. "I gather that they took some photos as evidence."

"But it's all a lie." 'Bu Ana repeated, and this time there was a note of desperation in her voice.

"Maybe so," he admitted. "But this country has a death-penalty for drug dealing. You would probably be acquitted but *somebody* would have to pay the piper for the death of The Playboy and the two little girls. Do you think your deaf friend would be able to present the sort of defence that would keep him away from a firing squad?"

'Bu Ana took a moment for the thinly cloaked blackmail to soak in. So, she was being made to choose between fighting to save the temple or to save Pak Kolok from being framed as a drug-dealer.

Nat's voice was full of bitterness: "It's no exaggeration at all to say that what we've brought to this village has been a curse."

The boss slammed his beer bottle onto the table with unexpected violence: "Your mistake, Nat, is that you think we should all be team-players. I don't have to be a team player because I'm the fucking coach!"

"If you don't think it was a curse," 'Bu Ana said slowly, "might I remind you of the girls' father, Pande...?"

The bottle wobbled on the table and, seemingly of its own accord, slowly toppled over onto its side. Nobody noticed as the beer leaked between the timber planks.

It was the boss's turn to look confused: "Who's Pande?"

As 'Bu Ana and Nat stared they had the impression that the boss's face was fracturing before their eyes, as if he was an image in a mirror that was slowly shattering. His expression became one of shock, as if somebody had grabbed him from behind and was shaking him by the shoulders. Suddenly aware of a rasping noise at the back of the room, Nat turned to see that the painting of the Sea Goddess was swinging from side to side against the wall. She watched, frozen in amazement, as it crashed onto the floor taking the shrine down with it.

>◇◇◇◇<

The boss grabbed the edge of the table to steady himself but Nat dragged him roughly away, shoving him outside: "Get out!"

"*Gempa*!" 'Bu Ana shouted; her English temporarily forgotten in her panic. Then, "Earthquake! Outside!"

Nat reeled forward as the ground rolled on a billowing wave. She grabbed hold of a pillar to keep from falling as she staggered across the room. She almost tripped over the boss who was doubled over, scrambling on all-fours towards the edge of the concrete floor. They all tumbled out onto the sand, relieved to get out from under the bamboo and thatch roof that crackled as if caught in a wildfire.

'Bu Ana's islander instincts warned her that they were still not safe. All around them spiky palm-leaves rained down and plummeting coconuts embedded themselves in the sand with the dull thud of distant artillery. The three comrades – so recently in bitter argument – now gripped each other like drunken friends as they scrambled down the short bank to the beach. With a deafening crack the *warung*'s pillars gave out and the roof caved in. The boss tripped on a root as he scrambled away and he landed face-first. His fingers gripped into the sand like a man desperately clinging to a cliff face. "Are we going to die?" he asked of nobody in particular. It struck Nat that his voice was childlike and strangely unemotional, merely requesting confirmation.

Then, suddenly it was all over. They held their breaths and strained their senses as they listened to a receding rumble; a giant juggernaut was labouring steadily over the distant hills, making its way into the centre of the island. Nat crouched, legs askance and arms spread for balance, in a surfing posture. Like many people who have just been through their first big earthquake, she was sure she would never take life for granted in quite the same way again. If the billions of tonnes of bedrock beneath her feet were capable of lurching up without the slightest warning, then there was truly little in the universe that could be entirely relied upon.

This intense subterranean jostling – the most powerful that even 'Bu Ana had ever experienced – had shaken all three of them to their core. To the Balinese woman it was suddenly easier to understand her ancestors' belief that their island was balanced on the back of the great turtle *Bedawang Nala*; the explanation was no less convincing, after all, than the scientific theory that the very fabric of the planet had shifted beneath their feet like a flapped carpet.

To the boss, coherent thoughts were impossible in the first panic-stricken minutes after the quake. With his belly flat against the sand, he continued to sense the distant rumble of the receding juggernaut after the others had ceased to hear it. It was as if the beach had retained the energy of that underground shuddering and the individual grains that had jostled together were now slowly settling back into their allotted places. There came a few intensely quiet seconds in which even the birds and insects were silent. The entire universe seemed to be waiting with bated breath. Praying that the earth-shattering juggernaut would not return.

Then, Nat broke the silence: "Oh my god! Look at the sea!"

The rock slab which had been about level with the hightide less than an hour ago now lay half a metre above the water. It was like a great, craggy beast that had risen to shake the sea from its back.

"Tsunami!" 'Bu Ana hissed, and it was as if she was afraid of waking that beast.

"We must get to high ground! Now!" The boss was on his feet with unexpected agility.

"We have to get to the resort to warn them!" Nat pointed out.

"There's no time. It could hit at any moment."

"I know you're going to fire me anyway, but we have to warn them."

Nat set off at a barefoot sprint down the beach. She knew that she'd be able to run fastest if she dashed down to the packed damp sand, but she had to force herself against all her instincts to run down into an area that should at this moment – by all laws of nature – have been under water.

Near the rock slab an old Balinese man stood staring at the empty, waterless beach. It struck her as strange because she assumed that the local people would understand the danger. Amid all the omens that dictated their actions, surely they would grasp that this was a *real* omen of truly terrifying proportions. She paused for just a moment, wasting precious oxygen by yelling at him to get up the hill, but she didn't wait to see if he moved before she turned to run onwards, ignoring the grating of the sharp rock on the soles of her feet.

As she ran she watched the horizon, expecting at any second to see the growing line of tumbling white water that would obliterate everything, herself included. She tried to control her breathing, straining her ears for the first hint of the doom that must surely be sweeping upon her this instant. From somewhere back in the direction of the Death Temple Nat could now hear the hollow clatter of the *kulkul* drum warning the villagers of an impending disaster.

She was halfway to the resort when she looked back over her shoulder, expecting the boss to be labouring over the sand behind her. Instead she could see his distant figure making directly for the tarmac track up the hill towards the village. 'Bu Ana was far behind the boss and Nat cursed when she saw that the Balinese woman was labouring across the sand with a large, unwieldy object supported on her head.

Nat would never forget the last part of that run, struggling across the soft sand above the hightide line on legs that burned as if her marrow had been turned to hot lead. Her mouth tasted of copper and she was breathing so hard that when she finally arrived she found that, nightmarishly, she was unable to yell out the warning. Running up the steps to the restaurant, she could only gasp and point. Dewi's jaw dropped when she looked towards the beach but she understood instantly and sent staff running to the suites. In one room they spent valuable seconds arguing with a *bule* couple who had almost to be forcibly dragged away from packing their suitcases. In another they found two surfers and the missing Suzie, struggling to knot a sarong across her naked breasts. Even this went almost unnoticed in the frantic rush to get the inhabitants of the Bali Moon Eco-resort running towards the hill at the edge of the village.

Only when they were sure that the resort was empty did Nat gratefully jump into the driving seat of the boss's pickup truck without sparing a thought for any cobra curse. Mercifully, the keys were in the ignition and, with Dewi riding shotgun, they accelerated along the dirt-track towards the village. Nat's eyes flickered constantly out of the side window, expecting a fearsome wall of white-water to appear at any moment. It seemed that the universe itself was conspiring to slow down their escape and as soon as the truck picked up speed Nat would be forced to halt so that stragglers could throw themselves into the flatbed. Worst of all, the track ran parallel to the beach and she was certain that they would be broadsided by a wave that would flip the big white Toyota like it was made of polystyrene.

Miraculously, it had still not appeared by the time they bounced onto the tarmac and Nat wrenched the steering wheel to begin the uphill race to what she only now dared pray might be salvation. When they reached the level of the first breezeblock house a woman was standing in the road with two wide-eyed boys and Nat skidded the pickup to a halt.

"Have you seen my husband Ibu?" she asked, as she leaned through the open window. "My husband Rahim…"

"Oh my god!" Nat stammered. "I'm so, so sorry. He went out on the boat didn't he? With four guests. I'd totally forgotten…"

Even as the woman's legs buckled, Dewi was out of the passenger door, helping to lower her onto the dusty verge at the edge of the road. "I'm sorry Kadek," she was saying, "but you have to stay strong for the boys."

The terrain levelled out up ahead and then dipped slightly so there was little point in going farther. Nat hoped that they were already sufficiently high over the beach by now. She secured the hand-break, leaving the engine running just in case and climbed out. She signalled to the passengers in the flatbed to stay seated just in case they had to make a quick getaway.

Nat could see the boss sitting on the verge farther up the road, still breathing hard from his run. He looked away to avoid her eyes. She was relieved to see 'Bu Ana nearby too. She was clutching the portrait of the goddess and Nat felt a momentary anger when she realised that the warung owner must have wasted precious time salvaging it from under the collapsed roof. This anger abated in the next instant, however, when she remembered that the portrait had been the first thing that had fallen. It had provided the crucial warning that allowed them to escape before the roof came down.

Vibrations crept into Nat's bare feet from the hot tarmac – a rumbling sensation that rose through her legs. Frozen in rapt horror, she watched as a churning maelstrom of water burst through the gap in the trees at the bottom of the hill. The air was filled with cracking and splintering as the village fishing fleet smashed into the trees. An entire forest was being ground through a sawmill. The water compressed into the narrow valley and rushed up the track towards them, darkly menacing with black sand and deadly with churning wood and tumbling rocks.

Despite the unfathomable force behind the wave it was clear by now that – just as the village founders had anticipated – the tsunami's power would be exhausted long before it reached the first houses.

>><><><<

The boss was first to arrive back at the resort – just as he'd been first to abandon it. The damage was not as bad as he'd expected. The concrete retaining wall on the beach had apparently taken most of the power out of the wave and its scalloped shape had done a surprisingly effective job of diverting most of the water around the resort.

Even so, part of the wave had driven up over the lawn with enough force to rush through the open restaurant, carrying furniture with it. It had swirled into the pool and swept up against the rock gardens that separated the suites from the lower poolside areas. After a quick glance around the boss congratulated himself for the design foresight that had ensured the guest rooms had been left high and dry.

Nevertheless, when he saw the destruction in the lobby beside the restaurant he was pleased that he'd taken the opportunity to slip away while the other evacuees were still sitting up on the hill. He'd reasoned very naturally that the first person back onto the property would be sure to make a priority of emptying the cash box in the office. The swooping thatched roof had held firm and as he stepped underneath the boss noticed that the driftwood chandeliers still hung, entirely unsullied by the carnage below. He picked his way carefully through the debris on the tiled floor, grateful for the running shoes that protected his feet from smashed bottles and splintered wood.

For a moment he thought the office door was locked from the inside but, shoving with his shoulder, he opened it enough to squeeze through. When he stepped in he could see that the wave had smashed in through the full-length window at the back of the office to jam the door shut from inside. The desk and chairs had been thrown against the wall, but it took the boss just a moment to spot the bright red cash box, embedded in the water-logged black sand that carpeted the room. It would be pointless trying to find a key among this devastation so, tucking the box protectively under his arm like a rugby ball, he turned to leave.

In that instant he heard the distant rumble of an approaching freight-train. It was a noise he'd known all his life from back home in the Western Australian mining towns. Then he paused mid-step, as his mind struggled to place the familiar roar within the context of the tropical island.

It was this moment of befuddled delay that saved him from being hit by the full power of the second – far bigger – tsunami as it crashed into the restaurant, stripping the antique wood from the concrete pillars and taking away the corner of the office. There was a split second when the boss – still clutching the red cash box –cringed next to a wall of blackened water. Then a grasping claw reached around the corner and hooked him out, like a fisherman plucks a whelk from a crevice in a rockpool.

>><><><><<

'Bu Ana too had slipped quickly away after the first wave receded, and she struggled back through the waterlogged bush to the ruins of the *warung*.

She leaned the portrait carefully against the splintered bamboo ridge pole that had formed her roof and, with barely a glance towards her shattered home, continued onwards to the Sea Goddess's temple.

As she stepped carefully along the top of the bank she noticed that her medicinal garden had been wiped from the face of the earth. Maybe this was as it should be. Nothing is permanently good or bad in life and, in the end, everything is destined to find its own balance. The medicine that she'd always tried to use for good in the community had ultimately come at a far higher price than she could have imagined. The three playboys who'd taken the mushrooms were merely pawns in the hands of gods and demons.

She herself would have to pay the price eventually too. But not today, she realised, with a sigh of relief: her worst fears were unfulfilled because she could see now that the old temple wall had inexplicably remained intact. She'd been cursing herself for the lack of devotion she'd shown by not fixing the crumbling wall, but now it became apparent that the breach had probably helped minimise the full-frontal force of that first wave. A solid, unyielding wall would almost certainly have been battered over but, with much of the power deflected through the gap, the temple appeared to have been saved. As she stepped inside she saw that the sturdy pinnacle of the altar had withstood the rush of water with the fortitude of a lighthouse. Protected on its leeward side, the ceramic figure of the Goddess of the South Seas was miraculously unharmed.

As Nyai Roro Kidul's devotee knelt to give thanks, she heard the rumble of distant thunder. It was the sound of impending karma. She steadfastly kept her head bowed in an attitude of prayer, refusing to look up even when the huge wave crashed over the rock slab and slammed through the temple wall.

>><><><><<

Putri Laut rocked gently in the vast natural harbour formed by the protecting bulk of the Javanese headland. Rahim and Yunus had both been busy preparing bait for four *bule* anglers and the tsunami had passed almost unnoticed below them.

Rahim recalled afterwards that, at one point in the afternoon, he'd had a sensation of weightlessness in his stomach as he felt the boat surge but when he looked around at the horizon all looked peaceful. He shrugged it off and by the time he was halfway through his next cigarette he'd forgotten all about it. Now that business was improving, he'd decided that he didn't need to give up smoking after all.

It was only two hours later when they were puttering back to the beach that Yunus, standing forward in the bow, noticed an unusual amount of floating debris and timber. Rahim looked towards the mountains, expecting to see the rainclouds that must have caused the flash-floods, but the peaks were clear.

Sensing that something was seriously amiss, he opened the throttle. His pounding heart echoed the labouring cough of the Chinese engine.

The water soon became more jumbled with trunks and pieces of boats and, despite Rahim's growing haste, they were forced to slow as Yunus peered ahead for floating obstacles. It was twenty minutes more before they could make out the destruction among the trees where the fishing fleet had been devastated. Yunus ignored the frantic questions of the four tourists as he balanced in the bow calling instructions back to his skipper.

"Look! Over there!" Yunus pointed to a speck about fifty metres off their starboard side. "Something swimming. I can see horns. It's almost impossible but could it be a *menjangan*?"

Rahim peered under his shaded hand. "Could be. But we don't have time..."

"Wait! It's a buffalo."

"Never mind. Keep going!"

"No! Look behind it. There's something behind the buffalo!"

Behind the strongly kicking pink rump Rahim could make out something bobbing in the water. It must be just a coconut though because a human would be shouting for help. So, he throttled ahead for the beach again.

It was only when Yunus shot a final brief glance back astern towards the swimming buffalo that he realised what he was looking at.

"Stop!" he yelled. "It's the deaf man!"

>><><><<

Like 'Bu Ana, Pak Kolok had also seen omens. As he walked out of his hut after his siesta he'd been shat on by a gecko. Everyone knew this was a bad omen but that wasn't all. The previous night he'd noticed that the voracious packs of wild dogs had deserted the beach. The growing heaps of waste food dumped at the back of the resort, had not only swelled their numbers but also seemed to have amplified their aggressiveness. It was unnerving how swiftly they were able to surround him and in recent nights he'd taken to carrying his heavy flashlight for defence. With their shining eyes and slavering fangs, it struck him that they looked like demons squabbling over a sacrifice.

Some of the guests had complained that the snarling and yelping was keeping them awake and the boss had arranged to hire off-duty policemen to shoot the dogs. The police chief would be onto a good deal, of course; in addition to a bounty paid by the resort, he'd certainly sell the carcasses for meat to feed either crocs or humans. This massacre would not take place until a time when the resort was empty of guests but, in the meantime, Pak Kolok had been advised temporarily to look the other way if he came across armed hunters on the beach.

So, when Pak Kolok had noticed that the beach was devoid of dogs his first thought was that maybe the hunters had been in action already. While his highland community was no stranger to earthquakes, his people had no experience of tsunamis and it was only when he saw the guests and staff abandoning the resort that he too headed for the hills.

Later, when his sensitive eyes noticed first the boss and then 'Bu Ana moving (with the portrait still under her arm) quietly away from the crowd, he decided he had a responsibility to check on Pak Gusti's precious buffalo. He found them after a brief search. The four animals had been swamped by the wave and, with their tethers pulled loose from the ground, they'd found refuge in a flooded hollow.

They were skittish but unhurt, and he managed to catch the ends of their tethers and was leading them gently back to their usual grazing place when he looked across the stream and noticed an old couple standing among the jumbled turmoil of the beach. It was Dewi's grandfather and the old woman Pak Kolok had seen him talking with on the beach so often.

What surprised Pak Kolok was the impression that they appeared to be waiting for something. The deaf man stopped in his tracks, wondering hazily why the old couple was staring so fixedly at the sea. As he followed the direction of their gaze, he saw a shimmering band of white spreading right across the horizon. He had no idea that secondary tsunami waves – sometimes well over an hour after the initial impact – can often be far larger than the first. Although the science was lost on him, the sheer power was not. Even after a lifetime of terrifying visions this was by far the most horrifying thing he'd ever seen. He tried desperately to yell at the old couple but no sound emerged. He watched in horror as they stood impassively hand-in-hand, as the mighty wave, two storeys high, rumbled across the sand towards them.

In later years, when Pak Kolok thought back to those terrifying moments, he was haunted by the impression that the old man had let out a great shout in the instant before the wave hit them.

He was right but – apart from the gods and the ghosts – there was nobody around to hear it.

"I am Ngurah Agung!" the old man had shouted defiantly. Then, straightening his back as the wall of water reared over them, he bellowed as loudly as his old chest would allow. "I was Ngurah Agung!"

An insight into magical realism Bali-style

This morning one of my neighbours popped around for a visit. Just as somebody in the west might bring cookies, she'd come to make offerings of *arak* and coloured rice to placate the demons that inhabit my garden at Writers' Treehouse.

What might appear to be some of the most outlandish aspects of *Driftwood Chandeliers* would not seem even remotely unusual to the villagers here.

One of the most important locations in the book is based on a 'ghost waterfall' that is a ten-minute walk from my house, and the spot where the freedom fighters arrived during the war for independence is on the reef in front of the village. One of our neighbours is commonly said to be married to a *wong samar* ghost and another old friend of mine (now, unfortunately, passed on to the other world himself) was personally familiar with the many ghosts that haunt our local beach at night.

All locations and characters in the book are fictional but the deaf security guard certainly bears a similarity to a man I wrote about in a *BBC* report from Bali's mysterious 'Village of the Deaf'.

The tsunami that forms the dramatic finale of this story is a more common occurrence than people might imagine. Also, it's not unusual for secondary tsunami waves (often considerably larger than the first) to hit land an hour or more after the initial onslaught. My description is not of one of the cataclysmic events that make the international news but is based on a much smaller – though certainly terrifying – tsunami that struck the coasts of Java and Bali in 1994.

While this is a work of fiction there are elements of inviolable truth threaded right through the story. The bizarre encounter between Nat and the 'demon of the bridge' (the king cobra), for example, was faithfully reported almost without change from an actual incident that happened to the author one evening on the way to the night-market.

Names, characters, events and incidents are the for the most part products of the author's imagination. Any resemblance to actual people, living or dead, or actual events is purely coincidental.

Only the demons and ghosts are real. For example, a singing ghost – the spirit of a foreigner – is well known to villagers here. It would have been helpful for the story if she sang in Portuguese or Dutch so that I could have tied her in to the history of the region. Those who have heard her tell me that she sings in French and, for some reason, I felt that it was important to remain faithful to this truth.

My characters are based on the sorts of people who live in the West Balinese village I fell in love with. Only the central character 'Bu Ana is perhaps an exaggerated invention since, even today, no Balinese in this village would dream of building a house so close to beaches that are still overrun by ghosts, demons, witches and a certain potentially wrathful goddess.

M.E. – The Writers' Treehouse, West Bali, 2023

About the writer:

British-born writer Mark Eveleigh (a fellow of the Royal Geographical Society) spent the first decade of his life in West Africa. He's travelled widely in Africa, Latin America and Asia on assignments for some of the world's most prestigious publications – including *BBC*, *CNN*, *Telegraph*, *Guardian*, *Independent*, *National Geographic* and *Conde Nast Traveller*.

He's authored and co-authored more than a dozen non-fiction books and guidebooks on Bali, Bangkok, Kenya, Borneo, Tanzania and Madagascar. His travel book *Kopi Dulu* (Penguin Random House SEA, 2022) told the story of his 15,000-kilometre journey by sea and land through Indonesia and was listed among the best books of 2022 by *Jakarta Post*.

With his wife Narina Exelby he was commissioned by *National Geographic* to teach a travel writing masterclass and their book *How to Become a Professional Travel Writer* was listed among *Wanderlust* magazine's 11 'Best travel books of 2022'.

If you enjoyed this book please visit the Amazon page and drop a quick review. It means a lot to writers!

Printed in Dunstable, United Kingdom